# TO CURE
# THEM ALL

# TO CURE
# THEM ALL

## DANIEL G. MILLER

STEIN AND DAY/*Publishers*/New York

Excerpt from *As I remember Him*, by Hans Zinsser, copyright © 1935, reprinted by permission of Peter Smith Publisher.

First published in 1986
Copyright © 1986 by Daniel G. Miller, M.D.
All rights reserved, Stein and Day, Incorporated
Designed by Louis A. Ditizio
Printed in the United States of America
STEIN AND DAY/*Publishers*
Scarborough House
Briarcliff Manor, N.Y. 10510

**Library of Congress Cataloging-in-Publication Data**

Miller, Daniel G.
  To cure them all.

  I. Title.
PS3563.I3767T6   1986        813'.54        85-43405
ISBN 0-8128-3074-1

Dedicated to the memory of H.D.D. and D.A.K.,
cancer researchers, colleagues, and friends.
Both died at the height of their careers,
of the disease they labored to vanquish.

I was able to please no one except the patients I treated.

—Paracelsus

# TO CURE
# THEM ALL

# CHAPTER
## ONE

A FTER THE Chemotherapy Conference on Wednesday afternoon, Dr. Henry Nyren returned to his office. He saved this late afternoon time for school-age children so it wouldn't interfere with their schedules. Sometimes, if he arrived late, he'd find the waiting room filled with kids doing homework. Today there would be only Maria. She hadn't shown up yet. Henry went to his desk and started to return the accumulation of phone messages.

A moment later the door to the waiting room opened, and youthful exuberance bounced in—straight black hair and bangs, shining black eyes, radiant smile, teeth set forward just a fraction so as to suggest an impish appearance. Henry's secretary waved the fourteen year old straight into his office, where she kissed him on the cheek as if she were visiting her father.

"Your folks showed me your report card. I'm very proud of you," Henry beamed. For two years he had seen Maria Fauci in and out of remission, through one complication after another.

"How about my report card here, Doctor Henry?"

"Maria, remember when you had to wear a wig and how you hated it? I told you that your hair would come back. You didn't believe me, but look how beautiful it is now. It's going to be that way again."

11

"Uh oh," she said.

"You've got too many 'blasts' in your marrow, honey. We've got to go through the chemo again before you get into trouble."

"Did you tell Mom and Dad? They're going to be, like, out of their minds."

"I'll explain it to them. The results will be good. And with a little luck it'll be the last time you have to go through it. Now let's see if we can work around your program at school. I don't want anything to interfere with your brilliant career. I know how much you want that scholarship to Marymount."

If I could design a daughter, Henry thought, she'd be as bright as Maria, as affectionate as Maria, as good as Maria.

"There is one thing," Maria said. "I wish I didn't have to lose my periods. I want to be like all the other girls."

"They'll come back, too. Just promise me that if anything bothers you—anything at all—you'll tell me. I'd rather you call me about even the craziest thing, instead of sitting at home and stewing about it. I know you hate to worry your folks—so ask me."

"I've got to protect them—they have enough trouble. I'm glad they've got Tommy, in case anything happens . . ."

"Nothing's going to happen. The first treatment's today. Let's go over your school schedule, so we can steer a clear path to Marymount."

ON THURSDAYS IT was customary for Henry to breakfast with Janine Williams, head of the Personnel Department. This morning he surprised her with an unusual request.

"How about going shopping with me tonight?"

"Did that come out of you, the greatest enemy of retailing in the United States?" Janine asked.

"It's Maria Fauci's birthday next week, and I'm afraid the poor kid's going to have to spend it in the hospital."

Janine looked down. "It's wonderful that you care so much

12

about Maria." She stirred her coffee slowly and spoke the same way. "However, I can't help thinking that if you had been as considerate with your own daughter—well . . ."

"You're right, and I'm paying the price. But that doesn't change things. With Maria, my feelings are so clear—and untangled. I swear, if she doesn't get that scholarship, I'm going to put her through college myself."

FOR THREE WEEKS Henry tried to get Maria into remission, without success. She was kept going with platelet and blood transfusions. She smiled through the side effects of the chemotherapy and continued her studies in the hospital with a tutor. Henry found it hard to maintain his usual upbeat demeanor. Instead, she was cheering him up.

"Don't worry, Doctor Henry. I'm going to be okay. I feel much better today, really."

"I'm sure you do, Maria. And tomorrow will be better still."

"The medicine isn't working this time, is it?"

"No, it's not." Henry was standing at her bedside, holding her hand.

"What are we going to do?"

"What do you think?"

"We're going to try different medicine," she said with a grin. "More time in the hospital, huh?"

"I love that chipmunk smile of yours. It won't be too long."

"It's not so bad. At least we get to see a lot of each other."

Her words struck Henry like a blow to the chest.

"It's not the same thing I had before, is it? That was scary. What did you call it?"

"Nadir sepsis—"

"Blood poisoning because my white count was low after the chemotherapy, right?"

"A grade of one hundred for my favorite pupil."

"Got a name for this new thing?"

"Nothing special, just low platelet counts. You're having a little bleeding, and it's safer to give you more chemotherapy here in the hospital."

"You wait and see—I'm going to be okay."

HENRY WAS UNDRESSING for bed when the phone rang. The hospital operator said, "The medical resident is calling."

Henry sighed. It could be anything.

"Doctor Nyren. It's about Maria Fauci."

"I'll be right over."

"No—I mean, she just died."

"What do you mean she died?" Henry shouted.

The resident, thrown by the anger in Henry's loud reply, said "Nothing happened. That is, I mean, everything was okay. It was like she just turned over in bed and died. I'm really sorry, Doctor Nyren."

"I'll be right there!"

Henry slammed down the phone, dressed quickly, and took the stairs two at a time. But outside his building, he stopped short. There was no reason for him to rush to the hospital. He knew what had happened. No platelets. She had been having bleeding in the skin, mouth, and GI tract. Then, a sudden massive and fatal cerebral hemorrhage. *Finis* to a scenario he knew all too well.

Instead of turning right toward the hospital, Henry turned left. He was numb with pain. After walking aimlessly for a while, he went into a Mexican restaurant and sat down. He ordered a margarita. He didn't know if the salt he tasted was from the rim of the glass or from his eyes.

14

# CHAPTER
## *TWO*

THE NEXT day was filled with the comfortable warmth of spring. Henry, with a full complement of patients to see that afternoon, had no time to dwell on the grim events of the previous night. That episode, as well as his grief, had to take its place in the files. Today's problems were now center stage. His office, on a high floor of the hospital, was small, bright, adequate. He sat at his desk reviewing the records of a new patient, also a child. The reports were favorable, and he was not sure why the mother had sought another opinion.

Henry's nurse, Ellen, brought the young mother into the office. Henry motioned to her to sit in a low-backed armchair across from his desk. Donna Stockman fussed with her skirt, waiting for him to speak. He got right to the point.

"The reports from your hematologists are very encouraging. It looks like"—Henry found the boy's name in the chart—"Randy is going into remission."

"That's what they told me, but I need someone else to tell me the same thing. Also, I've got questions, and they keep putting me off. The fact is, they just don't take the time to answer me. I mean, does remission mean cure? Why does Randy have to go on getting chemotherapy? What will be the effects of all this chemotherapy, later on? Has his brain been affected? How about children? I've

15

got a whole page of questions. I was told you talk to your patients. That's why I came."

"You're not wrong to get another opinion, and you have every right to have your questions answered," Henry said.

This woman was doing something that Henry strongly advocated: asking questions, standing up for her rights, refusing to be intimidated by doctors.

"According to the records, it's time to do another bone marrow examination. Did you know that?" he asked her.

"Yes. That's another reason why I came. I want it done here."

Donna Stockman brought her son in from the waiting room. No stranger to chemotherapy, he. Bald-headed and with dry skin, he looked like a little old man rather than the five-year-old he was. Ellen tried to distract him, but he knew what was coming. The mother held the boy's hand while Henry examined him and did the bone marrow aspiration. Henry did it quickly, but it was not something that could be done painlessly.

Henry peeled off the surgical gloves he had been wearing during the procedure and, as he washed his hands, overheard the mother comforting the crying boy.

"I know it hurts, darling, but it's over now, right?"

The child nodded agreement. She held his hand as he jumped down from the end of the examining table. She helped the boy dress, and then the child and his mother walked together, heads erect, toward the waiting room.

"Randy, stay with Grandma, while I talk to the doctor."

She came back into Henry's office and sat down, folding her hands in her lap, a woman used to waiting for a doctor's verdict.

This child had been through so much, and yet he had cooperated and quickly regained his composure. Henry had been impressed by the mother's tone, the way she comforted without babying.

"I'll have the results for you tomorrow, Mrs. Stockman. I'll be able to give you a definite opinion then."

"Is there such a thing as a cure in situations like Randy's?" she asked anxiously.

16

Henry turned and pointed to three framed photos on his bookshelf.

"This was Carol, age three, my first patient. She had leukemia. Then here she is at twenty, graduating from nursing school, and at twenty-two with her husband and baby. She had good medical care—and she was lucky. You need both." He was thinking of Maria. "Randy has had good care. He may be in complete remission now. Ask the secretary for an appointment for the same time tomorrow. I'll have the lab results, and I'll be in a much better position to answer your long list of questions."

There was intelligence and sensitivity in those gray-green eyes, Henry thought. He held out his hand.

A little disappointed that she did not get the assurance she sought on the first visit, her smile was tentative, and her grip, although firm, was moist. Anxiety had left its mark.

After Donna Stockman and the child left, Henry took a short break before afternoon rounds, the final chore of the day. He lit a cigar and went to a small table next to the secretary's desk where a coffee pot was kept warm. He poured a cup and looked around the waiting room as if surprised to see no patients.

Ellen was putting the examining room back in order. Finished, she joined him for coffee.

"I don't know why you light up that cigar of yours if you just put it out in two minutes," she said. "It still amazes me that you, of all people, should smoke."

In response, Henry sat down in one of the armchairs, stretched out his legs, took a puff, a sip of coffee, and said "Ahhh!" Then, to Ellen, "That's it for today."

"And you won't be in tomorrow?"

"Right. Tomorrow I'll be in Morristown."

"But you told Mrs. Stockman . . ." Ellen said.

"Dammit, I did. Be a pal. Call her, apologize for the delay. Make sure she understands it has nothing to do with any special concern about the results of the test. Give her an appointment for Wednesday instead."

"What time? You've got students the first part of the afternoon,

17

then Chemotherapy Conference, and a full schedule of patients after that."

"Make it at five-thirty then. I can't put her through still another day's wait."

THE TRAIN TO Morristown was the same dirty, red coach with the same shabby seats, their iron frames and wicker covers unchanged since Henry rode back and forth to college in New York. It had been a long time since he had taken the train to Morristown instead of driving, and it heightened the sense of nostalgia he felt whenever he went there.

At 9 A.M., the heavy traffic was going the other way. Henry's car was two-thirds empty. There were a few salesmen and a couple of strays returning home from a big night on the town, but most of the passengers were solid, somber, middle-aged black women going to the suburbs for domestic day work.

Henry was sitting in his seat, adjusting his memories, when an old man, his face a net of wrinkles, approached him from the end of the lurching train. He was dressed in conductor's trousers and vest with a gold chain, but he was wearing a shabby brown jacket. Holding the hand grip at the end of the seat, he bent over slightly to get a better look at Henry.

"Say, you look familiar. Are you—let me see . . ."

"I'm Henry Nyren, and you're Luther Tines. You were the conductor on the train all the time I was going to college. It's really good to see you again."

Henry rose to shake the old man's hand.

"Henry Nyren. Well, I'll be damned. I remember like it was yesterday. I'm retired ten years now. Can't get another job and too young to sit around and do nothing. I have a pass, ride the train every day, early, when I still have some energy. Sometimes I meet someone I know, just like now. Say, I was sorry to hear about your mother."

"Thank you. Her passing was peaceful. How did you happen to hear?"

18

"I go to the nursing home every day. I saw a lot of your mother there. She liked to talk about you. She was proud of you, working at that big cancer hospital in the city and all." Luther shifted his weight rhythmically with the motion of the train, as if dancing to a tune he knew by heart.

Henry leaned toward the retired conductor so they could talk more easily over the clickety-clack.

"Do you have someone at Pinebush?"

"My wife, well, she's got it . . . you know, cancer. They put her in the nursing home from the hospital. She's got it in the female parts, spread all over her belly. Nothing they can do for her, but they keep her comfortable there. People said I ought to call you. I was on the verge a few times, but Doctor Walton said there was no point to it."

"I'm going to Pinebush. I'd be glad to drop in and see your wife if you'd like me to."

"Would you? I'd sure appreciate it. We've got Medicare and everything."

AS HENRY STEPPED down from the train he was greeted by three stages of local history. The neat, red-brick train station with the slate roof still had some dirt paths around it, a few patches of the nineteenth century that progress had failed to pave over. Behind the station was the bumpy, two-lane asphalt highway that became Main Street when it ran into town. Busy with small trucks and housewives out shopping, it carried the daily rounds of the community. Beyond that was the turnpike with its fast-moving traffic. To the west of the station were the farms that produced fruits and vegetables for New York markets, and in the trees beyond, the farms ran into the country clubs. When Henry was a boy, the farmers had been the local poor folks. Henry could remember his father giving them credit in the pharmacy. But things had changed. With the increasing value of land so close to New York, the sons of the farmers had become real estate men. The boys who had been caddies and cooks and

19

helpers at the clubs were now members. They bought and sold the town businesses like the pharmacy that the Nyrens had owned. They also built the Pinebush Nursing Home on a tract of land for which they had no other use.

Pinebush was a rambling, one-story, long-term care facility built in the midst of what used to be scrub pine woods. As he entered the building that afternoon, Henry said hello to the members of the staff he recognized and thanked them for the care his mother had received. He looked for Delia Dean, a senior nurse at the home and family friend. She was giving instructions to the medication nurse, but as soon as she spotted Henry, she checked her carefully set gray hair, smoothed out her uniform, and sent her corpulent torso waddling down the corridor to greet him. Delia and Henry walked arm-in-arm together back to the nurses' station. He told her about meeting Luther Tines on the train and why he had come. Delia picked up the chart as they walked to Mrs. Tines's room.

"You've had it rough, Henry. First your wife and now your mother."

Henry nodded his head as all the obligatory things were said.

"Your lovely daughter must be all grown up by now," Delia smiled.

"She is," Henry replied.

"What is she doing?"

"She's working for a magazine, following in her mother's footsteps."

"I'll bet she's a darling. You must be closer than ever now."

"Yes," Henry said, taking the chart from Delia to signal the end of a conversation that was becoming awkward for him. She gave him an affectionate hug.

"I'll find Doctor Walton for you. You've lost weight since you were here last," she said. "Take care of yourself, Henry."

Henry smiled wryly. He had weighed almost the same since the last year of medical school, but was actually in better physical condition now. He was slightly above average height, though he was often described as being tall. Perhaps his posture gave the impression of height, or his high shock of straight black hair, which had the habit of falling over his forehead.

He had experienced every variation of fatigue when he was a student, intern, and resident, and he had discovered that, regardless of the effort required, exercise was the best antidote for fatigue and the best tonic for tension. He had become a determined stair-climber, bypassing elevators as often as he could, and he swam whenever he had the chance. Laps in the pool several times a week got the kinks out of his back, neck, and shoulders. The result was that he walked tall, with determination in his step. When he came down a crowded hospital corridor, people spontaneously gave way before this vigorous figure who sailed more than walked past them.

Henry stood outside Mrs. Tines's room for a few minutes reviewing the chart. She was bedridden and too weak to go to the dining room. A nurses' aide was feeding her pureed food.

"I'm Doctor Nyren," he said as he entered her room. "I'm a friend of Luther's. Why don't I come back after you've finished eating?"

"I'm finished now, don't have any appetite. Anyway, doesn't make any difference if I eat or don't eat. I keep right on losing weight. Except here."

She pointed to her abdomen. "Looks like I'm pregnant, doesn't it? I call it my tumor baby."

Henry saw the protrusion through the thin bed covers. He turned the covers down and palpated the mass; it was hard and immovable. Her legs were swollen; the tumor was obstructing the blood flow in the veins of her legs and pelvis. But her lungs were fine, and her internal organs were apparently functioning well.

When Henry returned to the nurses' station, Dr. Walton had arrived.

"I'm sure your visit cheered her up, Henry. A sad case there. She never knew she was developing a tumor, her pelvis just filled

21

up with cancer. We opened her up, then closed her again and sent her over here. We're managing to keep her pretty comfortable."

The nursing home was too hot, adding to Henry's discomfort. He had meant this to be a compassionate visit, a few kind words, that's all. Anything more would be butting in.

He did it anyway. "Doctor Walton, she'll be dead in two months at the rate she's going," he said. "I think with radiation therapy and chemotherapy she could have two or three good years. Why don't you have the oncologists at Morristown Memorial have a look at her?"

The older man sat down on the secretary's chair.

"Well, Henry, my philosophy about cancer is, if you can't cut it out then you've got to let nature take its course. That's what they taught us in medical school, and I haven't seen anything in forty-three years of practice to change my mind."

Henry had once viewed the elderly physician with deference; he had been Dr. Walton when Henry was in high school. But he couldn't defer now. He couldn't walk in and then leave like any other visitor. "This case could change your mind. We're getting excellent results with cancer of the ovary."

Horace Walton leaned forward in the chair, a glint of sharpness in his eyes. "You don't cure them, do you? I read the journals, and I know what people go through when they get those experimental drugs. You're going to make her go through hell just to give her a few more months, and then she's going to die anyway. Here she's at peace and in no pain."

Henry was still standing. He pulled up a chair and sat down and tried to match Walton's relaxed manner.

"Doctor Walton, I'm not talking about experiments. I can show you practical results. I'll have patients, who would have been dead but are now in good health, write to you and tell you if they feel it was worthwhile or not. Sure the treatment isn't as simple as a shot of penicillin, but in the two months that Mrs. Tines would be here dying, she's got a better than fifty-fifty chance of getting rid of that tumor for three or four years."

22

Mulling over his response, the older man stroked his chin. This was his first encounter with Henry in a professional capacity. "Now it's three or four years. A minute ago it was two or three years. You go and talk to her. She's a plain, trusting soul, and I'm sure you'll be able to talk her into it. When the Tineses ask me, I'll say you're the cancer expert. I won't say you're wrong. But remember, the family didn't ask for any more to be done."

Any thoughts Henry had about holding back were gone. He felt the same in-the-ring fighting spirit that always grabbed him when he encountered a patient with cancer, particularly after he had examined the patient and touched the cancer, sized it up. Could it be true? Could the cancer loom larger than the patient— assume an adversary position with the oncologist in which the patient was incidental?

Henry managed to keep his tone low-keyed and friendly. "Doctor Walton, I've got a good feeling about this lady."

"What does that mean?"

"There's something we can do for her. This case is what chemotherapy is about—time."

"Henry," Dr. Walton said, "that woman has terminal cancer."

"I don't like the word 'terminal.' Do you think of your cardiac patients as terminal?" Henry asked.

"That woman has an inoperable cancer."

"You can't operate on a diabetic, but you try to keep him alive. You can't cure someone with emphysema, but you try to keep him alive, don't you?"

"Of course."

"Why not a cancer patient? I'll tell you why, Doctor Walton. We all left medical school with a fatalistic attitude toward cancer. We weren't taught any better. But patients don't go to medical school. They just want a few more years of living. I don't have any trouble convincing patients, it's their doctors I can't convince. Doctor Walton, if you could give two or three more years to a cardiac patient, you'd consider it a triumph. Why not a cancer patient? Why not this woman?"

Henry took in a look that told him he had gone far enough. "Nothing personal, Doctor Walton."

"Don't worry about my feelings, Henry, but remember this, won't you? There is a difference. When I treat a diabetic or a cardiac, I don't make them deathly sick, and I extend their lives for years, not months."

Dr. Walton smiled thinly, and they shook hands. Henry said good-bye to Delia, who had returned while the doctors were talking. Then he left, promising to arrange the transfer.

"There he goes, Delia," Dr. Walton said. "Don Quixote. Can't leave well enough alone."

# CHAPTER
# *THREE*

HENRY STOOD outside the nursing home waiting for a taxi. Dr. Walton's remarks stayed with him. That practice-worn physician, encrusted with years of experience, wasn't entirely wrong. There were patients, including many with ovarian cancer, in whom he couldn't make a dent in the tumor. There was just no way to know beforehand who would have a brilliant response to treatment and who would not. In the cab, his encounter with Dr. Walton continued to force thoughts on him. You don't give up the struggle because you may not win. Dr. Walton or no Dr. Walton, Mrs. Tines was going to get her chance.

BY THE TIME he boarded the train to New York he was thinking of other things. He had ten patients hospitalized. Two were about to die, but he had some new drugs he could try. No reason to sign off on them. In two others, the cancer had just been diagnosed. He felt he could either achieve a cure or a long-term remission. For the rest, with various complications of recurrent cancer, he was buying time. He was at his best with these patients. Whether it was fluid in the lung, an obstructed bowel, or a fungal infection in the central nervous system, Henry would devise an intensive onslaught by physicians and surgeons with X-ray and laboratory support that could be compared only with a military assault. Napoleon against the Shevardino redoubt: the infantry, cavalry, artillery, and all the complicated logistics necessary to defeat an entrenched foe. Henry worked only with those colleagues who shared his aggressive attitude toward cancer, associates who knew that when Henry called there was something to be done and he wanted it done right away. It was also remarkable how often he was able to achieve his goal: malignant pleural effusion cleared up and did not return, intestinal obstruction was relieved, cryptococcal fungus infection was overcome. His track record for overwhelming redoubts was remarkable. However, when the attacks were over, the battles won, often he was left standing in the midst of ruins. There'd be little life left, and that would soon run out. But this never deterred him from seeking the next battle. What satisfaction was there for the physician if every cancer complication were overcome and yet the patient died? If you were Henry Nyren, there was satisfaction.

THINKING ABOUT HIS patients helped Henry to relax. Other thoughts jumbled onstage but were easily shoved into the wings. *His* patients—he was in control, he gave them life—what a fantastic thing. Sometimes he stepped on a few toes at the hospital or antagonized other doctors, as he knew he had Dr. Walton. But he did what he had to do. Cancer did not always have to win. In fact, he knew that if you never gave in, stayed with the patient all the way, to the very end, in a sense, cancer did not have to win at all. The human spirit could be extinguished, but it did not have to be crushed. That was the secret, Henry knew. Never leave the patient with no hope.

At Curie Hospital, only Paul Rosen fought as hard as Henry did to keep cancer patients alive. Henry wished he knew as much cancer biology, biochemistry, and genetics as Paul, who ran a research lab and was Chief of the Chemotherapy Division of the Medical Department. But Henry wouldn't change places with Paul. Paul was not in practice. He did not get involved in the lives

26

of patients the way Henry did. The patients Paul Rosen saw were those being treated for research purposes only; he did not provide the routine medical care. It wasn't the same.

Paul often told Henry no one could do it all. Research was a full-time job and so was patient care. In principle Paul was right. But Henry could not make himself give up either. It was patients that made his juices flow, that made him want to fight. Yet when he wasn't working on a research project, was caring only for patients, he felt trapped. Research raised his expectations, just as chemotherapy raised patients' expectations. Both were supported by the same hope—that something was going to happen that would make things better.

The recommendation Henry had made for Mrs. Tines was a conservative one. Actually, he would have preferred to take Mrs. Tines into Curie Hospital, skip over the conventional chemotherapy, and treat her with a new drug, streptokotocin. She had a tumor he could measure. She hadn't had previous chemotherapy so her blood counts were not depressed. The tumor had not spread to vital organs, therefore she would live long enough to evaluate the antitumor effect of the drug. Streptokotocin was toxic enough, but still it was a potent anticancer agent. Henry was not exactly pleased with himself for having recommended conventional therapy. It wasn't like him. His instincts were to go right for the jugular.

HENRY MOVED QUICKLY out of the PATH station at 34th Street into the faltering afternoon light. A glimpse to the left, West 34th Street. The sun was retiring beneath the New Jersey horizon like the other commuters. Five P.M. was no time to try for a cab. Predatory urban females would destroy you if you approached their foul yellow cabs. Onto a bus grunting its way across the waistline of the city to the East Side. Fifteen minutes later the bus had gotten from Eighth Avenue to Broadway. Henry couldn't sit still for more of the same. He plunged into the turgid stream of pedestrians flowing east and west. He elbowed his way

27

into the chatting, hustling, radio-playing, package-carrying mob, but he couldn't move any faster than the others. In the long run he would have made better time if he had stayed on the bus.

He hadn't tried to set his own pace in such a slow-moving crowd since he was a medical student coming in from New Jersey twenty-five years ago. Then he had walked for exercise: out of the tubes, crosstown to Bellevue, and then back over the same route at night. Almost a generation had gone by. He seldom used public transportation now. There was no reason for him to be on 34th Street. But as he shoved and was shoved, pushed and was pushed, his walk turned into an impromptu urban carnival. He was experiencing a sensation he had had walking in crowds in other places, other countries, among other peoples. There were no telephones to answer, no insistent illness to make demands. If there was sickness or disability around him, his eye would not take it in. No one expected anything from him: no achievements, no *deus ex medica.* In this protoplasmic flow, off came the stethoscope, gone was the white coat; he was down off the podium and down from the pedestal. Free and equal as on the first day of life or the last. It was exhilarating. The ripple of murmuring voices was a liturgy, and the background sounds an antiphony. It was, in fact, a communion.

When Henry came to Fifth Avenue, he stood and looked at the avalanche of down-streaming buses, absolutely the same as it had been decades earlier. As a student he had once reached this intersection, this very curb, in the midst of a surging crowd much like today's. Some of the traffic always turned right at this corner. That day the shadow of a bus turning the corner had flung a dark hypotenuse across the people standing in the right angle. The medical student knew the motion of every molecule on the street and how much room it needed. He would not move back an inch from the curb as the bus turned. It would get so close and no closer. The lumbering mass of power came within inches of his body as his feet stood their ground, but it did not touch him. He had again asserted his hegemony over insensate forces. A second

28

later his toes were run over by a cab whose driver was impatient to beat the light. Three broken toes, hobbling along for two months. A metropolitan stomp for childish behavior.

He was still capable of childish behavior, he thought. All day he had been thinking of that child's mother, Mrs. Stockman. What was her first name? If he'd caught it, he didn't remember. Why did he remember *her*? Why was he thinking about her? She was young, warm, and attractive. Hell, at least fifty women at Curie fit that description. But there was something about this woman that reminded him of Laura. Charm, yes, but also assertiveness and independence. Back to reality. Did he, or didn't he, have a date with Janine? He thought so, but sometimes things he was sure they had planned, he'd never even mentioned to her, and she hated that. He was trying to be more considerate. So he had to phone. When he got to Third Avenue, he turned north and stopped to call. The first booth had chewing gum in the coin slot. In its twin, the phone handle had been cleanly clipped off the cord. Well, he'd tried. Not hard enough, maybe. When he got to Janine's block he continued to walk east, past a five-story walk-up, a Chinese laundry, a tiny Italian restaurant, a bike shop, a mattress store, an empty store, and a candy store. Henry walked in, bought a cigar, and used the phone in an old, wooden cabinet in the back. The phone worked, there was even a seat. "Janine, I'm sorry to call so late," he apologized. "Are we on for dinner?"

"Sure. Did you get tied up? Where are you?"

The question made him feel like a child caught with his hand in the cookie jar. "Just up the block," he admitted.

Janine laughed. "C'mon up."

Janine's building was an old, red-brick apartment house with gargoyles on the roof, a concrete crenellated entrance, and a canvas canopy. It sat between two modern, expressionless, white-brick buildings like a properly dressed old maiden aunt seated between two husky nephews. Henry got a familiar wave from the doorman as he entered the building. He passed the elevators and took the stairs to Janine's floor.

Henry greeted her with a kiss. Janine went back to fixing him a drink.

"Did you just come from Morristown?" she asked.

"Yes," Henry replied, "the lawyer didn't take very long, but I got stuck at the nursing home."

"All this time?" Janine was standing on the kitchen side of a small counter that overlooked a tiny dining area and the living room. "You said it was just some legal formalities you had to take care of."

"There was this lady at Pinebush, a friend of the family's. She's got cancer. I thought I could help her."

Janine pushed the drink across the counter. "You know, you find cancer like a dog finds bones, and here I was thinking, Poor Henry, he must be so upset about all those estate problems and tax things and all those memories. I should have known better."

Henry sighed. All combat veterans have difficulty adjusting when they return to civilian life, but usually they have to do it only once. Henry's battle was every day, and he sometimes found it difficult to jump from the emotional storm of dealing with cancer patients and their families to the shallow *politesse* of everyday life. Even though Janine worked at the same hospital, her position in the Personnel Department distanced her from patient problems.

He took his drink and sat at the small table facing the living room. The floor was covered with some well-worn oriental rugs Janine had inherited from her parents, who had been people of means. There were many deep cushions, and small trees in large, glazed pots were artfully placed around the room. There were also bronze trays on legs, but little other furniture. The walls were filled with hanging plants, all thirsting toward the window, drinking in the light.

"Where do you want to go for dinner?" Janine asked.

"No place."

Henry walked over to her. He bent and kissed her on the neck. "I need you," he whispered.

30

"For what, an hors d'oeuvre?" Janine replied in a surprised tone.

Henry laughed. "Touché! What a nice way to tell me I'm a jackass. Let's have another drink." He reached over to his jacket for a cigar.

"My dear, with us everything is possible, but we are civilized. Have some brie. And if you're going to smoke that thing, you'll have to brush your teeth before coming to bed."

AS THEY WERE dressing the next morning, Janine said, "Henry, there's a great deal I can tell about you when we are making love."

"What do you mean?" he asked. He was looking through a dresser for a fresh shirt. It never ceased to amaze him how casually—almost clinically—Janine discussed sex. How different from Laura, who had relished shrouding sex with a penumbra that replaced visual impact with veiled imagination.

"Well, for example," Janine said, "I can tell when you are depressed or elated. I can even tell when you are not making love, but are really fighting cancer. How about that?"

"How can you tell?"

"It's just something a woman knows."

"And last night?"

"You had someone else in mind."

JANINE HAD BEEN at Curie many years, had met Henry at a time when he was just starting his practice at the hospital and needed a secretary. She recruited two good people, but they did not work out. Henry went to the Personnel Office to seek out the individual who was doing the hiring in order to complain. Instead he was gently informed that the secretaries reported it was a strain to work for him because he was impatient and because he spoke too rapidly into the Dictaphone. He resolved the standoff by inviting Janine to dinner. Janine was a year or two older than Henry and enjoyed her work in that it allowed her to use her intuitive knowledge of people. But personnel work wasn't creative enough for her; nor did it provide her with after-hours sociability. Her life outside the hospital was off-Broadway theater. She produced plays—sometimes alone, more often with others for whom the development of new talent provided a stimulus they needed and could afford. Janine had a son in boarding school in New Hampshire, who fulfilled her sense of family. All in all, her life had settled into a satisfactory pattern.

About a year after they met, that friendship, which at first had been casual, became a bond. Janine had taken a young actor home with her. She was, in her own words, selectively promiscuous. The man was someone she was sponsoring in a new production; she felt he had talent, sensitivity, and high standards. That time her intuition had been wrong. He beat her savagely and left her on the floor semiconscious and bleeding. She called her personal physician, who sounded annoyed and told her to go to a hospital emergency room. She was too mortified. Apologetically she called Henry. He came right over, cleaned and dressed her wounds, arranged for dental care the next day, and took her into his apartment for a week. He had the locks on her door changed and her phone number changed and unlisted before he let her return to her apartment. Henry felt he had done nothing special; but Janine was never again casual about her friendship with Henry. When Henry and Laura were married she was a guest at the wedding. Laura knew Janine was an old friend of Henry's and never asked any questions.

# CHAPTER
# FOUR

I N THE early morning it was a twenty-minute brisk walk along nearly empty streets from Janine's apartment to the hospital. Frequently they walked together, but since he had been away for a day in the middle of a busy week, he wanted an early start. It had been a good day, constructive, even relaxing, and yet, as Janine had said, he did find cancer like a dog finds bones. If you were obsessively involved with your work, and it centered around something that directly or indirectly touched almost everyone's life, encountering it constantly was inevitable. Still, for a few hours at least, Henry had been free of the hospital. Free in the sense that a bird is free to walk on the ground. But the hospital was his natural environment, and he functioned less well outside it. For him, the hospital was an arena, a place for a deadly and unequal contest.

Of course, there was no audience and certainly no displays or advertisements of any sort. In truth, hardly anyone knew that an encounter of Olympian proportions was going on. This particular hospital was unique in that it specialized in cancer. Within, there were scores of highly trained, competent, and dedicated physicians and surgeons. The attached cancer research institute housed scientists of international acclaim, and laboratory lights frequently burned twenty-four hours a day. In what way was

Henry Nyren different? He detested cancer with a fierce and personal loathing.

He did not cultivate this passion deliberately, nor was he by any mannerism or behavior other than an attractive man and a mature, responsible physician, well-liked by his colleagues and patients. He came from a family where feelings ran deep. His mother was passionate about religion and held strong views about many things. His father was an atheist who felt equally strongly about his convictions. At home, disputes laden with emotion were common. They frequently ended in the bedroom, and Henry, an only child, never knew if the cries that emanated from there were the result of pleasure or pain.

The single event that had turned the young medical student to the study of cancer was the fact that, at the very onset of his medical studies, he had himself developed Hodgkin's disease—an early case and successfully treated. Yet, despite his emotional involvement with the disease he spent his life treating, it was seldom apparent. Outside of this single obsession, his views on other subjects were reasonable and soberly expressed.

THAT AFTERNOON DONNA Stockman arrived at Henry's office a little early. She sat quietly in a corner, subdued by a blanket of anxiety, waiting to see the doctor and get the bone marrow report. Ellen went over to her.

"Doctor Nyren will be finished with the last patient in a few minutes. But he did say it was all right to tell you about the bone marrow. He knew you'd be anxious. There was no sign of leukemia." She smiled.

Donna tried to return the smile, but instead her face became taut, her breathing labored. She took a wad of tissues from her purse and buried her face in her hands, sobbing. Ellen sat with her for a moment. Then she took a cup and asked, "Well, what'll it be, cream or sugar, or both?"

By the time Donna entered Henry's office she had regained her composure.

34

"Thank you for having your nurse tell me the report on Randy. After she gave me the good news, I could have waited forty days and nights out there," she said.

She spoke calmly, but her face was still flushed and her eyes red. If he had known her better he would have put his arm around her, to frame the good report with human warmth. Instead he said, "You said you have a list of questions. Let's start with them."

"Well, in the first place, can you tell me what to look forward to—I think the word is prognosis?"

"In a child Randy's age, with an excellent response to the first course of chemotherapy, and who is continuing to maintain that response, the prognosis is excellent."

"Can you be a little more specific, Doctor Nyren?"

"You're right. I will be more specific. I'd say that if, after a year of intermittent chemotherapy, the remission holds, I wouldn't hesitate to use the word 'cure.'"

"Then he will need more chemotherapy."

"Yes, once the remission has been induced, the chemotherapy must be continued to forestall a relapse."

"Will he get sick again?"

"A little. There is some new antinausea medication that is very effective. He'll sleep through most of it."

"Can he have the treatment here? I know he's had good care at the other hospital, but I haven't, and I'd like to try to keep myself out of the loony bin during all of this. My husband, Randolph Senior, is in real estate. Rand's so wrapped up in his work that anything outside of it is not quite real. It's not that Randy's father isn't interested, but he can't deal with illness. He loves Randy—in fact he dotes on him. But when Randy got sick, his father insisted it was nothing, that he'd get over it. When Randy started bleeding and having high fevers, Rand started having three martinis before dinner instead of one. He used alcohol to cut the boy off. Then he started lashing out. One night when we were sitting outside Randy's room at the hospital while he was getting platelet transfusions, Rand said, 'Kids don't get cancer. You must have done something wrong.' He apologized later, but what with everything—I mean, I felt the pain as much as he did—that just destroyed me. God, who knows? Maybe I *did* do something wrong. I'm sorry, I shouldn't be bothering you with these personal things."

She took out a thumb-sized, L-shaped plastic tube, held it against her mouth, pressed the button and inhaled the vapor.

"Medihaler?" Henry asked.

"I had asthma as a kid. I grew out of it, except every now and then."

Henry waited as she gained control over her breathing. Her flushed cheeks were in contrast to her fair complexion. Their glow and her hair, by now in some disarray, reminded him of a woman just released from a sensual embrace. When she spoke, she looked down, as if she feared her eyes would give away too much. She was dressed rather demurely in a navy blue pleated skirt and a white silk blouse, with a single strand of pearls. Henry sensed in this woman a tension between sensuality and shyness that he found appealing. He was tempted to prolong the session, but it would have been unseemly. He led her to the door. He didn't know what it was, perhaps the eye contact, a second longer than necessary, or a trifle more than perfunctory pressure of the hand, but he felt unanticipated pleasure, and he gazed after her as she left.

BACK AT HIS desk, Henry picked up a small, crystal, egg-shaped paperweight from a pile of letters and passed it back and forth between his hands. He toyed with the idea of finding some excuse to speak with Donna Stockman again, but forced his attention instead to the paperwork on his desk. If only Maria had had a good, solid remission like the Stockman boy. And then he remembered that he hadn't given Mrs. Stockman an appointment for Randy.

He waited, giving her time to get home. When she answered

the phone, he realized how disappointed he would have been if he had had to leave the message with someone else.

"I didn't give you an appointment for Randy's next visit. How about next Thursday at four P.M.?"

"Fine. Also, I want to thank you for taking the time to answer my questions and, well, for your concern."

"I'm optimistic. See you next week."

He wanted to say more, he wanted there to be more, but he, who was never without the right words for a patient, didn't know how to bridge the gap that had developed between the physician and the man.

# CHAPTER
## *FIVE*

**M**ARLENE LOWELL'S long, hard Thursday started early. First thing, she lost some papers and had to spend a good part of the day looking before she found them. She took pride in her efficiency, and things like that bruised her self-confidence. It ended with two of her night-school students getting into a fight; and when she tried to mediate between the young women, both turned on her screaming and cursing. Several of the minor mishaps in between didn't help. She would forget it all by tomorrow, but right now she was tired. She walked down the long, dark apartment house corridor, then hesitated before entering the apartment. She wasn't sure she could take *them* this evening.

Marlene was in the kitchen cutting up an apple when her mother came in and sat down.

"I'm not going to say anything about the way you eat or how late it is before you have supper," the older woman commented.

"What are you going to say something about?" Marlene countered, sorry at once that she had given her mother the opening she wanted.

"Marlene, the way you're living—cooped up in an office all day, making statues—"

38

"Sculpting."

"—at night. You'll never meet anybody."

"Mother, have you had a pleasant evening?"

"Of course."

"Well, I haven't. I had a lousy day, too. And now I need some peace and quiet. I'm really not up to being tormented tonight."

"You're our only child. All your father and I want is for you to be happy."

"Happy! Has marriage made you happy? All your marriage gives you is someone to gang up on me with."

"Marlene, whatever you say is right."

"Stop it, please. Whatever I say is nothing. We're not having a conversation. You don't hear me."

"I'm your mother. I have to tell you when you're hurting yourself socially and when you don't take care of yourself. That ugly mole on your leg, for example. When are you going to have someone look at it?"

"You mean besides you? I've had that thing for years. I don't even know it's there except when you stare at it or say something."

"Marlene, your legs are your best feature—"

"Great, I'll learn to walk on my hands. Then I can introduce myself by shaking with my best feature."

"They shouldn't be marred by a blemish. Promise me you'll take care of it first chance you get. Doctor Green is a fine dermatologist, and he's right here in the building. He cured Mrs. Kelly's itching, and she raves about him."

"With the stream of men coming in and out of her apartment, no dermatologist can cure the kind of itch she has."

"Say you'll make an appointment with the skin doctor."

"No matter what comes out of his mouth, I'm sure it'll be you under the table throwing your voice. Why should I? It doesn't bother me. Besides, everybody's got moles."

"Marlene, this ain't everybody. It's my only daughter. Promise me."

"Sure, if you promise to let me lead my own life from now on."

"Absolutely. Don't I always?"

THE FOLLOWING MONDAY, Marlene was sitting in the first-floor apartment that served as the dermatologist's office, feeling almost nonchalant. Seeing a dermatologist can't be so bad, she thought. He's not going to poke around my insides, he doesn't care what goes on in my brain, and it's not like having a tooth pulled. So if he doesn't like that blemish and wants to scrape it off, it's okay with me.

Dr. Green's secretary asked her some questions and typed Marlene's replies on a card. Then she brought her into the examining room, gave her a paper robe, and told her to undress. Marlene couldn't see why she had to undress for the doctor to look at a tiny raisin attached to her leg. She hoped he wasn't on the freaky side.

After what seemed a good long wait, a smiling Dr. Berton Green walked into the room and introduced himself. No white coat for this young, trim ad for affluence. He was wearing a camel's hair jacket and brown slacks. Vacation-tanned, his hair better styled than Marlene's, he carried all the nonchalance she had had before being left to sit, wrapped in paper, in a cold examining room. Clutching the gown around her, Marlene felt as vulnerable as the last sardine in the can.

After a once-over-lightly skin examination, Dr. Green studied the black thumbtack-size mark on her leg and announced he would remove it then and there.

"At least we'll get it over with," she sighed. "The only thing that would have been worse would have been for you to say that it didn't have to come off at all. Then you'd have to deal with the great diagnostician in 7H."

Dr. Green raised a dark, trim eyebrow.

"Doctor Lowell," Marlene said. "My mother."

The secretary, who was also the medical assistant, came in and

40

had Marlene lie on the treatment table. While Dr. Green left the room, she scrubbed Marlene's leg and covered it with a sheet perforated by a hole. Then she focused the light. The black spot was centered in the hole like a bull's-eye.

Dr. Green returned, this time wearing a short white coat, simultaneously humming and chewing gum. "Just put your head back and relax. I'm going to inject some novocaine. You're not allergic to it, are you? After that, there'll be no pain."

Marlene put her head back and closed her eyes. A little pinprick, some tingling and a warm feeling, and then, it was quite true, no pain. But there were some pushing and pulling sensations; she knew something was going on. As the seconds went by, she felt perspiration accumulating on her forehead, and the muscles of her neck and back were becoming increasingly tense. From somewhere at the other end of her body, she heard the humming of a vaguely familiar tune. She opened her eyes just enough to see the side of the head from which the tune was emanating. It was a roundish head, with thinning, brown, curly hair and a large, tanned ear, apparently related to the tanned bald spot that showed through the hair carefully combed over it. The tip of a pointed nose was directed at her leg, and she could see the jaw in front of that large, tanned ear, vigorously chewing a jiggling bulge of gum. She tried to relax by focusing her mind on things she could see with her eyes half open. The ceiling of the room, the cabinet when she turned her head to the right, the washstand when she turned her head to the left. Then the side of the head again—the masseter, that was it. The chewing muscle. She remembered it from surface anatomy drawings in art class. She tried to amuse herself. Maybe he wasn't using a scalpel. But she couldn't relax. Her muscles were taut strings of anxiety. The noncommunication from the other end of the table was intolerable.

"Er—Doctor Green?"

"Yes? You don't feel any pain, do you?"

"No, but pain isn't the only thing that can drive you crazy. Try nerves some time. Or better yet, nerves, fear, and a wild imagination."

"This is just a minor procedure. There's nothing about it to upset you."

"Wanna bet? Right now, I can't make up my mind if you are amputating my leg or just digging a hole from one side to the other. I'm sure when you see light on the other side, you'll stop digging. On the other hand—if you're cutting that leg off, I'm sure you'll transplant one of the dog's legs I'm positive you keep in that white cabinet there."

"All I'm doing, Lena—nurse said you prefer that to Marlene, right?—is cutting off a piece of skin the size of your fingernail and about as thick as an orange peel. I'm almost finished. We'll have the pathology report in a week or so. You know, when you came in here, I had you pegged as a cool, calm, cookie—a real businesslike gal. How could a little thing like this bother you?"

A few minutes later Dr. Green put a flesh-colored bandage on the small, sutured incision. Marlene thanked him, dressed, and walked out looking cool and calm, her heart racing like an Olympic runner.

# CHAPTER
## *SIX*

"**I**T'S ROBERT Bauer, Doctor. Ann is having trouble breathing again. I don't know what to do."

Henry had been taking care of Ann Bauer's lymphosarcoma for three years. Things had been going well until the disease spread to the lungs.

"She was doing fine after we drained the fluid from her chest last week. When did this start?" he asked.

"She wasn't home two days and again she can't breathe."

"Why didn't you call me right away? You don't fool around with shortness of breath."

"She wouldn't let me. Don't bother him, don't bother him, she kept saying. But now I'm frightened."

"Bring her right into the office. We'll get a chest X-ray and see if the fluid has returned."

"I don't know if I can get her there, Doc, it's really bad."

Henry could detect the sounds of fear coming from a dry mouth.

"Her lips are cracked, and if I try to give her water, she pushes my hand away. She can't talk more than a word or two, the gasping doesn't stop."

"Listen, don't bring her to the office, take her right to the emergency room. I'll call and tell them to expect you and I'll meet you there."

Henry was thinking ahead. Why had the breathing gotten so bad so fast? Maybe it wasn't the tumor; perhaps heart failure was superimposed. Maybe she had developed pneumonia. He called the emergency room and left orders. All this time he was standing at a phone in the nurses' station, leaving the interns and residents waiting in the hall to continue rounds with him. When the patient arrived in the emergency room, he would again have to drop what he was doing. That day, after rounds, he had a mandatory hospital committee meeting, office hours, a pathology meeting, and two hours of research planned in the dog lab. How could he juggle the time? He couldn't. What would lose out? The research. What would be the result? Cumulative frustration. What could he do about it? Nothing. Every day brought some valid but unforeseen urgent call that punctured his bulging daily schedule. However, that day the time ticked by and no Ann Bauer.

When she did finally arrive, it was bad. Her husband couldn't stop apologizing for getting there so late. He had panicked and taken her to a local hospital's emergency room, but when they saw how bad she was, they gave her oxygen and kept her waiting until their attending physician arrived. X-rays were taken, deliberations were made and in the end, they decided they did not want to treat her. She was sent on to Curie. On the way, the ambulance had a flat, and another had to be called to complete the trip. Nothing was going right for Ann. She was sitting on the stretcher, legs drawn up, pale hands with blue fingertips clenched over her knees. Her face was beaded with perspiration, and all her energy was directed toward achieving the next breath. Emergency X-rays showed not only fluid in both sides of the chest, but tumor and possible pneumonia in both lungs. Her pulse was rapid, the neck veins were distended, and the blood pressure was low. A bad situation was made worse by heart failure. She was admitted to a single room in the hospital and put on the critical list. Ann was scared. Asphyxia is a bad way to go.

44

"Can I stay with her?" her husband asked.

"Sure, Bob."

Ann grasped her husband's hands and continued to gasp for air. The oxygen was helping very little. Henry injected digitalis intravenously. Then he removed fluid from both sides of her chest, but there was no improvement. Her blood pressure had fallen further. Blue, the color of oxygen-starved blood, was creeping up from her fingertips to her hands. It took about ten breaths for her to say, "Bobbie, is this dying? If it is, it's lousy."

Henry was on one side, her husband on the other. He looked at Henry with a wild stare. He opened his mouth but nothing came out. Ann didn't look at either of them, just straight ahead. She was in the same crouched over, sitting position as when she came in. Her staccato breaths could be heard through the thin oxygen mask.

"Am I dying, Doctor Nyren?"

"No, you're not. You're having a rough time. We've gotten you out of bad situations before, and we'll do it again."

He thought to himself, call the resuscitation team—put her on the mechanical respirator—pump her full of oxygen—try to hit that tumor with experimental chemotherapy or maybe mid-torso occlusion. The last was a new technique Henry was working on to give large amounts of chemotherapy to the upper part of the body only. But when he turned to the nurse, it was a different order that came out of his mouth.

"Are you sure you want to give morphine to a patient who is having trouble breathing?" the nurse asked.

"Yes, and call the resuscitation team immediately," Henry said, his urgent whisper reflecting the patient's anguish.

The nurse left and, in about two minutes, a different nurse returned and handed Henry the syringe containing morphine. Desperate thoughts continued to run through his mind. Wait for the respirator—God, this is terrible—she's strangling and I'm sitting here holding her hand. He injected the morphine intravenously.

"Where the hell is the team?" he shouted. "Where are they!"

45

"In the elevator—they'll be here in thirty seconds," she said.

There was nothing the nurse could do either. She was standing outside the room looking at the elevator, waiting. The lights over the doors traced the elevator's progress. It had reached their floor, then, unbelievably, it kept going. One, two, three, four floors farther. The lights indicated the doors were staying open. They were moving their equipment out on the wrong floor! She ran down the hall to call and tell them their mistake. Back to the patient's room—Dr. Nyren must know about the delay.

Henry was still holding Ann's hand. With the other he was holding a stethoscope to her heart, seeking the heartbeat that was not there. The nurse saw him look up at the husband and shake his head. She put her hand to her mouth to stifle a sob, lowered her head, and left. Henry came around the foot of the bed and put his hand on the husband's trembling shoulder for a moment, but there was nothing more he could do.

As Henry left the room, he felt like a length of fabric being strained to the tearing point. Did he have any regrets about what he had done? He had not been obliged to give her morphine until the respirator arrived. If he had waited, perhaps he could have kept the flame of life flickering a little longer. Wasn't that his job, his credo—his calling? The unexpected, the surprising, was always happening in cancer patients. Maybe it would have happened to Ann Bauer. Why didn't he wait? Was his skin so thin, his tolerance for a patient's agony so low? Had compassion clouded his judgment? There was another answer. He had tried the approach of respirator plus last-ditch chemotherapy many times under the same circumstances, and no one had ever recovered. The patients all developed brain damage and died in a few days or at most weeks. He clenched his fist to contain the dissatisfaction within and proceeded to the nursing station. When he arrived at the glass-enclosed area to make a note in the chart, Miss Flannery, the nurse who had questioned his order for morphine, glowered at him.

No love lost there, Henry thought. He did not care much for

46

Veronica Flannery either. She had the particularly annoying habit of reminding him with an arrogant air to do something that was perfectly obvious and that he fully intended to do. But she was damnably efficient, completely reliable, and when she had a comment about a patient you listened. She ran her floor with a firm hand, and patients were well cared for on her shift. Henry had once slipped and referred to her out loud as "the White Whale," his private name for her. Apparently she had overheard him—or someone had told her. It was daggers ever since. Miss Flannery *was* obese and had beady eyes, white hair, a very white face with no visible eyebrows, and a long, thin line for lips. In her white uniform, the description was apt enough.

WHEN HE LEFT the hospital floor, Henry returned to his office.

"Way behind schedule, Tara, I know," he said.

"There are several people waiting in the hospital lobby till we have room here."

"How many patients this afternoon?"

"Fourteen, sir."

Henry had the only secretary in the hospital who wore a sari and had a red *bindi* mark between her eyes. When she came to be interviewed he had hesitated, wondering if she would fit in. But Janine had said her typing was good, her grammar, punctuation, and spelling were superior, and he found her manner so pleasant that he hired her on the spot. Both Janine and he had been right. Tara's work was highly accurate, and the patients appreciated her warm, personal approach. About halfway through office hours, Tara buzzed him.

"Something important, Doctor Nyren. May I see you for a moment, sir?"

He enjoyed the soft, lyrical accent of her speech, but what she told him was not lyrical.

"Rosalie, the secretary in the Nursing Office, and I, have lunch together each day, and we have become rather good chums. She just called to tell me that Miss Flannery has submitted a memo of complaint to the Nursing Office. Rosalie said the memo referred to your treatment of Mrs. Bauer as euthanasia and claimed that your call for the resuscitation team was just a cover-up."

"Thanks, Tara. I'll respond to it at the proper time."

AT FIVE O'CLOCK, with Henry still in the midst of office hours, the telephone rang. It was Len Boyer, Chief of the Department of Medicine.

"Henry, the Nursing Office has just received a formal complaint about you from Miss Flannery. It states you performed euthanasia in the case of a patient named Ann Bauer."

"Yes, I already heard about it." Henry was not perturbed, just annoyed.

"Well, it has all the girls down there shook up. They tried to talk Miss Flannery out of it, but she gave them a blast, called them frightened little children. She has the gift of gab, you know, and when she is indignant, she's a terror."

"They're all master's degree-cum laude types in the Nursing Office, and Flannery's a street fighter," Henry said. "If they're afraid of her, it's understandable."

"The nursing staff has already had a meeting," Len Boyer went on. "It seems Miss Flannery knows the rules very well. First, the nursing manual instructions regarding medications state that morphine is not to be given to a patient in respiratory distress. And if a physician, regardless of rank, prescribes a medication that is incorrect either in kind or dose, it's a nurse's duty to inform the physician. If he does not provide a satisfactory explanation, she can refuse to give the medication but she cannot interfere with his access to the drug or his right to administer it himself, and that's just what happened. In such cases she is required to make a full explanation in the patient's chart and send a copy to the Nursing Office. She can send this in as a matter of record, or as a complaint, in which case it has to be reviewed by the Executive Committee of the Nursing Department. They can

48

either accept or reject it, but their latitude is very narrow if a complaint falls within the guidelines of the nursing manual."

"They accepted her complaint, didn't they?" Henry said.

"Yes."

# CHAPTER

# *SEVEN*

T HE ETHICS Committee of the Medical Board convened Tuesday, a week later, at 4 P.M., after surgery and after clinics, so that the maximum number of departments could be represented. Still, only six of the ten members made it. According to the hospital bylaws, five constituted a quorum. In addition to Dr. Boyer, there was Paul Rosen, whose counsel was highly valued and frequently sought. Adding a legal dimension to the group was Gilbert Costaine, the hospital attorney, who sat between Ralph Hardy, the affable Chief of Surgery, and Dr. Gregor Veit-Volpin, the aging, bearded, mustached, and very relaxed Chief of Radiation Therapy. Veit-Volpin had actually worked with Marie Curie in Paris. Peter Roland, the last member expected, finally came in. A professor at the medical school, he was not a physician but an ordained minister with a graduate degree in ethics and medical history. Although no one questioned his academic abilities, many felt that he was too much the observer in the field of ethics, never a participant. Nevertheless, physicians, particularly those involved in research, were turning more and more to his specialty for advice, as medicine made advances in organ transplantation and genetic manipulation. In addition, problems involving human experimentation cropped up all the time. The Ethics Committee had to take cognizance of the wide scope of ethical and moral dilemmas encountered in a large university medical center. There seemed to be even more of them at the Curie Cancer Center than most places.

Euthanasia was definitely one, but there were other difficult problems as well. If you are using a drug for the first time on human beings and do not know the correct dose, or the side effects, is that treatment or experimentation? How do you obtain consent from patients receiving these drugs without either terrifying them or misrepresenting the situation? If you think a drug can prolong life, is it ethical to give it to some patients and withhold it from others in the name of randomized, clinical trials? Where does therapy stop and human experimentation begin? Where does human experimentation stop—and scientific arrogance begin? Mechanical support of life allows surgery to become more and more radical. First a leg, then the pelvis, then hemicorporectomy—a man-made basket case. What next? The head of St. John the Baptist on a platter of "life-sustaining devices"? New research was brazenly peeking under the skirts of old ethics.

As the group gathered, Henry felt rather detached from the proceedings about to begin. He was busy, patients were waiting. But as soon as Len Boyer called the meeting to order and the formalities started, Henry began to feel uncomfortable. Actually, everyone in the room except Peter Roland looked uncomfortable. Next to Dr. Boyer was Mrs. Ashley, the elderly secretary he had inherited from the previous department chairman. He immediately got down to the matter at hand and had Mrs. Ashley read the statement from the Nursing Department.

How ironic, Henry thought, to be accused of euthanasia, he who tried harder, did more for his patients than anyone else. He assumed that under the circumstances the euthanasia complaint would be rejected out of hand. All the committee had to do was hear the complaint forwarded by the Nursing Department, note the problem of the resuscitation team going to the wrong floor,

51

reaffirm their position as being against deliberate euthanasia, write a report, and move on to other business. He expected that the committee would then take a quick vote to adjourn.

"Henry, would you please recount the events of the afternoon up to the patient's demise?" Boyer said.

Not so quickly settled, then, Henry thought. He swallowed his irritation and presented a matter-of-fact, abbreviated case history. As for his last hospital visit with the patient, "The morphine sulfate was administered by me in order to relieve the agony of the patient's terminal few minutes. I gave it with the expectation that the respirator would be there momentarily. My primary intent was to relieve suffering."

Paul Rosen spoke up first. "I have a question, Henry. Why didn't you wait for the resuscitation team to arrive? They would have sedated her and intubated her as well."

Henry's conscience had already wrestled with that one. "I'll admit my action at the time was influenced by the desperate circumstances. Talking about it now, it would appear to have been a reasonable alternative. Then, it didn't seem to be. I knew I was taking a chance with the morphine."

Rosen pressed further. "If she had been on the respirator, can you conceive that there could have been regression of the lung tumor with vigorously applied chemotherapy?"

There was no man Henry trusted more than Paul Rosen, so he let his guard down a little. "When any patient dies, I ask myself, Should I have done this? Should I have done that? I'll also admit that sometimes I experience bitter regret and remorse at not having used another approach. Yes, Paul, we could have given her chemotherapy, and it's conceivable that she could have been kept going a little longer. I'm all for learning as much as possible about these drugs, as you well know. With Ann Bauer I asked myself the same question, but I felt I could not let the agony continue. I had to relieve it, even at the risk of causing her death. Under the circumstances I did what had to be done."

"The pathologist estimated that eighty percent of the lungs

were replaced by tumor," interpolated Len Boyer, who had the autopsy report in front of him.

Paul Rosen understood Henry's motives. He also knew that Henry always went for experimental chemotherapy, that he had a remarkable ability to talk patients into accepting toxic medication and then working with them so that they would tolerate it—and if the protocol called for more, they would come back for more. Not every doctor could do that. But apparently even Henry had his threshold, and Paul would not deny him that badge of humanity.

"I have actually intubated and treated patients with comparable degrees of tumor involvement in the lung," Paul said. "And to the best of my knowledge not a single patient has recovered. I can document that if anyone so desires."

Dr. Boyer turned to the Chief of Radiation Therapy. "Do you think that radiation therapy to the lungs should have been used at this stage?"

Veit-Volpin exhaled a volcanic cone of pipe smoke. "Absolutely not. It would have killed her for certain. I would have refused to treat her." Then he leaned back in his chair, took his pipe out of his mouth, and threw back his head. "But, on second thought, perhaps you should have called me. If she had had at least one treatment to the lungs, you could have blamed us and not that stupid morphine, and we could have avoided all this. You know, if the power fails, Radiation Therapy is blamed. If there is interference with the electrocardiograph machines, or even with the television sets, Radiation Therapy is blamed. If Miss Flannery had been goosed by an invisible hand, I am sure the thought would have occurred to someone that we were behind it. So why not blame this on us also? Besides, I don't take things quite as seriously as Henry, and I would be glad to exchange places with him. I don't think Henry is enjoying this at all."

"Thank you, Gregor," Dr. Boyer said somewhat hastily. "I think we have concluded the factual presentations. I'd like to ask Peter Roland to comment on the events described against the background of current thinking regarding euthanasia. But, if I may be blunt, please keep it short. It's been a long day for all of us."

"I presume from Doctor Boyer's introduction that this is the fanciful part of the presentation," Roland said. "It's not necessary for me to define euthanasia for this group. To permit someone to die without pain would seem to be a natural extension of the basic function of physicians, to prolong life and relieve suffering. It is only when the relief of suffering and the prolongation of life are contradictory that the question of judgment comes into the picture. In the case we are discussing today, it is without question that the suffering was so great that it required a maximal effort to relieve it. However . . ."

The bastard is enjoying this, Henry thought. Probably the greatest agony he's ever experienced is having a library book overdue.

"However, there is a dilemma because it would appear that biologic life could have been extended by the use of mechanical respiration. The question at hand, therefore, is, was this incidental euthanasia—that is, the fortuitous acceleration of death under circumstances designed primarily to alleviate pain or suffering? Or was this active or purposeful euthanasia—that is, direct measures instigated to terminate life?"

Ralph Hardy interrupted. "With all due respect to philosophy, Peter, if what Henry did was incorrect, half the medical staff would quit this hospital. Do you really think we have to go into a detailed analysis of this problem?"

"I don't think this meeting should be perfunctory." It was Paul Rosen again. "If a complaint had not been made, we would not be here. It's no great secret that euthanasia is practiced frequently in this and other hospitals. Euthanasia by omission is done with the tacit approval of all. How it is carried out varies from case to case, from doctor to doctor, from hospital to hospital, and there are few guidelines to help us in these dreadful situations. I think we need all the help that Professor Roland can give us, precisely

54

because it's not just an occasional problem for us. It's a problem that comes up in one form or another almost every day."

"Thank you, Doctor Rosen," Roland said, and tried to contain a smile. "I think it should be stated that any act taken with the deliberate intent of terminating life, even if merciful rather than malicious, is never condoned by law. When carried out by a physician it is labeled assault or manslaughter. However, in point of fact, no physician in the United States has ever been convicted of such a charge, and I believe the same is true for Great Britain."

Gilbert Costaine was making notes on a white pad. He didn't expect any legal problem here, but he had to be sure nothing was said or done that would get out of this chamber where it could, in distorted form, reach the state legislature and fray the purse strings of the medical school, or reach the press and harm fund raising.

"As for the Church's stand on euthanasia," Roland said, reaching for some notes, "Pope Pius XII said something relevant to today's discussion. 'If there exists no link, through the will of interested parties, between the induced unconsciousness and the shortening of life, and if the action of administration of drugs brings about two distinct effects, the one of relief of pain, and the other the shortening of life, the action is lawful . . .'"

Roland was about to quote from Erasistratus, a third-century physician who took poison to end his suffering from cancer, after writing a moral justification for doing so, when Veit-Volpin, impatient with the whole affair, puffed heavily on his pipe and shot a stream of smoke in his direction. Roland was indignant about the smoke signal. He expected better from one with a fine European education. Still, he sat down. Only the set of his lips betrayed his resentment at being deprived of the feeling of scholarly—and spiritual—superiority he usually got from Ethics Committee encounters.

Len Boyer rose from his chair and said to the speaker, "Thank you very much, Peter." He looked at Henry and nodded toward the door. Henry understood and left the room. Then Boyer turned to his colleagues. "We must now decide whether this complaint is justified or not. If, by majority vote, it is concluded that this complaint is justified, that is, that this was purposeful euthanasia, then we are obliged by our bylaws to forward the complaint to the Medical Board for further action. If it is found to be unjustified, the matter is summarily terminated. Now, gentlemen, will you please signify by raising your hand if you believe this complaint to be justified?"

# CHAPTER
# *EIGHT*

WHEN VERONICA Flannery heard the results of the committee meeting she was furious. However, there was still another strategy she could use.

In the small office of the attendant in charge of autopsies, the phone rang. Georgie Martin, a young pathologist, picked up the phone and heard the voice of his opposite number at the Medical Examiner's office.

"Georgie, what the hell is going on up there? We just got a call from a nurse at your hospital saying a patient with cancer of the lungs had died after receiving an injection of morphine and did we want to investigate the case? Don't you know that we have between ten and twenty murders a day in this city to investigate, plus another dozen deaths under suspicious circumstances? I think that place must be getting to you. Maybe the whole staff ought to take a month off."

THE NEXT TWO days passed quickly for Henry, with hospital rounds, committee meetings, and patients in the afternoon. He was looking forward to his four o'clock Thursday appointment.

Randy wasn't very happy when he walked into the waiting room. He had just had a venipuncture for a blood count. They had left the needle in the vein, and the short, plastic connecting tube had been taped to his arm so that he wouldn't have to be stuck again for chemotherapy. It was just a small convenience, but something that had never been done with Randy before, and the mother appreciated it even if the boy didn't.

The blood counts were good, and the chemotherapy went easily. Henry had also injected antinausea medication into a small bottle of intravenous fluid that was dripping slowly.

"We'll let the rest of this run in. It'll take about ten or fifteen minutes, and then Randy'll be all set. Do you have a car here?"

"I left it at my mother's on East Eighty-eighth Street. We planned to go there first for a while."

"Let me drop you off. I'll be ready to go by the time this is finished. It'll be hard getting a cab at this time of day."

"No, that's really too much. We'll manage."

"I have to go that way anyway. I live on Park and Eighty-first. Stay with him, Ellen." Then, to the mother, "When you're ready, come down to the main lobby entrance and I'll drive by."

Ellen thought, Well, I never saw him offer to do that before.

Henry took off his white coat, hung it behind the door in his office, and put on a suit jacket. He walked over to Randy and tugged on his foot.

"That wasn't so bad, Champ, was it?"

"I still don't like it," was the drowsy but succinct reply.

"DO YOU STAY here often when you come to town?" Henry asked as they pulled up before the building.

"Not since Randy got sick. We used to. I took courses at the Art Students League. Now, well, I still paint at home. I manage to get back once in a while, and I do keep working. It's been therapy for me through all of this. In fact, I'm in a competition at the League right now."

"Would it be out of line for me to ask if I could take a look at your entry?" Henry inquired.

"No, I think that would be just great." Then, rethinking her response, she added somewhat hesitantly, "I'll check the dates and find out if it's open to the public. I'll let you know soon."

58

Henry got out and helped to settle the sleeping boy in her arms. Her smile of thanks filled him with warmth.

Since Laura died, there had been no one to fill the space she left. His daughter, Eve? She was hardly a source of joy. Janine was important in his life, but he wasn't in love with her. The truth was, he had no way to replenish the store of compassion he expended on his patients.

Henry started for the garage, a short distance from his building. He stopped for a traffic light and started up when it changed, only to have a cab, trying to beat the changing signal, cut in front of him. He jammed on the brakes and missed the cab by inches. Another of New York's random perils, he thought. As he got underway again, an old scar on his shin started to ache. It acted up now and then if he jammed his leg down the way he just had, or sometimes after running up a flight of stairs, or when he was tired, and, occasionally, when he thought about Laura or Eve.

IT WAS TWELVE or thirteen years ago, he couldn't remember exactly. The small auditorium in the old, white, stone mansion in the East 70s was filled with parents. The school was small, with limited facilities, but very selective. Eve, like all its graduates, would be headed for one of the Seven Sisters colleges. The occasion that evening was a series of dances given by the fifth and sixth grade classes. As the last act, six girls came on stage, Eve among them, dressed in bright pink trousers, loose white blouses with oversized, scalloped collars and cuffs, and large black bow ties, and they tapped. They tapped their hearts out. They would have been a credit to any vaudeville house. The parents were clapping in time with the music. It was a showstopper. Eve, hammering the stage with her scrawny legs and heavy taps, caught sight of her parents for one fleeting second, her mother smiling and clapping, her father with his head down. It was just bad timing. Henry, who had been beaming at his child's performance, had put his head down momentarily to cough into a handkerchief. Still, the truth was, Henry hadn't been terribly

59

attentive all evening. After the first two dances his mind had started to drift back to the hospital. There had been an incredibly difficult case in the operating room, a patient of his with cancer of the pancreas.

Once during the performance Laura had noticed Henry staring out into space, and had jabbed him in the ribs.

"Henry," she had said sharply, "for God's sake, rejoin the human race!"

And he did. He really tried to be there for Eve.

There was a subplot to the evening. There were few occasions when all the parents gathered in such a good mood, and the headmistress wasn't going to miss this opportunity to do a little fund raising. But it was getting late. By the time the tap dancers had finished their first two numbers, some parents were starting to leave, and Myra Lee Russell couldn't have that. So before the girls started their third number, she went on stage, hugged them all, and benignly sent them packing so she could make the appeal that she would reinforce at the reception in the downstairs hall.

However, the six tap dancers were not to be put off so easily. If you carefully select your students for intelligence, initiative, and maturity, they are not going to be readily shunted aside. Therefore, on the way downstairs, Mrs. Russell was surrounded by six shrill-voiced, insistent, sweaty, skinny young girls bouncing up and down in their shiny, bright pink pants, yelling "It's not fair. It's not fair!"

One more thing was true about Myra Russell: she could visualize consequences. She knew if she didn't resolve this, six sets of parents would be treated to the same display, other parents would see and hear, the entire tenor of the evening would be spoiled, and her fund raising would go down the drain.

"All right, girls, now listen to me. I wanted it to be a surprise. When everyone's downstairs, I'm going to ask them all to stand around in a circle and you're going to do your last number."

Squeals of delight. "Oh, thank you, Mrs. Russell!"

"But," the headmistress added, "I want you to do it without the

60

repeat after the last section. I'll turn the tape off there. It's getting late."

A few groans. Then a chorus of okay's and all right's.

The parents dutifully formed a large circle in the reception hall, its polished stone floor well suited for tap dancing. The six flushed youngsters clattered their protruding metal taps like fillies at the starting gate. Then they began their number, their happy faces reflecting their triumph as they struck their staccato beats and did their struts, leaps, and turnabouts. Henry and Laura were standing at the inside edge of the circle, an arm around each other, enjoying their daughter's performance, when Henry's beeper went off. It had to mean disaster in the recovery room. He looked at Laura, shrugged his regret. She understood. He turned and, excusing himself, parted the circle to leave. Henry was just a few steps beyond the perimeter of the group when he heard clattering feet behind him and turned to face Eve, who had broken ranks to chase him.

"What's the mat—" He didn't get to finish. Eve grabbed his sleeve with one hand and the front of his jacket with the other, and pulling back as hard as she could, kicked him in the shin. Then she turned and ran to her mother, sobbing.

Henry, his shin throbbing, had to leave. Laura took the child to an anteroom and comforted her. She knew the dynamics of the situation very well.

"He wasn't walking out on you. He enjoyed every minute of it. He loved your performance, Eve. Honey, he was not deserting you."

"He hates me. He hates me!" she cried.

"No, he doesn't. We both thought it was great and you were wonderful. I know how you feel, but—"

"There's always a 'but.' He does this to me all the time! I know what you're going to say—but, Melissa's father's a doctor, so is Joanne's, and Patty's, and you didn't see them run out."

"Your father's different. He has people's lives in his hands," Laura replied.

61

"Everyone's but mine!"

In the cab taking him to the hospital, Henry looked at his leg as best he could in the dim light. There was a deep gash in his shin. He tied it with his handkerchief to staunch the bleeding. He knew it should be sutured, but when he got to the hospital, all he could do, before the emergency overtook his entire attention, was to wash it and bind it tightly with a bandage. The result was a wound that healed slowly and left a broad scar that even now ached when memory kicked it.

# CHAPTER
## *NINE*

IRENE DESFRENNES sat upright in bed and reached for the clock. This noontime hour was all they could steal from the day.

"I've got to move that mirror," she said, as she set the alarm. "The first thing I see when I get up is an apple sitting on top of a corn flakes box."

Irene's analogy was not inapt. She was a large girl, her frame square, her face rosy and round. Roger Floyd raised his head, which had been half-buried in the pillow.

"Mmm, you are substantial," he murmured.

"When I look at you," she said, "I get furious. Ankles like Nureyev, a body like Tarzan, and a head like Adonis. I look like a lady wrestler next to you. Whoever said love was a form of narcissism was crazy. Maybe I remind you of your mother, or more likely your father. I don't understand why you want to go out with a lady wrestler."

Half-listening, half-dozing, Roger said, "Maybe it's because I need protection."

"That does it!"

With a swoop of one arm she took his pillow and threw it on the floor. Then she jumped on him, biting his ear and neck and holding his legs tightly between her thighs. "You want a lady wrestler, you've got a lady wrestler."

Half an hour later, as they lay next to each other quietly, Roger said, "It's the most fun you can have without laughing."

Irene lifted her head to look at the clock. It was 1 P.M. "We're going to be late for clinic."

"Everybody is late for clinic. I'm sure we won't be the last ones there."

"Yes, but the female staff has to show how much better we are. You know all we minorities are paranoid."

"Some minority!"

Irene was out of the shower and dressing rapidly, combing out her long, brown hair and sweeping it into a bun. Roger, waiting for her in his white hospital coat, picked up a paperback book from the dresser and put it in his pocket.

"I'm going to return this to Father Noyes today."

No one watching Irene and Roger leave the apartment building, their demeanor serious, stethoscopes, pens, flashlights, tongue blades in their pockets, would have guessed they were just minutes past a midday romp in bed.

"You know," Roger said, "Father Noyes is the only person I've met at Curie who will talk to a patient about dying. This is a weird place, mostly because of people like Henry Nyren."

Irene shook her head in disagreement. "I don't think it's weird. I'll tell you something. When I first came here I thought I would find it depressing to work in a cancer hospital," she said. "But there's an atmosphere of hope around this place."

"How about the atmosphere for the doctors? The place is getting on my nerves. I like to feel I'm helping people once in a while. The effort that goes into one patient who isn't going to make it—I can't see it. It's too much mustard for one hot dog!"

Irene liked to walk with her arm around Roger's waist when they were out strolling. Now she remembered the circumstances and stopped herself. "Whenever we talk about Curie you always sound so negative. Sometimes I think we work in two different hospitals. You remember that boy with the bone tumor they flew in from Greece? The one I sat up with all night when he got his chemo? He's going home tomorrow. Complete remission. We're going to have a party for him. He's as bald as a melon but there's no more tumor. Was that too much effort?"

"Okay, but who knows when it's going to come back?"

"Oh, please. That boy was at death's door and now he's fine. Ask the family if it was worthwhile. They'll say it was a miracle. Maybe he's cured, maybe it'll come back. Who knows how much time anyone has? You keep looking at the half-empty glass. The spirits of the patients around here improve just because they know something is being done for them."

"Try telling that to Nyren's patient, the one who had the skin reaction after an injection of bleomycin. He looked like a boiled lobster. We can't even find a place on his skin to inject the morphine," Roger continued. "Nyren's got the old-time religion all right—a shaker and a mover. I don't say you can't learn a lot from him, but there's no way you could go to the extremes at other hospitals that he does here. He thinks he's got to cure them all. He doesn't know when to quit. He loses sight of the patients, all he sees is the cancer, and if he thinks he's going to lose, he goes crazy. He won't let people die."

Roger was not enjoying his residency at Curie. Meeting Irene was the one bright spot in a grim year. It was fascinating to study the biology of cancer, no denying that, but taking care of cancer patients was another matter. He moved quickly up the steps to start his afternoon clinic and rounds and get them over with as soon as possible. Roger gave chemotherapy late in the afternoon after checking the blood counts of the day. Almost all the drugs he was called upon to use lowered the white blood cell count and the platelets. Some of the newer anticancer agents affected other organs. Any slipup in dosage, however minor, could be devastating. However, learning to be an oncologist meant not only knowing how and when to use these toxic medications, but also being able to sustain a compassionate attitude toward suffering patients during long periods when your own emotions were being drained. On the Chemotherapy Service, Roger felt wiped out at the end of every day.

VISITORS DIDN'T HAVE to leave until 8 P.M., and it was only a little after five. It was really better to give the medication after they'd left, Roger thought. Then you didn't have relatives to deal with. Mrs. Kreutzer was going to get 10 milligrams of streptokotocin intravenously. He hoped they'd have the damn IV going so he could shoot it into the tubing. Her veins were like silk threads.

"Miss Flannery, where is the streptokotocin for Kreutzer?" Roger asked at the nurses' station.

"It should be in her medication drawer, but it seems to me you used it all for another patient yesterday. You know we don't store special medications," Flannery added, pleased to be able to tell him off.

"Oh, Christ!" Roger groaned. "Do you have anyone you can send for it?"

Flannery was annoyed. "And who would you suggest? Would you like me to go and leave the floor uncovered? Or my aide? She can't tell an entrance sign from an exit. You'd trust her to fetch an experimental drug?"

"No need to get nasty about it, Miss Flannery. I was just hoping I didn't have to run to the other end of the building. I was supposed to be off an hour ago."

"You should have thought of that before you went to medical school. None of you young fellows want to do a stitch of work more than you absolutely have to," Flannery replied.

The last thing Roger needed right then was an argument with the White Whale. . . . He would see his other patients first, get the streptokotocin, and see Mrs. Kreutzer last. He got through most of the patients quickly. There were just a few left, all Nyren's patients, all last-ditch, desperate cases. On his way to pick up the medication, he stopped off at Father Noyes's office.

Roger found Father Hector Noyes at his desk in the large,

66

book-lined chaplain's office. The priest moved to a chair next to the sofa and motioned to Roger to sit down.

"Evening, Padre. I can only stay a few minutes, I wanted to return your book," Roger said. He took a thin paperback out of his pocket. "Also, I wanted to tell you, I don't think Tolstoy ever saw anyone die of cancer. The drama that he puts into Ivan Ilyich's final moments is phony. I've never seen anyone have the Ben Hur type revelation he describes."

Father Noyes got a bottle of sherry and glasses from a cupboard. As Roger spoke, a thin smile appeared on the priest's boyish face.

"I'm not sure you really know, Doctor Floyd. I've administered the sacraments to quite a few dying patients, and many have told me that they felt more at ease, could see things and understand things that they'd never appreciated before. Perhaps you don't understand the meaning of 'grace'?"

"Now, just a minute, Father." Roger got up from the sofa and paced. "Up to a point, our backgrounds are very similar. Maybe my theology is puerile compared to yours, but nobody graduates from St. David's Academy without at least once getting 'high' on grace. I know how powerful it can be. But that's not the point. You were giving the last rites to people who had a fatal illness but were in control of their faculties. That's entirely different from a revelation during the last few moments of life, which is what Tolstoy was describing."

"The light and serenity don't have to come with the last breath. It's not the timing but rather the transition that's important, from a soul in torment to a soul at peace. It's a recurring theme with Tolstoy."

Father Noyes went to a bookcase, took down a volume.

"Look at this—"

"Sorry, Father, not now. I have a few more patients to see, and then I'm going to dinner with Irene Desfrennes. I'm running over an hour late now."

"Just one thing I'd like you to think about, and I'll let you go. Do you think your attitude may be biased by your experience in this hospital and your lack of experience elsewhere? It's different with people dying at home. Here we use morphine and Demerol to relieve pain. Love can be just as strong an anodyne, and we have only very small doses of that in a hospital. Possibly you haven't seen enough yet. Just keep your eyes open. By the way, Doctor Floyd," he added, "if you have more calls to make and Doctor Desfrennes is waiting for you, please ask her if she'll come and wait for you here. This sherry is better than the hospital's, and I have a pretty good Scotch if she prefers that."

Roger was pleased. "I'll call her. I'd feel less pressured if I knew you were keeping her company."

Irene, dressed and waiting, knew well the uncertainties of a doctor's schedule and welcomed Father Noyes's invitation, especially when Roger told her it would be another twenty minutes before he would be finished.

Back on the hospital floor, Roger met Henry Nyren leaving the room of one of his patients. Henry told him that he had seen them all except Mrs. Kreutzer.

"The nurse told me she hasn't gotten her streptokotocin. You didn't forget?" Henry asked.

"I didn't forget her, but I did forget the drug. I'm headed for the special drug pharmacy now."

"It's not necessary. I already picked it up. I was going up to leave it for you at the nurses' station."

"Just one quick question, Doctor Nyren. Mrs. Kreutzer has CA of the breast with metastasis to the liver and brain. She's completely out of it. She's so close to the end, why give her any medication? Why not let nature take its course?"

"I discussed her case at chemo conference last week. Weren't you there?"

"No, I, ah, missed that one."

"Roger, you've got to go to those meetings. That's the time to ask that kind of question, not now. In any case, Paul Rosen found it to be an effective form of chemotherapy in animal tumors, and we've got to give it a chance in patients."

68

"What good is giving an experimental drug to a dying patient? Maybe the drug is a good one, but giving it to a patient who is about to die seems pointless."

"We've gone over that one too. Not once, but many times. If you work here, it's because you believe it's worthwhile keeping cancer patients alive. The unpredictable is always happening and could happen for this patient."

"The trouble with that is the unpredictable can be bad as well as good. Well, thanks for saving me a trip," Roger said, taking the drug from Henry. "I'll do it, but you might as well know my heart isn't in it."

"You'll get there, just keep at it."

ROGER DIDN'T PURSUE the argument. Kreutzer was Nyren's patient. Besides, now he'd be finished in only a few minutes. He took a disposable syringe from the medication cart and drew up 10 milligrams of streptokotocin from the vial Henry had given him. Then he carefully sheathed the needle with a plastic cap and took an alcohol sponge with him to her room.

The patient's husband was standing outside the door. Damn. No way not to stop for a minute.

"Good evening, Mr. Kreutzer. Doctor Nyren asked me to give the new medication to your wife."

"Is that what I signed the papers for yesterday?"

Old Professor Kreutzer was as tense as he was thin. A very private man, he never used his academic title.

"Yes," Roger said.

"She looks bad tonight. Won't Doctor Nyren be here?"

"He was here before, and I'm meeting him here in the morning. Don't worry, there'll be good coverage by both doctors and nurses through the night. Doctor Spencer is on tonight."

With that he peeled away from the husband and walked into the room. Roger was relieved to see that the IV was running. He approached the bed. The patient's eyes were closed, and she was breathing softly in comatose repose. The skin of her face was tightly drawn so that the outline of the bones in her nose, cheeks,

69

and forehead was clear. But the skin had no marked pallor because of the deep jaundice, which made her look suntanned. At a casual glance, one might think here was a thin, well-tanned lady taking a nap—except for the intravenous fluid dripping slowly, like tears, into her veins. Roger lowered the railing at the side of the bed, turned down the bed sheet, and exposed the rubber portion of the tubing that connected with the needle in the vein. He wiped this with an alcohol sponge and inserted the needle of the syringe containing the medication. With his left hand he pinched off the plastic tubing higher up so that the medication would not flow backward, then withdrew the plunger of the syringe slightly. There was the reassuring appearance of blood in the tubing showing that the pathway to the bloodstream was intact. Having in a few seconds deftly made these preparatory moves, Roger slowly injected the contents of the syringe. When the syringe was empty, the needle was withdrawn and recapped. Like all disposable syringes, it had to be destroyed lest it find its way to the underground needle market. Roger Floyd was ready to leave. One last backward glance at the patient.

Hold it.

# CHAPTER
# *TEN*

**M**RS. KREUTZER wasn't breathing. Roger put his stethoscope to her chest: no heart sounds. A fingertip on the cornea: no reflex. He pinched the neck muscles: no reaction. Try resuscitation. No go. No phone in the room, get to a phone . . .

"How is she, Doctor?"

Roger brushed by Mr. Kreutzer without replying, ran to the phone at the nurses' station and dialed quickly. His message was immediately iterated by a soft, but urgent, voice on the public address system: "Code blue, Room 802. Code blue, Room 802."

Roger was already on his way back to the room to try again to resuscitate Mrs. Kreutzer. Elevators stopped and discharged their passengers, then went nonstop to the fifteenth floor where two nurses and an anesthesiology resident from the intensive care unit were waiting with the respirator that had never reached Ann Bauer.

The electrocardiograph technician heard the call, put down her coffee, slipped on her shoes, and pushed her wheeled equipment toward the elevator. The senior assistant resident, Wally Spencer, left the bedside of a surgical patient on the fourth floor. He used the stairs to go up, taking them two at a time.

Spencer arrived first. Eighth floor nurses were already in the room giving artificial respiration with an emergency kit. The resuscitation team moved in. The brash young resident, followed by a nurse assistant, pushed the floor nurses aside and yanked the headboard off the bed. He positioned himself behind the motionless patient. He lifted her head and roughly thrust a lighted laryngoscope down her throat so he could place a tube into her trachea and hook her up to the respirator.

"Lift her shoulders a little so I can get a shot at this. Not that way—lift her fucking shoulders, I said! Hold it, that's it. It's in. Gimme a syringe. Okay, let's hook it up."

The accordion-pleated black bag in the cylinder groaned its slow, awkward imitation of the lungs. The ECG technician was attaching electrodes to the patient. Wally Spencer was hurriedly doing a cut-down on a vein in the right side of the neck, getting ready to put a thin plastic tube into the pulmonary vein to determine the degree of congestive failure. Sweat from his forehead dripped into the wound. He mumbled, "Don't make no difference," but mopped it up with a gauze pad anyway. Roger Floyd was calling for the epinephrine that he was going to inject with a long, thin needle directly into her heart. A nurse was wheeling in a defibrillator. Another was monitoring the blood pressure: there was none. But as soon as the respirator was hooked up, there was a flicker of circulation caused by the motion of the lungs. Yet another nurse was adding dopamine to an IV bottle. "That should do something for her pressure," she said.

Everyone had a job to do and was doing it. The technician was looking at the never-ending tongue of paper coming out of the mouthlike aperture of the electrocardiograph machine. "She's in ventricular fib."

"Everybody—hands off," Spencer called out. "I'm going to sock it to her."

Two flat, platelike discs were placed on her chest.

"Ready—go!"

The patient's body contorted for a second as the high voltage of electricity stimulated all of her muscles, including the heart. Spencer looked at the ECG.

72

"Hit her again. Hold it! We're getting something."

For a few seconds the jagged peaks of fibrillation signaling useless thrashing of cardiac muscle were replaced by a meaningful pattern of auricular and ventricular activity. A manometer was registering the pulmonary vein pressure. The respirator was pushing and pulling pure oxygen. The patient's chest was silently rising and falling, mimicking life. And, during each pressured minute, Mrs. Kreutzer's cancer was rooting for them, wanting its blood supply back.

Not this time. The irregular but coordinated cardiac activity was again replaced by the jagged lines of impending cardiac death.

"Hit her again—once more," Spencer said aloud to himself, as he applied the defibrillator.

A continual beep from the ECG.

"She's straight lining," the technician said.

"No B.P. Pupils fully dilated and nonreactive." This from the intern who had come in to assist. Wally Spencer and Roger Floyd looked at one another. Roger had started this, and he had to say when.

"Okay, it's quitting time. Thanks everybody."

They all took their equipment, not talking, nothing to say—a silent retreat of white uniforms, white equipment, black accordion bag, electrocardiograph machine, defibrillator, retreat of the tanks of oxygen, medication cart, and assorted poles, bottles, and tubes. A clear, unequivocal defeat.

Maybe the next time.

Roger turned to the eighth floor nurses.

"Please call Doctor Nyren and tell him what happened."

Roger walked to Mr. Kreutzer, who was huddled against the far wall of the hospital corridor. As he approached, Mr. Kreutzer spoke.

"What's happening? All those people going into my wife's room. What happened? What happened? Now they're going away. Is she better?"

"I'm sorry, Mr. Kreutzer, your wife is dead."

"What do you mean, dead?" The old man's voice neared a hysterical edge. "You went in there, you came out, you started a small riot, then you called off the riot, and now you tell me my wife is dead. She wasn't dead when you went in there."

With deliberate calm, Roger said, "She was on the verge of dying for the last forty-eight hours, Mr. Kreutzer. She just happened to die about the time I was giving her the injection."

"No! Just a few days ago she said she was tired and wanted to sleep. But Doctor Nyren said that with the medication she had a chance of coming out of the coma. He said she'd talk to me again. Why give her medicine? To make her die? She could have done that by herself!"

He stopped, inhaled deeply, appeared to fill up with a tremendous amount of steam, and then he exploded.

"She's dead? Die? She didn't die! You killed her! Help! Police! You killed her! Help! Help! Murderer! Murderer!"

He began pummeling Roger with his fists. Roger grasped his hands and held him. Nurses and aides came running. Mr. Kreutzer was still hysterical and shouting. Patients and visitors cautiously peered out to see what was happening.

Suddenly, Mr. Kreutzer's voice receded to a terrible whisper. "Hitler couldn't kill her, Dachau couldn't kill her. She had to come here to get killed. She didn't do anything over there to get punished, and she didn't do anything here either."

He allowed himself to be led to the patients' lounge. Sympathetic staff members offered him coffee, a sedative, the telephone. Could they call someone, could they do something for him?

"Thank you, thank you, you're all very kind. I apologize that I could not control myself. This is a kindly place, a kindly place, yes. A kindly concentration camp. Oh, I don't mean it's your fault, any of you. You are victims yourselves. You are like the *Sonderkommandos*. I'm sorry I blamed you. I'm sorry I blamed you, young man. I apologize for upsetting the hospital. But you don't know. You couldn't understand if I told you, and I couldn't ever live through trying to tell you. But would you sit down, my young

**74**

doctor? Can I talk to you for a minute? Can you sit here for a moment with me.?"

"Sure," Floyd said, thinking the old man wanted to ask him about the medical events that led up to his wife's death.

They sat in a corner of the visitor's alcove on two green rattan chairs set at right angles to each other. There was a waist-high green plant between the chairs, and the men had to turn slightly as they leaned over to face one another.

"When my wife left the camp," Alfred Kreutzer began, "she was taken to a shelter for displaced persons. That's where we met. I survived the same camp, but I had never seen her there. Once we met, we never left each other's side. At first she kept saying 'Why me? Why did I live and not the others? Why me?' After a while she stopped that, but whenever she'd get depressed or thought back too much, she'd say 'I owe God a death.' She was a wonderful person, but always tense, on guard. Then, when she got breast cancer, the tension seemed to disappear. One night she said to me, 'I'm paying back what I owe.'"

"Doctor Nyren told me Mrs. Kreutzer was the most cooperative uncomplaining patient he ever had."

The husband continued as if Roger had not spoken. "Me, I'm a different person. I'm an historian, I teach at City College. I'm inquisitive, and when something happens I want to find out as much as I can about it. So when my wife developed breast cancer I read all about the different kinds of breast cancer, the different stages. It didn't take me long to find out she had ignored it for too long. Then I read about the different forms of treatment—surgery, radiation therapy, and chemotherapy."

Mr. Kreutzer stood, and turned toward the window behind his chair. "Once I started reading, I couldn't stop. Gradually, I started to think like my wife used to. Why her? Did she really owe God a death? What was breast cancer, really? Was it just an arrow randomly shot into a crowd, striking my wife? Or was it something else, a metaphor for sacrifice, perhaps, and here is where I would appreciate your patience, Doctor. Excuse an old, tortured man who may have lost his mind. I started to read in my own field. I was amazed to find references to breast cancer wherever I looked. In ancient Egypt it's described. There were references to breast cancer in Assyria, in cuneiform tablets found in Nineveh. The *Ramayana* described treatment for breast cancer in ancient India. The wife of Darius, king of Persia, had breast cancer. Herodotus wrote about it. Even the name 'carcinoma' came about because of breast cancer. Did you know that, Dr. Floyd?"

"No, sir, I didn't." Roger was getting a little uneasy.

"Hippocrates wrote about a tumor, a red swelling of the breast that reached out with destructive claws like a crab—'*karkinoma*' he called it. So much suffering for so many centuries."

The old man pulled a grayed handkerchief from his pocket and wiped his rheumy eyes. "I read of the efforts of doctors through the ages to cure it, all of them hurling themselves against a mountain. So you see, young man, you are not of the only generation of physicians that struggled against breast cancer." He folded the handkerchief and returned it to his pocket with some effort.

"Maybe my wife was right all along. Maybe we are wrong and our ancestors were right. Maybe God does demand sacrifices. Eh, what about it? Maybe His name is Moloch. Maybe she did owe God a death. What do you think? I'm crazy, right?"

"I don't know, sir. I don't think you're crazy, but I think you're wrong."

He helped the old man up and walked him back toward his wife's room, holding his arm. With nothing more to say, he left him there and walked to the nurses' station. Henry had just arrived.

"He's over the worst of it, Doctor Nyren, but it was pretty bad. A lot of shouting and hysterics."

"I have taken care of Sarah Kreutzer for four or five years, and I know something of what they've been through. I don't see how he held together so long. I'm going to spend some time with him. You did your best, Roger, you don't have to stay."

76

AFTER HE SAT and talked with Alfred Kreutzer and then sent him home a little calmer, Henry went back to his apartment. He called his answering service hoping there would be a message from Donna.

Why hadn't he heard from her about the art show? Should he call her at home? He suddenly felt lonely. He could call Janine, or invite Eve to dinner. The hospital was having a fund-raising gala to which he had been invited. There was a manuscript he had to complete, and the library was beckoning. The University Club was only a few minutes away.

But this loneliness was specific. He was lonely for someone he had met only a few times, had never spent any time with, and with whom he had no personal relationship.

He opted for the University Club, there was still time for a workout. This evening he swam harder than usual, pulled on the Universal weight machine till his muscles burned, then submitted to twenty minutes of Big Boris. Towel wrapped around his waist, he hopped onto the white-sheeted massage table.

"Boris—do your worst!"

"A pleasure." The beefy hands came down like chopping knives.

THE NEXT MORNING at eight, before leaving his apartment, he dialed Donna's number. Her husband answered.

Henry hung up. He waited half an hour and called again.

"Yes, this is Mrs. Stockman."

"This is Henry Nyren. I was hoping to get a message from you about the art show. I'm looking forward to it."

"Er—I haven't taken the measurements yet. I could call you at your shop later this morning."

He had blundered—her husband hadn't left yet.

She was married. Remember that, Henry.

# CHAPTER
# *ELEVEN*

**T**HE INTERCOM buzzed.

"It's for you, Doctor Nyren. It's Mrs. Stockman."

Henry closed the office door, sat down at his desk, and swiveled the chair to face the window.

"I apologize about this morning," Henry said.

"No problem. I'm sorry I couldn't talk."

"No, I shouldn't have called. But when I get an idea in my head—I was just anxious to know if it's on or off." He tried to sound as if he weren't all that anxious.

"It's on. There are two showings. One this coming Sunday and again the next Sunday."

"Is this Sunday okay?"

"It's fine, but next week would be good too. My mother and Randy are coming then. It's not my husband's cup of tea. But it might be more fun if we went as a group."

"No, this Sunday will be fine . . ."

HENRY WAS WAITING on the steps of the Art Students League when Donna arrived.

"I have just a few hours," she said. "Randy and his father are at a ball game and I'm going to meet them at mother's."

"We'll make the most of it."

They made their way through the crowded hall.

"How do you like it?" she asked.

They stood before her entry. Donna did still lifes, large flowers against distant landscapes or next to familiar objects, a kind of wish-I-could-be-Georgia O'Keefe style. This entry was a large blue dahlia. Next to it was a letter ripped in half.

"I could stand here all day and imagine stories that go with that painting," Henry mused.

"I try to create only beauty, but it always comes out bitter-sweet," she said.

They spent another forty-five minutes browsing, and Donna introduced Henry to several of her art school friends.

"It's a beautiful day. Are you in the mood for some fresh air and a stroll back uptown?" he asked.

"That would be great, Doctor Nyren. I've still got an hour and a half."

"Look, we can't have you calling me Doctor Nyren on such a beautiful afternoon. Henry is better."

They were on 57th Street, walking toward Sixth Avenue.

"It tilts the relationship away from the professional side, doesn't it?"

"I hope so," he said, turning north toward the park.

She smiled slightly, but didn't answer.

"How about lunch at the Café de la Paix?"

"Then we'll never get back in time, if we're going to walk."

"Let's walk then."

Central Park on a warm Sunday afternoon—joggers, cyclists, strolling couples of every age. In that convivial atmosphere, it was only natural to feel close.

"I want to be up front with you, Donna." It felt good to say her name out loud for the first time. "First, I'm not in the habit of going out with my patients or members of their families. Neither do I have a continually growing list of female companions. Quite the opposite, in fact. But I do have a very strong desire to get to know you. I hope we can be friends."

"It would be good to have a friend," Donna said quietly.

"Does your husband share your interest in art?"

"I think he looks on it as competition for my attention. Sometimes I feel I am neglecting my responsibilities when I paint."

"I thought what you did looked quite professional."

"Well, I work at it. I don't win any prizes, but just being selected for a show is a reward in itself. I paint at home or, when I can, in the Botanical Gardens in the Bronx. It's not too far from Riverdale, and the mood is better for me there."

"Were you raised in New York?" Henry asked.

"Yes. Right on Eighty-eighth Street, where my mother lives. In the same five-story walkup. Actually, it's nicer now than it used to be. It's been fixed up a few times. My mother's there all alone. I've got two brothers who live out of town, we don't see much of them. My father had a little hardware store on First Avenue, 'Janocek's,' but he passed on, and the store was sold. Mother's in good shape though, except for her arthritis. Maybe she'll make corned beef and cabbage for you some Sunday—if she likes you," Donna said with a smile.

"Janocek?—making corned beef and cabbage?"

"Her maiden name was Sullivan. She and my father were childhood sweethearts. At least that's the story. I don't know what went wrong, but by the time I arrived, things were not so hot between them. There was a lot of fighting in the house. Usually over the boys, or over money. The store wasn't doing well. What I remember is, that when I had an asthma attack, they would stop fighting. Sometimes I think that's why I developed asthma. Sounds weird, huh?"

"It happens," Henry replied.

By this time they were up to the boathouse in Central Park.

"I'd love for us to take out a rowboat, but I guess there's not enough time."

Donna nodded. "I'm enjoying the walk."

"Me too . . ."

They left the park at 79th Street, passed the Metropolitan Museum of Art, and continued up Fifth Avenue.

80

"Were you raised in New York also?"

"No. Morristown, New Jersey. I'm an only child. My father had a pharmacy and my mother used to help out. They went at each other once in a while, too. I went to Columbia undergraduate and NYU for medicine, and I've stayed in New York ever since, so I feel like a native."

They stopped at an umbrella'd ice cream cart on the park side of Fifth Avenue, then continued walking, munching ice cream bars.

"It's funny how things work out. I wanted desperately to have a good marriage, with happy, healthy children, and also—to tell you what a dope I was—I thought you had to have money to feel secure and avoid arguments. Anyway, I grew up fast with Rand. I gave up school for him. I was studying art at Hunter. He was older, solid, a successful real estate man. Then his antagonism, and Randy's illness, and my guilt feelings, well . . ."

"You shouldn't feel guilty about anything."

"When a marriage isn't working, I know a woman doesn't automatically have to feel guilty, but this one does. I—we're—trying to make it work for Randy's sake."

She paused for a moment, then said, "Whew! I just let it all out, didn't I! I think I said too much."

"I don't think so," Henry said. "I'm grateful you felt free to say what you did. There has to be someone with whom you can drop all the masks and be the person behind them. That kind of friend I don't have. I hope we can do this again."

They were at 88th Street now. They would be at her mother's building soon. "I'm just down the block. And, well, there's one more important thing to say."

"What's that?"

"I agree with what you said about how good it is to be able to talk freely with someone. I loved our walk, and I feel comfortable with you. I would like to meet you again."

"So would I."

"But I want to say something even if it's completely inappropriate and the farthest thing from your mind. I'm obliged to you

81

as a physician, and I like you as a friend, but there's a lot of pressure with Randy's illness, and I'm trying to hold my marriage together, and Rand is trying too. I can't take more pressure. What I'm trying to say is, I couldn't handle having an affair."

# CHAPTER
# *TWELVE*

HENRY, ELATED at getting to know Donna and not put off by her parting words, started his day in a rosy mood. After rounds he sat in a small conference room with Roger Floyd and two interns. They discussed briefly what was happening in each of their problem cases. One of the interns, Jim Belmont, presented a new case.

"The patient is Frank Walsh, a thirty-six-year-old Caucasian police officer living in New York City. He was transferred here from Bellevue for the treatment of lung cancer."

Belmont went on to describe the history, the findings on examination, and the results of the laboratory tests. Then he turned to Henry and said, "I think this disease is very malignant. It's only three weeks since surgery, and he has fluid in his chest and enlarged hilar nodes as well. The fluid was checked for cancer cells and it was positive. He's not a candidate for further surgery and the cancer's too widespread for radiation therapy. Maybe we ought to leave him alone."

Henry balanced Frank Walsh's chart on his knee. Even on his best morning that kind of remark was, to him, like waving red flags in Pamplona.

"What do you mean, 'Leave him alone'? What do you think we're running here, a nursing home? A first-rate team of surgeons sent him here from a top-notch hospital. Why? For us to leave him alone? People come here from all over the world because they want that one more chance, because they know we're doing things here that are not being done elsewhere. This patient was sent here because we have a program of intensive chemotherapy plus radiation therapy for the treatment of lung cancer. Sure we'd prefer patients with no metastases, but if we picked only winners we'd have damn few cases. Doctors refer to us the cases they can't handle. Our job is to take them all. At any rate, this patient is suitable for the program. We are definitely not going to leave him alone. We are going to give him a full course of streptokotocin and follow it with radiation therapy."

"Streptokotocin?" Roger said. "After Mrs. Kreutzer? I'm not about to touch that drug again. Why not something a little less deadly, like Adriamycin and vincristine?" Roger was boiling with resentment.

Henry thought, I'm damn near ready to toss this Roger over my shoulder with one horn, but he restrained himself.

"Those drugs would not do much. We'd be wasting time and the patient has little of that. We would also be wasting his bone marrow. Besides, you missed the point I was making. They can give conventional treatment in any hospital."

"But why streptokotocin? I've been involved with that drug in four cases, and they've all been disasters." Roger couldn't let go of it.

"I could use some experience with Adriamycin," Belmont said.

Henry stared them both down.

"Do you know what your problem is? You don't know what chemotherapy is all about! Maybe some place else you can give any cancer drug, in any dose, and then say afterward, 'The patient didn't respond.' But you can't get away with that bullshit here. At Curie we either treat with an effective drug or with experimental drugs or we get the patient out of this hospital. Get that through your heads! We're not here to make meaningless gestures."

84

"How about that mid-torso occlusion you're always raving about?" Roger threw at him.

"Your sarcasm's misplaced, Floyd. I've never raved about mid-torso occlusion. I was under the mistaken impression that your presence in this hospital signified you would be interested in new developments in the treatment of cancer. That approach isn't ready yet. Walsh is going to get streptokotocin."

"I think we should stick to the first principle of medicine, *Primum non nocere*—do no harm. That drug spells trouble and I'm not going to administer it."

Somehow, Roger Floyd's challenge was just what was needed to calm Henry. He took a deep breath and tried for a conciliatory tone.

"I don't think you're being quite fair, Roger. You're reacting to your experience with Mrs. Kreutzer. I know how hard that must have been, but it *is* the responsibility of the resident on the Chemotherapy Service to give the experimental drugs. I can't order the intern to do it. I'm going to write my reasoning in the patient's chart. I'm sure by tomorrow you'll see that's the way to go."

"I intend to state my position in the chart also, Doctor Nyren."

WHEN ROGER RETURNED to their apartment that evening, Irene was already there. She was still in her white skirt and blouse, and a small, gray paging device was clipped to the waist of her skirt. She was preparing dinner.

He kissed her perfunctorily, then flung himself down on a chair with his legs straight out before him.

"I'm quitting. Tomorrow. I'd leave tonight if I could."

Irene sat down at the table. "Oh, come on, that Kreutzer business has you all upset."

"No. That just crystallized it all for me. I want out of this hospital. I want out of oncology. I don't get any satisfaction out of making people sick with chemotherapy that's not going to cure them anyway. I'm sick of running around measuring tumor

85

nodules that are getting smaller while the patients are dying. At Curie, it's the tumor first and the patient second."

"That's not true."

Roger was on his feet now, stalking the room. "It is true. Kreutzer wasn't the first patient I've killed with chemotherapy, but she is the last. I'm just not a believer. I can't fool myself any more about buying time, or how important it is to show that we can get tumors to decrease in size because that means it's a step in the right direction. I don't see anything on the road marked chemotherapy except dead ends, preceded by snake-filled swamps called side effects."

"Well, then, I don't see what you see," Irene said. "I see X-rays of lung tumors and then see the tumors disappear. I feel cancers in the abdomen, and then they are gone. My patients handle the side effects and don't complain too much. It's true I don't deal with the experimental drugs the way you do, but all the drugs I use were once experimental. You make it sound like it's all a fraud."

Roger was still pacing. "No, it's not all a fraud. But some of it is. I know the patients want it. To them it's a lifeline. Do they actually feel better? Sure they do, but, Christ, Nyren could give them Drano and they'd feel better. Did you ever see him with patients? That salesman's pitch, the Rasputin look, and the hair flopping over his eyes? When he gets through telling them how much better they're going to be, they could walk on water or fly to the moon. And Mangoli, there's another one. Those bedroom eyes and quicksilver voice—he holds the ladies' hands and loves them into remission. I tell you, those guys could sell you anything. The patients buy it and that's okay. But Nyren and Mangoli and the rest of them are all under the delusion that it's chemotherapy the patients are buying. It's ten percent chemotherapy and ninety percent suggestion. That doesn't apply to Rosen. He doesn't flim-flam anyone. He honestly believes he's getting somewhere with chemotherapy. If he wants to spend his life that way, that's fine."

He sat down hard on his chair. "I don't!"

PAUL ROSEN'S OFFICE was cluttered with makeshift bookcases and a desk piled high with manuscripts, journals, and correspondence. There was also a couch he used when he worked late. Right now it was covered with small piles of papers and journals.

"Come in, Roger," Rosen said. "Clear off that chair and sit down."

"Thanks for seeing me on such short notice." There was a lot of tension in the way the young man gripped the arms of the chair.

"You made it sound important. I heard about Mrs. Kreutzer and her husband. That must have been a tough situation for you."

"I still feel bad about that. I know she was on the edge and would have gone over anyway, but I didn't want to be the guy that pushed her. Then the husband panicking and calling this place a concentration camp—well, there was just enough truth in it to hurt."

"First, Roger, I don't know that you did push her over, as you said. I doubt it."

"But streptokotocin is toxic to the heart," Roger replied. "We know she had tumor in the heart—the pericardial tap was positive for malignant cells. I think she went into ventricular fibrillation as a result of the medication affecting the tumor in the heart."

"Even if what you say is true, you were still operating within the doctrine of reasonable and acceptable risk. Every time a patient is given any medication or goes to surgery or has an injection for diagnostic purposes there can be a bad reaction. In a patient with cancer, the risks are greater. Treat a patient with tumor in the intestine, in the heart, or in the brain, and you may get a ruptured gut, cardiac arrest, or a massive brain hemorrhage. Those are the risks we have to accept if we're going to make progress in cancer treatment. The Kreutzer case was unfortunate, but that part about the hospital being a concentration camp is a lot of crap. All disease is punishment without crime. If Mr. Kreutzer is a reasonable man, I'm sure he'd be the first to admit it."

Roger sat still for a minute. Then he said, "Well, my purpose in coming was not to discuss the Kreutzer case. It's about chemotherapy for Frank Walsh, Doctor Nyren's patient with metastatic carcinoma of the lung. We had a little set-to yesterday. We haven't resolved it. Essentially the dispute—"

"Roger, I already know about it. And you don't have to give Mr. Walsh the streptokotocin. I had coffee with Henry Nyren this morning, and he told me he was going to administer it himself today."

"Look, there's something else, Doctor Rosen. I know how important the work is here, but it's just not for me . . . If, someday, the barbed-wire fence marked 'cancer' swings open for me, I'd want to be here. But right now . . ." He shook his head.

Rosen leaned back in his chair and tapped a pencil on his desk. "If you leave now, you'll be putting an unfair burden on your colleagues who will have to do your work, Roger. You'd also be throwing away a year of training for your Boards."

Roger leaned toward this senior staff physician whom he so much respected. He was no longer argumentative.

"I have a suggestion, Doctor Rosen. I have six months to go. There's a friend of mine at Metropolitan Hospital who's had two years of medicine. Then he thought he wanted pediatrics. But he's changed his mind. He wants very much to get into medical oncology. His name is Duncan Comfort. I'd be glad to go into pediatrics. His chief agreed to release him if he can get a qualified replacement. Would you be willing to do the same? You'd be getting an enthusiastic assistant instead of a guy who keeps fighting the system." Roger smiled ingratiatingly.

"For something like that we'd have to ask Doctor Boyer. That's a decision for the department head."

"Yes, I know, but he'd turn right around and ask your advice. Everyone asks your advice around here."

Paul looked hard at Roger for a long moment then he nodded briskly, "If he asks my advice, I'll say he should allow you to do it."

88

# CHAPTER
## *THIRTEEN*

A S HENRY walked down the corridor to talk to Frank Walsh's wife, he met Paul Rosen, slightly stooped, shuffling quietly in his tan crepe-soled shoes. Paul wore these shoes in the laboratory and walking in the Maine woods—in fact, everywhere. There were some yellow laboratory stains on his white coat; he didn't see them because he was color-blind. Paul raised his hand in greeting.

As they walked down the hall together, Paul said, "Did you know Roger Floyd wants to leave Curie—now?"

"I heard he was in to see you. I thought it was about Walsh. It must be harder on him than I thought. Well, he wouldn't be the first member of the house staff to find it too rough here. Anyway, I'm off to see Frank Walsh's wife. C'mon along."

"MARY," HENRY SAID, this is Doctor Rosen. He's familiar with your husband's case."

Mary Walsh and Paul shook hands.

"I just saw Frank and gave him an injection," Henry added. "He's pretty chipper today. Why do you look so upset?"

"Could we go into the visitors' lounge? I gotta have a smoke."

As she lit her cigarette, her hands fluttered. Mary Walsh was in her mid-twenties, but because of her slight frame, fine features and long hair, she could have passed for a schoolgirl.

"I've got a problem and I need your advice. Last month I missed my period and I ignored it. I've been so upset with Frank's troubles that I've been irregular. Now, I missed another one. I got a urine test and I'm pregnant. Frank doesn't know. Should I tell him or not? I know he'll be happy for a minute, but then he'll start thinking, and pretty soon he'll be in the dumps worse than ever."

Paul stood with them but said nothing.

"You mean he'll be happy that he's going to be a father, but then he'll think that he'll never live to see the child?" Henry said. "Well, I'm not going to let him think that, not ever. We're going to keep him so busy with treatment and tests that his morale is going to stay up regardless of his condition. And now you're giving him an extra reason to fight. Look, Mary, I don't know how long Frank has. I'm not going to tell you it's going to be as long as eight or nine months. I'm not kidding you or myself, but it's your job—and mine—to give him as many happy and good days as are humanly possible. The emphasis is on life and nothing but life. Now you take it from there."

AS HENRY AND Paul entered the doctors' dining room, Paul said, "I feel the same way you do about doing the maximum for the cancer patient, but with Walsh the treatment isn't going to make any difference, and I wonder if we shouldn't have given him the option of spending the few months he has left with his family. How long can we refuse to admit to him that he's dying?"

"Hell, Paul, when was the last time a patient asked you if he was going to die? They just don't talk like that."

Paul didn't reply until they had found themselves a table in a quiet corner. "I'm not sure that it's in the patients' best interest for them not to know the truth."

"The truth," Henry said brusquely, "is like castor oil. Some

90

people can take it straight, for most you have to disguise it, and some can't stomach it at all."

NUMBER 416 WAS a three-bed room. Frank Walsh had the window bed on one side of the room. There were two elderly men on the other side who talked to no one except their visitors and who weren't very interested in listening to Frank. It was not that Frank dwelled on his medical problems, he just liked to talk. Since he came into the hospital it seemed that the hardest thing was to find someone to talk with. He answered a lot of questions, the same damn questions from one doctor after another. But talking, the thing that made you a human being, he couldn't find anyone to do that with here. He tried going into the patients' lounge to smoke. Mostly old men and ladies watching TV. Maybe they were afraid to talk to one another. Someone might mention the big C.

Talking was what made his job as a cop bearable, even enjoyable. On his beat he was not only the defender of law and order, he was also the judge, social worker, marriage counselor, and labor relations arbiter. Sometimes he felt like a squire, as if he actually owned the neighborhood. Being on good personal terms with the inhabitants meant that he could talk, drop in for a few minutes, grab a cigarette, have a drink, hear the gossip, give advice. The girls liked to talk to him too, about their kinky johns and about their great plans for the future. The only one he could not talk to was his wife. He clammed up as soon as he got home. Here he was, probably the greatest talker on the New York City police force, and when he was alone with his wife he had nothing to say. All he *could* say to her was that everything he did was for her.

"Then why don't you talk to me?" she would complain.

"That doesn't mean I don't love you. I worship you."

"Don't worship me," Mary would say, "I'm not God or the Mother of God, and I'm not your goddamn mother. She has you so browbeaten you can't open your mouth in front of her for fear of saying something wrong. You told me that yourself. You can say anything you want to me. I never criticize you. I just want to be part of your life. Why can't you tell me what you did all day? Why can't you talk to me?"

Frank would look at her and say, honestly, "I don't know why." Then he'd reach for a cigarette.

Frank looked down at his chest. He opened his pajama top. He couldn't see where the scar started. It just kind of sprouted out of his chest, just below his collarbone, then it looped gracefully under his arm and stopped somewhere on the back of his chest. The night of the operation seemed long ago to him. Christ, he thought, if only I hadn't walked into the liquor store that night.

JUST A STROLL through the alphabet streets and he'd be through with his shift. He should not have let his partner leave early, but what the hell, he thought, it was the kid's first wedding anniversary. As he passed the Good Cheer Liquor Store, he didn't turn his head, he kept walking. Two youths, Afros and jeans, standing still in front of the old, black clerk. They were all standing too still. He was sure he had been spotted.

The shop had one window front and an entrance passage that ran along the brick wall of the next building. Frank stood on the street side of the brick wall. He was able to get a narrow glance into the shop without being seen. He called out, "Herman, you okay?"

"Everything's all right."

A reply too loud with fear.

Frank knew there was a back exit from the store. He hoped the two knew about it also, and that they would grab the money and take off. That would be okay. No one would get hurt. But they just stood like statues in front of the counter with their backs to the door and their hands out of sight. Nobody moved. In three strides Frank was in the store, revolver in hand.

"Police! Stay where you are. When I tell you, put your hands in the air real slow."

92

He remembered that he should move for cover. The floor of the shop was filled with open cases of wine, the specials on whiskey stacked four feet high, and straw-lined barrels of imported liqueur in fancy bottles. The tall set of blue jeans didn't budge. But the small one standing at his side—probably the spotter—fell to the floor behind a piled-up case of wine bottles. He knocked over a case from the top, and the bottles crashed to the floor. Frank saw him, crouched, and fired, but the figure was moving fast among the stacked boxes, barrels, and tables filled with bottles. Frank fired again. More crashing bottles and shadows. Then a sign lit up in his brain: "Keep an eye on the big guy." As he turned to see what the tall set of blue jeans was doing, he knew it was already too late and he had been outfoxed. All he saw was a flash. He felt a pain in his shoulder and keeled over. Two sets of blue jeans and denim jackets blurred past him. He managed to fire off another shot as they ran from the store, but all he did was shatter the glass windowpane. The crashing sound of the glass added to the noise of the burglar alarm that Herman had set off.

It seemed like a year before the squad car and the ambulance arrived. Frank was soaked with blood. It wasn't his shoulder. He was hit in the left chest. He was coughing up blood, but he never lost consciousness.

The ambulance crew gave him plasma intravenously, checked his airway, and gave him oxygen. The squad car ran ahead of the ambulance like a ship's prow through the sea of traffic. He figured they had called ahead because when they got to the hospital they didn't stop at the emergency room. Hospital staff met him, put him on a stretcher, and took him straight to the operating room, undressing him as they moved along the corridors and while in the elevator. In the operating room they sat him up to take a chest X-ray, and he blacked out for a minute. When he came to, he was on his back again looking into the glare of the operating room lights. Dark green shadows, green-veiled faces with covered heads. Funny, he didn't feel any pain, and he wasn't upset about anything. Everyone was busy but him, and he felt he had all the time in the world. Then the repose of anesthesia.

WHEN THE PHONE rang in his office, Henry didn't wait for Tara to answer it. This was a call he and Donna had arranged. If her admonition had not put him off, neither had it stopped her from seeing him whenever she could.

"Henry, I made it to the city and I'm free."

"I had a hunch it would work out. I've made reservations at the Edwardian Room at the Plaza."

"I told Rand that I was going in to see mother, that she was sick. I had to bring mother in on all of this. I'm calling from her apartment now."

"Shall I meet you there?"

"No. Let me meet you at the Plaza. You'll meet mother another time. She's wonderful, but she's not the easiest person in the world to deal with. There's something else I want to tell you about. It's bothering me."

"What is it?"

"I think I was followed down from Riverdale. It would be just like Rand."

"What makes you think so?"

"Well, when I drove off my block and got to the parkway, a little, silver Honda was behind me. There are so many little cars I wouldn't have noticed, except this one had two extra headlights slung under the front bumper. They looked like bug eyes, so I noticed them even though they weren't turned on. The car stayed right behind me when I went down the Harlem River Drive. That's when I became suspicious. When it followed me off the drive at Ninety-sixth Street, I was almost certain. It pulled into that garage at Ninety-first and York."

"I use the gas station there. Just sit tight and I'll call you back."

Henry took a cab to the Mobil station across the street from the ASPCA Hospital. Sure enough, the little, silver Honda with the underslung bug eyes was parked there.

"Hello, Louie, how are you?" Henry greeted the attendant.

"Okay, Doctor Nyren. What can I do for ya?"

"Whose Honda is that?" He pointed to the little car.

94

"That one? It belongs to Doctor Aiello at the ASPCA. Why d'ya ask?"

"Coincidence maybe. A friend of mine thought that little car followed her down from Riverdale."

"No coincidence. Doctor Aiello lives up there. Also got a practice up there. So he goes back and forth."

"That's good, Louie. Thanks."

Henry called Donna from the phone booth in the station.

"False alarm, Donna. The car belongs to a vet at the ASPCA."

"Are you sure?"

"As sure as I can be. It's not likely that the veterinarian is working for your husband. I'm just around the corner from you now. All right if I come up? Don't worry. I can handle your mother."

In a few minutes he was flying up the five stories on feet that barely touched the steps. The door was open and Donna was waiting. She took him by the hand through a large, old-fashioned eat-in kitchen, into an inner room that probably had been a living room at one time but was now a workshop. There was a large skylight, which made it good for that purpose.

"Doctor Henry Nyren, this is my mother, Annie Janocek."

"Pleased to meet you, Mrs. Janocek."

A small woman in a simple, green, floral cotton smock tied at the waist bounced up from one of the two sewing machines in the room and looked Henry over without a word. There were garments all over the place, on racks, some in piles. In the center of the room, right underneath the skylight, there was a large cutting table on long legs with some high chairs around it. Donna had been sitting on one of them having coffee.

Mrs. Janocek's puffy cheeks were in contrast to her thin torso. She was looking at Henry through glasses with large, red aviator frames, a shape not usually favored by women. Donna waited. Henry looked at the glasses.

"Mother wears glasses to sew."

"To see, you mean," she answered snappily.

"And she takes in sewing."

"In the old days I took in sewing. Today, I'm a subcontractor."

She still stood there with a prim, stiff expression, holding her wrinkled hands with gnarled joints in front of her. And no formal greeting to Henry.

"I'd say you're a forty-four long." She tilted her head and squinted at him.

"Forty-four regular."

"Get another tailor—here, take my card."

Henry reached out for the extended hand that held an imaginary card, and his face opened into a large, spontaneous grin.

"Good for you, Doctor Nyren. It's 'Henry,' I know. Have a seat."

Henry sniffed. "That's a wonderful smell."

"I don't smell anything. Donna, you smell anything?"

"Not a thing, Ma."

Mrs. Janocek patted Henry on the shoulder.

"Very good. Natural shoulders. No padding."

She laughed again. "What'll you have to drink? How about bourbon? It's my favorite. They say I shouldn't with the cortisone, but at my age, what the hell!"

"Bourbon's fine. Neat, please."

"Donna, you know where the stuff is. Bring it in. And I want you to have a drink like a normal person. Stop with the white wine. You're not at the country club now."

Mrs. Janocek looked at both of them. "Look at the two of you. All dressed up."

There was a twinkle. "What a compliment, getting all fixed up just to see me."

The three of them were sitting on the high chairs around the cutting table. A pile of fabric was pushed aside to make way for a bowl of pretzels.

"Now you don't want to go to the Plaza. My daughter doesn't like that kind of place. Do you, Donna?"

"I love it."

"Don't listen to her. She's really Secondhand Rose. Look here,

96

Henry. They got candles on the tables there. You'll burn that nice suit. Or you'll get wax under your fingernails. And face it, the food could be better. Now, if you just take off your coat and Miss Fancy Pants here kicks off her shoes, we'll have some of that corned beef and cabbage you've been dying to taste."

# CHAPTER
# FOURTEEN

THE TWO surgeons pored over the opening they had created in Frank Walsh's chest to reach the torn lung. "It's not bad. He'll be okay. It's just the apical segment of the upper lobe. He'll never miss it," one said.

But it was the other man who was doing the actual surgery. "Something's funny here. The bullet went in and out of his chest, and there are good clots along the path, but this section around the bullet hole is hard and white."

"Maybe he's got some old tuberculosis. A lot of cops get TB. The bullet hole probably went through an area of scarring."

The operating surgeon looked closer. "Here, take a look at this. This isn't TB—it's lung cancer. The guy who tried to kill him may have saved his life."

"I don't know. Look at these lymph nodes."

Frank's age did make a difference. A few days after surgery he was in fine shape. He forgot quickly how miserable he had been in the recovery room and how weak he was when he tried to get on his feet. Now he was walking around, sitting in his bedside chair, and feeling like his old self. It was Sunday morning and he walked around the room for a while, trying to get back the strength in his legs. Then he went back to bed for a snooze.

When he awoke, his wife, his father and mother, and his brother and sister-in-law were all sitting in the room.

"Well, hello there. Come to take me home, did you?"

There was an uneasy silence for a moment. Frank sat up in bed and looked around. "Well, don't look so goddamn glum. I'm glad you've all come to see me, but this isn't a wake, you know. I'm feeling better. Hope no one is disappointed. Also, I hope you brought me something to eat. Jeez, this place has lousy food. Now, if one of you doesn't open your yap and say something, I'm going to tell you about every nurse that walks into this room and every thought that goes through my head when they bathe me, when they change my sheets, and best of all when they bend over my bed. Oh, you are a great bunch, you are."

Mary and his brother, Jimmy, spoke simultaneously and said exactly the same thing: "We didn't know what to say, Frank."

"We still haven't gotten over the shock of what happened," Mary added.

Then Jimmy again. "We didn't know you were up to talking, Frank. We'll fill you in on the news if you like."

"Yeah, that's what I want to know. Did they catch those two guys? Was anyone else hurt? Also, who got my beat? I got some more news for you, too. Did you know they've got six cops in this place right now? Three bullet wounds and three multiple stabbings. Three and three, ain't that neat? I know about every one of them. Let me tell you . . ."

Frank was talking again. The best index of his recovery. After a while the hospital aides brought in dinner. It wasn't worth chewing, but the family used the arrival of the tray as an excuse to leave. They promised they would bring some decent food the next visit. He'd given them the full treatment, let them all know that old Frank was back again. But none of them did any talking, particularly his father and brother. He couldn't figure it out.

THE NEXT COUPLE of weeks the surgeons came in daily on rounds. They checked his incision, took out the drain and later the stitches. One day the surgeon who had done the operating stopped in. They chatted a little. Then the doctor told him.

"Things aren't as simple as they seem, Frank. You see, we fixed up that bullet hole all right, but when we were in your chest we found a tumor. We took it out, but that doesn't mean it's all gone."

"Does that mean I'm going to have another operation?"

"I can't tell you. We're transfering you to Curie Hospital. There's a Doctor Henry Nyren there who's the best one in town for cases like yours."

"This tumor. Is it cancer? I mean, what kind is it?"

"They have to do some more studies at Curie and get it all figured out. Then they'll tell you the whole story."

The buck, a perfect pass.

AT CURIE HOSPITAL, just as had been promised, they were busy "figuring things out." Frank got to know Henry Nyren and extended himself in a friendly way so the doctor would think well of him. But he couldn't quite break through. The self-assured doctor never seemed to get too close. There was that shock of black hair he was always pushing back. But he never pushed it back far enough to reveal what was really in his head. Frank couldn't get that feeling of mutual confidence he usually had with people, at least when he was in charge, making *his* rounds, on *his* beat. With Henry Nyren, he wasn't being told the whole story. Maybe others didn't feel that, but cops are trained to sense things, or they would never survive in the jungle.

"Doc, sit down for a minute, will you? I have to have some answers," Frank told Henry one day after receiving his injection of streptokotocin. Henry pulled up a chair and brushed his hand through his hair.

"When I was in Bellevue they told me I had a lung tumor," Frank said, "and that's why they were going to transfer me here. When I asked them if I had lung cancer, they said you people at Curie would figure all that out. Now I'm asking you, what have I got and what's going on?"

100

"You do have a tumor, and we are treating you to keep it under control." This was Henry's standard opening shot.

Frank wasn't satisfied. "You've got to give me more information, Doc. I can't go on that. I want all the facts. I was taught something about gathering evidence, at John Jay College, and I'm very interested in the case at hand."

"For example?" Henry asked. The motors were churning. Down deep, where metabolism throbs like the diesels of a destroyer, a signal was received. This guy was not going to be satisfied with pat answers, Henry realized. He was not going to be neutral territory on which Henry could engage the enemy.

"For example, this tumor, is it cancer?" Frank said.

Henry replied from his store of careful phrases. "Cancer is a scare word, and people have the impression that it's always fatal. Well, there are some tumors that look benign under the microscope but act malignant. There are others that look malignant under the microscope but people live with them for many years. It's not just what it looks like. It's how it behaves."

"How is this one behaving?" Frank asked.

"It's too early to tell." Henry passed his hand through his hair again but appeared relaxed. His answer was a bold-faced lie. The cancer was acting in a very aggressive and malignant fashion. "We are treating it with drugs so we can keep the tumor growth suppressed and keep you feeling well and active for a good long time. For the foreseeable future anyway."

"You've been doing a lot of detective work on me the last few weeks. Haven't you figured out yet if this tumor is a good guy or a bad guy?"

"Look, Frank, suppose you see a man coming out of a building. He's dressed in an Indian outfit and he's carrying a tomahawk in his hand. He might be criminally insane, or he could be an ordinary guy dressed for a costume party. But he would definitely bear watching, as a suspicious character, right? Well, we're not going to take any chances here. We're going to treat this tumor and hit it hard."

"It seems to me I'm right back where I started," Frank persisted. "I just want to know if this is lung cancer or not. Can you at least give me a straight answer to that question?"

Henry was in a ticklish spot. Not many people pressed him the way Frank was doing. "You do have lung cancer, Frank, but those two words don't tell the whole story."

"Well, cancer is cancer. I guess that's all I have to know."

"No, it's not. It hasn't spread outside of the chest, and that's important. We may have it in a stage where there's a chance to control it."

"I think I ought to tell you something. I was home for a few days before I came here. When I was home I called the police surgeon. I told him my uncle in Boston just had an operation on his lung and they found cancer and they didn't get it all out. That's what I told him because I figured that was the story with me. You know what the surgeon said? 'Don't wait too long if you want to visit him. I'd give him three months, six at the most.' Now you know that didn't make me feel good, but I didn't crack up either. I figure it's the truth. Can you tell me otherwise?"

Frank Walsh was steering a collision course.

"I can't play that game, Frank. I won't ever guess how long anyone has to live. Suppose someone had told that to Arthur Godfrey thirty years ago when he had surgery for cancer of the lung? I'm going to keep you alive and well as long as humanly possible. I promise you that. But how long that will be, I can't tell. I just want you to fight this thing with me. The medicines are strong and have side effects. If you're not feeling well, don't get discouraged—it's the medicine, not you. You'll feel better in a few days." Henry was steaming full speed ahead through waters he knew very well.

"I always figured I would die with my boots on. Somewhere up in the attic," Frank said, pointing to his head, "there's a small, dark room that I keep locked up. On the door there's a sign that says, 'Someday you'll be killed.' In that room are three things—a table, a chair, and a bottle. Like I said, I keep this room locked up, and the rest of the attic is a big cheerful place with flashing lights, pensions, kids, wife, grandchildren, and lots of family parties. When I was shot in the chest, while I was in that ambulance bleeding all the way to the hospital, I figured I was going to die and that was that. I didn't panic. I opened up the door to that little room and sat down, had a drink, and relaxed. Then when I woke up, smiles all around. I felt great but it didn't last. Now I'll tell you what I can't stand. It's going in and out of that little room in my head. It's too painful. I can go in and relax and take things as they come, or I can stay out and fight, if it's really worthwhile. That's why I want you to level with me. Now what do you want me to do, Doctor Nyren?"

"Stay out and fight. I need you to fight this thing with me. Look, nobody knows how long they have to live, not you, not me, not anybody. But you've got to believe this thing can be licked, that you can get better. You've got to have hope. If you give up and go back into that little room, neither of us has a chance. I'll guarantee that. Look, I'm willing to fight with everything I've got. What do you say?"

"I'll sign that contract," Frank said, finally changing his course to follow Henry's lead.

Henry left all fired up and enthusiastic as if he had won another convert, but down deep Frank knew he was being conned. He knew that Henry really believed what he said, and he wanted very much to believe it, too. It's just that he didn't.

I feel a little sorry for that guy. He's going to be very disappointed, Frank thought. Then he relaxed and imagined he was pouring himself a drink. Frank fell asleep in the little room.

# CHAPTER
# *FIFTEEN*

H ENRY WAS spending a good deal of his time in animal surgery. Mid-torso occlusion, his new technique for safely giving chemotherapy to the upper half of the body in very high doses, was working out. Since the drug would circulate only in the upper half of the body, there would be no nausea and vomiting as the stomach and intestines were spared, and enough bone marrow would be preserved in the lower half of the body to avoid a dangerous drop in blood counts. Use of this technique would be limited to tumors that had not spread below the diaphragm. The procedure, researched in small niches hastily carved out of his patient-care responsibilities, was close to being ready for its first trial in a human being.

Animal surgery sometimes referred to as the dog lab, was a large, well-ventilated inside room with no windows. The walls and ceiling were encased in beige tile; the floor cement was covered with gray deck paint. There were three operating tables in a row and three complete OR teams. Supervising all was Dr. Luis Gomez, an old aristocrat and a refugee surgeon from Republican Spain, who had never gotten his license to practice in this country. The facility was the best of its kind to be found anywhere. All the new Curie strategies for surgically attacking cancer were meticulously perfected here.

Henry was delighted at the progress they were making. They were up to 100 milligrams of streptokotocin and ten minutes of occlusion. That was ten times the human dose—certainly an otherwise fatal amount—and the animals were tolerating both the chemotherapy and the procedure well.

"What time do you want to start tomorrow, Doctor Gomez?" Henry asked.

"In Seville we made the first incision at seven A.M." Dr. Gomez replied, turning his acutely angled V-shaped face to Henry.

"I'll be here at seven. You go ahead. All I do is inject the drug."

"The vials are all here, awaiting your attention." He pointed to a stand that held all the equipment used for mid-torso occlusion and a box with ten vials, each containing 100 milligrams of streptokotocin.

HENRY ARRIVED AT the dog lab a few minutes after seven. Dr. Gomez was already gowned; the dog—a large, red-brown mongrel—was anesthetized and draped. The assistants were in place. As soon as Henry entered the room, Dr. Gomez made an incision over the femoral artery and prepared to insert a catheter with a balloon tip into the aorta. Henry gowned up quickly and saw that the abdominal tourniquet, which resembled a large blood pressure cuff, was in place. He was getting ready to mix the medication and draw it up into the syringe when the phone rang.

One of the laboratory assistants, in the pajama-type attire common to all operating rooms, ran to the phone.

"It's for you, Doctor Nyren."

"Take a message."

"It's a Mrs. Stockman."

"Okay." Henry stopped what he was doing and walked to the wall phone. "Hi, Donna! What's up?"

"Randy has a temperature of a hundred and one. He used to have fever with the leukemia. I'm frightened, Henry."

105

"Look, Randy is entitled to pick up a bug like any other kid. Bring him in. We'll check his blood, and I'll look him over." He glanced over to the table. Disappointed eyes said he was holding up everything.

"Can I take him out with a fever?"

"Yes, come in as soon as you can. Tara will find me."

Scuttlebutt around the lab had gotten back to Henry that although his ideas were good, he didn't spend enough time working on them. He walked quickly back to the table.

"Sorry for the interruption. Okay, inflate and occlude and start timing."

Everything was going well. The dog was showing no immediate effects of the chemotherapy or the temporary loss of the blood supply to the abdomen and lower half of the body.

Dr. Gomez seemed pleased. "Very good, Doctor Nyren. Would you like me to do the bone marrow or will you?"

The phone rang again. "If it's for me, take a message!" Henry called out. It was Tara, relaying a call from the hospital. While they were finalizing follow-up plans, the laboratory assistant who had taken the call handed Henry a note: "Tara says: Frank Walsh scheduled for 10 milligrams of streptokotocin this A.M." Well, at least he wouldn't have to make a special trip to get the drug. He reached over to the stainless steel table, where all the paraphernalia for the mid-torso occlusion was kept, and picked up a vial of the medication.

Dr. Gomez caught Henry on his way out. "You know, Doctor Nyren, time makes no difference to me. I can operate day or night. What is important is to get the work done with the minimum of interruptions and the greatest concentration on our goals. This is a good technique, perhaps even a great example of surgeons and chemotherapists working together for the conquest of cancer."

"Well, we'll see what happens," Henry replied, a little overwhelmed by the surgeon's hyperbole. The implied criticism didn't escape Henry either. Still, there were forces beyond his control.

106

When he had left, Dr. Gomez murmured, *"Muy ocupado—hacienda demasiado."*

A Puerto Rican laboratory assistant nodded and said, "Yes, he spreads himself too thin."

IT WAS STILL early. Henry would give Frank Walsh the medication before rounds. He would be glad when Roger Floyd's replacement arrived and he'd be spared these tasks.

The policeman was sitting up in bed, reading the newspaper.

"That stuff you gave me last week wasn't so bad, Doc. I've had hangovers worse than that—only booze never shot the hair off my head."

Henry had the syringe filled with the diluent and was mixing the medication at the bedside. A tourniquet around the arm, an unprotesting, bulging blue vein received the silent thrust of the intravenous needle, and the orange-red fluid was quickly injected.

"That's it. It's all over."

A few minutes of banter, then Henry returned to the nurses' station to make an entry in red ink in the chart, indicating that the medication had been given. He sat down and wrote: "Streptokotocin administered. No immediate untoward reaction to the intravenous injection of 10—"

Then he knew. He had not given Walsh 10 milligrams; he had given him 100 milligrams of streptokotocin. The vials prepared for patient use contained 10 milligrams, but he had taken the vial from the dog lab. He had intended, when he reached for the 100 milligram vial, to use just 10 milligrams and discard the rest. Henry's first thought was, I've killed him—I wasn't paying attention and he's a dead man. Adding a zero to the ten in his chart note, he looked at it in black and white: "100 milligrams." Damn.

"This dose was given by me in error," he wrote, his hand surprisingly firm. "I had intended to give 10 milligrams."

He then wrote orders requesting that Frank Walsh be placed in isolation since his white blood cells could be expected to disap-

**107**

pear, making him a sitting duck for infection. He alerted the blood bank that he might need platelets if the patient started bleeding. He went to the nurses' office and ordered special nurses to stay with Walsh around the clock. He told the nursing registrar to send the bill to him.

If Henry had struck down a child with his car he couldn't have felt worse. How could he have done a thing like that? It was inexcusable. For years everyone had been telling him, you can't do everything. They were right. It wasn't fair to the research, and it definitely wasn't fair to the patients. He couldn't do both, no one could. Why did it take an act of mayhem for him to believe it?

The next two weeks were hell. Henry canceled all his research procedures and, except for patient calls, was virtually incommunicado. What was left of Walsh's hair fell out. He suffered terrible nausea and vomiting. His white blood cells disappeared almost completely. The platelets fell to very low levels. He urinated and defecated blood. He was anointed by a priest, seen and decorated (through the glass window) by the Police Commissioner. The family checked to see that his insurance was paid up and the benefits properly assigned to his wife.

Most of the time, especially at first, he was mercifully unconscious, but when he was awake, he felt his throat was on fire—not so far from the truth—and that his muscles had turned to jelly. Everything hurt: breathing, swallowing. There was no question of moving.

BUT FRANK DID not die. By the third week he was on the way to recovery. He was going to make it.

Henry internalized his anger at himself. He ate poorly and looked haggard and grim. But he, too, would make it. The cancer decreased in size somewhat, but was still there. It was going to make it too!

# CHAPTER
# SIXTEEN

**T**HERE HAD been other emotionally bruising cases. He still felt the pain of Maria Fauci's demise. Since Laura, he hadn't healed as quickly afterward. Since Laura, he hadn't known the emotional exhilaration that could displace other concerns.

Until Donna.

Their evening meetings in the city were too infrequent and were taking their toll on both Donna and Henry. She hated the lying, and he worried that the infrequency of the meetings would cool and finally freeze their relationship.

Tonight was one of those rare opportunities for her to come into the city. They didn't go to her mother's, they were afraid they'd never get out. They met at *Il Monello,* a restaurant she liked.

"You don't look well, Henry. Are you okay?"

"I'm going to be. Let's get something to drink." He forced a smile.

Donna could discern a weariness in his shoulders. His laughter did not soar. It was tethered.

"Something's bothering you. Even your phone calls recently— your voice, it's been, well, grim. And sometimes I felt our conversations were kind of perfunctory. Is it us?"

"No. It's everything else. Now is when I need you, when the

bricks come falling down on my head. It's my work—mainly one case where I did something very wrong. I gave a patient a nearly fatal overdose of chemotherapy. He went through hell, and I did too."

"Is he going to be all right?"

"He's recovering. He could just as well have died. It would have been my fault."

"But he didn't die. You should feel relieved," she said.

"Of course, I'm relieved that he didn't die, but I'm still upset that I could have made such a mistake."

"Maybe you're reaching for too much, trying too hard," she said.

As she spoke the image flashed through his mind of trying to direct an experiment in the dog lab and at the same time collect the chemotherapy to treat Frank Walsh. "Please don't give me that line! It was an out-and-out disaster I created."

Donna stiffened. She was not prepared for this kind of heavy scene. She tried to be up to it.

"Please, I'm only trying to help," she said. "I know a little. I went through it with Randy. And that was only once. I still go to pieces, like when he had that fever for just one day. I know your entire life is made of Randys, but isn't there some pay-back?"

"You're right, Donna. The Randys—the cases that turn out well—are what make it worthwhile. That, and the chance to be with someone like you. Just being with you makes me feel better."

It was true. He loved to look at her. She was as beautiful when she frowned as when she smiled. The warmth and softness of her hand excited him. The way her dress fell against her thigh or abdomen could leave him momentarily breathless.

By the time they had finished dinner, Henry's mood had improved markedly. The laughter was unfettered, the smiles were not competing with frowns. But as they were about to leave, Henry put his hand to his head.

"I've loused up again. I was supposed to meet my daughter tonight, and I forgot to call and tell her I couldn't make it."

110

"Call her now and apologize. It's not late. Drop me off and go to her. I have to get going in a little while anyway."

After leaving Donna at her car, Henry tried calling Eve. No answer. He went back to his apartment and called again.

"Eve, I apologize," he said as she answered.

"Henry, it's like all the other times in my life when you ran out on me. You didn't even think enough to call."

"I know. I'm as big a disappointment to myself as I am to you."

"The only difference now is I don't have any expectations of you like I did when I was a kid, so it's really okay. I know I'll always play second fiddle to your patients, but I'm not upset."

"Eve, I've got to be honest with you. It wasn't a patient this time. I had dinner with a woman I met recently that I like a lot."

"Why is it I feel the arm pushing me away from you is getting longer and longer?"

"I owe you a lifetime of apologies. This is just one more."

"It's none of my business. But it reminds me of when I first learned about Janine and how bad I felt for mother. Now I've gotten to know Janine, and I feel bad for her. I don't think females in any category get too much out of being close to you."

"Nothing has changed with Janine. We're still the same friends. With Donna, it's different. I'm trying to build a relationship with her that will have some meaning. If you'll let me, I'd like to talk to you about it some time."

"The next thing you'll tell me is that she's married."

AS DONNA DROVE home she was clear about one thing: her life had been so complicated by Randy's brush with death that she wanted a respite from any source of anxiety, and her relationship with Henry could lead only to anxiety. She was past the stage of feeling friendly toward him out of gratitude. She had gotten to know the man behind the white coat, and his attentions were flattering. She could sense his ardor growing, and she had to admit to a reciprocal excitement, but she recognized in Henry a man with a take-charge personality who would soon have her

111

tied up and neatly wrapped in his emotions, and she wasn't going to let things just happen to her, not again. After her marriage six years ago, she awakened to a set of circumstances beyond her control, and not all to her liking. If this continues, she thought, then sooner or later I'll be sleeping with him. Do I tell Rand? Do we get a divorce? What happens to Randy? Why do I think he wants to marry me? Maybe I'm just one of a string of affairs for him. It could be his life-style. After all, being a doctor is a great way to get to know people. This time I'm not going to let someone else decide my life for me.

As she drove up her block in Riverdale, Donna thought, What a dull street. Every house was a small, stone Tudor, with only minor variations on the same architectural theme. Some had wooden crossbeams painted white, others brown or gray; some had white stucco to show off the wooden beams; some had one chimney, some two; some had open porches, others enclosed porches, and still others no porch at all. Each brown or gray stone fortress had a little army of evergreen men—rhododendrons, arborvitae, spruce, yews—to safeguard the inhabitants' precious privacy. But what struck Donna as the essential difference between the city and here was people. Where were they? Could they all have died? Did they go away? Or were they simply all holed up? Tonight was no different from other nights, Donna reminded herself. She had until now just managed not to notice that the city had what she wanted—life.

Why are we living here? she thought, as she pulled into her driveway. We're too young to be here. There were lights on in the house, but the blinds were, as always, drawn. Lights off upstairs. Randy was asleep; that was good. She walked to the side entrance near the garage, but the screen door was locked from the inside. Hell! She walked around the carefully trimmed lawn and up the stone steps to the highly shellacked, large, oak front door. As she put her key in the door, she thought, Funny, I thought the lights were on.

At Donna's first step into the house, all the lights came on, and she was greeted by cries of "Surprise!" The living room was festooned with streamers and balloons. The welcoming shout was followed by "Happy Birthday" sung in a variety of keys, then the crowd of guests gave way to reveal a table set with her best linen and a large cake and candles in the middle. A smiling Rand came to greet her with arms extended, and gave her a resounding kiss to the cheers of all the guests.

She stood openmouthed, couldn't find anything to say. Her thoughts had been so far from this. Her birthday was Friday, tomorrow. She looked at Rand.

All she could say, rubbing her hand across his head, was, "You had a hair cut!" Whatever she said at that moment would have been fine, and this domestic touch struck a favorable note. The relatives and guests burst out laughing, and the hired musician at the piano started to play.

Donna carried off her part. She was in fact magnificent. Rand took a glass of champagne and stood aside to make a toast. To get everyone's attention, he took off his glasses and tapped the silver of the coin-shaped frames against the champagne glass. "A toast to my wife, for the wonderful life she has given me—and for the gift of our son, who we treasure more than ever."

Later, in the quiet of a bath, Donna tried to assimilate the evening, from dinner with Henry to the party. Rand had gone to a lot of trouble. Why didn't that make her love him the slightest bit more? Because no party could change the fabric of their marriage. However, this one had emphasized its density. There could be no way to fit Henry in. Being married to Rand was made up of an occasional gesture of affection and nastiness in between—but it was her marriage, and that was that.

Henry called several mornings the following week. Each time Donna was out. When he finally found her in, there was no opportunity for them to meet because he was going to a medical convention for a week. He promised to call when he returned. Maybe he would, she thought, but she would make it her business to be out of the house mornings. There were two weeks before

Randy's next visit to Henry. By then, she'd be ready to make it clear to Henry that her relationship with him had to be professional only.

EVE HAD A job in the copy department of a magazine founded by her mother. She was not especially gifted, but she was a plugger and on her own level good at coming up with new ideas. All members of the magazine staff were free to contribute articles to a column called "The Arts—Fine and Not So Fine," and she had had a few of her entries chosen for publication. She never sat down and deliberately planned what she was going to do. Something would strike her, and she would go after it like a terrier. She was like a terrier in other ways too; she was temperamental and snapped easily. She even looked a little like one, petite, with tight, curly hair.

Saturday evening Eve had a Category II date ("Okay, 'cause I've got nothing better to do"). Category I was "Possibilities," and Category III was "Only because I'm desperate." She had stayed over at her date's Greenwich Village apartment but made an excuse to leave first thing in the morning—noon sharp. She was going uptown to a Sunday afternoon cocktail party where she expected to find some Category I's, and she wanted to go home and change into something sure to snare one.

The day was warm and bright and Eve decided to hike uptown. In good spirits, she walked briskly up Sixth Avenue, enjoying the sights. She spotted a young woman sitting with her heels resting on a rung of a high stool, bending over a small stone, polishing it by hand. Next to her on an easel was a piece of plywood covered with black velvet, on which were hung carved stone pendants and bracelets of copper and silver. Eve's idea lamp switched on. She went over and inspected the woman's wares, impressed as much by how engrossed she was as by the pieces themselves.

"Hi. Your stuff's good."

"Thanks." The woman's eyes remained on the stone she was polishing.

114

"Do you sign your pieces?" Eve asked.

"Somewhere on every piece there's an 'M' for Marlene," the young woman replied, still not looking up.

Eve picked up a small piece of polished marble. "I'll take this pendant. It's marked six dollars, right?"

"If that's what it says."

"I have an idea, a proposition, actually. I'd like to interview you."

"What on earth for?" Marlene Lowell sat upright and for the first time looked at Eve. She put the small piece of marble and the polishing cloth aside while she tucked Eve's six single dollar bills in a small leather purse, which she stowed in the pocket of her jeans.

"It's nothing weird," Eve went on. "I work for a magazine, *The Outrageous Decorator*, and they have this monthly column on art, any kind of art. I'd like to do a story on you, a jewelry maker on the streets of New York."

"I'm not really a jewelry maker, I'm a sculptor. I do the marble pendants and the cameos. Those bracelets I buy from someone else."

"That's even better," Eve replied, her enthusiasm growing. "It won't take long. All I need to know is who you are, why you do what you do. We'll just chat."

"I don't think so. I'm not an interesting person."

"Your work's interesting. Look, all I need is something about your background, your parents, your boyfriends."

Marlene laughed. "My parents are superboring, and my boyfriend is a friend who is a boy—who I've known since we started fooling around together when we were thirteen. You think your sophisticated readers would enjoy hearing about that? Besides, I'm not going to stop what I'm doing or leave this spot on my best afternoon of the week."

Eve, the terrier, could turn into a bulldog. "Listen, if you're serious about selling your things, I'm really offering you about twenty-thousand dollar's worth of free publicity. I'll guarantee, when I'm finished, you could sell pet bricks with 'M' on them. You could open a store if you wanted."

"Well, maybe you've got something." Marlene began polishing the marble piece again. "But not this afternoon."

Eve thought for a moment. She wasn't ready to toss aside the idea of the cocktail party. Prospects for finding a Category I were not easy to come by. She put away the pendant and turned again to Marlene. "Suppose I go away and let you do your work and come back about six-thirty? We could have a bite together and that would be it. I have a small budget. I could give you fifty dollars for the interview."

"No money. You made your one good point. Stick with that."

# CHAPTER
# SEVENTEEN

O N A clear, crisp morning a few months after his trip to Morristown, Tara brought the mail into Henry's office. Henry, with his characteristic restlessness, was pacing back and forth between his desk and the window, Dictaphone mike in hand, working on a pile of correspondence that seemed never to diminish. Tara slipped most of the day's mail to the bottom of the pile on Henry's desk but held out two pieces for him to look at immediately.

"Our score for success this week has been quite high," she said. There was a letter from a doctor in California telling Henry that a patient he had treated two years ago for metastatic carcinoma of the colon was still doing well. And, enclosed with a box that contained a large jar of peach-plum jelly, there was a letter that said, "Dear Dr. Nyren, I want to thank you for seeing my wife and the advice you gave Dr. Walton at the nursing home. The missus and I walked out of the hospital three weeks ago. She gained twenty pounds. Her belly isn't swollen anymore. I know I have you to thank for it." It was signed Luther Tines.

Henry turned off the Dictaphone and read the letters again.

"It's nice to win one once in a while."

"Two," Tara said, smiling.

"Two," he acknowledged with a grin. "By the way, when is the next appointment with the Stockman boy?"

VEIT-VOLPIN WAS standing in the hallway puffing clouds of smoke from his pipe while holding his hand over a "No Smoking" sign. "Are you sure you want to go through with this, Mrs. Evans?"

"Of course I do. How else am I to find out what goes on in the hospital and the institute? When we moved to New York, I made up my mind that I was not going to be merely the social adjunct to the director of the hospital. I've had enough of that. Besides," she continued, "there are so many important things going on around here. I know if I apply myself I'll find a meaningful niche, perhaps in the Social Service Department, or in the library, or in the Rehabilitation Department. Perhaps even in a laboratory— that's my fantasy, even though I know the director's wife doesn't have enough pull for that. But I'm an inquisitive person, and I'm going to all the lectures I can, until I get saturated with the place. Then I'll know where I fit. I've chosen you for my guide because you are supposed to be the most outspoken and knowledgeable person here."

Gregor Veit-Volpin, eyebrows thick as his mustache, was enjoying his current assignment. "I am afraid you will find out very soon that I pretend to know more than I actually do," he said and with a courtly half bow led Mrs. Evans into the auditorium where medical students were gathering. They walked toward seats in the back where they would be able to talk, his pipe issuing streamers beneath the "No Smoking" signs.

"A few tips I can give you," Veit-Volpin said as he crossed his legs and turned to Mrs. Evans. "Some say it's the same, others say it's different, but to me it's a hospital like any other hospital, except it has no obstetrics department. Pediatrics, keep out of. It's the only place I do not go. I can't stand the sight of little ones with tumors."

Mrs. Evans acknowledged his advice with a slow nod. Pediatrics would be the next place she would visit.

118

The old man with the pipe continued. "Then there is the Research Institute. Well, what can I tell you? It's a bunch of laboratories where the doctors from the hospital go for an ego trip. Since your husband never asked me, I'll tell *you*. Medicine is a jealous mistress, and Mother Nature is a bitch. Always doctors try to make love to them both at the same time. But it doesn't work. This business of clinicians doing laboratory research is pure nonsense."

"But Morgan tells me what a fine cancer researcher you are, Doctor V."

"Ah ha, I have a great bibliography. What I do is go to Doctor Weil and say, 'The Russians say radiation therapy works better when the tissue is supersaturated with oxygen, so why don't we try radiation therapy plus chemotherapy and oxygen? And we will be one step ahead of them.' Doctor Weil assigns this to Doctor Fran Li Park. Frannie puts a graduate student on it. We all put our names on the paper, and presto we are cancer researchers. I am not a cancer researcher, Mrs. Evans. I am a cancer research broker. I bring clinical problems and laboratory people together. But myself, I'm content to run my department."

"I'm getting a marvelous tour of Doctor Veit-Volpin," Mrs. Evans said.

"Great research does not always come from great research institutions. My apologies to your husband, but he must know this and so must you. Do the great symphonies come from Juilliard or the Eastman School of Music? Do great masterpieces come from the art academies? Why don't they? All the masters are at those places. I'll tell you why. Because Mother Nature is not only a bitch but a promiscuous one. She never sleeps with the right people. She'd rather pick some despicable wretch working in a dump than a *grand seigneur* in a palace. Look at Madame Curie herself. She worked in a garage. Papanicolaou's work was ignored until he found someone to champion his cause. Ludwig Gross worked in an obscure laboratory in the Bronx. When he claimed that he had found a virus that caused leukemia, he was considered just another refugee crank."

"Oh, come, Doctor V., your Russian background is showing. Does every creative person have to slosh around in despair in order to be worthy of a grain of newly discovered truth?"

"No, Mrs. Evans, but it helps. Why don't we leave this place and go back to my office for a brandy? This is going to be a terrible lecture."

Just then Paul Rosen walked in, entering from the back of the auditorium. As he passed Mrs. Evans and Veit-Volpin, he greeted them. The pipe smoker groaned under his breath.

"Trapped, like the kulaks in 1929," he said good-naturedly, settling back in his chair.

Paul Rosen's lecture on cancer was actually an introduction to cancer chemotherapy. Not only did he talk about pharmacology and tell of the early discoveries that led to the current advances, but he also stressed the requirements for clinical research—the discipline and training needed to evaluate the patient's response to treatment, so important in chemotherapy because the response was seldom all or none. That would be easy. Instead, it was a critical question of degree and duration of response. And, if it was an experimental program, how did it compare with established forms of therapy? This was Paul Rosen talking about what he knew best—cancer chemotherapy as a clinical science.

Mrs. Evans leaned over to Dr. Veit-Volpin.

"He's muttering. I can hardly understand him. And the students—they seem to have the lecture on mimeographed sheets."

"You have to listen carefully," Veit-Volpin replied. "What he says is pure gold, but a speaker he is not. Last year's students wrote down his lectures and then mimeographed them, like *samizdat*. Nyren should know about it, these notes."

"Adriamycin, bleomycin—I thought the term 'mycin' was a label used for antibiotics," Mrs. Evans whispered to her companion.

Veit-Volpin answered in his normal tone of voice. "Correct, my intellectual ballerina. Those drugs are derived from bacteria, just like antibiotics are, but they are more active against cancer."

120

Mrs. Evans, who had brought a clipboard and legal pad, was taking notes.

"I'll have enough material from this lecture for ten of my fund-raising talks," she said.

Dr. Veit-Volpin was not impressed. "For that kind of talk you only need baloney. So you should see me. My father used to run a delicatessen."

When Paul finished, students crowded around the podium to speak to him. Long after the auditorium had emptied, he would stand there with the remaining students, patiently answering every one of them.

Mrs. Evans bundled up her notes, put her pen away, and then turned to Veit-Volpin.

"I do have a question for you, my Intourist guide. If we are doing such wonderful things with surgery, radiation therapy, and chemotherapy, why does it seem that more and more people are dying of cancer?"

"My father used to tell me there are always two answers to a question. One is the answer that is on top and the other is the secret answer. The answer on the top is that we are not seeing patients early enough so we can diagnose and cure them while the cancer is still localized. Also there are not enough wonderful centers like the Curie Hospital where patients benefit from the latest advances in the scientific treatment of cancer. But the secret answer is different. The secret answer is that we are making cancer faster than we can get rid of it, and we always will. It's like automobiles. We manufacture automobiles faster than we can get rid of them, so we have tremendous junk yards. So it is with cancer. We manufacture tremendous amounts of cancer with the air we breathe, with what we eat, what we work with, what we smoke and drink. And so we will never be able to cure it faster than we make it. Therefore, we need gigantic repair shops and junk yards. And we call them hospitals."

"You, Doctor V., sound wretched enough for Mother Nature to cuddle right up in your lap, light your pipe, and whisper her secrets in your ear."

"Mrs. Evans, who ever heard of a woman, even a promiscuous woman, giving anything away to a seventy-year-old man?"

As they walked out together she said, "I think I have to learn more about Doctor Rosen. I hear his name wherever I turn. But he is not a department head, he's not a full professor at the Medical School, and his name doesn't even appear on the table of organization. Yet it seems that no decisions are made without consulting him. Why is that?"

Veit-Volpin replied, "Again there are two answers. The answer on top is that he has superb judgment. But the secret answer is that he is the soul of the hospital."

"If he is the soul of the hospital, then what is Henry Nyren?" she asked.

"Ah ha! I knew you would ask that. Whenever there is a difficult case, everyone says 'Consult Doctor Nyren.' 'Call in Henry.' Right? But, I ask you, who does Henry consult with? It's like theology—there are seraphim and there are angels, and one is higher than the other. But who can remember which is which?"

# CHAPTER
## EIGHTEEN

**M**RS. JULIA West and her companion were standing on the platform at the Como railroad station, waiting for the train to take them to Switzerland. At Interlaken, they would make a connection to Wengen. The last fifteen minutes of the journey would be by cogwheel train up the side of the mountain in which the village nestled. There Julia West would stay for ten days at Dr. Schlager's sanitorium and have her annual checkup.

"Isn't this going to a lot of trouble for a checkup? I mean, you could have had it when we were in New York."

"Lilly, stop whining like a child. I don't have to answer to you."

Mrs. West's gaze drifted from the younger woman to the mountains that framed the lakes she loved ~o much. "There's only one thing wrong with Lake Como," she said, "too many Italians."

"That's pretty silly, isn't it?" Lilly Peel replied. Here, Lilly was a companion. At home in New York or Denver, she would have been a maid or housekeeper. Although not well educated, she knew nonsense when she heard it.

"Since we discovered that villa at Bellagio, we don't have to bother with other places," Mrs. West said.

"If you like it so much, why don't you learn Italian?" Lilly was not going to be ignored so easily.

"You must be crazy. You know I don't like Italians. I like the countryside, the food, the villa, the music. The weather is marvelous. Now if everyone spoke English, everything would be perfect."

"If they all spoke English, they'd still be Italians."

"Oh, Lilly, you just don't understand. Now, where is that man from Cook's? He's supposed to handle all these traffic problems. I can't be bothered communicating with the natives."

"Okay, okay, I think it would be better if I look for *him.* After all, he has a sign on him, and we don't. All he knows is to look for an overdressed, gray-haired lady who looks like she owns the joint and a skinny clown who wears long skirts."

Lilly quickly located the Thomas Cook agent, who apologized profusely and explained all the arrangements for their compartment and for dining and the connections at Interlaken. The train arrived, so he finished his explanations as he escorted Mrs. West and Lilly to their compartment.

The man from Cook's did not neglect to tell the conductor who his new passengers were. Then Mrs. West took over, subjecting the agent to five minutes of strongly voiced complaints, all trivial. When she was done, he bowed, made his farewells—*"Arrivederle, signorine!"*—and bounded off with obvious relief. Mrs. West and Lilly sat back in their tidy, private quarters.

"The trip won't be long. We'll be there in time for dinner," Mrs. West said, putting a cigarette into a long holder.

Trips in easy stages were her secret to traveling in comfort. Never more than six hours if she could help it, rail or air. On their way to New York, there would be a short stopover in London.

"That means only one meal on the train—too bad. Trains rustle up my appetite, and the food on these trains beats most of the stuffy joints you drag me to," Lilly said, fidgeting.

"They do serve plain, wholesome, and hearty portions of French and Italian food on this train, which unsurprisingly match your peasant tastes. Now, shut up for a while and let me enjoy my cigarette and cognac."

124

Julia West enjoyed her "unsinkable Molly Brown" reputation. But it was, in fact, a put-on. Her mother, Denver born and bred, was in that image, but Julia, although born in Denver and thoroughly familiar with the family's ranch properties, was educated in the East and had married and settled in New York. She donned and doffed the rough-tough style as it suited her. The family had accumulated wealth by purchasing nondescript cattle farms just before World War I. The war saw a great boom in beef prices, and from then on the family empire never ceased growing. Now, Denver was to Mrs. West only a place for vacations and occasional business trips, but she cultivated the folklore of the West and, since she had no peers as close friends, she used her pseudoroughneck style to establish a camaraderie with Lilly and her other servants. She was a strong but lonely person. Traveling created the illusion of meaningful activity. The mechanical kinds of problems it entailed could usually be solved with bullheadedness and money. She liked the part of the world she was in now. She recognized the Italian lake country and adjacent Switzerland as the last place in the world where she could find civilization as she wanted it.

As the train pulled away from Como and headed for the St. Gotthard pass and the Alps, the mist-covered lakes bordered with lush greenery and baroque villas disappeared behind a rugged wall of mountains. In a few hours, all was snow. The train strained up a steep grade, or crawled slowly through a pass, and then seemingly relaxed along a level stretch, as if gathering strength for the next ascent. They got off the train at Interlaken on a day smoky with the haze of lightly falling snow. The Jungfrau was there somewhere: you could barely make out its outline through the milk-glass screen of clouds.

The town had some of the same dreamy qualities of the lake country she had just left, but she was not there just to visit. The appointment for her annual checkup at the sanitorium at Wengen was two days from now.

"Come on, Lilly. There's nothing doing here today. Let's check in, and tomorrow I'll take you for lunch at the most beautiful spot in the world."

THE NEXT MORNING they went as far up the Jungfrau as they could get by car. From the tiny village at the end of the road one could see an adjacent mountain peak. On this clear day, it almost seemed close enough to reach out and touch. The sun was shining brightly. There were people sunbathing and lunching in an eagle-shaped hollow drenched with golden rays and surrounded by snow on all sides.

"That's it, Lilly. L'Aiglon. That's where you and I are going to have lunch. When you are up there you feel like you're sitting in God's lap."

"Maybe *you* do, but to me it seems like a hell of a lot of trouble to go for lunch. I'm not the bikini, sun-worshiping type, and you ain't either."

"It makes no difference. You'll like it anyway. It takes just a couple of minutes to get there." Mrs. West was using a silver-headed cane as a walking stick.

They walked down the crooked cobblestone streets, which looked like stony carpets carelessly flung onto the ground, to a ledge covered with a shed containing a cable car. The cables connected to the adjacent mountain peak just a few hundred feet away.

"*Guten Tag, Gnadige Frauen!*" the operator said.

"Yes, well, that's enough of that! Please take us to L'Aiglon," Mrs. West said.

"I am very sorry. The cable car is out of order. The motor is broken."

"What's going to happen to those people?" Mrs. West nodded toward the crowd already on the other side. None appeared perturbed.

"Oh, the engineer will be here in about an hour, and he will fix it, maybe another hour, it will take. But by then it will be too late for you to go. Certainly there will be no lunch then."

126

"Well, what would happen if someone there"—she waved in the general direction with her silver-headed cane—"had an accident or got sick?"

The operator explained that in such a situation, he could operate the car manually with a lever and ratchet device in the cab, but that it was *strengstens verboten* to do this with a passenger, unless it was a dire emergency.

"I think I understand. Still I want you to fetch—"

The operator looked puzzled. She had taken him one step beyond his multilingual vocabulary.

"Go and get the engineer, *now!*" She underlined her order with a large wad of neatly folded bills.

"Gladly, *Gnadige Frau,* but please, it will take two hours still."

Mrs. West nodded. The operator affixed the sign to the shed saying the cable was out of order, and he left.

Mrs. West turned to her companion. "Lilly, let's get going."

"Get going where?"

"Just take the basket and get yourself into this cab. We'll operate it manually over to the other side." Mrs. West got in and snapped off the safety latch on the three-foot-long lever of the ratchet device. Lilly looked at the lever and gears on the ceiling; she glanced to the peak where the cables terminated and at the nothingness below.

"I think you're nuts. All this just to have lunch over there? I'll go with you just to show you I've got as much guts as you have, but I'm not going to knock myself out with that barbell up there."

"Then get out of here. I don't need your deadweight."

Lilly stepped out, muttering, "Remember, it's your goddamn idea, not mine."

Mrs. West slammed the cab door shut, reached through the opened window of the cab, and released the brake on the ground. The cab lurched forward from its mooring, and she started rocking the lever back and forth. She never stopped once for the thirty-five minutes it took to traverse the short span. As she stepped out of the cab, some people who had gathered to watch applauded. Others sitting in the wings of the eagle just looked at her and shook their heads.

Later that afternoon, without batting an eye, she paid a sizable fine for this stunt. The next day a limousine took her to the sanatorium in Wengen, a pleasant village nestled on a plateau jutting out from the side of a mountain. The sanitorium was a plain, stone building that had been built for tuberculosis patients but was now run by Dr. Klaus Schlager, who specialized in wealthy patients. They came for checkups, for physiotherapy, or to receive his "tissue extract injections," regarded by the socially cognizant, but medically ignorant, as having rejuvenative powers. The injections were believed to be beneficial for an endless number of chronic illnesses. Actually, what Dr. Schlager did was to provide the facilities of an old-fashioned spa in an up-to-date setting: exercise, physiotherapy, mineral waters with a mild laxative effect, and enforced rest. Anyone would benefit from such attention unless it was used as a substitute for needed medical care.

During the stay, a physical examination and laboratory tests were conducted and tissue extract injections were given according to the "deficiencies" revealed by the examination. These injections were harmless placebos whose only effect was to add to the illusion of unique care and attention. But the physical examination was a good one done by physicians hired for that task. It was performed with great attention to the comfort of the patient, with one portion of the examination done each day—just the way Julia liked it.

"What is it? Wednesday? That's bust and belly day, if I remember. Yup. Monday was bloodletting day. Tuesday they clean the cobwebs out of the attic. I never knew I had so many openings in me. I looked through so many optical tubes and heard so much pinging in my ears, I thought they were trying me out for the job of submarine captain in the Swiss Navy."

Lilly picked up a cigarette. "You can't smoke here, but I can.

128

Say what you want—I know you like it here—I think this place is a funny farm. If they try to put a finger on me with their polite, Kraut manners, I'm going to kick them right in the behind."

Julia West ignored her. "The electrocardiogram and the chest X-ray today, and this afternoon they examine my chest and my belly and then, tomorrow, the rear end and transmission. Friday, I see Dr. Schlager for my report and for my tissue extract injection, and we'll be off for home on Sunday."

DR. SCHLAGER WAS a courtly, silver-haired man who had been the company physician for the giant Sandoz Pharmaceutical Company in Basel. There, he developed a special talent for caring for executives. He had retired from Sandoz and, fulfilling a lifetime ambition, had opened this sanatorium in the shadow of the Jungfrau where he administered very little medicine and much tender loving care to wealthy patrons from all over the world. But now and then a problem would arise.

"I am pleased to tell you, Mrs. West, that your results were superb," Dr. Schlager said on Friday. "As a matter of fact, you won't need any tissue extract this year, but there is one thing that should be looked into. There was some blood in your stool. Also, you have a slight cold that, while trivial, would preclude giving you the tissue extract injections even if you required them."

"How come no injections? Wouldn't they help with this cold? Blood in the stool doesn't bother me, it's just hemorrhoids. I've had the blood for over six months now."

"Well, we give the tissue extract only when we find a deficiency that needs treatment. Also, we never give it to anyone with a respiratory or other kind of infection. It may prove too powerful if given to a body that is fighting an infection."

Behind that mumbo jumbo was the fact that Dr. Schlager was no fool. Julia West did not have hemorrhoids. Painless rectal bleeding in a sixty-five year old with no evident cause is cancer of the bowel until proven otherwise. He made every effort to avoid giving his extract to any patient with even the suspicion of a malignant disease, lest the therapy be linked with a fatal illness.

"Because of the rectal bleeding, I would suggest that you have the lower colon examined with a proctoscope. Doctor Miescher examined you last year, if you recall."

"If I recall! How can you forget the rear admiral who harpooned you? But really, I'm not up to it. I'm a little under the weather with this cold and, quite frankly, I don't want to be bothered."

"As you wish, Mrs. West. We don't want to inconvenience you, but I want you to understand that this is our recommendation."

"Thank you, Doctor Schlager. I'm going to continue with my plans. My companion and I will leave on Sunday. When I feel up to it, in London, or more likely New York, I'll have it looked into, preferably by someone with a smoother manner than your Rear Admiral Miescher."

# CHAPTER
# NINETEEN

W HEN MARLENE Lowell came home one night, a week after the mole was removed, her mother had a message.

"Doctor Green would like to see you."

"Did he say when?"

"His nurse said that, whenever you come in, go down and he'd fit you in."

"That's service," Marlene said. Suddenly she felt woozy.

"Why are you sitting down?"

"Nothing . . . I was on my feet a lot today."

"Marlene, I'll go with you."

Marlene sighed and stood up again. "Please don't. He just wants to check his work. I'll be right back."

She walked into the office, and this time it was filled with patients. The year before, Dr. Green, fresh from his residency, had scouted this middle-class section of Queens, found there was no dermatologist within two miles, which meant over twenty thousand people in the high-rise buildings as potential patients, and took over the lease on the office of a general practitioner who had recently died. It had taken six months for his patient load to reach capacity. It was eight-thirty when Marlene came in, and ten when he saw her.

131

"Sit down, Marlene. Let's see your leg. No, don't get up. I can examine it right here." He bent over and peered briefly at the scar with a penlight. "It looks fine." He hesitated. "The biopsy report came in today."

She could sense that he was tightening up.

"It wasn't an ordinary mole." He retreated behind his desk and sat down.

"What was it?"

"The mole we removed was a melanoma."

"A what?"

"Melanoma. It's a kind of cancer."

"Skin cancer's not serious, is it?"

"Melanoma is not the ordinary kind of skin cancer. Ordinary, small skin cancers are usually no problem, but even a small melanoma can sometimes get you into real trouble."

"What's all that mean for me?"

"Probably nothing. We got the whole melanoma out and the edges of the skin were free of tumor cells. But you should know that some specialists advocate removing a wide margin of skin around a melanoma to assure against its recurrence."

"That's what I mean. What's the chance it will come back?"

"To be perfectly honest, I can't tell you. Some melanomas are low-grade cancers and have very little inclination to spread, and of course others are not. I think we ought to keep an eye on it. I'd like to see you in two weeks."

Marlene headed upstairs to the apartment. In the elevator, she was aware of a dryness in her mouth, a pulling in the back of her neck, and pulsations in her fingers and temples. But by the time she entered the apartment, she was calm.

Her mother was sitting in the living room with the newspaper open on her lap, some knitting in her hands, watching television. "What did the doctor say? One leg is as beautiful as the other now."

"He said it was malignant. The mole was a cancer."

Her mother put down her knitting, got up slowly, shut off the

132

television and, clenching the newspaper, sat down again in the same spot.

"He said it's going to be all right, didn't he? There isn't any danger?"

"He told me he has to watch it, but it's all out and there is very little chance it will come back, so there's nothing to worry about."

"Exactly! If it was cancer or malignant and it isn't there any more, it's like it wasn't cancer. So you shouldn't even say it. Oh my God, you really had cancer of your leg? What am I going to do?"

"Forget it. He told me not to worry, and that's what I'm doing. Just put it out of your mind. Anyway, what do you mean, what are *you* going to do?"

"Put it out of my mind! How can you talk like that? It will always be on my mind. Why did you have to tell me? How could you do a thing like that to me?"

"I'm sorry I upset you, okay?" Marlene said, thinking, How could I forget I'm dealing with someone with the emotions of a ten year old.

"You should see other doctors, get other opinions."

"He gave me other opinions. He said some doctors remove a large piece of skin around the mole, but I don't want more surgery."

"Now where are you going?"

"To Ronnie's."

"When will you be back?"

"Tomorrow."

"Again? You think that looks nice? A single girl staying overnight at a boy's apartment? You don't know how your father and I worry about you. Why do you let him take advantage of you like that? He's such a nobody."

"If he was a somebody, it'd be okay, right? Look, make believe I'm going to a psychiatrist. When you're upset you go to your shrink. You tell me it helps you deal with your emotions, you come out feeling better. I'm tired and upset right now. I'm going to spend the night with Ronnie. I'm going to have an emotional experience, and when I come back tomorrow, I'm going to feel better."

"What does a psychiatrist have to do with staying overnight at someone's apartment? I didn't say Ronnie was bad. Why, I wouldn't even mind—I mean, you look at things so different. It's that college and everything."

"Look, Ma, the only thing I learned at college that was important was to say what I think, and for you that's impossible. But that doesn't mean we don't understand one another. I think we do."

"Well, you and Ronnie have known each other since you've been kids. I know you don't do anything bad, you're just good friends."

"You're right. We're just good friends. We don't do anything bad. We do something good. Do you want me to spell out the details?"

"Marlene, you're just saying those things to aggravate me."

"I told you we understand each other, Ma."

THE DOG STUDIES were still going on, but Henry felt that if he had a suitable patient for mid-torso occlusion the Clinical Investigation Committee could be persuaded to approve the new technique for use in human beings. Therefore he was delighted when a doctor called to refer a patient who sounded ideal. The referring doctor had assured Henry that the cancer in this basically healthy man was localized to the muscles of his shoulder, that he had had conventional radiation therapy and chemotherapy with no improvement, and that he refused surgery. With mid-torso occlusion he could receive ten times the conventional amount of chemotherapy without life-threatening side effects. Henry, always striving to up the dose and to control toxicity, had said again and again to Paul Rosen, "If I could only give more, I could kill that goddamn tumor." This would be his big chance.

But it was a disappointed Henry Nyren who closed the door of

134

the examining room and walked to his office. The patient had an enlarged liver and spleen, absolute contraindications to a giant tourniquet around the abdomen that would raise intra-abdominal pressure and possibly rupture those organs.

"Tara, who's next?" Henry asked. "I hope that's the last one."

"You're done for the day," Tara replied. "Would you like to see tomorrow's list?"

Henry held out his hand and smiled, resigned to the inevitability of tomorrow's lists. "I see Stanley Kaprowski on the list again. I bet he won't show up. Did you call his mother to remind her?"

"Yes, but there's no answer. I've called at least a dozen times."

"I don't think the boy is alive any more. She signed him out against advice, and when she promised to bring him back to the office I could tell she was lying. Stupid woman."

"Doctor Nyren, could you really have done anything more for the boy in the hospital? You kept saying he had end stage Hodgkin's disease. That it was in his bones and bone marrow and that nothing was helping . . ."

"But he needed transfusions and pain medication and medical attention."

"I was here when you explained all that to her, and you know I'm on your side always—well, almost always. But that day I was cheering for her. She said he needed his mother more, and she was right. So when you admitted to her that there was nothing more you could do . . ."

"I never said that. When she asked me outright what the odds were, I admitted they were very slim but that I wanted to keep trying, and she said, 'No thanks, I want him home.' Well, that's her privilege, of course, but I thought we could keep him comfortable, free of pain, and give him better care in the hospital."

"Your blind spot is showing," Tara said. "I'm sure Stanley was happier at home with his mother and the other kids around him."

"Okay, I get your message," Henry said. "Stanley could have lived only two or maybe three weeks without active medical support. It's months now, and we haven't heard a word from his mother. If he doesn't show up tomorrow, drop her a note. Try to find out what happened."

IT WAS AFTER five when Henry finished seeing patients. He was alone in his office, things were quiet, but there were still messages that needed his attention. He sat behind the desk, lit a cigar, blew away the smoke, and concentrated on the notes left by Tara:

1. I wrote to Stanley's mother.
2. I made an appointment for a new patient, Julia West, who will be flying in from London.

That made him think about his last patient today—whom he had referred for Phase I chemotherapy, which meant treatment so new that not even the correct dose in man was known, much less the toxicity or effectiveness. The man was not too bright, and Henry had talked him into it. Now he felt guilty. Maybe Paul was right about giving patients a choice. The tranquillity of the evening, which Henry had been looking forward to, was sinking in a sticky sea of self-doubt and recrimination. The note about the new patient coming from London meant only that another problem case was coming. The chance to call Donna this evening and speak to her without anything else preoccupying him was gone. He brutalized what was left of his cigar against the side of the wastepaper basket.

# CHAPTER
# TWENTY

WHILE DONNA was consciously and deliberately trying to cut herself off from further involvement with Henry, he was becoming more enthusiastic than ever about her. It was true that he had not contacted her very often, which she had interpreted as a lessening of zeal, but in fact, it was nothing of the kind. It was simply the way Henry went about his life. The patients with the most urgent problems got his attention first, then the others, then his research—always trying to elbow into first place but never quite making it—then his personal life. Janine had accepted this order of priorities, as had Laura, although not without protesting from time to time. Only his daughter, Eve, had objected strongly. He had naively assumed that anyone he was close to would understand what his work entailed and that Donna, like the rest, would patiently wait her turn.

Henry paid meticulous attention to his patients, to their emotional as well as their medical needs. He always cautioned his students to pay attention to detail—"It can be the difference between life and death," he would tell them. But he couldn't manage to carry the principle over into his personal life.

DONNA AND RAND had been out for dinner with friends in a restaurant in Dobbs Ferry and were on the way home. During all

137

the time that Randy had been ill, they hadn't gone out in the evening. They had only recently started to again.

"Boy, were you polite tonight." Rand gripped the wheel angrily as they drove down the Saw Mill Parkway. "I expect you to shake my hand and thank me for a lovely evening. You were as cold as ice to everyone. They're the same people who were at your party. What's wrong with you?"

"I don't know." Donna withdrew deeper into her seat.

"You weren't this moody when the kid was sick. You should be happy now," Rand pressed.

"Maybe it's just beginning to hit me. Could we drop it, please?" She reached into her purse for a cigarette, lit it, and inhaled deeply.

"You promised—" he said.

"You're right, you're right," Donna said, and flipped her lit cigarette out the window.

The car rolled into their driveway. He left it outside, taking care to lock all four doors before going into the house.

"I don't know why you don't put the car in the garage," Donna said. "You know how many cars have been stolen in this neighborhood."

"If you used your brain, you'd remember there are two cars in the garage already. Besides," Rand snapped, "I think I can handle that risk." He opened the side door of the house. When Randy became ill, they had hired a sleep-in maid. She had stayed on. It was her car that accounted for the garage being full.

They got undressed silently. The first to get into bed, Donna turned to the wall. When Rand got in, he spooned himself around her. He stroked her arm from shoulder to elbow, soft, slow strokes. She moved closer to the wall.

Rand tried to embrace her. "You haven't been in the mood for a long time."

"If it's sex you want, just put a pillow over my face and go ahead," she snapped. "I'll make believe I'm somewhere else."

138

"That's a lousy thing to say." He turned away from her. Amazingly, only minutes later his even breathing told her he was asleep.

For Donna it was not that easy. She twisted and stared into the dark. That *had* been a lousy thing to say. More, it was vulgar. She had never acted that way before. She could still wipe it all out by a soft touch, a kiss—he wouldn't mind being awakened for that—but she couldn't make herself do it. I've got to resolve this, she kept repeating to herself. I've got to.

Maybe she did sleep eventually. She couldn't really tell. Finally, dawn came.

In the morning she busied herself getting Randy ready for kindergarten and making breakfast for all of them.

"The bus will be here in a minute, have some cereal before you go. Drink the juice first, Randy."

"I don't like All Bran—it's yech!" He had a jacket on and wore a pilot's helmet to cover his baldness. Donna was thankful the hair was beginning to grow in again. "I want Sugar Pops."

She reached for the box he was pointing to.

"For God's sake, put some milk in the bowl. Don't just grab them with your hands."

"No milk."

"There's the bus." Donna whisked him out the door.

Finally she sat down with her husband, who hadn't said anything to her since last night. "Rand, I'm sorry I was so rotten to everyone last night at dinner, and especially to you. I really am sorry. Okay?"

He took off his glasses and polished them with a paper napkin. "You spoil everything, and then you think you can apologize and everything is just fine."

"Please, I don't want to argue with you. There's been something on my mind. I want to go back to school. I want to take courses in the city. Maybe at the New School or the Art Students League again."

Rand got up from the round table in the kitchen alcove, brushed his head against the lighting fixture, and slammed some bread into the toaster.

The kitchen was crisply modern, with gray octagonal floor tiles and light gray cabinets with chrome fixtures. In contrast, an old wooden wheel with lights affixed hung over the round, chrome-trimmed table in the alcove. Donna's mother had given it to them for their first apartment. Rand detested it—it didn't fit with his everything-has-to-match sense of orderliness. Rand was tall and frequently made it a point to hit the fixture with his head when he got up from the table. Donna, in turn, made a point of keeping it. In the end, the stupid fixture was always a convenient starting point for an argument.

"If that's all there is to your foul mood," he said, "why didn't you open up before? What's stopping you?"

"That's a good question," Donna responded without trying to answer him. "How long can we keep Charlene?"

"Donna, Charlene is not the issue. Look at all the money you're saving me by not buying a simple, decent light for the kitchen. You know damned well we can afford Charlene if we need her!"

Suddenly Donna was sitting in an empty kitchen with dirty dishes for company, feeling deliciously happy. It had been so ridiculously simple. She could go into the city whenever she wanted. She didn't have to slink around or lie. Well, a few half-truths might be necessary, but she could resolve her feelings toward Henry in a mature way.

Donna arranged for early evening classes at the Art Students League. Rand assured her it was no problem for him to be home with Randy. Donna started to take phone calls in the mornings again. And Henry called. "This is the best news ever," he told her when he heard her plans for school. "Let's celebrate with dinner."

"I'd love to," she responded, with more enthusiasm than she had intended. "I start on Tuesday."

"I can't do it until Friday," Henry said, looking at his desk diary.

140

"No good. Rand is coming in with me."

"The following Monday, then?"

"Fine," Donna said, suddenly wishing it were sooner.

TWO WEEKS AFTER Eve interviewed Marlene, they met in a café in the Village. Eve had completed the article and was eager to clear it with Marlene. The days were longer now, and it was still light. They moved a small, round table near the window of the café and pulled over two wire frame chairs. Marlene put her glasses on and bent over to read. She said, "Do you think this will fly? I mean, 'She's both a modern-day Myron and a practical Praxiteles'? I'm not exactly a classical Greek sculptor. And then jumping to Daniel Chester French, I mean, it's a little ridiculous. Why not Michelangelo or Della Robbia?"

"Della Robbia! That's terrific! Why didn't I think of that? Most of your stuff is *bas relief*. I wouldn't have gone as far as I did if you hadn't shown me the pictures of the marble busts you did. Also, remember I warned you I took a course once that was heavy into sculpture. I know a little. I didn't compare you to Jacob Epstein or Jacques Lifschitz. Your style is definitely classical."

"Yeah, but I'm just as practical as all of them. They all worked for money."

Marlene exchanged the pencil she was holding for a glass of red wine. If this was important, she thought, I'd write all over it. But it's nonsense. It won't be published. And even if it was, this is not how you get commissions. Anyhow, what do I have? A lousy stool on a street corner. So relax, let the kid do what she wants.

She turned to Eve, who was busy fishing an onion out of her martini with the blunt end of a cocktail stirrer. The onion popped out and scurried across the table as if it had little feet. Eve squished it with a napkin, rolled it into a little ball and put it in the ashtray.

Marlene said, "So that's what you want to do—write? Move up from editorial assistant to staff writer, and then from a studio to a one-bedroom—"

"You've got it. I've got this ambition to be independent of my father. I moved back to New York from California two years ago. After my mother died, I went to school in L.A., lived with my grandparents. Then I was offered this job, and I'm back in New York again."

"You can't make it on your salary, he subsidizes you, and you resent it, right?"

"If it was just that, it would simply be another case of a spoiled kid—boring. Then you'd resent me, 'cause you tell me about living in your parents' apartment in Queens, two jobs, and all that. But at least you get along with your family."

"Famously," Marlene replied, and finished her wine.

Eve had smoked a cigarette about halfway down and then let it burn in the ashtray. Finally she put it out.

"You won't believe this, but I hardly know my father."

"Being away in California for years doesn't help."

"No, that's why I went to California. I never got along with him. He's a doctor, the kind of doctor who practically lives in the hospital—a cancer hospital no less—and forgets he has a family."

"Cancer—my unfavorite word."

"Someone in your family?" Eve asked.

"I just had a skin cancer removed from my leg."

"Skin cancer's not so bad, is it?"

"No, it's nothing. Let's change the subject. You were saying about resenting your father?"

"He ignored me. And there was another thing. My mother and I were very close, and when I found out he was shacking up with this horse-faced society dame that works in the hospital, I could have killed him. So when my mother died, I split. We talk. Sometimes I even talk to his old girlfriend. In his own way he tries, but we're on different wavelengths."

"You know, Eve, your story is more interesting than mine."

142

# CHAPTER
# TWENTY-ONE

"**WELL, THAT'S** it for this morning, Duncan. You know you fit into this place like you were born here," Henry said, gratified that he had a resident assisting him whom he could count on. They started walking back to the nurses' station.

"I feel I'm in the right place, and Roger is happy in pediatrics. Irene keeps me posted."

"Is she still seeing that guy?" Henry asked.

"They're engaged. They'll be getting married at the end of the year."

"Well, that's one wedding I won't be invited to." Henry laughed.

TARA WAS MAKING notes of phone calls, and Henry was looking over the charts of the patients due that afternoon. As usual the new patients were scheduled for the end of the session. It was almost five when Tara introduced Henry to the woman who had flown in from London, Mrs. Julia West. Henry took her medical history, and the nurse then accompanied her to the examining room. The examination included an inspection of the lower twelve inches of the colon by proctosigmoidoscopy. In skillful hands, no periscope or bombsight searches more carefully for its target. Usually, sighting this target is paradoxical, in that its destruction means life.

But not in Mrs. West's case. It was not an early localized tumor Henry saw protruding from the wall of the colon. He saw a purple-red, angry, blood-and-mucous-covered protuberance facing him defiantly: "Here I am, come and get me!" The hulk moved, it pulsated with each beat of Mrs. West's heart. If Henry could, he would have crawled through the instrument to grab this incarnation of his loathing and torn it out of her gut with his bare hands. Henry made his notes and then quietly asked, "Tell me, Mrs. West, why didn't you go to a rectal specialist or surgeon with this problem, rather than a chemotherapist?"

"When I left the sanitarium in Wengen, I knew I had cancer. I could tell from the shifty way that director spoke to me. They don't want any trouble in those places. He was in a big hurry to get me out of there."

"I'd say he was a pretty astute clinician," replied Henry. "Intermittent, painless rectal bleeding in a sixty-five year old with no hemorrhoids, well . . ."

"I understand. At the Royal Marsden Hospital they proctoscoped me and said I had a bleeding polyp that was likely to be cancer, and that it should be removed by abdominal surgery. I told them I'd have it done in New York. But first I wanted to read up on cancer. Once I had, I decided I didn't want an operation. I wanted to be treated with chemotherapy. I called Doctor Rosen's office for an appointment because when I mentioned chemotherapy in London I heard his name. But his secretary informed me that he doesn't see private patients and recommended you. I must admit I'd been having rectal bleeding for months before I went there, and the thought that it might be cancer had already occurred to me several times. But I promptly put it out of my mind."

Henry sat listening to her, thinking that with all her wealth and education she suffered from the same denial of illness as everyone else. It was a universal affliction.

144

"The Swiss doctor did jolt you into action," he said. "Perhaps you should be thankful."

"I'll consider it," Mrs. West said.

Most of the cases Henry saw were the result of failure to remove the tumor before it had metastasized, waiting too long before doing something about the pain or lump or bleeding that wouldn't go away. Sometimes the cases of personal neglect were so outrageous that he wanted to say, "You goddamned fool—you signed your own death warrant." But of course he never did. He had a special feeling of compassion for those trusting souls who had been told by their doctors, "It's probably nothing. Come back and see me in six months."

Julia West had dressed and was sitting with Henry in his office.

"Frankly, I resented the possibility of such a hostile intrusion in my life, one that would make me do something I didn't want to do. There are very, very few things I do that I do not wish to."

"All right," Henry said. "We understand the situation up to now, and we know something has to be done, but this business about choosing the method of treatment—"

The intercom buzzed and Tara announced, "Mrs. West's son is here and wants to know if you have completed your examination and if he may join the discussion."

Henry looked at Mrs. West, who nodded.

"By all means, send him in," Henry said.

John West, a no-nonsense businessman in his mid-thirties, came in, greeted his mother, and sat down.

"I was explaining to your mother that she made a mistake in deciding what kind of treatment she wanted and then choosing a physician specializing in that form of therapy."

Henry turned from the son and addressed Julia directly.

"That tumor, almost certainly cancer, is operable and must come out. It may be completely curable by surgery. At any rate, there is no indication for chemotherapy at this time. Chemotherapy is used only after a tumor has spread and cannot be com-

145

pletely removed, and then only in some circumstances. You will never find a reputable cancer specialist using chemotherapy instead of surgery if there is any chance that the tumor is localized. I'd like to call Doctor Hardy for a surgical consultation and then see if we can get a bed for you at the Curie Cancer Hospital."

As Mrs. West heard Henry out, she looked relaxed. Then she laughed. "I was remembering something my brother once said to me. 'You're not a complete fool, Julia, just from the neck up.' I'll admit I haven't handled the situation well, but I've done a lot of thinking about it. I figured surgery might be in the cards, but I wanted to avoid it if I could. I came to see you because I'd rather have a chemotherapy specialist say I need surgery than hear a surgeon say it. So I accept your opinion and thank you for it.

"The next point is the Curie Cancer Hospital. I don't want to go there. I'm depressed enough about having cancer without going to a hospital where everyone else has it. The University Hospital is affiliated with the same medical school, isn't it?"

Henry nodded.

"Good enough," Mrs. West said, "I had no control over this intruder's arrival, but I can choose how I will handle this unpleasantness. I will have the surgery done at the University Hospital. I have nothing against Doctor Hardy—I am sure he is a perfectly competent surgeon. However, according to my information, Dr. James Blair is Chief of Surgery at the University Hospital, and if you approve, or unless you tell me someone who is better, I'll go ahead with him."

Henry looked at this determined woman for a long moment before he spoke—carefully. "Doctor Blair is an outstanding abdominal surgeon and is certainly qualified to do the job. But you are wrong about Curie. It's not a depressing place. It happens to be a very optimistic place with a hopeful atmosphere. Patients find this attitude contagious. They know that they are in a hospital that specializes in cancer and that every facility and specialty that might help them is available here. Please don't misunderstand. University Hospital is excellently equipped and has an

146

outstanding staff, but there is not the same driving commitment with regard to cancer that you find at Curie."

John West spoke up for the first time. "What Doctor Nyren says makes good sense, Mother. Why don't you follow his advice? I think it would be good to be in a hospital where everyone has an optimistic attitude."

"It's my attitude I'm concerned about, not that of everyone else in the hospital. Doctor Nyren made my decision for me. Doctor Blair is highly qualified, and they lack nothing at the University Hospital, and that's it."

Mrs. West asked Henry to make the necessary arrangements and got up to leave.

John West stayed put. "Mother, may I have a few moments alone with Doctor Nyren?"

"I don't see why that is necessary," his mother replied. "I'm sure there is nothing to be said that I should not hear. I have assumed, justifiably I hope, that there is absolute candor on everyone's part."

"Mother, you had a private talk with the doctor, and I think I'm entitled to a little of the same. I assure you nothing will be said that you couldn't hear. But perhaps I have apprehensions and concerns I'd like to express to Doctor Nyren." Then he added with a determination similar to her own, "You either grant me these few minutes now, or else you'll inconvenience both Doctor Nyren and me by forcing me to contact him privately at another time."

Mrs. West did not reply but took her purse and walked out to the waiting room.

John West sat still for a few seconds. Then he said, "Doctor, what are her chances?"

"That's not a good question, Mr. West," Henry replied. "I'll sharpen it for you. First, what are her chances of getting through the surgery? Better than nine out of ten. Then, what are her chances of cure? Not too good. If you catch colon cancer early, then the chances of cure are about eighty percent. But for patients like your mother, who have cancers that are ulcerating or bleeding and where symptoms have been present for several months and neglected, the five-year survival rate drops to about thirty percent. And if at the time of surgery the surgeon finds that it has spread to the liver, it drops even lower. So you see that it all depends on what we find at surgery. Unfortunately, she waited more than six months before mentioning it to a physician, that doctor in Switzerland."

"I can't believe it. She's so efficient about everything. She's been running all the family business interests since my father died." John West sighed. "I don't have a good feeling about my mother's problem," he said. "I don't like what she's done so far, and I don't like what she's doing now. She's really trying to run the show, isn't she? And everything she's done so far has been wrong."

# CHAPTER
# *TWENTY-TWO*

JULIA WEST blinked her eyelids a few times and looked around the room. Everything was distorted and out of focus. Her mouth felt terrible, and every time she took a breath there was a stabbing pain in her abdomen. She tried to talk but only a whisper came out.

"Did they do the operation yet?"

"Yes, Mrs. West," her nurse replied. "It's all over. You've been in the recovery room all day, and you're back in your own room now. It's seven o'clock, you're doing just fine. I'm going to clean you up a bit now."

The private duty nurse cleansed the patient's mouth with a lemon-flavored glycerine swab, then sponged and powdered her moist torso around the large abdominal bandages. She changed the bedclothing and then combed the patient's hair. Considering that it was only eight hours since the lower portion of her colon had been cut out, Mrs. West looked quite good.

"Thank God it's over," Mrs. West murmured, and she fell back to sleep. It was about 4 A.M. when she woke again, feeling more alert, but very weak. She could still taste the anesthesia when she exhaled, her throat was sore and any movement caused flashes of pain in her bandaged abdomen. The nurse gave her a small dose of Demerol, and she dozed again lightly, waking every time her pulse was checked or her temperature or blood pressure taken. The 6 A.M. bed bath was a blessing, she thought, as the nurse sponged her gently.

At six-thirty, a murmur of voices was heard in the hall.

"That will be Dr. Blair and his staff making rounds. We'll be ready for them," the nurse said, tidying up as if for a military inspection.

The door to the private room opened. The charge nurse entered first with a clipboard holding the order sheets for each of the patients they would visit. The procedure of this impressive entourage was formal and ritualistic. The junior residents in surgery entered next, moved to the bedside, removed the bedclothes, and checked the bandages and the various plumbing connections to see that all was prepared for the inspection by the Chief. Two senior assistant residents entered and stood at the foot of the bed. Finally came the entry of Dr. James Blair, chatting casually with his senior resident while his Janissaries waited. His casual manner changed as he approached Mrs. West. He checked the bandages, touched all the right places, and assured his assistants that everything was in good order. Then he bent over the bed rail and looked directly at the patient. Mrs. West was alert and poised to ask questions, but she waited to see what he would volunteer first.

Dr. Blair did have information to volunteer. He began with a few words of assurance and ascertained that she was as comfortable as could be expected. Then: "Mrs. West, we were able to remove completely the tumor in the colon and it was a cancer. We also were able to put together the two ends of the colon so that you will not have to have a colostomy. We did everything that could possibly have been done for your benefit. But I'm afraid the cancer had already spread to the liver. There is nothing more we can do for you."

"Thank you for being so honest, Doctor Blair."

"Are there any questions you'd like to ask me?"

"No, thank you. I have no questions."

150

Dr. Blair and his group left the room in the reverse order in which they had entered.

"There is no substitute for complete honesty," he said in the hallway. "Tell the patients the truth in the immediate postoperative period, and by the time they recover from surgery they will also have recovered psychologically. They will then be able to cope with their illness because they have all the information they need. But before you tell them, be sure they are completely out of anesthesia and can comprehend what you are saying."

Mrs. West comprehended very well. She saw his words in red letters, ten feet tall: "THERE IS NOTHING MORE WE CAN DO FOR YOU." A picture flashed in her mind. It was 1922 in Denver. She was eleven years old and had sneaked into town to watch a hanging. She saw the body hanging from the rope and remembered a very tall man bending over her—just as Dr. Blair had bent over her—saying, "Well, there is nothing we can do for him."

The nurse noticed that Mrs. West was restless. Her expression hadn't changed but she was moving her body just a bit, this way and that. "Is there anything more we can do for you, Mrs. West?" she asked.

Julia West stared at the nurse. It was now twenty-four hours since surgery and the recovery room. She had had several injections of Demerol for pain. Although she was carrying on rational conversations, the stress of surgery plus the medication left her with less than normal control. In a few minutes she had gone from repose to despair, despite the fact that she had girded herself beforehand for bad news. Somehow, that it was not a surprise didn't help.

The nurse continued to try to be helpful. "Perhaps you'd like to see the newspaper or the television."

The newspaper was accepted, and she stared at the headlines. Large letters stood out: "THERE IS NOTHING MORE WE CAN DO FOR YOU." The large black letters quivered for a moment and then melted and poured down the page. Mrs. West glanced at the television. A robotlike female with a metallic grin was placing something in a washing machine and lifting something out. The mechanical form in skirt and apron then held a box up to the screen and large letters gave out a noisy, pulsating message: "THERE IS NOTHING MORE WE CAN DO FOR YOU, MRS. WEST."

Julia West gripped the side of the bed. There was a roaring in her head as she fought to reassert control.

"Thank you, there is something you could do for me," she said to the nurse. "I'll need a robe. You said I would be getting out of bed tomorrow, and I don't want to use this old one. I have a red silk one at home. I can't ask the maid to bring it, she's too stupid. You can be back in less than an hour."

The nurse, who had been sitting quietly at the bedside reading, said, "I'm really not supposed to leave you."

"Certainly you can leave me. You leave me alone when you go to eat, don't you? We'll be all set for tomorrow. Just be sure the window is open a trifle so I can breathe."

The nurse hesitated. Mrs. West snapped at her in a low, hard voice, "It's very simple. You have two choices—you can either leave and get the robe, or leave and not come back."

The nurse did as she was told.

Julia West looked around the room, then closed her eyes. A moment later she opened them. There was no need to think things over. She had worked it all out before she came back to New York. If it was a tumor, she'd see a cancer specialist. If he said surgery she'd go to a surgeon. If the surgeon said operate, either they would get it all out or they wouldn't. If they got it all out, fine. If they didn't get it all out, she was set for that, too. No cancer was going to whip her into a lump of flesh whimpering for pain medicine. Goddamn it, she thought, I'm in charge, and I'm going to stay in charge.

A hand was slowly extended, reaching for the automatic bed control. She pushed "Down." The bed sank quietly downward, stopping a few inches above the floor. Then she pressed "Raise

Head," and she was slowly raised to a sitting position. She pushed the side rails, but they wouldn't move. She looked for some mechanism to operate but could not find it. The effort exhausted her, and she had to rest for a few minutes. She could not remove the catheter in her bladder but she removed its connection with the drainage tube. The intravenous tubing taped to her wrist was easier; she simply pulled the tubing out, needle and all. It swung to and fro from the hanging IV bottle, spraying its contents on the floor. One more connection to sever. The gastrostomy tube was attached to a suction device, and she disconnected it as she had seen the nurses do. Again, she rested for a moment. "I'm in charge," she whispered.

She closed her eyes momentarily. There was no question about her goal. All her thought and energy were concentrated on completing the difficult journey that she estimated to be about ten feet. She remembered the trip on the cable car to L'Aiglon, and thought that this one would not take as long. Given the side rails, there was only one way to the floor of the room, by going over the foot of the bed. This she did on all fours. When she reached the floor, she tried to stand up, but could not. Her legs were too shaky.

Slowly, she began to crawl along the floor. With each forward push there was pain and breathlessness. One arm and one leg. Free will. Another arm and leg inched forward. No suffering for me. She compressed her lips into a thin white line. Her arms could not hold her. She lay on the floor and pushed herself forward with her thighs and legs. Another foot. My fate is my own. Another foot. Another foot.

The windowsill. She rested for as long as she dared, then drew herself up, her arms supported by the windowsill. The gown was tied from behind and reached down to her thighs. The catheter dangled between her legs. She reached for the slightly open window. It glided up easily over her head. She breathed in deeply. How good the cold air felt. Not a second's hesitation or doubt. Mrs. West closed her eyes and propelled herself forward.

153

# CHAPTER
# TWENTY-THREE

F RANK WALSH had been discharged from the hospital after recovering from the streptokotocin treatment. The lung cancer was still present, but he was actually in quite good shape. He knew a decision was going to be made about additional courses of chemotherapy. Right now he felt fine. The nausea and vomiting, the fatigue, were over. The anemia and low white blood count were also things of the past, as the policeman's basically healthy body rapidly recovered from the toxic side effects of the new cancer-killing drug. He was back home again, and although he was on complete disability, he had recovered his good spirits—largely because Mary was well along in her pregnancy. Maybe he'd get to see his son yet. He was talking again, to anyone who would listen, about the nice vacation from work he was enjoying.

Today was a follow-up visit at the hospital. Henry was going to see him, not in his office but in Chemotherapy "D" Clinic—the section of the large Outpatient Department where patients on special experimental drug programs were followed. Had the tumor regressed any, stood still, or started to grow again? Was he ready for additional treatment? Streptokotocin was only a part of the new aggressive program for the treatment of lung cancer. Had the side effects been sufficiently repaired so that he could

154

take more chemotherapy? Frank was thinking about all these things as he waited his turn, but mostly he was thinking how happy he was that he was going to be a father. Mary was sitting with him, her hands folded neatly on her round belly. She smoothed out the folds of her dress and pulled down the hem, an unnecessary gesture reflecting her discomfort at being in an alien and threatening environment that was going to rob her of her husband. How many wakes had she been to? After all, you don't grow up in Richmond Hill, Queens, without knowing the score. There were cops' and firemen's families all around you. Her father had made it to retirement, but few firemen were as lucky as he—never even needed hospital treatment. That made her mother lucky, too. But her mother, like Mary, had been prepared to be a survivor.

She didn't need anyone to tell her, "You're young, you'll marry again," "Better save your money for the baby," and definitely not, "If you need anything, let me know." There was just here and now to take care of. Tomorrow would take care of itself.

The trouble was today was enough to make her anxious. It was too bad their roles as husband and wife were so frozen. He never talked to her about his fears, and she had no one to talk to about hers. If he is going to die, she thought, I could accept that, but I could help him live for now. Oh, I could give him so much, if he would let me. I'd feel better, too. As it is, I feel so goddamned useless and helpless.

"Mary, you look like you're wearing a shroud of dark thoughts. Are you troubled? Do you have morning sickness?" Frank asked.

"I don't have morning sickness anymore. I'm fine Frank, I'd like to talk to the doctor after he examines you. I never see him, and you don't tell me what he says." That was all she could squeeze into the narrow channel of communication between them. Then she looked straight ahead again.

"I promise, if he starts some new treatment or if there's any change, I'll call you in. Why bother the man? Look at that lineup of people trying to get at him, will ya? I shouldn't be sitting

155

here—I should be walking around, getting this place organized."
Frank kept talking. It was the shield he needed.

It wasn't what she needed.

"Oh no you don't!" Mary the survivor finally surfaced. "Little Miss Muffet here is going to sit on her duff right outside the examining room, and when the doctor comes out I'm going to nab him."

Sure enough, when Frank's name was called, Mary followed him and waited outside the office while Henry examined him.

As soon as Frank entered the examining room the sparring began, with Henry on the defensive. Frank asked him about the patients he had left behind in the hospital. He remembered all their names. Then he sent regards, again by name, to the nurses on each shift. Along with his ability to talk, Frank had a prodigious memory: names, books, dates, he was never at a loss for material. In his own good time, he got around to himself.

"I'm feeling fine, Doctor Nyren. I'm glad to be home and all, but the hospital and the treatments weren't so bad. I gotta tell you one thing, though. You made it sound worse than it was, with all those explanations and consent forms to sign. You should have just gone ahead and done what you had to, without all that buildup. Yes, sir, I'm sure if you've got what I've got, this is the best place to come to."

Finally he got down to it, his voice deliberately casual. "By the way, Doctor Nyren, did the medicine do what you expected it to?"

"When I'm done, Frank." Henry went on with his examination. Finished, he looked at Frank's chart, the X-rays, and the blood count results. Then he sat down, brushed back the shock of black hair with his fingers. The gesture gave him a few seconds to arrange his thoughts.

"This much is clear, Frank. There's no evidence that the tumor is progressing at this time."

Frank sat on the edge of the examining table. He hadn't gotten dressed yet. He was smiling.

"Good old Doctor Nyren, you're playing with me. I'm a little

156

hurt by that. I think of myself as a professional, too, and a good one. But you're talking down to me. What I really want to know is, will I be needing any more chemotherapy?"

Henry was holding his head back, looking up at the ceiling, thinking, This is one patient I haven't sized up right. "It's a good thing I don't have any other patients like you," he said, managing to smile at Frank.

"Let's get down to brass tacks, man to man now," Frank said.

Henry put his lips together for a second, combed his fingers through his hair again. "You'll need more treatment, Frank. You have a tumor we can measure, and it's going to start growing again."

"Cancer, you mean."

"You wanted the facts. Here they are. We can measure the size of this cancer, and it doesn't make sense to wait to treat you. The best thing to do is to give you more chemotherapy. There is one thing more. The kind of cancer you have frequently spreads to the brain. There probably are small seeds there now. The chemotherapy doesn't get to the brain. So after the chemotherapy, we are going to give you radiation therapy directly to the brain, and that should prevent any neurological problems from developing. It should knock out the seeds before they grow into real tumors. We wouldn't want anything to interfere with your gift of gab. Besides, who knows what other literary genius you have tucked away?"

Frank was getting dressed. "Now, my good physician—and, I feel, my friend as well—you've got it through my thick skull about all this chemotherapy. What I want to know is, what results have you gotten in other cases like mine? Plain and simple. I know you can't cure it, but how much longer do I get for all this?"

Henry had tacitly agreed to the patient's terms for the discussion. "Okay, more facts," he said tersely. "Patients with your particular kind of cancer who are treated this way do better in the sense that they stay out of the hospital longer, they don't have brain metastases, they live a better day-to-day life. In terms of duration of survival, I can't guarantee any great improvement. The treatment is a step in the right direction—not a big step, but a real one. However, the fact that we can change the course of lung cancer, the fact that our patients haven't developed brain problems, that's important. I'm talking to you straight now, just the way you wanted it."

"I mean, no miracles or pie-in-the-sky business," Frank interrupted.

"All right, I'll tell you why it's worth all this trouble to me and the other doctors here. This is the first time we've been able to make even a dent in lung cancer. If we've learned how to keep it out of the brain, then there may be strategies we can develop to hold it down in other organs. If we can put enough small steps together, we might just be able to control this disease. Fighting cancer is trench warfare, Frank, we fight for every inch."

Frank was dressed and ready to leave. "I'm not sure it's worth it to me, Doc," he said, in a soft, nonchalant way as he looked down at his sleeves, adjusting his jacket. Then he looked up at Henry. "By the way, would you say a kind word to the missus? She needs a little cheering up. And one more thing, Doctor Nyren. Would you do us the honor of having lunch with us on Sunday? I'll pick you up and drive you back to the city."

"You don't have to do that—I'll drive out."

"No, I'd like to. That way, if we want to, we can talk without the missus around. How about it?"

Mary wasn't able to carry it off. When Henry came out of the office, she looked at him for only a second with tear-filled eyes, then kept her head down so he wouldn't see the tears. Henry told her that her husband "had a way to go with that tumor," and Frank said, "Don't worry, we'll handle it okay."

They stonewalled her.

But as soon as the Walshes left, Henry realized that he had gone along with Frank's attitude toward Mary, and that it was wrong. It had taken him years to realize that the typical male attitude toward disease was wrong. It was as if to share any of the details of their infirmity with a spouse was an admission of weakness, as if their illness didn't affect anyone else. And so most male patients kept their wives away from the doctor. However, when the men were ill and housebound, they wanted attention. The wife was caught in a dark well of anxiety with no enlightenment from either her husband or the physician.

THE NEXT SUNDAY Henry was enjoying lunch at the Walshes' apartment in Bayside. The view of Long Island Sound sparkled with sun and sails. Not a word was said about his illness. There was a good deal of joking, stories about New York, comparing childhoods in Brooklyn and Morristown, appreciating Mary's cooking and baking. Henry let his hair down a little and spoke about the early days of his marriage to Laura.

Driving Henry back to the city, Frank said, "Doctor Nyren, do you mind if we stop at Avenue C first? I'd like to show you my professional life. Also, I got an itch t＾ take a look at the liquor store where that bastard plugged me."

Henry and Frank stopped in front of the closed Good Cheer Liquor Store. The window had been repaired and the storefront painted.

"You know, I don't feel a damn thing," Frank said. "It's like it happened a million years ago to somebody else."

They drove uptown, and Frank double-parked in front of Henry's 81st Street apartment house. They both got out of the car. Frank walked over to Henry and put out his hand.

"I want to say good-bye."

"You mean good-bye good-bye, don't you, Frank?"

"As we were driving up First Avenue, Doc, I had a wonderful thought. You saw my neighborhood. It's really my town. I care for those people. You know what I was thinking? If you, the monsignor, and me, made rounds together, you know, we could solve ninety percent of the problems in that neighborhood. Ah, what rounds they would be. They would be like those Grand

Rounds of yours at the hospital, only grander. We would make a team that could banish illness and heartaches and fears. It would be a great, great thing." Then he said "You know, I finally talked to Mary. I told her about our conversation at the hospital. She listened to me and I listened to her. We talked out everything, and it's like we never knew each other before. So it's not a bad good-bye, Doc. It's a good one."

"But it isn't my way, Frank. You went to a lot of trouble to tell me this, and I appreciate it. You could just have walked out and not come back. I know you thought it all through, and you're not going to change your mind. Now I've got to tell you, I meant what I said the first time we had a talk. I believe in fighting every inch of the way."

"I know you do, Henry, but you're not fighting just my lung cancer. You admit it, you're waging war on all the cancer in the world. Just this one battle is being fought on my body. Look, how can I explain it to you? I'm a law-and-order guy, and what I like best is peace and quiet. If I tried to knock out of my beat every scale that cheats a little, every payoff, every kickback, every under-the-table deal, you think I'd have peace and quiet? I'd have mayhem, and everybody'd hate me. The whole world is a balance of good and evil.

"Now I've got a lot of good things in me, and I've got this rotten thing that you want to wage war on. But if I let you, I'm the battlefield, and I get blown away in any event. You get what I mean? Doc, I want nature to take its course. There are certain laws of nature I wasn't familiar with and didn't understand, but I do now, and I have to obey them. I hope to God you win your fight. Maybe some day you'll be able to change those laws."

This time it was Henry who put out his hand. Full of admiration for Frank, he said, "My door will always be open to you. I'll be there to try to help you if you need me, any time you want to come back to my turf."

"And another thing, Doc. You remember that little room I told you about, the one with the table and the whiskey bottle in it, the

160

one I figured I'd wind up in when my time was up? Well, I don't need it any more. You broke down the door and cleaned it out, and now Mary keeps it filled with flowers, and I'm gonna keep it noisy and busy, and every day will go as God and Nature want it to. And that'll be just fine. Mary's gonna have wonderful stories to tell that little fellow."

# CHAPTER
# TWENTY-FOUR

**M**ARLENE HAD been educating herself. First she'd gone to the public library. She asked the reference librarian for a medical dictionary. There she looked up melanoma. "A tumor made up of melanin-pigmented cells," she read. "When used alone, the term refers to malignant melanoma."

Not much help, she thought. "Is there a medical book, something about various diseases?" she asked.

"Try the *Home Medical Encyclopedia*." The librarian gave it to her. The encyclopedia did not tell her much more than she knew, all couched in simpleminded terms. She went back to the reference librarian and let it out.

"Look, my dermatologist just removed a malignant melanoma from my leg. He did explain something to me, but to tell the truth, after he used the word 'malignant' I don't think I heard a thing. I want to read up on it, and what I've seen so far has not helped at all. What do you suggest?"

"You should go to the library at the Academy of Medicine. It's open to the public. You'll find everything there. The library is at a hundred and sixth and Fifth Avenue."

Marlene had been too impatient to take the subway. She hopped into a cab that took her to the impressive red brick and white stone corner building housing one of the best medical

162

libraries in the country. Up the elevator to the library. She slowed down as she approached a long, dark mahogany counter. Would the librarians be helpful, condescending, antagonistic? She did not have much experience with any aspect of the medical profession or its cadres. As it turned out, the response was just more New York.

"You want a book on melanoma? Look it up, there's the file with the index cards."

New York she could handle. She chose a number of books at random and wrote down their names. Some were out, but several were available. Plenty of material for her fishing expedition.

When she first started reading about melanoma it was like opening the door to a closet filled with fascinating secrets. Upon close examination, the contents soon became even more interesting. Why had it occurred on her leg? Malignant melanoma occurs more frequently on the lower legs of females than males, since women's legs are exposed to sunlight more than men's. Also, malignant melanoma almost always occurs some time after puberty, and yes, that mole first appeared when she was a teenager. And melanoma occurs more frequently in fair-skinned people. Marlene's hair was brown but her skin was remarkably fair, and in the sun she burned rather than tanned. She skipped over the next section, which explained why albinos never get melanoma, and over the parts dealing with the biochemistry of melanin. As soon as the book got too technical she put it down and picked up another. Each brought out another aspect of this, the most important disease in the world to her. She kept reading and discovered that melanoma was not a human affliction alone, but was a common cancer in all animals: fishes, fruitflies, chickens, dogs and cats, and in gray horses the most common form of cancer. It was as if malignant black teardrops were falling indiscriminately on all the earth's creatures. The next book said that melanoma was the most rapidly increasing cancer in the world, but could not say why. More exposure to the sun, perhaps, or more ultraviolet light getting through the diminishing ozone

163

layer in the stratosphere—the result of billions of big and little burnings of fossil fuels, the molecules of long-dead plants and animals smoking up to the heavens to grasp an atom of oxygen and start all over again. No matter is ever lost, all matter is always changing. What was she but a victim of the process?

She was about to put away this volume when a paragraph caught her eye. "The first written mention of melanoma occurs in the Babylonian Talmud, 3rd to 4th centuries A.D. To wit, 'berry-like swellings of the skin call forth the angel of death.' To literal-minded readers such a dire consequence for a common occurrence would cause much consternation. In the 12th century, the French Talmudic scholar Rashi added this reassuring commentary, 'Not all berry-like swellings of the skin are fatal, only those that develop daughters.'"

Thank God, she thought, I did not have daughters. And she closed the book.

When Marlene picked up the next book, the five-finger exercise ended with a slam of the keyboard. "Pathology, prognosis, and surgical treatment." Suddenly she sat up very straight. These were the questions she needed answers to. This was what her life depended on. Her eyes hurtled through this section.

She had to get to Dr. Green. She called from the phone booth in the lobby of the Academy building, got the answering service, and found out that he would be in the office at five.

Marlene thought, there's no use waiting in his office. It'll be packed with patients. I've got a better chance of getting through to him by phone. But where should I call from? Not home. *She's* there. She could hear a submarine two miles away, and without sonar. Dammit, why don't I have a place of my own, why am I such a wimp? I can't call from a phone booth. I just can't.

In the end she went back to her office. She arrived at 5:30. The place was empty. She made her call.

"Is this the office or the answering service?" Marlene asked.

"The office," came the dry reply.

"My name is Marlene Lowell. I'm a patient of Doctor Green, and I've got to speak with him."

164

"Is this an emergency? The doctor is very busy with patients right now."

"Look, I'm not dying this minute, but I'm very upset, and I've got to talk to him."

"Unless you use the word 'emergency' I'm just supposed to take messages."

"Please," Marlene was pleading now. "Tell him it's very important that Marlene Lowell speaks with him tonight."

She sat back and waited for him to return the call, drinking cup after cup of coffee.

Several cups later, he did.

"This is Doctor Green."

"Hello, Doctor. This is Marlene Lowell. I'm sorry to make it sound so urgent but I've got to have answers about that biopsy report or I'll go bananas."

"Okay, shoot."

"Well, for starters, don't you think I should have a chest X-ray and a blood count and liver tests to be sure that this is stage one of the disease? Then about the biopsy. How deep did it go? What Clark's level was it?"

"I see you've been reading. Well, that's okay, just as long as you don't frighten yourself—which I think you already have."

"Like I told you before, Doctor Green, I can deal with the facts. I can't deal with my wild imagination. I mean a lot of these things I figured out for myself before I even went to the library. Like being sure the tumor didn't spread anyplace. And even though it was just a spot on the skin, how deep did it go? In my imagination that was just a little, black tip of an iceberg that you cut out. I'm not putting you on the spot, am I?"

"No, not at all. Only, well, I don't have too much time now."

"I'd be glad to come by when you're not too busy and have you explain it all to me."

"No, no, no, that's okay. I'll tell you now. This was stage-one disease as far as I can tell. It has not spread, but to make you feel better, come by and we'll get a chest X-ray and some blood counts. With regard to how deep it was, it was Clark's level two,

165

minimally invasive, which means a ninety percent chance of cure."

"Or about ten percent chance that it will come back," Marlene said. "And if it comes back, that could be bad news, right?"

"Could be," said the preoccupied voice at the other end of the line. He was obviously trying to terminate this conversation and get back to his patients.

"Remember," he added, "I told you there was more that could be done in the way of surgery. What I did was minimal. I didn't even use a skin graft. I don't think you need any more done. However, if you want to get other opinions, I'll give you some names."

"No, that's okay," Marlene said. At this point, I think I would be satisfied if we got a chest X-ray and some blood tests and they were all normal. When can I come by?"

"Just call my secretary, and she'll take care of it."

"Can I speak with your secretary while I'm on the line?"

"Sure, hold on, she's with someone now." And Dr. Green put her on hold.

Marlene waited, satisfied that she was making progress.

After some minutes: "Miss Lowell. Doctor wants you to have some tests. Can you come in tomorrow? I'll have it all arranged."

"Fine. When will I get the results?"

"Oh, in about a week."

"A week? Why so long?"

"It just works that way. You've got to go to the lab for the blood work and to another office for the X-ray. Then the results are mailed back to us. I'll call you as soon as they're all in."

Marlene had the tests and waited out an anxious week for the results. They were normal. However, the results did not dispel her apprehension. Like her imagining that the tumor was an iceberg and only the tip had been removed, the results of the tests only removed the tip of her anxiety.

166

# CHAPTER
# *TWENTY-FIVE*

**M**RS. WEST wasn't dead. She hadn't seen the eight-inch glass wind deflector across the windowsill. As she threw herself forward, she jackknifed over the edge of the wind deflector, hit her head on the concrete outside window ledge, and was knocked unconscious. Her son found her when he came to visit.

John West's shouts brought nurses and doctors running. Mrs. West was picked up and put back in bed, this time with restraints and sedation. The nurse was fired and replaced by two other nurses and her factotum, Lilly. Psychiatric consultation was mandatory in all cases of attempted suicide. The psychiatrist spent a few minutes with Mrs. West. Not finding her case interesting, he wrote "exaggerated reactive depression" in the chart. He left after writing some drug orders that would assure her not disturbing the hospital staff any further as long as she was there. Not one suggestion was made that might have been helpful to the patient.

Julia West came to her own aid. Her candor as intact as her life, she told her son about Dr. Blair's visit, what he had told her, and how she had exercised the option she had prepared for just such a contingency. Her only regret was her clumsiness. John West listened but said very little. He had learned young to show restraint in front of his parents. However, when he left her, it took only a couple of drinks to make up his mind.

Tara took his call. "Doctor Nyren is on rounds now, Mr. West. Yes, I understand it's urgent. I'll do my best to contact him for you. If I can't get him right away, I'll be sure that he calls you between eleven and eleven-thirty."

At eleven o'clock Henry returned to his office with Duncan Comfort, now completing his training on the oncology service.

"Doctor Nyren," Tara said, "John West called, said it was very urgent for you to call him back. I didn't interrupt you on rounds because it seemed to me that the urgency was his and not the patient's."

Henry nodded affirmation of her decision, but returned the call without further delay.

"Hello, John. How's your mother? I know she went to surgery yesterday."

"She tried to kill herself."

"She what?"

"Came damn close to pulling it off, too."

"What happened?"

As Henry listened, he became more and more angry and exasperated.

"Well, you know, doctors are not big on criticizing one another, but I have to agree with you. That was a heartless thing to do."

"Will you come over and see her?" John West asked.

"Yes, I'd be glad to see her, but you must call Doctor Blair's office and tell them you've called me to come for a consultation."

"I'm going to tell them the family is very upset, and we've just got to call someone else in at this point."

"Tell them whatever you want to. I'll have a few choice things to tell Doctor Blair myself."

Then he hung up and turned to Duncan Comfort, talking and lighting a cigar at the same time. "Do you know what that self-righteous, shot-in-the-ass-with-himself Blair did? His first post-op visit to Mrs. West, less than twenty-four hours after surgery, he walks in and tells her the cancer has spread to the liver and that there's nothing more they can do for her. Then he walks out. She says thank you for being honest with me, and as soon as he leaves she tries to jump out the window. That pompous bastard is more malignant than cancer. I'm sure that somewhere in his weasely mind he thinks that cancer is punishment for some sin and that he's God's instrument of retribution."

"Who is Mrs. West?" Duncan asked. "Do I know her?"

Henry filled Comfort in. "I didn't want her to go to University Hospital in the first place." he said. "And I never would have chosen Blair, but she was determined. Duncan, do you know what he actually accomplishes with his so-called honesty? He disassociates himself from a case in which the results will be less than perfect and therefore an affront to his self-esteem. More important, by saying there's nothing more to be done, he's destroying any hope that the cancer can be controlled, and no one can live without hope. Not you, not me, not precious Doctor Blair."

"Quite a cop-out from someone who's considered a top surgeon." Duncan shook his head.

"Blair is a virtuoso in the operating room all right. He can dissect, cut, stitch, and sew. He collects ooh's and ahh's from his admirers in the OR—how quickly he can operate, how little blood is lost, how good the wound looks. That's all fine—but he should have someone else see his patients, talk with them, and care for them before and after his concert performances," Henry said, waving his cigar like a baton.

Duncan shifted uncomfortably in his seat. "Can you explain to me why he's *numero uno* at University?"

"I don't know. I think he's a number one son of a bitch! He uses the truth as a towel to wipe his hands with. Then he flings it in that poor woman's face and walks away. He just doesn't give a damn. Now I've got a patient with two burdens, cancer in the liver and cancer of the soul. I don't know which will do her in first."

WHEN HENRY LEFT Duncan and walked across the street to the University Hospital, he took his foul mood with him. He hoped he would not meet Dr. Blair. Nothing good could come of an encounter at this time. Maybe when he had calmed down, he would talk with Blair. Better yet, he would invite him to Grand Rounds, and in a scholarly manner they would discuss the pro's and con's of what to tell the cancer patient. Perhaps he would also invite Father Noyes. Henry was feeling a little guilty. This wasn't his first dealing with Blair. He'd known the man's attitude toward treating cancer. Perhaps if Henry had strongly suggested someone else, Mrs. West would have listened.

When Henry got to the eighteenth floor, the first person he saw was John West standing near the door of his mother's room. West, on the lookout for Henry, came down the hall to meet him.

"If that damn nurse hadn't left my mother's side, none of this would have happened. I'm glad you're here, Doctor Nyren—for my sake, too. I'm angry. And because I haven't seen Blair, I'm taking it out on everyone else. Mother is asleep. She's been sedated. We've got two people to sit with her and do any chores she can dream up. They understand that at all times one of them must be in the room."

"I wouldn't have been too hard on that nurse," Henry said. "I can't imagine many people not obeying an order of your mother's. Our job now is to put her in a frame of mind so she won't want to try that again, convince her that her life now is worth living. She has to know that there is treatment—that there is hope!"

"What do I do about Doctor Blair if he's pulling one way and you the other?" John asked.

"I don't think it will be like that. If past experience is any guide, you won't be seeing much of Doctor Blair. He will be quite proper, and he won't interfere with anything I want to do."

Henry walked into the room and examined Mrs. West, who, except for a bruise and goose egg on her forehead, was apparently none the worse for her harrowing experience. The surgical team had checked her for internal bleeding and looked over the wound. They were monitoring her blood pressure and pulse and checking her hemoglobin level frequently to see if any internal bleeding was occurring. Henry noticed that a lock had been fastened to the window.

He left the room and walked down the long corridor to the nurses' station. He sat down to write a note in the chart and to outline his recommendations for chemotherapy. Someone bent over his shoulder.

"Good evening, Doctor Nyren." It was James Blair, and his tone said he was looking for a fight.

# CHAPTER
# *TWENTY-SIX*

"HELLO, DOCTOR Blair. I've just written a chemotherapy consultation note. But of course that wasn't why the family called me. They called me because of the suicide attempt."

"If you had told me she was unstable, I wouldn't have told her about the cancer."

Blair's big frame moved around the nurses' station with the assurance of the college boxer he had been. He pulled a chair around so he could sit facing Henry full on.

"I don't think she is unstable—but if I had asked you not to tell her until I had given her the options for therapy, would you have held back?" Henry said. He didn't relax his hold on Mrs. West's chart.

"Of course not. You know we always tell the patients the truth unless they are *non compos mentis*." Blair stood up again, as if to meet his rising level of adrenalin.

Henry stood, too. "Then you have to take the consequences of your action. I won't be so blunt as to say you pushed her out the window, but a little more circumspection and the entire episode could have been avoided."

"Okay, Nyren, that's quite enough."

But Henry was not in a mood to be stopped. "The point I resent more than you telling her that the cancer had spread to the liver is telling her that nothing more could be done for her."

Blair was bristling with indignation. "That's the entire truth, and I think she is entitled to that!"

"Even if there was nothing more *you* could do, couldn't you even have the courtesy of considering that something useful could be done with chemotherapy? Don't you understand the implication of saying to a patient that nothing more can be done? You're a goddamn doomsday machine."

Blair exploded. "Goddammit, Nyren, shut up! I'm suppressing my gut impulse to kick you out of this hospital. I hate zealots and especially medical zealots. Do you think you and your colleagues at Curie have a franchise on the right way to treat cancer? Do you think you've been given some divine revelation on what's right and what's wrong? Frankly, I think your judgment has been distorted by a prolonged involvement with a dread disease. You're obviously emotionally involved with cancer to such an extent that you've lost your objectivity, if not your marbles. Mrs. West is a dying woman."

"Are you blind?" Henry shot back. "Can't you see the difference? Mrs. West is not going to die this year and maybe not next. Now, if you have no objections, I would like to have Mrs. West transferred to Curie."

"None at all," Dr. Blair replied coldly, turning away from Henry with the hauteur he wore like a suit of armor.

Henry slammed Mrs. West's chart down on the desk and left. The angry exchange with Blair had only sharpened a perception that had never wavered in all his years of dealing with cancer patients: hopelessness leads to despair, and despair causes pain that is as real and intolerable as any physical distress.

DURING AFTERNOON ROUNDS, Henry ran into Father Noyes.

"Henry, you look upset. How about retreating to my *sanctum sanctorum* for a spot of sherry?"

Henry grabbed the opportunity to put what happened to Mrs.

173

West out of his mind. But he found himself telling Hector Noyes about Blair.

"There was so little meeting of the minds, you'd think we came from different planets."

"Sounds to me like you were both arguing from entrenched positions. Perhaps he tells his patients too much, and you don't tell them enough."

The priest leaned back in a rocking chair he had bought in a secondhand furniture shop on First Avenue and waited patiently for Henry to think that over.

Henry did before he shook his head. "If patients ask me for statistics on how long they are going to live, which they don't, I couldn't tell them. Statistics can't pinpoint any single individual's fate."

"But maybe they want to know in a general way. If you don't tell them two or three years, maybe they'll be thinking two or three months and suffer unnecessary anxiety. They'll adapt differently. I don't think people are as afraid of death as you might think, Henry. They don't want to suffer. They fear pain, not death."

"Well, I'd like to hear what you'd tell the patient if you were in my shoes."

"I'm not in your shoes, and you're not in mine, I know little about your work, and I suspect you know less about mine. I wouldn't think of asking you to administer the Sacraments, and I don't think you should ask me how I would act in your place. The patients need us both, although I'll admit that, proportionately, my role is small—not as small as those who ignore me think it is, though. I am useful. That's presumptuous—my *work* is useful. All the while you're treating the cancer, I am treating torment with love, and despair with hope. When the time comes that *you* can't do any more, my therapy becomes even more important. Clearly, we both have the same goal, to support the patient."

Henry accepted a second glass of sherry, trying to get Blair out of his mind.

174

"You're lucky, Hector," Henry said. "You can deal with the problems of suffering as an uncontested authority figure. Nobody fights with you, everyone wants what you are selling, and you don't have to worry about collecting bills."

"That's how it looks to *you*—the grass is always greener, et cetera. Did anybody ever curse at you because you failed them? And you have failed them, you know, every one of them that dies. But they curse me as a representative of a failed God. It makes no difference if your patients take their medicine sincerely or not, as long as they take it. I know I'm being taken in by the 'lay it on me' type characters. Sometimes I'd just like to walk away, but I can't."

"Sometimes I wish I'd become a dermatologist."

Father Noyes knew with whom he was dealing. "If you were a dermatologist, you'd specialize in all the incurable cases of skin cancer. You can't escape your fate—oops, little lapse of free will there. But I'll level with you, Henry, the greatest torment I find in this hospital is in my own soul. How can I answer Job's question, put to me over and over again? 'Why did God do this to me?' It's difficult enough to answer the adults. But the mothers who ask why their children must suffer and die..." He shook his head. "I would be a fool and a hypocrite if I gave them the bovine response that cancer is God's will. No, cancer is a caprice of an insensate Nature. God didn't cause cancer, and God can't cure it. But God's love can make suffering bearable. I can help cancer patients find comfort in the words and prayers that have comforted others because I'm with them and I believe it."

Henry lit up a cigar, something he rarely did in the hospital outside his own office. Then he leaned over and touched his glass to the priest's.

"We always arrive at the same point, don't we? Even if we can't cure it, we can always make it hurt less."

"You know, Henry, I'm glad to see you smoke. It makes you more human, seeing you share one of mankind's little failings."

"Everyone needs some comfort, Hector."

175

HENRY FINALLY GOT his chance to use mid-torso occlusion on one of Thomas Mangoli's patients, a Nisei woman in her forties with lymphosarcoma localized to the lungs. The situation was reminiscent of the Ann Bauer case that had had Henry brought up on euthanasia charges. It was as if Nature were giving him another chance. This case was perfect. The patient had had all conventional forms of treatment; every drug caused some regression of the tumor, but it always came back. If a massive dose of chemotherapy could be used safely, it might be able to clear the tumor once and for all.

The operating room was very quiet at the start, with the patient on the table and two nurses at her side. The anesthesiologist and an assistant entered and got underway. Dr. Gomez came in to observe. The vascular surgeon, then Henry and the chemotherapy resident, arrived. The wide abdominal tourniquet was underneath her, but not yet encircling her abdomen or inflated. A cardiologist, a neurologist, and an ophthalmologist came in to monitor for complications. The physiology team set up their equipment to measure the degree of effectiveness of the occlusion. For this purpose they would use radioactively labeled albumin injected intravenously into the arm. Then, during the procedure, they would take blood from the leg and if no radioactivity was detected, it meant the occlusion was complete. By the time the procedure was ready to start, there was hardly a place in the room for Henry to mix his medication.

"Commence occlusion." Henry heard his own voice and felt a moment's wonder at its utter calm. Following the procedure worked out for the dog lab, the catheter was threaded into the aorta and the balloon at its tip inflated. The abdominal tourniquet was placed around her waist like a corset and inflated. The radioactive albumin was injected into the upper arm, and no leakage was detected. Henry mixed the chemotherapy, this time deliberately preparing a massive dose. With this experimental injection he would again be launching a patient into unknown hazards. However, it exhilarated him to see the culmination of

176

two years of planning and research. The ten-minute wait passed slowly. During the last thirty seconds, Henry's eyes were fastened on his stopwatch.

"Release occlusion," he ordered.

Everything went off without a hitch. Suddenly a voice boomed out of the intercom connected to the visitors' gallery above the operating room. It was Veit-Volpin's. "Is that Henry's mid-torso madness? Twenty people I am counting in this OR. And if you're all going to send bills to this woman, a million dollars it'll cost her for this circus. But who knows? Maybe I'll eat my words. After all, I was the one who said it would never succeed, the revolution."

Later, in the hall, he said to Henry, "I want you to know I voted against approval of this project by the Clinical Investigation Committee. Ah, I knew you could do this thing and give bigger and bigger doses of chemotherapy, but what you really didn't know, and what you still don't know, is if bigger and bigger doses mean better results. I ask my intuition and it tells me no."

THE PATIENT RECOVERED from the procedure. The blood count did not fall, and the tumor did shrink remarkably. But in a few weeks it started to grow again.

Henry was disheartened. As he walked down the hospital corridor, he met Tom Mangoli coming from the patient's room.

"Cheer up, Henry. At least we didn't do her any harm. And we tried something new. That's why she came here, and maybe in the long run we bought her some time."

"That wasn't what I was after," Henry replied.

"I know, but dammit, Henry, you can't cure them all."

Mangoli, everyone's choice for a leading man, was a few years younger than Henry, but this was canceled out by the ample gray streaks in his carefully groomed hair. His practice was as large as Henry's; however, he managed to avoid most committee assignments, and, while he would cooperate with new research projects, he would not get involved with their development.

"Look, we'll have more patients coming in who will be suitable, we'll get one whose tumor is more sensitive to chemotherapy," he said.

Of course they would do more cases. The technique had worked perfectly. After all, she was only the first case, and the dose was not the maximum that could have been given, but down deep Henry had a sinking feeling. Everything had gone as planned, but cancer was going to win again.

# CHAPTER
# TWENTY-SEVEN

URING THE next three months Henry and the chemotherapy team tried mid-torso occlusion on twenty-one
patients with varying types of tumors. The technique
did avoid the dangerous drop in the levels of white blood cells and
platelets that occurred with large doses of chemotherapy, and
there was tumor shrinkage—occurring in almost every patient—
but it did not last. As Henry sat in his office writing a report on
mid-torso occlusion, he thought it was like shooting twenty-two
caliber bullets at a tank. It doesn't make any difference how
many I shoot, I still won't make a dent. And that's all I've got—
twenty-two's. The worst part of this is that it doesn't lead to
anything. Why don't I get the hell out of research!

That night when Henry returned to his apartment, he looked
around as if seeing the place for the first time. Twenty-year-old
furniture, fading and peeling paint on the walls, no change since
Laura had decorated it shortly after Eve was born. At first he
had wanted to keep everything as it was. After a while, he paid no
attention at all. It was basically a fine apartment with large
rooms and many tall windows. The living room was long, with an
arched entrance, and from the corner window you could see all
the way down Park Avenue to where the Pan Am building sat
like a monarch at the end of a palatial hall.

Suddenly he wanted all of it changed—he wanted his whole life to be different. It was because of Donna, this feeling so alive again. Dissatisfaction with his life at Curie was pushing him toward a change there, too. In a little while Donna would be finished with classes and he would go to meet her, but right now his thoughts focused on the frustration of the mid-torso occlusion research. Old Veit-Volpin was right—it was mid-torso madness. His intuition had been on the mark and Henry's way off it. So stupid. That offer from Phoenix was looking better and better. He looked around the room again. Yes, he definitely would do something about the apartment.

DONNA WAS WAITING, as she usually did, just inside the entrance of the school. She loved these meetings with Henry, even if they weren't as frequent as she had expected when she first started coming to the city. Sometimes a week would go by without her hearing from him. Then there would be a long phone call laden with apologies. There was competition for his time, she knew that well by now. But when he was with her, his attention never wavered. For a few hours, nothing existed except their being together.

One thing struck Donna as strange. Henry had never asked her back to his apartment. There had been nothing more than a warm good-night embrace, sometimes ardent it was true, but that was it. She couldn't know how important her presence was to him, or that he feared that if he came on too strongly with her, he might lose her. When Henry was with her, he was as emotionally insecure as a schoolboy.

Thoughts of Donna, and what he was going to say about Phoenix, displaced Henry's other concerns. They went straight to a small café carved into the basement of an old tenement a few blocks from the Art Students League. It had bare brick walls, a stone floor, and a haphazard collection of tables and chairs. The irregular shape of the place also made room for a number of booths, which provided privacy. They sat in one of these quiet

180

corners, across from each other. A wax-encrusted metal cup with a short glass tube was affixed to the wall. The candle it held was taller than the cup, so the flame moved with the air currents, casting shadows across the table, engulfing them, pulling them together.

Henry put his hands across the table and held hers. He shifted his body to try to get comfortable in the small booth.

"I'm going to Phoenix for a few days to give a talk. How about coming along? You'd be registered under your own name, in your own room, no problem with long distance phone calls."

"It sounds exciting," Donna said. "But how could I work it?"

"Maybe the art school can give you a reason."

"Maybe it could. I almost won a prize once, and the school showed the picture at an exhibit out of town. That was quite a while ago. I could say I was invited to show a painting in Phoenix and ask Rand to come. If he says 'yes,' the show would suddenly be canceled. But a 'yes' isn't likely. If he says he can't come, which is what I think he'll do, then I'm free." This will be my first out-and-out lie. Why don't I feel guilty? Donna wondered.

"Do you think you could ever leave your husband?" Henry said.

Not just his asking, but the utter seriousness in his eyes, surprised Donna. She took a long moment before she answered.

"It's not just Rand, there's a son, a home. Randy is the sticky part."

"But he's all right, and he's going to stay all right. You'd get custody."

"I can't be sure," Donna replied. "Besides there are a lot of complicated feelings mixed up with Randy. I could never do anything that would hurt that boy, and if I thought I *was*, well, I wouldn't be anyone you'd want to be around."

"But we're lucky, he's young enough to adjust to a change."

"There's something even more basic, Henry. There's a lot I don't know about you, about where I fit in," she said, lowering her eyes, taking her hands from his and putting them around the glass of sherry she had ordered.

181

"I love you," he said quietly.

"I know," she answered "I feel it." Then she hesitated a moment, his words had caught her unprepared. "But the truth is I don't know you very well. I look forward to being with you, I'm happy when I'm with you, but I don't know ..."

"Do you care for me at all?"

"Of course I do. But love, well, I need more time." She opened her purse to get a cigarette, but the tightness in her chest made her reach for the L-shaped vaporizer instead.

Henry wanted to smile, to reach over and touch her—but he didn't—he sat and waited for what she would say next.

"Yet time is the one thing we don't seem to have much of," Donna said after a moment. "In a way I feel this is a repetition of what happened to me six years ago, when Rand swept me off my feet. I said 'yes' and I'm still wondering why. I can't let that happen again. I hope I've learned something these last few years, but as I said before, the stakes are higher now."

"Okay, I won't rush you. But there is a reason why Phoenix is so important." He leaned back and looked at her intently. "I'm not going out there just to give a talk. They're interviewing me for a job, to take over Oncology out there."

"You'd leave Curie?" Donna asked.

"I would if you and Randy came with me. We could start a new life together out there, the three of us. I've thought for a long time that I've needed a change. This isn't anything sudden."

He stood up, stretched one arm over his head, arched his back, and then sat down beside her, nudging the table a bit to make more room.

Donna made room for him, but at the same time seemed to be backing off, both physically and emotionally. This time it was she who felt there was something that should be said, but she couldn't find the words.

He smiled, then laughed quietly and took her hands.

"We're a pair. We're so damn jerky about our emotions, verbally and physically."

Donna relaxed a little and smiled in return. "You can't help the way you're brought up. But tell me what you were thinking before."

"I've often thought that I might be more effective somewhere else. Without the research pressure and with more time to devote purely to patient care. I've put in my research time, paid my dues. It's true, research picks me up, but then it slams me down. In the end there's nothing to show for it except a bunch of reprints. I'm ready to work at beating up on cancer full-time, devoting all my time to patients. That's what I really want to do at this stage of my life."

Donna believed him, and for the moment Henry believed it too.

Donna's eyes were bright with admiration, maybe even love. His passion for his work touched her. He was so different from Rand, who spoke with passion only when he quoted something from the *Wall Street Journal*. However, she still had reservations, and she felt them keenly. Was she up to entering his world?

Did she want to?

She was driving home, still very perturbed as a result of this evening's meeting, when she started to laugh. I'm going home, she thought, to hitch up my smoking, adulterous underpants, and see if I can lie my way to Phoenix.

WHITE, RECTANGULAR STALAGMITES bursting out of the sand flats, that's how Phoenix appeared as the plane cruised into this sparkling center of the Sunbelt. Henry and Donna were greeted at the airport by Dr. Lane Maddox, hospital Chief of Staff and the man trying to talk Henry into moving out there. He had done part of his training at Curie and knew Henry from those days. Maddox was a gastroenterologist who had devised a technique for operating on the early stages of cancer from within the colon. He was only one of several outstanding men who were giving the new medical center in Phoenix a prominent national profile. They wanted Henry's image to sharpen that profile in oncology.

Henry introduced Donna Stockman as a friend. He kept glanc-

183

ing at her, trying to see whether she was uncomfortable. There was no problem. She was more relaxed than he was.

As they drove to a downtown hotel together, Maddox was being expansive. "What it comes down to, Henry, is either you like Phoenix or you don't, 'cause oncology-wise you can do anything here you can do at Curie. More—listen to what I tell you—here you've got independence, and you've got it two ways. We've got independent funding, don't need the National Cancer Institute or the American Cancer Society. We've got clergymen who believe in us and companies that believe in us and lots of plain people, too. Last month we raked in six hundred thousand dollars. All I had to do was make four appearances. Now, cancer's what they want to hear about. And Henry, you'd knock 'em dead. Talking about independence, you'd have your own department. I mean, we're free of the committees. Oh, we got 'em all, but the difference is, they'd be your committees, you'd run them. Spend as little time on 'em or as much as you like. You'd see as many patients or as few as you'd like. Build up your Oncology Department to whatever size you like. Henry, this is a dynamic, hard-working, hard-hitting place. And you'd fit in. You know about half the staff already. God, you wouldn't need more than ten minutes before you felt at home. And the lady here, she'd love it. They all do."

Maddox dropped them off at the gleaming Sheraton Tower. They walked together to the registration desk, where Henry was given two cards for the reservations that he had made. With an awkward smile, he showed both cards to Donna who was standing stiffly at his side. They were for Rooms 1304 and 1305. She filled out one of them. Rand had to know where she was in order to be able to contact her if need be.

The cocktail reception at the country club was pleasant, and so was the sit-down dinner afterward. There were thirty-five guests, who were easily accommodated in Maddox's sprawling, white-arched modern version of Southwest Spanish architecture. They left late, Henry feeling more and more awkward as they approached the hotel. He started to light up a cigar in the

184

cab, remembered Janine's admonition about brushing his teeth and Donna's asthma, and stuffed the cigar back into his breast pocket.

"The weather's really great out here," he said.

"You said that twice already." She reached over to hold his hand. She found his embarrassment endearing. Leaning close to him so the driver wouldn't hear her, she whispered, "I do love you, you know."

They walked through the lobby hand in hand and then up to their rooms. They kissed and went into their adjoining rooms with a look that said we'll be together in a moment.

For some reason, the connecting doors, which they had opened when they checked in, had been closed by the maid. The door was locked on each side with a sliding bolt. Both parties would have to slide back the bolt for the door to open. Henry waited a few minutes and went to the door, opened the bolt on his side, and called for Donna. There was no reply. She was in the shower and couldn't hear him. He waited, and decided to use the phone. But, tense as he was, he dialed the wrong number, got an empty room and no reply.

As Donna put on her nightgown she looked at the door wondering when Henry would knock. Her heart beat fast as she stood there waiting. She was surprised that there was no communication from the other side. She dared herself to tap on the door. Finally she did. But at that moment Henry was flushing the toilet and didn't hear her.

Although Donna sometimes found Henry's reticence appealing, she couldn't understand why he, who had taken all the initiative so far, would stop now. Still, she thought, he has to do things his own way.

Henry, for his part, was overjoyed with her first-time declaration of love and, not wanting to push his luck, went to bed.

BREAKFAST THE NEXT morning started awkwardly for both of them.

"I tried to call you last night. You didn't answer."

185

"Henry, the phone never rang. I knocked on your door, you must have heard me."

"I didn't. Maybe it was when I was in the bathroom."

They stared at each other for a moment, stood up, and, eyes filling up with laughter, they leaned over the breakfast table and kissed. Anyone looking at them would have thought they were newlyweds.

# CHAPTER
# *TWENTY-EIGHT*

THE DAY was filled with lectures and rounds for Henry. He reported his results with mid-torso occlusion, a technique so far unknown outside of Curie. He presented it as a new approach to cancer chemotherapy that showed some promise, and with better drugs—who knew? Then lectures on the good results in the treatment of breast cancer and the continuing tough job with lung and colon cancer. These were things they knew, but they liked Henry's style, the authoritative way he handled his material, and the personal anecdotes to which they could easily relate. The same firm rapport between him and the staff continued on rounds. There was no question that the job was his for the asking.

Donna spent the day getting to know the city, trying to find a scene relating to her interests and talents. She went to the museums, the art schools, spoke with some artists whom Maddox's wife arranged for her to meet, and visited some studios. There was more going on than she had anticipated. She did not allow her thoughts to wander to the complications that could envelop her.

There was another dinner that night, this time at a restaurant. Maddox and the other doctors drove Henry and Donna back to the hotel in two cars. Henry invited everyone to the hotel lounge where they had a few more drinks. Two of the men were with their wives. The third had a woman friend with him, not much older than Donna. It was a very compatible group. In fact, Donna felt comfortable with all the people she was meeting. She felt accepted, at least at that level and at that moment. Her only apprehension was that Henry's ineptness last night would return once they were alone.

When they went upstairs Henry said, "I've got something for you, and she followed him into his room. He gave her a silver Indian necklace.

"I bought something for me, too," she said laughingly as she went into the adjoining room and came back with a tall silver comb done in the same style as the necklace. The doors were open now.

"It's a little too much with the necklace, but what the hell, they're a good match. I bought some other stuff for Randy. I didn't get any for you. I just couldn't see you in it."

She picked up her gift and started back toward her room. Henry touched her shoulder and, as she turned, took her in his arms. "No closed doors?"

She shook her head. "No, but give me a half a sec." She closed the door halfway.

After a few minutes Henry went to the doorway. "Donna?"

"Come on in."

He pushed the door fully open. She was standing next to the bed, wearing a beige satin nightgown trimmed with lace. Behind her was the night table lamp. The backlighting made the satin nightgown shimmer.

Henry stood there a moment, not daring to speak or even breathe. Then he gathered Donna in his arms and quietly moved to the bed. He contained the sense of urgency that came from waiting so long. He wanted this to be right. He held her until her muscles were no longer taut, until her breath was no longer staccato, until her arms voluntarily moved to embrace him. The softness of her body, the sensation of her heart beating against

188

his chest, the velvet warmth as she cradled him between her legs overwhelmed him with desire. He was so focused on extracting every molecule of joy from this moment that had a surgical incision been made across his back he would not have felt it.

Donna's pleasure was heightened by a residual sense of the forbidden. Although she hesitated for a second at the moment of penetration, her thrust then was all the stronger because it was accompanied by the cry, "But I want to!"

THE NEXT DAY Maddox drove them to the airport, still effusive. Henry promised to consider things carefully and to write to him within two weeks. Only when they were airborne did they start to talk about the past couple of days.

"What about you, Donna? Could you live there?" Even as he asked the question, he knew he was oversimplifying the situation.

"Henry, let's be fair. That's not the question. You must know that. From your point of view our relationship isn't complicated. But my problems won't be solved by going to Phoenix or any place else. Besides, when we talked about this trip, I said, think of it for you only. My situation is a completely separate one. So the questions have to start with you. What do you think about the offer?"

"I could be plenty busy out there, work twenty-four hours a day if I wanted. They've got all the patients anyone would want, and they've got good people in all departments. I could be a big fish in a small pond."

"At home you're a big fish in a big pond."

Henry smiled and gently touched her arm. "There's something else, and Maddox missed it completely. You don't do research all by yourself, at least I don't. In Phoenix I'd be a one-man research team, and I've got to interact with other people who understand cancer. You think you've got an idea of your own, you never do. It's give and take. You're challenged, you're prodded, you're stimulated—finally something happens. Did you ever go to a

189

carnival where you sat in an electric bumper car, and there were forty or fifty other bumper cars, and when the juice was on you all slammed into one another? Then at the end everyone yelled how great it was? Well, oncology is something like that. At least for me it is. I'm not a solo operator. I need everybody else. Curie's not the only place I could find it—but not out there. There're no Paul Rosens out there, no Veit-Volpins. Donna, I need the critics, the skeptics, the nitpickers."

"How about that other pitch—you know, giving up research and sticking only with the patients?" Donna asked.

Henry didn't reply for a moment. He pushed back his hair and looked out the airplane window before speaking. "I don't know how to express it. Sometimes I hate research and wish I had never had anything to do with it. I can't tell you why I keep coming back to it. I really would like to be the kind of person who could accept that job, ditch research, and care only for patients. I'd also like to be the kind of normal human being who could enjoy golf, go fishing, or do any number of things normal human beings do. I'd like to be a different animal, and when the frustration builds up at Curie, I think how nice life could be someplace else. But God help me, I can't do it. I've got to stay at Curie and take my chances." He hesitated. "The only other scene that interests me is one with you in it. I did hear what you said, and I won't imagine there aren't any problems."

Waves of emotion flowed over Donna.

She did love Henry. Perhaps she would never know him the way she knew Rand, whose words and behavior were so predictable—only the party he had made for her was a surprise. Still, she couldn't say how she would react if forced to choose between Rand and Henry. All she knew for sure was that Randy would weigh heavily in the balance.

"What are you doing now?" Donna asked as she watched Henry writing in a notebook he had placed on the fold-out tray. He was busy crossing out, erasing, rewriting.

"Making some notes for a new research proposal. It's for a grant application I've got to complete."

190

"We won't be side by side once we land, you know."

Henry turned in his seat and looked at her for a long moment without saying anything. Then he put away his pen and the notebook, still without speaking. Finally, taking her hand in his, he said, gently, "I was trying to pretend to myself that our being together isn't going to end when we land." He sighed, and smiled. "I can't concentrate. Nothing I wrote makes any sense." He raised her hand to his lips and kissed it.

"Sometimes," he said, "I think that the only thing in my life that makes any sense is you."

Donna sat pensively, then turned to Henry. "It's not very pleasant to think about going back and meeting in the shadows again."

Henry squeezed her hand. An uncertain future sat between them like a third passenger.

# CHAPTER
# *TWENTY-NINE*

**T**ARA STOPPED Henry as he came into the office. "Look at this card we got from Stanley's mother!"

He took the card and read it aloud. "Don't bother us no more. Stanley got better without your medicine."

He looked at Tara. "What does she mean, Stanley got better? Stanley is dead. Do you think she's blocked him out?"

"I don't think mothers block out their children, even uneducated mothers. But her note makes me wonder what happened."

"Wonder all you like, there's only one way to find out. Tara, I know this is above and beyond, but I want you to go up there Saturday and find out. Bring presents for everyone and win them over. I'd go myself, but we both know I wouldn't get one foot in the door. If that kid is alive, tell the mother how much I love that lousy little bastard, and what a fine boy he is, and that I would like to see him. We'll send a hospital car for him."

He felt a slight tingle of the old excitement when every new patient was a new opportunity for triumph.

After rounds on Saturday, Henry went back to his apartment to wait for Tara to call. When he walked in, the first thing he heard were peals of feminine laughter.

"Hi, Henry!" Eve called out.

Why the hell couldn't she say "Dad"? Besides, why was she here

192

and with whom? Then he remembered—at least the why part. A few weeks ago, during one of his brief conversations with her, Henry had invited Eve to give him some ideas on redecorating the apartment. Not only wouldn't his time-short arrangement with Donna ever allow them to do it, he also thought there was a chance the project might somehow bring him and Eve a little closer. However, he found that all he had done was let the camel, or rather the camels, into the tent.

"Henry, meet Pauline, Greta, and Ilana, all from the staff of *The Outrageous Decorator*. Mom's legacies, you might say."

Acknowledgments all around, then: "You're gonna love it, Dad! Look at these fabrics. And the color! It will be mostly shades of green and white, with really striking accents."

"Sounds just fine!" He gave Eve a hug, thinking, be gracious, be gracious. He swept his hands toward the rest of the apartment. "It's all yours!" he said. The last thing he heard as he retreated to the bedroom was, "I saw the perfect thing for that corner in Lightolier."

Seated in the armchair in the bedroom, he read the paper and waited for Tara to call.

The decorating project had not gone exactly as he had planned, he was hardly involved, but Eve was in her home again, she was being friendly. Exuberant sounds were floating back to the bedroom—he had nothing to complain about.

EXACTLY AT NOON, Tara called. He had no great expectations that she would have anything important to relate.

"Doctor Nyren, I'm here with Mrs. Kaprowski and her family. Stanley looks just fine to me. He is running around with all the others, and it would appear he has no disability."

"That's impossible. Let me speak to him," Henry said.

"His mother told me he was deathly ill when they took him home from the hospital, and that they were very lucky to get him away from you. Then he caught the measles from one of the other children, and he became even sicker. They thought he was going

193

to die. One morning the fever broke, and from that day on he improved steadily. In about two months he gained twenty pounds, felt fine, and went back to school."

"Let me speak to him!"

"I'll try," Tara said. She came back on. "Sorry. He doesn't want to. I'm afraid he blames you for making him sick with all that medicine. And he also says—"

"Tara, hold it. I don't care what he says. Promise him and his mother anything, but get them down here."

"I have that situation in hand. His mother and I are getting better acquainted. In a little while, we're going to go shopping on Ninth Avenue where she lived as a little girl. Then we'll bring Stanley to see you at the hospital."

"Tara, you are marvelous."

Henry sat down at his desk and began to think. The potential importance of this phone call was starting to dawn on him. Spontaneous regression of Hodgkin's disease—a rare phenomenon for any form of cancer. He had read about it, but this was his first chance to see this remarkable event with his own eyes.

SLIM TARA, IN her delicate lilac and red sari, and chunky Mrs. Kaprowski in her blue jeans and tennis shoes made a wildly improbable pair as they came into the outpatient building dragging twelve-year-old Stanley behind them. Both women were smiling. Stanley was muttering under his breath, but there were red cheeks and bright eyes above his down-turned mouth. Henry spoke to the mother for a few moments, and then motioned Tara and Mrs. Kaprowski to chairs in the waiting room.

"You two ladies sit out here. Stanley and I will only be a few minutes."

Henry turned to the boy with his friendliest smile and, placing his arm around Stanley's shoulders, led him into the brightly lit, windowless examining room that had to contain some frightening memories for Stanley.

"Sit down, Stanley. You look really good. How do you feel?"

194

Stanley took a quick look around and headed for the door. Henry, who had anticipated the possibility that the boy would decide to try a getaway, was standing in front of it. Stanley looked up at him and yelled, "Doctor Nyren, you're a prick!"

"You shouldn't talk to your doctor that way," Henry said, controlling an unexpected impulse to laugh. Surely, he thought, some patient before this one had wanted to say exactly that to him, but lacked Stanley's openness.

"I almost died here. You put mustard in my veins."

"Nitrogen mustard—it's a medicine."

"You tried to kill me—and don't tell me you didn't. I heard the interns talking. They said, 'You got to inject the mustard fast,' and then they squirted it into my veins and then I got sick. I told my mother all about it. And how the kids in that place died. I saw them carrying them out, making believe it was nothing. But I knew what was going on. I begged her to get me out of there."

Henry stood and listened as Stanley let it all out. What a hospital must feel like to a child, he thought. It would do no good to explain to Stanley that he was in the pediatric ward because he had something wrong with him, and that sometimes they had to make you sick before you got better—in Stanley's case treatment had not worked at all. How could he explain to Stanley that when his mother took him home he was dying of Hodgkin's disease?

"I know it was tough on you in the hospital," he said, latching onto Stanley's eyes. "I promise I'm not going to do anything bad to you now. Your mother is a better doctor than I am. She made you well. I just want to look you over and see if I can learn from your mother's treatment."

The plain truth worked. Stanley took his shirt off. Henry examined him thoroughly and found no enlarged lymph nodes. The liver and spleen were normal. The areas of bone that had been destroyed by Hodgkin's disease were neither tender nor swollen. When he was in the hospital you couldn't touch those parts of his body without his screaming. Then, he could hardly move; now, there was no sign of abnormality. It seemed to be a true, complete remission, of eighteen months duration. It was not the result of any treatment, it appeared to have occurred spontaneously.

Henry needed X-rays of the bones, to compare with the films taken in the hospital, and blood for biochemical and hematological testing. People in the research labs would want blood to see if he had antibodies against cancer cells and to determine his immune status.

"Stanley, I want to explain something to you. You've got a secret in you—how you got well—that might help a lot of other kids who are sick now the way you used to be. All you have to do is let me take some X-rays and some blood from your veins."

"Help, murdaaa! Ma, he's going to kill me again. Ma, Ma!"

His mother came running in. Henry had explained to her about the blood tests and X-rays, and she had agreed. But she couldn't quiet the kid either.

Tara came in and instantly cut through the mood of panic. "Look, Doctor Nyren will leave the room. Stay just a little while longer, Stanley, then you can go back to your house and have the ham and kielbasi and cakes and everything."

"No! Now! I wanna go now!" Stanley reached for his shirt.

"And the big surprise!" Tara cut in. "The bicycle."

"What bicycle?"

"We're getting you a bicycle. But only if you're good. You wait here with your mother. The nurse will be right in. We simply want to take a little blood from you and then some X-rays. After that we can go directly to the bike store. Think about what color you want."

Henry walked out of the room, holding up three fingers. In about five minutes, Tara came out with Stanley, his mother, and three tubes of blood. She was leading them to the Radiology Department.

"Blue. I want a sparkly blue one," Stanley said. "With orange reflectors. And a shiny basket."

When Tara and the Kaprowskis went off in search of the perfect blue bike, Henry called Len Boyer to explain the circumstances of the case.

"I agree," the Chief of Medicine said. "This case should be presented to Medical Grand Rounds as soon as the tests are completed."

"I'll arrange it," Henry said.

Tara returned in an hour. "Stanley has his bike. Bright blue. They're on their way home. I put all three of them in a cab."

Henry took Tara's hand, bowed deeply, and kissed it.

THIS NEW LIFE-STYLE that Donna had opted for was filled with complications. There were times when she'd fall asleep in Henry's arms—and awake with a start, too late to go home. She would go to her mother's apartment, call home with an excuse, and stay over there. As snarled as her life had become, Donna would have been content for things to stay as they were—but she knew that sooner or later something would happen. There were so many "almosts."

One bright, chilly Sunday, not long after her return from Phoenix, she and Rand had gone supermarket shopping, and the back of the car was filled with brown bags. After parking the car in the driveway, Rand bounded out, took an armful of groceries, and went to the side door. Juggling the bags, he rummaged through his pockets.

"This time I don't have the key."

It was usually Donna who couldn't remember where she had put her keys.

"Here, take mine." She handed him her key chain, and went back to get some more bags from the car.

In a moment Rand was beside her.

"What's this one?" He dangled before her a shiny new brass key to Henry's apartment.

Donna stared dumbly for a moment and then, stumbling

across the words, said, "Oh, that one. It's—oh, sure—it's the key to the studio at the art school. They lock everything there."

"Oh," Rand said quietly.

His eyes were altogether silent.

# CHAPTER
# *THIRTY*

HERE WERE certain times in Henry's career that he considered D-Days. They were so important because they were occasions that might lead to a significant victory. He considered his decision to push on with streptokotocin one of these. Mid-torso occlusion was a landing that had been rebuffed. Now there was Kaprowski. What kind of D-Day was this? The victory had been won. *All* he had to do was find out how!

When the time came for Grand Rounds, Henry found himself uncharacteristically anxious. He had given many Grand Rounds before, and they were always sweatless exercises for him. This morning he had actually forgotten to shave. Rubbing his chin in apprehensive thought on the way to work, he discovered the oversight, bought a disposable razor, and, feeling stupid, took his shirt and tie off in the men's room and shaved. He felt even more foolish when he nicked his chin and had to go back to his office with a piece of toilet paper sticking to the wound. He sent Tara to find a more acceptable flesh-colored Band-Aid.

Medical Grand Rounds were not rounds at all. Historically, rounds referred to physicians' bedside visits to hospitalized patients. However, bedside discussions could have a disconcerting effect; patients' fears would often distort what was heard. Therefore, Grand Rounds were now carried out in an auditorium, with the patient brought in only briefly or, more commonly, with appropriate visual aids in place of the patient. In Stanley Kaprowski's case, there was nothing to demonstrate, and bringing this healthy but decidedly antagonistic child before a collection of physicians ran a fair chance of becoming disruptive. Usually, following the clinical presentation, a visiting specialist from another institution would discuss the case and present the relevant research. Today, however, because the phenomenon was so rare that there were no specialists on the subject, Henry would discuss the spontaneous regression of cancer.

John Wissler, an intern, had put on a clean set of whites for the occasion. He mounted the podium and presented Stanley's case history. After that, the radiologist showed Stanley's X-rays at the time of his last hospitalization and compared them with the current X-rays, which were completely normal. The pathologist projected images of several slides of the diseased lymph nodes and was vigorous in defending the diagnosis and assuring his colleagues that this was indeed a valid case of Hodgkin's disease and not a misdiagnosis—the usual explanation of so-called miraculous cancer cures.

It was Henry's turn. He got to the heart of the matter quickly. What had brought about this rare and miraculous event? Hypotheses were abundant. There had been reported cases of spontaneous regression of cancer where it was believed that the patient's own hormones had caused tumor regression, or where tumors had outgrown their blood supply and starved to death, or where there had been immune reactions against the cancer. In other cases, it appeared that bacterial infections had produced toxins that destroyed the tumor, or that infectious viruses attacked the cancer cells, as might have occurred with the measles in this case. But as he got to the end of his presentation, the weakness of his conclusions, the lack of any final resolution, and his inability to say why or how it happened, made him appear muddled.

There was another reason why Henry seemed to drift off at the

200

end. Sometimes, when dealing with his adversary, he would start off scientifically, as he had just now, but as he moved in closer, a wave of irrational thoughts would swirl into his mind. Why was cancer so strong and his assaults so feeble? Why was cancer so smart and he so dumb? Why was it that cancer could live forever? And why did it, sometimes, sneak away in a gigantic biological mockery of him and all his efforts?

That's what spontaneous regression meant to Henry. It was his villainous opponent mimicking and taunting him: "See how easy it is? Why can't you do it?" So many of his patients died, so much effort went into the attempt to save them. So often he was just a fingertip away from a cure when the patient was cruelly wrenched away by his ruthless opponent in a casual display of power.

Henry grasped the edges of the lectern, deliberately speaking slowly now, in an attempt to hide his roiling innards.

"We need all the help we can get—from each one of you—in remarkable situations like this one. If we understood the mechanism of spontaneous regression, we might be able to use it for treatment. The clue for a cure is here, but no one has been able to take advantage of it."

Dr. Len Boyer stood up. "Thank you, Doctor Nyren, for your review and hypotheses. Are there any further comments or remarks?"

There were many comments and questions, but there was not a single suggestion from that collection of talent on how cancer research could profit from the Stanley Kaprowski case.

As Henry left the podium he had a letdown feeling. Not only were there no research suggestions from all that talent in the audience, but everyone rushed off afterward. The case hadn't excited them the way he had hoped. He should have known better. Scientists are interested in their own research gardens, not anyone else's.

One person remained in the room. Paul Rosen sat in a corner scribbling notes.

201

"Want to go for coffee, Paul?" Henry asked.

"Okay. I've been thinking about this case, Henry. I've got an idea."

"Then the hell with coffee. Let's sit here and talk."

"There's too much coincidence here," Paul said. "The measles had to have something to do with the remission. But plenty of pediatrics patients have had measles, and it didn't make them any better."

"I know. I looked into that angle," Henry replied.

"My hunch is that it's something different," Paul said. "There's an article I read recently, some botanists at the University of Connecticut have come up with a plant extract that repairs damaged cell membranes and inhibits cell division. Repairin, in fact, is what they call the stuff.

"What's the connection with measles?" Henry asked.

"They mentioned that certain viruses stimulate cells to produce repairin," Paul said. "Maybe the measles virus stimulated the body to produce repairin, which in turn suppressed the Hodgkin's disease. I can't guess why it worked in this patient and not others. I'm going to contact the U. Conn. group and see if they'll send us some of the material. We could ask Weil to take a look at the data, see if he thinks it's worthwhile putting it through a preclinical screen. And if it's active in the screening program, or if it has any effect on animal tumors, Henry, would you be willing to do a Phase I trial in man?"

"It's a very thin thread, Paul." Henry looked down at his hands. He'd been left holding so many broken threads already. A thread as thin as this one could break so easily.

He looked up at Paul. "I'd grab it," he said.

# CHAPTER
# *THIRTY-ONE*

**M**ARLENE LOWELL was upset for weeks after Dr. Green told her that the mole removed from her leg was malignant. But after three follow-up visits and a great deal of reassurance by the dermatologist, she began to relax. She put the skin cancer in the same category as getting caught once in an undertow and fighting her way out of it, and the time she was trapped in an empty subway car with two young toughs with rape in their eyes, only to have a transit cop walk into the car on his rounds. She figured everyone collects a series of near catastrophes. You don't sit home and hide from the world; you do the best you can and move on. The fact was, she felt rather good about her leg problem. It was something else she had overcome, like the measles, joblessness, and virginity. She felt, as she approached her twenty-seventh birthday, that at last she had it all together. She knew she had talent—not world-beating, but respectable enough so that sooner or later she would find a niche for herself in the art world. She was also pleased that she had turned down Ronnie's halfhearted proposal of marriage. Marlene had a better self-image than he did, and she did not feel like becoming his sole means of emotional support for the rest of her life.

She was a big, full-breasted girl with a slightly broad face and dark eyebrows. Put her in a black bodice and skirt, give her longer brown hair, and you could easily imagine her holding her own in a seventeenth-century tavern. Cut her hair short and dress her in a tailored suit, and she would be right in place at an executive's desk. In either case, she brought a certain authority and competence to a situation.

On Saturday, Marlene was back in Greenwich Village with her high stool, easel, and velvet-covered plywood square filled with jewelry. This was where the action was, the people, the color, the odors. It was street entertainment, music, art, and theater—a new show every minute. The roar of lumbering vehicles as they came out of huge warehouses fringing the West Village sounded just right; quiet would have been inappropriate. Appropriate, too, were the far-out displays, some inside the shops, some outside, and the old, immigrant leftovers sitting at open windows like still-life images. Marlene was not just a spectator, she was part of the scene. As she sat polishing a pendant, she became aware that she was stopping from time to time to scratch her leg. When she looked down, all she saw was the small, red scar from her operation. But the third time she looked, she saw a small pimple about an inch from the scar. Probably from the adhesive tape, she thought, but I'll see Dr. Green next week, and he'll give me something for the itch.

Marlene had counted on getting some ointment from the doctor and saying good-bye.

"THE LEG LOOKS fine," she said, "but it itches. I think I got a pimple scratching it."

Dr. Green moved the stand with a small spotlight closer to Marlene's raised leg. He picked up a magnifying glass, pulled up a round, stainless steel stool, sat down and looked. He saw a red, raised spot, about one-sixteenth of an inch in diameter; two pinpoint black flecks were apparent. Three thoughts rushed through his head, the second two hard on the heels of the first. First, she is going to die. Second, don't tell her anything to upset her. Third, I don't need this kind of problem in my office.

204

"Pimples like this sometimes appear around a scar just from the adhesive tape . . ." he said.

"That's what I thought."

"But when they happen around the site of a melanoma, they have to be biopsied again."

"You mean it's come back again?"

"In cases like this I'd like to get another opinion. There is a melanoma specialist at the Curie Hospital, Doctor Kolonymus. I'll write down his name and telephone number. I'm going to send him your biopsy slide."

"Does this mean a piece of skin is going to have to be removed, like you said? What happens then—a big scar, or a graft? Does plastic surgery fit in any place?" The pounding in her heart had started again.

"Maybe yes to all those questions. Doctor Kolonymus will give you definite answers. He's the top melanoma specialist in the city, actually in the whole country."

MARLENE LEFT WORK early to keep the appointment with Dr. Kolonymus. As she got into a taxi on Fifty-ninth Street, her chief concern was the inconvenience of it all.

Why was Dr. Green making such a big deal out of this? What about the skin graft? Well, after, I could cover it with makeup, but I'd probably have to be in the hospital. Oh, hell, that meant I'd have *her* to deal with. Maybe they'd put a "contagious" sign outside my room. And then, *I guess this means I really have cancer.* Marlene had never thought about Curie Cancer Hospital for herself. Anyone she'd ever heard of who went there, died. It was a place to keep away from, like the Tombs or Bellevue or Central Park at midnight. A place for losers.

The cab drew up beside a canopied entrance to the tall hospital building, one of several interlocking, related hospitals, research laboratories, and teaching institutes clustered together. "The garment district of medicine" was the way one of the hospital administrators put it. But if this was the garment district, it was *haute couture.*

205

Entering the lobby, Marlene thought it was strange for a doctor to have his office in a hospital. All the doctors she had ever known had their offices in apartment houses. She had never even been in a hospital before.

"Doctor Kolonymus, please?" she inquired at the information desk. She was directed to one of two banks of elevators that flanked the lobby. One was apparently for the hospital proper, and the other for a building that was reserved for outpatients. The formality of the environment and the need to come to a hospital for a consultation for a tiny thing like a skin problem increased her apprehension. By the time she reached the office she felt like her mother's daughter. She sat down and found some of the same magazines she had read in Dr. Green's waiting room. That's a good sign, she thought. Maybe it's not so different. It's only a doctor's office and I'm only going to be here once, so take it easy.

Dr. Kalman Kolonymus was a tall man in his sixties with a creased, hatchet face, rather like an Indian chief. His voice was deep and soft, and Europe was hinted at more by inflection than accent. He carefully examined the small, red, raised area on Marlene's skin. He examined the back of her knee and felt for lymph nodes in her groin. He also palpated her liver, listened to her lungs, and did a neurological examination. He was looking for evidence of metastases.

"Miss Lowell, I want to tell you something about melanomas. There are some that are very malignant, and cells from a small black mole can spread any place in the body. I don't see any evidence of that here. Other melanomas are sleepyheads, by which I mean they have a tendency to recur locally, and they don't do very much. This would appear to be the situation in your case."

"Doctor Green explained about the removal of a large piece of skin to be sure it's all out, and then a graft. Is that what you're getting at? I want to know everything. I think I can take it."

"Yes, that's right, but that's not the entire picture," Kolonymus continued, in his fatherly and direct manner. "The purpose of the

206

wide excision of skin is, as you said, to be sure that it is all out locally. But more has to be done. Once the tumor has shown a tendency to recur, you have to be one step ahead of its growth. We can't be sure that cancer cells haven't gotten into the lymph nodes. That's the way they spread. To do that we have to examine the lymph nodes in the back of your knee and in your groin. Only when we know that these show no evidence of malignancy can we be reasonably sure that we will have a complete cure."

"Does that mean you have to biopsy lymph nodes behind my knee and in my groin, two more little cuts like the one in my leg?"

"I'm afraid it's more than that. To take a biopsy is to take a small piece that is representative of the whole, but to be sure that your lymph nodes have no cancer, we have to dissect out all the lymph nodes of the groin and all the lymph nodes behind the knee. It's more than a biopsy. It's a complete removal. It leaves a long scar. It won't be unsightly in a year or two, but it may cause swelling of your leg."

"Please excuse me, Doctor Kolonymus, but all of this is happening too fast. I'm sitting here, I'm following you—but I feel that we're talking about someone else. Maybe I'd better ask you a few questions before it really hits me. I guess the big one is, what would happen if I did nothing?"

"Well, it's possible that the little collection of tumor cells that looks like a pimple would hang around for years and do nothing. But, frankly, I doubt it. It's more likely to start growing and get darker, and then other dark spots would develop and appear in different areas of your leg. It would spread through the lymph nodes to other parts of your body, and, well, at that point it would be a threat to life."

"All right, suppose I go through with the operation—or should I say operations?"

"If the lymph nodes are negative and you get through the next two years without any trouble, chances for cure are high."

"And if the lymph nodes are not negative?" she asked hesitantly.

"Let's go one step at a time. There are endless possibilities. I'd

207

have to read a textbook to you to present adequately every conceivable consequence, and all that would do would be to raise anxieties that in all likelihood would be unwarranted."

Marlene was sitting on the edge of the chair with her hands clenched in her lap. "How about X-rays and chemotherapy? Do they come into the picture?"

"Possibly, but not now. We are doing something that on the face of it may seem extreme in view of what we see. Just a pinhead spot on your leg, and I'm proposing extensive surgery. But we're trying to achieve the most when the tumor is minimal."

Marlene, who had no such plans, said "I was thinking of taking a vacation. Can I postpone this until I come back? Can we watch it for a few weeks?"

"What you're asking me for is time to make up your mind. I can't go along with that," Dr. Kolonymus said gently. "This should be done as soon as possible, if only because of the outside chance that yours could be one of the more aggressive melanomas. I'd like you to call me no later than tomorrow and let me know."

Marlene knew suddenly that if she left without making a decision she would drive herself mad between now and the time she had to call him back. And she would still come to the same decision.

"Okay," she said. "I'll go through with it. What do I have to do?"

Dr. Kolonymus sent her back to see his secretary, who filled out an admission form and then told Marlene she could go home and they would call her when a hospital bed was available, probably in a few days.

Marlene had been anxious when she got to Kolonymus's office. But when she left, it was no longer anxiety she felt. What had occurred was an assault on her personality so overwhelming that no room remained for anxiety. As she pushed the elevator button, she thought, There's a different human being going down this elevator than came up.

She had made a contract that would change her forever; she had been transformed thoroughly and pervasively into a cancer

208

patient. She was no longer an observer passing through. She was part of the scene—just as she was in Greenwich Village. She was being drawn into the walls, the carpet, the elevator, and would soon be part of the surgeons and operating rooms and nurses and bedpans and bottles with tubes and needles and knives and bandages and medicine and pain and helplessness.

My job, she thought. And my sculpture. Oh my God—my mother! Marlene stopped and leaned against the hallway wall. She felt faint. She wouldn't let herself. But she needed to let all she felt out, to talk to someone. She had parents with whom she lived, and Ronnie with whom she slept, and people she worked with, but in all this city of over seven million people, there was not one person whom she felt close enough to turn to. She suddenly felt very alone, very defenseless, and very scared.

IT WAS EARLIER than usual when she got home. She had not been up to teaching her night-school classes. She was looking forward to Saturday and Sunday at her stand in the Village and then apartment hunting. Marlene had finally decided to move out. But she had to get past this first.

Her mother and father were finishing dinner.

"Do you want something to eat?" her mother asked.

Marlene didn't want dinner.

"How come you're home early?"

"I had to see a doctor. I had some trouble with my leg."

"What kind of trouble? It's healed beautifully. You can hardly see the scar. By next summer no one will even notice it. Your leg looks so much better now than it did with that ugly black thing. Aren't you glad you took my advice? I only wish you'd take my advice about other things."

"I'm thrilled I took your advice. Your advice has changed me from an ugly, frustrated twenty-six-year-old spinster with no prospects, due to a horrible quarter-of-an-inch mole on a leg, to a brilliant, sparkling and beautiful cancer victim followed everywhere by doctors, nurses, and undertakers."

She hadn't planned that.

"Please don't use that word," her mother said. "Why should you talk about cancer? What you had was a little mole, a plain old birthmark. It was removed, that's all. What kind of trouble?"

"It's come back in a different place on my leg, and they have to remove a piece of skin and also the glands in my knee and the glands in my groin. There're going to be scars all over my leg, and my leg is going to be swollen when they're finished and probably always. I'm going into the hospital in a few days. But don't worry about anything. I'll take your advice."

Her mother had just taken a big spoon from a vegetable plate. Now she shook it at Marlene.

"Why did you go to the dumb dermatologist downstairs? He's such a miserable, money-grabbing bastard. When you start with him you're never finished. You know what Mrs. O'Connor told me? He's a real swinger. Isn't that disgusting? You should see a real doctor."

"I didn't see Doctor Green. I saw a specialist he sent me to. That's where I was today."

Mrs. Lowell was unstoppable. "And he wants to cut up your leg and your knee and your privates, and you're going to let him? A specialist Doctor Green sent you to? Are you crazy? He's probably one of his buddies, also a swinger. Only this one is a bigger swinger. Well, let me tell you. I'm not going to have my daughter be touched by one of his playboy buddies. Making a big deal out of a little mole because they need lots of spending money. Don't you think Doctor Green gets a cut? It's all a racket. Isn't that right, honey?"

Marlene's father spoke only when spoken to. "I think you've got to do what the doctor says," Gus Lowell offered limply.

"See, your father agrees with me." At this point Mrs. Lowell decided she had to take action. She was also protecting herself. She was the one who had sent Marlene to the doctor in the first place, and ever since she heard the word "cancer" in association with Marlene, the thought was there: It's my fault.

"Listen, Mrs. O'Connor's sister, the one who lives in Rego Park, she had a breast cancer operation a few years ago and she's

210

absolutely fine now. I'm going to call her and get the name of her doctor. You see what happens if you're a dope and let the doctors do whatever they want to? Look at the super. Five years ago they said he was going to die and they would have to cut his leg off, God forbid. He's an idiot. He let them cut his leg off, and did he die? No, he's jumping around here like he always did. Those doctors are crazy."

Mrs. Lowell rushed into her bedroom. Marlene heard her mother's agitated voice tinged with a note of hysteria as she spoke on the telephone. Marlene got up and made herself a martini and poured a beer for her father.

In a few moments her mother emerged, smiling triumphantly.

"I had a hard time getting him. First, I got Mrs. O'Connor. She gave me her sister's name. Then I got her sister, and she gave me the name of her doctor. Then I got the doctor's answering service. He wasn't in the office, and they wouldn't give me his home telephone number. But I gave them such a cock-and-bull story that I finally got through to him. And you know what? He was very nice. He told me that he didn't do that kind of surgery, but he agreed with me that it was a terrible thing that such a young girl should have all those things done to her. You see, he agreed with me. I know what I'm talking about. He told me that there was only one man in the whole city who specialized in melanomas, and he told me about this doctor. He raved about him. He said he's a wonderful person who doesn't do any more cutting than he has to, and he's not like your neighborhood retail-store doctor. He's got his office right in a hospital. People come to him from all over the world. He does big operations. Why, he'll take a look at that little thing on your leg and fix it right in the office. All this fuss about cancer. He sounds like a real God to me!"

"What's his name?"

"Here, I've got it written down. It's Doctor Kalman Kolonymus."

"That's the one I saw today."

Her mother screamed.

# CHAPTER
# *THIRTY-TWO*

"**I** CAN only stay a minute," Eve said as she came into Janine's apartment. "I'm having dinner with Henry and Donna tonight. Isn't that cozy?"

Eve sat down at the small table in the dining area.

"You think not?" Janine stopped and looked at Eve.

"I'm an emotionally uptight little person," Eve said as she shook her head, making her tight curls jump like springs. "It took me years to get used to you, I'm just starting to understand my father. And now there's Donna . . ."

"Why don't you try to establish a good relationship with the two of them? Donna should be easy. You don't have any history to get past."

"Does Henry talk to you about Donna?" Eve asked.

"Your father talks to me about everything. I'm his mother confessor." Janine's even voice offered no clue to how she felt about that role. "Look, I do think Donna is good for him. You've met her, haven't you?" She walked around the table to the refrigerator. "How about something to drink? I'm going to have some wine."

"Okay, half a glass for me, and then I've really got to go. And, yes, I've met her," Eve said. "She's a very nice-looking blonde, a little older than me, early thirties maybe. But she acts older. She's got a husband and a kid. You know about her son?"

Eve reached for the glass Janine held out to her. "She's got to have something, to be able to carry off the kind of relationship she has with Henry, go to school, and keep the home fires burning—more power to her. But how about you? I don't know how you stand for it. Don't you ever get the feeling you're just the Greek chorus in Big Henry's life?"

Janine filled her own glass and answered with a smile. "I guess you would look at it that way, but I don't. I have a job I enjoy, a decent income. I have a son who's a healthy heterosexual male, and I expect to be a grandmother some day. I have Henry and two or three other friends I can call on whenever the mood for male companionship strikes me. So you see, who's peripheral to whom depends on where you stand. I also think it has something to do with age. At your age, my relationships were much more intense also. But while we're getting personal, I know your father would like to see you married. Anything on the horizon?"

Eve laughed. "C'mon. Every guy I meet in New York is either an animal or gay—what I'd call Category III. It's very hard to upgrade them."

"You will. Just wait and see."

When Eve got up to leave, Janine hugged her. "Come back soon," she said. "You're as close to a daughter as I'll ever get."

FOUR DAYS AFTER she saw Dr. Kolonymus, Marlene received a telephone call from the hospital admissions office. They had a bed for her. Could she be in between one and three?

Marlene was ready. She had had a good weekend in the Village. The early fall weather had been sunny but cool so she felt cozy wearing her poncho. She had been able to sample all the aromas of the Village—the delicious pastry shop smells, the sweet, earthy odors from the fresh fruit and vegetable stands, the spices from the shops of the Indian merchants, and the smells from the French and Italian restaurants. The cops hadn't hassled her, and the toughs didn't steal anything. The tourists bought a lot. The college kids were back, and she liked to bargain with them without ever turning any of them down. A man who had bought one of her little marble heads recognized it as relief sculpture, and gave her some nice compliments on her work. That felt good.

What the hell, she thought. It has to be done, so let's get it over with.

AFTER THE ADMISSION routine, a pleasant gray-haired lady in a blue smock escorted Marlene to her room on the sixth floor of the hospital.

"Are you a volunteer?" she asked.

"Yes, I love it. They do wonderful work here."

"Anyone in your family . . . ?" Marlene hesitated.

"Me. I have a colostomy and no trouble. I never miss an opening at the Met or a sale at Saks. You'll be fine, too, when you leave."

Marlene nodded hopefully.

She was introduced to nurses, examined by interns, more blood was drawn, more X-rays taken. Then she met the immunology team and had to sign a consent form for some blood and skin tests they wanted to perform. They wanted to check her immune system and her resistance to disease, they explained.

"Okay, anything you want. In for a penny, in for a pound, as they say at the Stage Delicatessen," she joked, covering her anxiety.

Marlene signed the surgical consent forms and had just started to unwind when her mother came in full of instructions, self-pity, and self-recrimination. Mercifully she was displaced by the surgical resident who came by to do his physical assessment. He told Marlene the operation would be the next day. She asked for Dr. Kolonymus and was told she would see him tomorrow. The anesthesia team came in next. Then a nurse brought her a sleeping pill and told her mother that Marlene had to get her rest. Marlene could have kissed the nurse.

214

# CHAPTER
# *THIRTY-THREE*

**T**HE NEXT morning, after the operation, Marlene was awake, but still drowsy and hoarse as a result of the anesthesia tube that had been placed in her trachea. Now she could feel the soreness in her leg and her groin. It wasn't as bad as she expected.

Someone was turning her on one side and then the other. The nurse told her they would be getting her out of bed later that day. Her mother sat with her for long periods of time, helped her with the bedpan and with liquids and, mercifully, did not talk.

FINISHING MORNING ROUNDS a bit early, and even more interested than usual in what his friend was doing, Henry walked briskly down the corridor connecting the hospital to the laboratory building to visit Paul. The repairin research had started.

Technicians were taking mice out of cages and measuring tumors with calipers. Others were injecting animals according to various dose schedules, all the time on the lookout for side effects that might signal problems if repairin were used in patients.

"Well, what do you think, Paul? Anything there?" Henry asked.

"Still too early to tell. Weil says it has some activity in tissue culture. That's a start."

Jarrett Weil, the third member of their triumvirate, was the basic scientist. Rosen was the bridge between the laboratory and the hospital, and Henry was the clinical investigator. However, repairin had been discovered by botanists who were not doing cancer research. Neither were Watson and Crick doing cancer research when they unraveled the double helix, or Jacob and Monod when they discovered how genes are turned on and off. The message that Nature was sending was crystal clear: cancer is part of life, inseparable. Like it or not, it is flesh of our flesh and bone of our bone. All basic science is cancer research.

One of the technicians came over to ask Paul a question. Afterward, Henry said, "Paul, there's pressure from the Animal Care Department. Avery Stemple wants to try out repairin in dogs with cancer. It seems that, at the last research conference, you mentioned that it might have some activity in animals with breast cancer and lymphomas, and he's got a lot of dogs with those diseases."

"That's true," Paul replied. "No cures, but it seems to be having some effect. Yes, it would be good to try it out in larger animals. We'd get data on side effects and dosage that could be useful in patients. All depends on the supply. We'll see if they'll make enough of it at U. Conn. for large animals. It's worth looking into."

THREE WEEKS LATER repairin started to arrive in large quantities, and Avery Stemple's large, round, red face was beaming in anticipation of being involved in a hot research project.

"Avery, where in the hell do you get all those dogs with cancer?" Henry asked.

"We write to all the vets in New York, New Jersey, and Connecticut and tell them what we're doing and what good care the dogs get here. Then when they get a dog with cancer they give

216

their clients the option of destroying the animal or sending it here for keeps."

"Let's go back to my office. I'll show you what we're up to. Also, I just got a gift, a fresh box of Havanas."

They walked past the clean but acrid-smelling kennel area, through animal surgery, to Stemple's office.

"We've got three dogs with measurable tumors that we're giving repairin to. A nine-year-old bitch, mixed breed, with breast cancer—very common in dogs, but not so malignant as in people—and two male boxers, seven and ten years old, with lymphomas. Boxers get more cancer than any other breed."

Avery showed Henry the data. "We started with one milligram per kilo of repairin intravenously every other day, and we're up to twenty-five milligrams per kilo for ten doses. At that dose the dogs develop chills and fever, so we stopped there. We've seen no change in the breast cancer, but in the boxers the lymphoma masses have gotten smaller. We have at least twenty-to-thirty percent decrease in lymph-node size so far."

"That's promising, Avery. You may be onto something."

TWO WEEKS LATER Henry was back in the Animal Care Department, and Avery was giving him a follow-up.

"It's about the same, Hank. We have six dogs on treatment now. Nothing in the breast cancer. The ones with lymphomas have shown some regression of tumors, but still no cures. In the two original boxers, the tumor is starting to grow again."

Henry tried to hide his disappointment. "Well, none of the dogs has died from the stuff, and there's been some antitumor effect, so I think it's worthwhile keeping at it."

DONNA AND RAND were sitting at the round table in the kitchen. Randy was asleep. Rand had been hinting all through dinner that he had something to tell her, which Donna found unnerving. Was he going to tell her he knew about her and Henry? That

217

wouldn't surprise her; sooner or later he'd have to find out. In fact, she often thought of telling him and getting it over with. But things had been going so well with her at school, and Randy was fine; she didn't want to rock the boat. In fact, even with Rand things were better. He seemed happier, more cheerful, somehow more alive. For a long time she had regarded him as an automaton and because of that felt no obligation and certainly no guilt toward him. But with the man speaking to her now, she felt some undeniable connection.

"I wasn't sure, so I didn't tell you," Rand was saying, "but it's all falling into place. Do you remember what I wanted to be when you first met me?"

"An architect," she answered, still wary of where this conversation might be leading.

"I was making too much money in real estate and I loved you too much, so I said 'the hell with it.' But it never left my mind."

"You never said anything about it all these years."

"It seemed out of the question. There was nothing to talk about."

"And now?" Donna was almost afraid to ask.

"That's what I'm excited about. We've made a pile of dough in real estate, and our little firm is being taken over by Merrill Lynch. They're buying up real estate businesses all over the country. When they were talking to us about selling out to them, they listed all the advantages. One was, we could easily transfer to any office that had an opening. The second was, if we wanted to acquire new skills, we could work part-time and they would pay the tuition if we studied something even vaguely related to the business. I said 'Architecture?' and they said 'Fine!' I got a list of schools that would take part-time students and a list of offices with openings, and I came up with a good one—Phoenix! What do you say to that?"

Donna didn't say anything. She poured herself a cup of coffee, holding one hand with the other so it wouldn't tremble. Her first thought was: My God, he followed us out there, and this is some

218

sort of trap. She asked, "Is all of this serious? And why Phoenix, of all places?"

"Why not. It was the only city where there was a place for me in the office and at a school. The weather will be just great for the kid."

Donna sat there, poured some sugar into her coffee, and stirred the spoon slowly. Maybe it is just a coincidence. Maybe he really does want to make a move. My God, Rand could do it and Henry couldn't. She still didn't say anything.

"Well, what do you say?" Rand asked.

"It's all such a surprise. Can I hold off comments till the dust settles?"

"Sure. I'll can it all if you don't want to go. By the way, happy anniversary. Remember?"

"Happy anniversary," Donna said. "You certainly have a knack for surprises."

Donna stared at the ceiling all night. Amazing, amazing, amazing, she kept on repeating. Here I've been worrying what to tell him, and he's the one who drops a bomb! Phoenix, of all places. It's crossroads time for me. If I say no, then I've got to tell him. If I take my chances with Henry, if I marry him, Rand will leave and go to Phoenix. A clean break like that would avoid a lot of messiness for me and Randy. We'd move into Henry's apartment—that is, if Rand would really leave. If I lead him right, I think he would, and then I'd have Henry and the city.

But do I really want to buy into that? I guess the bottom line is, do I love Henry enough to do it? Talking it over with him wouldn't help me decide. I know he loves me. It really is such a strong love that it makes up for a lot. And I know he needs me. But what about Rand? I know this is his big chance to break out, the same as I needed a chance to break out. What'll I do?

Word came from the back of her mind. Randy.

THE NEXT MORNING at breakfast Donna didn't say a word. Her head hurt from lack of sleep, and her expression discouraged conversation. Rand acted as if nothing had happened. She'd asked for time, and he'd give it to her. Quietly he finished his breakfast and got ready to leave.

He walked down the short, inside steps leading to the side door off the kitchen and into a small mudroom where winter things were kept. He picked a light coat off a hook.

Donna stood up and called out, "I'll go!" Then she fairly collapsed in her chair. She put her head down on the table and sobbed between wheezing breaths.

Rand ran to her. He got down on one knee, put his arm around her shoulders and his head next to hers, and kissed her. Then it came to her, like an arrow hitting the mark. Of course he knows about Henry and me. That's why it's Phoenix—he's rubbing my nose in it.

"WHAT WAS THE report on my pimple?" Marlene asked, as Dr. Kolonymus came into her room.

"It was malignant," he said quietly.

"Did everything go all right?" she persisted.

"Everything is going to be fine. I am expecting some more reports today from the lab, and when I come back tomorrow I'll give you the entire picture."

His manner was so candid, no patient would guess he had all the reports he needed for a decision.

The next morning about ten o'clock Marlene was out of bed, cheerful and relieved it had been so simple. Why was her mother taking it so hard? Everyone else was so pleasant and relaxed. And she had such a small bandage over the wound on her leg— and not a very large one on her groin and nothing at all behind her knee. It couldn't have been a very large skin graft after all. About ten minutes later, Dr. Kolonymus came in and introduced Dr. Robert Sandburgh from the Rehabilitation Department and Miss Emily Wyeth, his assistant. The three gathered around the bed and then closed the curtain dividing her bed from that of her elderly Armenian roommate. Suddenly Marlene felt scared

220

again. Everyone looked so damned somber. Dr. Kolonymus forced a small smile.

"This is the situation, Marlene. We removed the skin lesion, and it was a recurrence of the melanoma. It had begun to spread. There were several tiny growths around the original site, like daughters. Before proceeding with the skin graft we took a biopsy from the groin. There was one dark lymph node that looked suspicious."

"Don't tell me, I can guess."

Dr. Kolonymus nodded. "We then explored deeper and removed many other nodes and they were all negative. The groin is as far as the tumor has gotten, but it has gotten that far. There was no point in doing a skin graft."

"Why not? Does that mean you got it all out?"

"Marlene, when there's a tumor in the lower leg and tumor in the groin, there have to be cancer cells in between, and the pathologist told us this is a very malignant tumor. The only way to get rid of the rest of it is to remove your leg. There is no other way."

Marlene turned pale. Just when you think you're home free, you're caught, she thought.

Then she found her voice. "You used the word 'daughters.' 'Only the ones with daughters call forth the Angel of Death.'"

She stared into space as she spoke. Dr. Kolonymus had the good sense not to ask her what she meant.

"Doctor Sandburgh here is going to tell you how we'll get you on your feet again. But first I'm going to have Miss Wyeth from Rehabilitation speak to you."

"Marlene, I know this is hard to take," the young woman said. "I'm going to be seeing you a lot and help keep you up and moving. By the way, what's your occupation?"

"I'm a sculptor," Marlene said absently.

"That's great. We'll get you up and working so fast you won't believe it. Tomorrow, if it's okay with you, I'd like to introduce you to a girl who had the same operation two years ago."

Dr. Kolonymus put his hand on her shoulder. "We shouldn't delay. We should do the operation this week."

For the next few days Marlene was quiet and withdrawn. She would not allow herself to think ahead. She listened to the news a lot. When she wasn't dozing from the sedatives, she tried to watch television but found she couldn't. The staff tried to keep her busy. They introduced her to several rehabilitated amputees, but she couldn't bring herself to identify with them.

The day before surgery, she was busy with blood tests, X-rays, a visit by the anesthesiologist again, and finally the nurse holding the consent form for her to sign.

Marlene held the consent form in one hand and a pen in the other. Up to this moment she had been resigned to the amputation. It had been explained to her by the doctors, the social workers, the psychologists. But now she froze.

"I can't sign this. Please take it away. I have to think for a few minutes."

She got out of bed very slowly, first one leg, then the other. There was no pain in either leg, and both functioned as they always had. She put on her bathrobe and paced up and down the hospital corridor, pressing down on one leg and then the other, reassuring herself.

I can live like this for months, maybe years, all in one piece, she thought. Then: I have cancer. I'm going to die if I don't have that operation. But what it comes down to is that I'm more afraid of losing a leg and becoming a cripple than I am of dying. I want to live the way I am as long as I can. I can't sign a consent to tear myself into half a body tied to a wheelchair, just for time. I can't do it! she screamed inside her head.

Marlene walked to the nurses' station. Walked, walked, walked, comfortable, firm, secure steps. The nurse was there at her desk and so was Marlene's consent form.

"Nurse, I'd like to leave the hospital. Now."

"You mean sign out against advice?"

"Yes. It's my right, isn't it?"

222

The nurse was flustered. "Will you wait just a moment? I have to check."

She went down the hall to an office where a group of nurses was having a meeting. Among them was Miss Flannery, recently promoted to supervisor. If there was one thing Veronica Flannery knew, it was the rules.

In a few minutes the floor nurse came back to Marlene. "I'll have to notify Dr. Kolonymus, but you do have the right to sign out against advice."

She walked around her desk, found a form, and gave it to Marlene, who signed it with determination. Meanwhile, the nurse was calling Dr. Kolonymus. She found out he was in surgery and could not be reached. She turned to Marlene, "I can't keep you here, but it would be better if you waited for your doctor."

Marlene thrust the newly signed release form at her.

"I have to leave now," she said. "Tell Dr. Kolonymus I'll explain everything to him later."

Marlene dressed as quickly as she could, then found she could not escape without passing through the hospital finance office first. She took that in her stride, and, as if by a miracle, she was out on the street in front of the hospital.

THE SUNSHINE WRAPPED itself snugly around her from head to toe. The cool air ventilated every pore of her skin; she forcefully inhaled the street air in order to dispel the hospital odors. It felt so good. Every deliberate step assured her she had done the right thing.

The next day she went back to work. She felt just fine.

For about two days. Then her mother began badgering her to get other opinions. Marlene thought perhaps it would be a sensible thing to do. Over the next few days she saw several doctors who also advised amputation and a radiation therapist who did not want to treat her at all.

The next week she took a vacation in the Bahamas. It would be

223

fun-in-the-sun, no cancer, entertainment every night, easy relationships, sex whenever it came along. But it didn't turn out that way. The weather was fine; the beach and ocean were great; the entertainment was thoroughly professional—but the men that came along were sleazy, and she didn't find their sexual advances and fraudulent passion any more convincing than her own devil-may-care stance. Besides, there was a throbbing in her right groin that made her freedom incomplete.

# CHAPTER
# THIRTY-FOUR

**T**HE SMALL sound within Marlene became more insistent. You panicked and ran, she told herself. But there is nothing to run to, no hope. You can't run away from the cancer. It runs with you. The hospital is offering you a way out—at a price. She went home.

But she did not return to Curie.

Instead, she worked and sculpted harder than ever. Only when she was working could she escape. She stayed with Ronnie often, but he had changed toward her. His lovemaking was not as passionate and spontaneous as it had been. It was somehow too meticulous, and he spent a long time in the shower afterward. One night he was for the first time impotent, and still he took a long shower.

My God, he thinks he's going to catch cancer from me, Marlene realized. She dressed and left.

Ronnie was not the only one. At work, no one ever spoke about her cancer operation, but somehow they knew, and some women would not use the same ladies' room as she or drink from the same water fountain. She also sensed that others went out of their way to avoid her, as if consigning her to another sphere, breaking their ties with her now so that they would not feel so bad "later."

One evening she went home after a long and tiring day, hoping to slip quietly into the apartment and go right to bed, but her mother and father were quarreling in the kitchen. Nothing unusual about that. In the foyer, she heard what they were quarreling about, and it so shattered her that she left silently, leaving the door ajar.

She stayed in a hotel that night, and the next morning she called Dr. Kolonymus for an appointment. He was in his office and told her to come right over. This time, she thought as the taxi sped to the massive white building, it looked like a tower of hope. She went to his office with determination and told him what had made her sign herself out of the hospital and what had happened. She started in a clear, strong voice, then stopped short and covered her eyes with her hands. Her body shook with soft sobs. After that release: "I could take the stupid people at work. Ronnie, well, once an idiot, always an idiot. But my parents! I went home last night. They didn't hear me come in. They were yelling at each other in the kitchen. You know what about? Graves! Cemeteries! They were arguing about where they were going to bury me."

Then she wiped her eyes and looked up. "I just can't go on like this. I once read a poem about fighting against that dark night. I want you to help me fight.

"I thought I could live it up until it was time for me to check out. It was a great plan. I really thought I could carry it off. But I couldn't. I'll go along with whatever you want to do."

She was in the hospital the next day and operated on two days later. This time her recovery was slow. She could not get out of bed unless she was lifted. This the nurses did twice a day. During surgery, they had first completed the exploration of the lymph nodes in the abdomen to be sure there was no further spread. This would have precluded the amputation, but there was no such evidence, so the operation was carried out as planned.

Over the following few weeks her physical and psychological recovery was better than she could have believed. She was looking forward to being discharged and resuming her life.

226

THE HOSPITAL ART show was an annual affair. It was held in the main dining room, so the entire staff and ambulatory patients could see it during the day. In the evenings, a series of parties was held there, and it was then that most of the paintings were sold. A committee of prominent artists decided on the many awards. There were so many that everyone received something, either an award or a letter of commendation. The art show was a great morale booster.

Henry had tried to get Donna to put some of her things in the show. She did not yet feel comfortable in his environment and declined the invitation to participate or attend.

Eve wasn't too happy about going. With her well-developed aversion to the hospital, it was an effort for her, but she agreed to accompany her father.

The reception they attended was one of the few social events of the year where the entire medical staff gathered. Happily, it was going well. Eve was surprisingly friendly and relaxed, and Henry was enjoying himself also. Tara was part of Henry's little group, and about halfway through the evening, Janine, who had been helping to sell tickets at the door, joined them. Eve left the group to look at the exhibits—there might be a story there somewhere. She stopped before a black velvet panel with relief sculptures and put her hand to the pendant hanging from her neck. Then she went back to get Henry. She tapped him on the shoulder and drew him away from the group he was chatting with.

"Henry, come look a minute."

Eve pointed to Marlene's work. "I know the artist who did these. She's the person I bought this from." She showed her father the marble pendant.

"I interviewed her for the magazine. She can't be a patient here. Maybe she's a volunteer. Please find out," Eve urged.

Henry looked at the name: "Lena Lowell."

"I don't know who she is," he said. "Let's ask Mrs. Lieberman. She's in charge."

They walked over to the desk at the entrance.

227

"Lena Lowell? Oh, yes, she really is someone special. Very talented. Art isn't just a hobby to her. She's the star of occupational therapy. She's going home in a few days. She's a patient of Doctor Kolonymus."

Henry spotted Dr. Kolonymus and his wife talking in a small group.

"Kalman, can I see you a minute? My daughter, Eve, thinks she knows Lena Lowell. Mrs. Lieberman says she's a patient of yours."

"Lena, you call her? Yes, she is my patient. Marlene Lowell. She was here earlier this evening. She has malignant melanoma. We had to remove her leg. With any luck we'll have a cure."

"Her leg was amputated?" Eve was stunned. "That doesn't seem possible. I just saw her in Greenwich Village a short time ago. She was fine."

"She's in room six-twelve," Dr. Kolonymus said. "Why don't you say hello? A visit would do her good. I think she'll be going home at the end of the week."

"I'll go see her now," Eve said.

"I don't think you ought to do it now," Henry said. "It's late. There are some people here who haven't seen you in years. I'm sure you can pick a better time to visit her."

The first words to rise to Eve's lips were, "Cut it out, Dad!" But she blocked them. Instead, she said, "If I don't go now, I don't know when I'll see her."

THE DOOR OF room 612 was open. The elderly Armenian lady had gone home, and a middle-aged woman with many visitors was on one side of the room. The curtain dividing the area was drawn. Marlene was in bed reading the "Apartments for Rent" column in the *Times*.

"Marlene? Hi, can I come in?" Eve asked. "I was at the art show downstairs and saw your things. I couldn't believe you were sick. It seems like only a short time ago," Eve said, clasping the pendant.

Marlene put down the paper and looked at Eve. A short time ago! It was as if meeting Eve had happened to another person in another world.

"C'mon in. Remember how uninteresting I told you I was? Well, I wish it were still that way. But I'm okay. Sit down."

Eve pulled a chair over to the bed. "That article I did on you, it didn't get published. It should have, though. I thought it was really first class."

"Please, no more good news. I couldn't take it."

Marlene was happy to see this silly kid who apparently liked her. "I'm about to be discharged. But I'm not going back home, or to that office. And I'm through teaching others how to make graven images. I've just been going through the papers, looking for a place where I can live and set up a studio."

"I'd love to scout for you—I'm good at that," Eve said impulsively. "Let me pick some out, and all you'll have to do is look at them and say yes or no."

EVE REJOINED HENRY, Janine, and some others who had remained to the end of the party. Her face still wore an expression of astonishment.

"Were things bad up there?" Henry asked.

"I still can't believe it. Losing a leg like that—and now she's ready to go out and live on her own. What guts."

"It's a shame," Janine replied. "If you can think of any way I can help . . ."

Henry also tried to be supportive. "I'll stop in and see her tomorrow. Perhaps if I speak to her about rehabilitation, talk about positive things, it would help her morale."

Tara was going to say, "A sculptress—well, then, it could have been worse, couldn't it?" But she caught herself just in time.

JARRETT WEIL MOVED through the crowded hospital cafeteria, carefully balancing his tray, and sat down at a table with Paul and Henry.

"I've been looking for you, Paul. We went over the repairin results, and it just hasn't panned out. I know how keen you've been on the stuff, but we don't think we can do any more with it. Sorry, old man."

"Don't make it sound personal, Jarrett. This wouldn't be the first time an idea of mine didn't work out. I don't think I'm ready to quit on repairin quite yet, though. The antitumor effect *is* slight, but I'm going to try to boost it by using it in combination with other anticancer agents."

WHEN HENRY RETURNED to his office late that afternoon, Julia West was on the line.

"Hello, Mrs. West, how are you doing?" Henry asked. "Dr. Stuart's last letter from Denver said you were holding your own just fine."

"Now, no samples from the honey bucket, Henry. I'm not as good as I was a couple of months ago—considerably less energy— that just means I'm down to normal for most other people."

"Are you continuing to take the chemotherapy?" Henry asked.

"Yes, I am. It's probably doing something. That's what I called you about. My son set up an endowment for chemotherapy research out here, and we are seeking a scientific advisory board from all over the country. I'd like it if you would accept an invitation to be the first member. How about it?"

"I'd be honored."

"John'll send you the details."

"I look forward to his letter."

"The first disease to be studied will be cancer of the colon. Nothing wrong with that, is there? The Wests are never completely altruistic, don't you know? But in the long run, all you brains will make the policy. Want to know what else I'm doing? Well, I started a free cooking school on my ranch. We bus in city girls from Denver. We started out last July as a summer program. It's gotten to be so popular we're going to keep it going. The best damn thing I ever did. It keeps me entertained—and

230

well fed too, mind you. Also, it costs a whole lot less than those stupid trips I used to take."

After the call Henry turned to Tara. "Put that case in the 'win' column."

Among the patients who became part of the fabric of his life, the win column was short lately. He had lost too many, Frank Walsh among them. But that one wasn't a total loss, Frank Junior looked his spitting image in the picture Mary Walsh had sent Henry. Stanley Kaprowski, on the other hand, was not a complete win. He had become a juvenile delinquent. He had been brought to family court several times, always for the same offense—slashing the tires of cars with M.D. plates.

# CHAPTER
# *THIRTY-FIVE*

THE NEXT time Donna came to the city she did not go
to the Art Students League first, but directly to Henry's
apartment. She carried a bag with things for dinner. The
decision had been made, and she couldn't put off telling him any
longer. He could be there any time now.

Henry arrived home early. Tonight he thought he'd rest for a
few minutes, then go to meet her. However, as soon as he turned
the latch and opened the door, he heard rattling in the kitchen.
He immediately perked up.

"Donna!" he called. "Skipping class?"

"Yup," came the reply from the kitchen.

Henry threw his coat on a chair and made right for the kitchen,
kissed her, and gave her a bear hug that lifted her off the floor.

"Watch out for the lungs!" she laughed, taking a noisy breath
as she straightened out her blouse.

They walked hand in hand into the dining room. It was just
getting dark. The lights of Park Avenue sparkled through the
long windows like clusters of stars. Henry moved to the liquor
cabinet.

"I don't want anything to drink, Henry. I made some coffee.
Let's go to the kitchen," Donna said.

"Henry, something's happened."

Henry knew that if Rand had become suspicious it would not have been difficult to find out about them. All he had to do was follow her one evening.

"It was too good to last," she said. "I knew something was going to go wrong. I used to get the willies thinking about it."

"Tell me what's happened!"

Donna told him the whole story, and Henry saw immediately that it was immaterial whether or not Rand knew. Henry had been upstaged and outmaneuvered—whether deliberately or inadvertently made no difference. He was going to lose the most important thing in his life.

"I feel like I've been shot out of the sky. And for all we know it's just a coincidence."

"No, Rand knows, all right." Donna was resting her elbows on the table, her head in her hands. Henry put his arm around her shoulders.

"He would never just come out and say it, never make an accusation. That's not his style. He's never done that during our entire marriage. Once I got into an argument with his mother. It was just before we were going on vacation. I was furious, and I walked out of the house. As I backed out of his mother's driveway, I clipped her fender. I think it was an accident, maybe it wasn't. The next day, Rand turned around and bought his mother a new car and told me we didn't have any money for vacation. That's the kind of thing he does. I wish he'd scream or shout. Just get it out and get it over."

She kept on shaking her head. "I couldn't sleep at all the night he dropped Phoenix in my lap, and then I didn't sleep last night tormenting myself about telling you."

"Why did you give him an answer right away? We didn't have a chance to talk it over together."

"Henry, darling, I've had this discussion in my head a hundred times. Don't you think I've looked at each point over and over again? Down deep in my bones I knew what I'd do when it happened. Besides, I can breathe being sad and unhappy, but indecision strangles me."

"I'm in love with you, Donna." Henry caressed her shoulders. "I always will be."

"Before I got married, when Rand and I got serious, my mother once asked me, 'Are you in love with him?' I said, 'Sure, I love him.' She said, 'There's a difference. Are you in love with him?' I said I didn't know the difference. But, oh, my God, I do now. If somebody asked me even now, how do you feel about your husband?, I'd say, well, I don't hate him. I just get numb when I'm near him. If only life were simpler."

Donna leaned her head against his chest.

"I thought if we took it slowly we could create a new family, you and Randy and me," Henry said.

"That's the problem, don't you see?" Donna spoke softly. "Randy is close to his father. Rand spends a lot of time with him, and they both love it. One of my chief joys, outside of you, is seeing the two of them together. I know I told you some things about Rand that make him out to be cold and indifferent, but that's just because he never shows his feelings, except with Randy. Poor Randy doesn't have too many friends, and his dad has stepped in, and the boy needs him. I could never do anything that would spoil that. And there's no way I could leave Randy."

Donna took a breath. "I owe them both something, Henry. Sometimes people have to sacrifice a lot for loyalty, don't they? Even each other."

She raised up her head. Henry kissed her very gently—then brusquely pulled away. "Goddamnit, I'm not going to take this lying down. I just can't let you walk away. I'm going to have it out with him face to face."

"Henry, please. What do you think will happen? Do you think he'll give in? Are you going to have a fight to the death? You're not two rams on a mountaintop. You know who'll really get hurt? Me."

"What *can* I do?" Henry said, his voice rising with frustration.

"Listen to me. Let it be. Let's see how things work out. Let's see what happens."

"I know what'll happen. Every day we'll drift further and further apart. And if I don't fight for you, every day I'll regret it."

"Please don't—you can't win. It'll make everything worse."

"You want me to stand by passively, do nothing?" Henry said, eyes flashing.

"Just be patient—something will work out for us. Do it for me."

"How can you give up so easily?" Henry shouted.

She lowered her head. "You make me sound treacherous." Her voice broke. "Or even worse, like someone who is just playing around."

He lifted her chin and stroked her cheek, finally accepting what he could not change. "Will you be happy, Donna?" he said.

"Happy?" She shivered. Her face was compressed with sadness, like a face at a grave.

He thought for a second about Janine. She would have cut through all this in a flash. *"Fin de l'affaire* and that's it!"

He wasn't prepared to do that. "This doesn't mean I'll never see you again," he said.

"Oh, no. I've thought that all through, too. Mother still lives here, and I'll come back to see her as often as I can. Same time next year?" she smiled wanly.

"And there's Randy. He'll still have to have his checkups," Henry said.

"Isn't it horrible to have to be grateful for that!" Donna broke down, sobbing spasmodically, her breathing getting bad.

Henry picked her up in his arms and carried her to the bedroom. He wished it were on another planet.

# CHAPTER
# *THIRTY-SIX*

"LENA, I found it! A studio on Perry Street," Eve said.

"Remember, I'm on crutches," Marlene said.

"It's a first floor walk-in. No steps. High ceilings and big windows. There's a parking lot for trucks across the street, so there's no building to shut out the sunlight. It used to be some sort of shop, but it's partitioned off in back for a bedroom and a kitchen."

"How much is it?"

"Don't worry, the price is right. Get a pass, and I'll pick you up at the hospital entrance."

Marlene had been transferred from the hospital to the extended care unit where the rehabilitation people continued to work with her. She stalled about going home, but she could get out on a pass whenever she liked.

Marlene signed the lease straightaway. Perry Street and the surrounding neighborhood in the West Village were made up of small artisan shops, warehouses for the nearby docks, and light industry, all mixed with some old residential buildings. The streets were cobblestone; the sidewalks rectangular slabs of slate, approximately horizontal. The sidewalks were often used for parking because the streets were so narrow, but on weekends the area was deserted. You could easily get to the shops on

236

Bleecker and Hudson Streets. It was a great area for strolling, Marlene thought, even for a person with one leg and a prosthesis.

"I like everything about this place," Marlene said, swinging lightly around the barnlike interior on her crutches. She could not manage the prosthesis very well yet.

"Wait till we paint it and fix it up," Eve said, flushed with pleasure. "I'll bet if we had a party here one evening and passed out brushes, we'd have it all done in no time."

"I'd love to have you help me, but I don't think I'll be up to partying for a while. Besides, I have something else on my mind right now. I had an opportunity tossed into my lap, and I don't know if I'm up to it or not. Doctor Morgan Evans came to see me a few days ago. I met him briefly when he stopped by my panel at the hospital art show with his wife. She bought the large piece, the horse and rider—you know, the one that looks like one of the Elgin marbles. Doctor Evans asked me if I was a professional artist, and, well, I'm not going back to that office or to the school, so I said 'Yes, I am.' He asked me if I would do a bust of his wife for her sixtieth birthday. He asked if I could do it in marble, and I said yes again. Of course I'm not *sure* I can, but I'm going to give it one helluva try. I'm charging two thousand dollars. I figure it will take about three months."

"Two thousand dollars? I'd charge more for three months' work," Eve said.

"If I were in a real studio with others around, assistants—but on my own—I think I may have bitten off more than I should have," Marlene confessed.

"Let me help you," Eve said. "I'd love to be your assistant. I bet I'd be good at it, too."

Marlene did need help, but she declined. "I couldn't handle that for a lot of reasons, mostly psychological. What I need is a partner, Eve. Someone to work with as an equal. If I had an assistant it would be someone who leaned on me for initiative and decisions, and I'm not in a position for anyone to lean on me." She tilted to the side precariously. Righting herself, she laughed.

"Okay, so we'll be partners," Eve said. "I'll be the business partner and you're the artist. And I can still be your assistant. You could teach me how to do some of the donkeywork around the studio. I'd love to help with the Evans job."

IN THREE WEEKS, with a lot of help from friends and a few hours' time from hired local workmen, they had a functional studio, attractive in an unfinished sort of way. Then they started doing the bust. First Eve and Marlene visited the Evans's apartment. Eve took photographs of Mrs. Evans, and Marlene started to work on the clay model, until she got the right expression, the right hair styling. There were many visits and many changes until everyone—including Dr. Morgan Evans—was satisfied. At last Marlene completed the final clay model. It was as good as anything she had ever done. She was feeling well, her spirits were high.

After a lot of practice after work, sometimes going late into the evenings and on weekends, Eve had learned how to be a useful assistant. Slowly and carefully they did the transfer from clay to marble. And then Marlene took over again, doing the final sculpting and the hand pumicing she was so good at.

When they first got underway, Eve, proud to show her surrogate mother what she was doing, had invited Janine to visit the studio and meet Marlene. Today Janine had left the hospital early to meet with a new theater group in the Village. On the way, she stopped by the studio. Eve hadn't returned from work, but Marlene invited her in for coffee.

Janine settled herself on a cushioned stool. "I think it's so lovely that Eve has found a good friend who brings out her best qualities."

Marlene handed her a cup of instant cappuccino. "I really owe Eve a lot," she said. "I'd like to do as much for her some day."

"Don't make your arrangement sound one-way. You're doing something for Eve, too."

"I suppose so, in a way," Marlene said reflectively.

"More than you think," Janine replied. "That one had a diffi-

238

cult time getting her act together. I've been the unobtrusive observer for many years—since she was born, in fact. This is as stable as I've ever seen her. Really, she used to be an emotional acrobat!"

"When you sculpt, it's easy to talk," Marlene said. "We've been doing a lot of both. It's marvelous therapy. Eve has told me of your special relationship with Doctor Nyren."

"No euphemisms, my dear. We're old lovers. No great heights of passion, more's the pity, but it lasted."

"Eve told me you never wanted to be more than friends."

"Good Lord, the girl's a fool! I'd have married him if he'd asked me. But he never came close. Anyway, he has someone who's right for him now, and I'm okay as I am."

The bust was completed the first week of December. It had taken more than three months of hard work. Both Marlene and Eve found it difficult to believe how well their first endeavor turned out. The head had been impressive in clay but in marble it was luminous and graceful. There was Mrs. Morgan Evans at sixty, the face showing the contours of age but without a wrinkle. It was the image that she projected of herself, attractive, strong, with a slight smile and raised brow as if she were asking a pleasant question. In fact, as you moved around the bust the expression actually changed. Dr. Evans had tears in his eyes when he saw it. Mrs. Evans kissed Marlene.

Other people liked the bust, and within six weeks Marlene and Eve had two more commissions. Marlene's rehabilitation was progressing too. She still made some relief sculptures for pendants, and with her prosthesis she could go back to her old stand on Sixth Avenue whenever she needed a change. There, feeling the pulse of the city again, it was almost as if nothing had changed.

The winter months flew by in a flurry of marble chips, bits of plasticene, and the whir of the polishing wheels. Marlene could make her way about the city herself and could even manage the subways.

The first new commission, by a friend of Mrs. Evans, had been completed, and they were now working on a bust of Dr. Wheaton Delaney, Mrs. Evans's son-in-law, the president of a small New England college. The graduating class was giving the bust to the college. The two were also working on their first speculative project. It was to be a marble figure of an infant with its arms extended.

Marlene had gone to Massachusetts to do the clay model, and Eve had started shaping the marble. Marlene returned to town on a dark, cold, snowy afternoon. The lighted studio looked warm and inviting.

"Welcome home," Eve called out at the door. A cab driver stood holding a large box while Marlene was closing her purse.

"Hey, lady, where do you want me to put this? It's heavy. What have you got in there? Rocks?" He turned to Marlene, who was just starting to make her way out of the cab.

"Put it just inside the door," she told him. She wouldn't take any assistance, but as she got out of the taxi she muttered some expletives under her breath to reinforce the special effort she had to make to get out of the cab by herself. When both legs were planted on the ground she held the door frame, bent her head, and lifted her body out of the cab, then grabbed the top of the cab door and stood straight. She continued across the tilted sidewalk, covered with wet snow, and walked very carefully into the studio on her own.

Once inside, she peeled off her heavy coat with its wet-wool odor and her boots. She went behind the bedroom partition, took off her prosthesis, and got into a baggy sweater and slacks with one leg pinned up. She took a pair of crutches and swung out to a couch on the other side of the partition. It faced a wall with a Franklin stove. This corner of the studio was arranged as a living room. Across the bedroom alcove was the wall with the kitchen.

"How about something to drink? You must be exhausted," Eve said.

"I'd love something, but aren't you going home?"

"Not in this snow. I've already had a couple of martinis to

240

warm me up, and I made us a real good dinner. Let me show you what else I did."

Eve indicated the blocked-out marble ready for pointing. "It's a beautiful stone," she said. "I was lucky to find it. Now let's take a look at what you brought back."

Eve unpacked the large cardboard box the taxi driver had brought in and took out the clay bust of the young college president. Again, in the visage of the bust there was that glint of personality that for a second made you forget it was inanimate.

Dinner was good. The drapes of the twelve-foot windows were closed, shutting out the storm. Wind lashed sleet against the windows. The small stove and the candles made the studio cozy.

"I think I'd still be a basket case if you hadn't dropped by that night at the hospital," Marlene said. "I want you to know I'll always be grateful to you."

"What you don't know, Lena, is that for the first time in my life I feel like a complete human being. I was always peripheral to my successful parents, not quite needed as a child or an adolescent. This is the best my life has ever been."

They both felt awkward at these confessions, and they busied themselves cleaning the dishes, sweeping the floor, listening to the news, and making small talk. Eve made another pitcher of martinis. They sat on the couch and sipped slowly. Eve looked at Marlene with tears in her eyes, put her arms around her, and kissed her. Marlene returned the kiss, then stiffened a little when Eve did not relinquish the embrace. Eve kissed her again, on her neck and then on the lips. Marlene felt a wave of embarrassment that was pushed aside by a flood of affection, and the two slid from the couch to the floor. Eve took a large quilt from the bed, and the two pairs of arms, two torsos, and three legs remained together through the night.

In the morning nothing was said of the previous night, but a new tenderness entered their relationship. Eve went off to her job at the magazine. The snow had fallen, the sky was clear, and the air was crisp. Marlene was going to go shopping in the

241

neighborhood and then in the afternoon make some jewelry. She needed a change from sculpting.

Marlene noticed that she had become physically stronger—probably from the effort of using the crutches and prosthesis. She could sculpt for long periods of time and not get tired. She could cook, clean, and still put in a full day with hammer and chisel or pumicing stone. It was a source of satisfaction to her that she was up to so much hard work.

Something else surprised her. She was able to concentrate in a way she never could before. She had always been able to get her work done, but this kind of concentration, four or five hours at a time, was a new experience for her. She had heard that artists and writers and musicians sometimes were able to get into their work in an all-consuming way, achieving a concentration as precisely focused as a beam of light, so fine it illuminated one object only. There were no aching muscles, no stinging scars, nothing unsightly or ugly, and no ticking clocks, no dripping faucets, no street traffic—just perfect harmony of hand on metal and stone. No analgesic could do as much, no narcotic could come close. The only requirement was that she had to be alone. When the experience came to a close, she could feel herself coming down, and she couldn't control that either. Afterward she would take a cup of coffee and sit quietly, in a kind of tranquil detachment, amazed at what she had achieved.

Her best work was always done in this altered state of consciousness. It was as if under these circumstances she could do nothing wrong. Intuitively, automatically, she made the right moves. On several occasions she found herself thinking, If I had to go through the cancer, the surgery, all the torment, to come to this incredible experience, it was worth it. The next question always was, Would I do it again if I had a choice? And always the same answer: That's not a fair question.

# CHAPTER
# *THIRTY-SEVEN*

URING THE remainder of the winter, the bust of the college president was completed. Marlene and Eve also worked carefully and lovingly on the figure of the infant. Henry hadn't seen Eve so happy since she was a child.

"Here's an invitation to show our stuff at the Seaman's Institute, of all places." Marlene was reading the day's mail.

"I guess that's me. They're having a fund-raiser and asking artists in the Village to help. Well, I'm your business manager. I submitted some photos, and I see they liked them." Eve was pleased with her initiative.

"If I had more energy, I'd do it." Marlene gave a deep sigh and pushed herself back on her chair. "Lately, I work for half a day and I'm bushed."

Eve responded, "Maybe you're not resting enough or getting the right vitamins." Then she thought for a moment. "You know, I think you've lost some weight this last month. Have you been to Doctor Kolonymus recently?"

"I'm seeing him every two months, and he says I'm fine. There's nothing to worry about on that score."

"Well, packing a solid meal might beat nibbling all day long. How about going out for dinner to that new Greek place on Bleecker Street?"

"HELLO, HENRY? I have a young woman with melanoma who has liver metastasis. I think she needs chemotherapy. Can you see her soon?"

Dr. Kolonymus had a chart in front of him with a diagram of a torso, on which he had drawn an enlarged liver. Laboratory results showing abnormal liver function tests were listed next to the figure.

Henry replied, "Is there evidence of metastasis anywhere else?"

"We haven't done an extensive workup yet. The white count and platelets are good, but the hemoglobin is down to eight grams. This is a fast-growing tumor, I'm afraid. I saw her six weeks ago and she was fine."

"We may want to admit her. She may be suitable for one of the research protocols. Let me look at her records. What's her name?"

"Marlene Lowell."

The name jogged Henry's memory. "She's a friend of my daughter's. She's the one Eve went to see the night of the art show. In fact, I saw her once myself."

"I didn't make the connection when I called you, but I remember now. I'm afraid it's a bad situation."

WHEN MARLENE RETURNED to the studio she had some news.

"I just saw Kalman, the kindly Kolonymus, and he's going to fix me up. But he said I have to go into the hospital for a few weeks, so you'll have lots of time to fool around in the studio all by yourself."

With deliberation, Eve rested her chisel and stubby hammer next to a block of marble, from which a head was emerging, and got down off the stool. Slowly she wiped her hands on a towel that was in the big pocket of her smock.

"Why do you have to go into the hospital?" The fatigue and the weight loss she had noticed suddenly became ominous.

Marlene sat sideways on the couch. Sitting always relieved the

244

pressure of the prosthesis. "He just said it's my blood, that I'm anemic and I need some shots for my liver, and that they could do the job better in the hospital. I'm not afraid of the place any more, you know. Best of all, I don't have to pay for it. This time it's on the hospital. The part of the hospital I'm going to is paid for by federal funds, so it doesn't matter what kind of health insurance you have." She showed Eve the tan admission slip in a light-hearted way.

Eve read it, just managing to keep her feelings under control. There was a welcoming sentence and then it said:

| | |
|---|---|
| Patient's name: | Marlene Lowell |
| To be admitted to: | 8th Floor, Curie Hospital |
| Responsible physician: | Chemotherapy Section, Phase II Team |
| Charge to: | Cooperative Chemotherapy Group B NCI Protocol 128-1201 |

Eve had heard "eighth floor" all of her life and knew that Henry's experimental chemotherapy patients were hospitalized there. "That's fine, I know you'll get good care there," she said quietly, while hammers were pounding her eyeballs and a chisel was picking away at her heart.

THE ADMISSION ROUTINE was familiar to Marlene. She brought along her own pajamas and toilet articles and things to read. She said, "Hi, I'm back again!" to the nurse who had drawn a blood specimen from her during her first hospitalization, but the nurse didn't remember her. A different volunteer took her up to the eighth floor. No, she didn't need a wheelchair. She was fine. This floor didn't look like the one she had been on. It was divided into sections separated by frosted glass partitions. There were also some single rooms off by themselves. A small sign on the wall said: "Phase I and Phase II Studies." She wondered if Phase II was better than Phase I.

245

"Phase II," she said to the volunteer. "Sounds like the name of a smart boutique."

The volunteer smiled as she took Marlene to her room. This room had six beds instead of two. Each was divided by a partition for privacy, and in the center of each room there was a desk with a nurse and a nurse's aide.

Shortly after she got into bed, Dr. Kolonymus came in. He briefly examined her again, and then sat down and explained why she was in that part of the hospital.

"I'm not going to be your doctor this time, Marlene, but I'll still come and see you. I think you know the doctor who will be in charge. It's Eve's father, Doctor Nyren."

"That's a relief. I feel better already," she replied.

Henry came by about an hour later, greeted her cheerfully, and introduced her to his assistant and the intern. He also introduced two other people whom he referred to as a chemotherapy nurse and a protocol secretary. All of this attention raised Marlene's spirits. Then he left and the hospital routine began.

Henry looked at the results of the initial workup and reviewed the treatment and evaluation plan with the chemotherapy residents and fellows. Kolonymus was right. The outlook was bleak. He thought how happy Eve was in her new-found partnership with this young woman. He remembered how Eve had acted, as a teenager, when her mother had died, and he thought, Well, it won't be the same as losing someone you love. He felt he should tell Eve the whole picture, otherwise she'd feel left out again. The chemotherapy fellow would tell Marlene's parents, and the patient would be told only that they were going to do their best to make her feel better.

OVER THE NEXT few weeks Marlene's deterioration was striking. She lost an additional twelve pounds; her face became sunken and jaundiced. The medication was having no effect. As Henry had predicted, the white blood cell count fell, and the bone mar-

246

row aspiration, negative for cancer cells when she came into the hospital, was now positive. Cancer was flagrantly displaying its might.

"Eve was here a little while ago," Marlene told Henry one day. "She looked so damned sad I had to cheer her up and reassure her I was not going to kick the bucket. Is there something she knows that you're not telling me? I hope not."

"I haven't spoken with Eve," Henry replied. He reminded himself to warn Eve about what might happen at any time. He picked up Marlene's hand to check her pulse. "How are you feeling now?"

"I don't have any pain, but I feel weaker than when I came in, and I'm so tired I could sleep all day."

"The medication takes a lot out of you," Henry said. "Remember, I told you that at the beginning. Sometimes I call it the head-banging syndrome—it feels so good when we stop treating you with all those powerful drugs with their side effects."

"That's good to know. I think I can take it awhile longer. I'm so anxious to get back to work. Eve says she can't do the work without me. I think she can do a lot."

"You seem to bring out the best in her. Sometime you'll have to tell me your secret, Marlene."

"Please call me Lena. Only my parents and people who don't know me call me Marlene. She reached for a cup of water. Henry saw that the cup was empty, filled it, and handed it to her. "Thank you. This weakness, Doctor Nyren, I feel as if I'm drifting away from everything and everyone."

IT WAS AGAIN time to go over the status of all cases on the service. The resident on the Chemotherapy Service, Gene Graybel, reviewed Marlene's hospital course with little confidence.

"... and with a WBC of one point nine and platelets of eighty thousand, we can't continue the chemotherapy. Did you see her this morning? Jesus, she's got so many black spots on her, it looks

247

like freckles. It's on her chest and her back and her face, even on her scalp. Does anyone have any additional suggestions for therapy?"

Henry turned to one of the fellows working in tumor immunology. "How about it? Does immunotherapy have anything to offer?"

"Well, we are getting good results with immunotherapy in cutaneous melanomas," the research fellow said. "But when there are widespread metastases like this one, we aren't able to touch it. And frankly, I don't want another negative result. The straight answer is, we don't have anything to offer."

Henry said with a sigh to the resident "Okay, Gene. Keep up the methylprogesterone—it won't affect her counts. Put her on a pre-coma regimen and keep the IVs open. Let's see if we can keep her out of renal failure."

MARLENE SLEPT MOST of the time. When Eve came to visit her again the next day, she was not just sleeping, she could not be roused. The nurse was in the room and confirmed that she was in coma. Eve spoke to the intern. He told her they were going to move Marlene to one of the single rooms and that she was dying. Eve moved back to Marlene's bed and stood quietly for a moment with her head bowed. She picked up Marlene's hand, still warm and supple, with callouses in funny places, held it for a moment, then slowly kissed it. She looked at the long fingers, the nails that had been filed short. Suddenly she felt that the hand was melting away. She glanced up at Marlene's face for a moment, and it seemed as if she were fading into the bed sheets, as though she were disappearing. Eve felt faint. She put down Marlene's hand and left the hospital as quickly as she could.

When Henry and Gene Graybel came onto the floor, Marlene was already in a single room with a special duty nurse. Her blood pressure was falling, and her heartbeat was barely perceptible.

"Gene, call her parents and tell them she's on the critical list. No, be more specific. Tell them she's terminal and could die at any time. Call me if anything happens."

248

In the hospital lobby, Henry ran into Paul. "That friend of Eve's is pretty bad. I don't think she'll make it through the night. I'd like to tell Eve what's going on."

"I saw Eve leaving a while ago. She looked pretty upset."

"Did she say where she was going?" Henry asked.

Paul shook his head. "Sorry."

"I wish she had waited for me," Henry said.

He couldn't help Marlene, but he could have offered his daughter comfort and a better understanding of what was happening. He wished he had talked with her before, as he had planned to.

"I'm going to try to find her," he said to Paul.

Henry used the phone at the information desk. He got no answer at Eve's apartment. He looked in the patients' card file at the information desk. It had Marlene's home phone number. He called. Someone picked up the phone. He said, "Hello?" He heard a muffled cry, and the phone clicked off. He left the hospital immediately and drove to Perry Street.

He parked on the broken-up sidewalk behind a truck. The lights were on in the studio. He heard a crashing sound. He knocked and something was thrown against the door. He tried the door, but it was locked. Henry shouted for Eve to let him in. The bolt on the door slid open. As he entered, Eve backed away to the center of the large room. Her dress was torn and dirty, her hair and face covered with white dust. Henry stepped over the chisel that had been thrown at the door. Eve stood with a stubby hammer in her hand. Every piece of marble and all the plaster casts in the studio had been smashed. The rods of the pointing equipment were bent.

"You fucking bastard! I hate you!" she cried. "You and that goddamned torture chamber you call a hospital. I know. She's going to die. Of your beloved cancer. You really love that disease, don't you. You're happy when someone gets cancer. More blood, more biopsies, more amputations, more research, more papers, more grants. A tumor is just a tumor, and maybe it will kill you. So what? People are dying all the time. But you make it hell. I've seen it all my life. And I never knew until now. I never knew," she

249

said, pointing to Henry, "all those times when I tried to get your attention, when I thought you were lost in thought. You were praying to your god, weren't you? Why couldn't you leave her alone? Why did you cut off her leg? Why did you take her back in the hospital? Maybe she would have lived another year."

"She wouldn't have, Eve. You've got to believe that she created more, and lived more, in the year after her amputation than she did in her whole life. Lena said that. She knew the score. She knew what was going on."

"Eve!" He approached her. "Be reasonable."

"Don't come near me! Do you know what I've been doing with this hammer? I was killing you with every head I smashed!" She choked on a sob. "I loved her. I loved Lena."

He reached out to comfort her. She flailed the air with her arms. "Keep away, keep away!"

Her sobs overcame her speech. The hammer dropped from her hand, and she sank to the floor. Henry helped her up and brought her to the couch. He took some vodka from a cabinet and poured it into a glass for her. Without lifting her head, she knocked it out of his hand.

# CHAPTER
# *THIRTY-EIGHT*

H ENRY DROVE back to the hospital and went to his
office. He turned on the light near Tara's desk. The door
was open, and his office was dark. He could see the
bridge over the East River outlined against the night sky.

Maybe she should have had radiation therapy at the beginning, he thought. Maybe if she had been given chemotherapy
before the tumor recurred, we could have prevented the relapse.
We never even tried immunotherapy.

Henry thought of all the times he had become upset when a
patient died. Even though he knew that the patient was going to
die and the death was inevitable, there were always the self-
indictments and the circular arguments—if I had done this, if I
had done that. Hadn't he outgrown that? He didn't think he could
feel that much pain now. He gazed out the window, as he often
did during the day when he had a minute's rest between patients.
He could achieve a moment of distraction by projecting himself
into the life of the bridge. The continual movement of the distant
traffic was somehow reassuring to him, like the continuity of life,
tragic end games notwithstanding. The pinpoints of moving
lights seemed to be traversing the span of human existence. He
had to pull himself back into the room, and reality. He walked to

Tara's desk and sat down, sliding back and forth on the casters of her chair.

At that moment it seemed to him that his entire career had been a Herculean effort of monumental futility. He had tried so hard, so deliberately, so determinedly; he had sacrificed so much. He wasn't sure if he still had a soul or not. His entire life was the single-minded pursuit of the leviathan—with a toothpick. There have always been diseases more powerful than physicians' therapies. In his own days as an intern, children with bulbar polio had died in his arms, he as helpless as their terror-stricken parents. How many syphilitics had he seen with dementia because arsphenamine was often an ineffective drug? And what use had he been to the patients with meningitis who died promptly after being admitted to the hospital? Why hadn't he wrung his hands in despair then?

And was cancer really such a terrible disease compared to the scourges of other eras? What a puny killer cancer was compared to the plague. Plague, still the world champion, with an undefeated record. A quarter of the world's population killed in the fourteenth century, over twenty-five million people. Had any cancer caused a mob to tear a health commissioner to pieces as happened during the plague of Milan, or to burn churches or sacrifice children?

Why was Henry so beset by this insignificant foe of mankind, certainly no threat to its existence? Only five or so million deaths a year, out of a world population of about five billion. Cancer was a very private disease. It did not disturb governments or the general peace. It caused hardly an ecological ripple. Cancer created its devastation deep in the heart. Mass death is comprehensible only as statistics, but a single death can strike with unutterable pain. That was the despair that held Henry in its grasp and fired his wrath.

Why didn't his internal mechanisms for keeping this pain at arm's length work as well as those of his colleagues? Although he had developed Hodgkin's disease as a young man, he thought very little about it. Few people knew about the Hodgkin's episode

252

other than his parents and the doctors who treated him. Paul Rosen knew and, of course, Laura had known. Perhaps Henry felt his cure had in some inexplicable way imposed an obligation upon him. It was true that he had come to believe that he had been fighting cancer all of his life.

Henry hit the desk with the flat of his hand. He couldn't believe that with all his experience he would still be thinking like that. Just like the old days. And the old days included the endless recriminations he had inflicted on himself because he had taken Laura on that unnecessary trip.

THE FLIGHT FROM Florida was bumpy. The warning sign had flashed on, instructing passengers to fasten their safety belts, and the stewardesses were hurrying to their seats.

"I hate these medical trips," Henry said. "They're supposed to combine business and pleasure, but the business is trivial and the pleasure is negligible. And now this lousy weather for the trip home. I don't know why you're so cheerful, Laura."

He shifted his lanky frame restlessly, loosened his tie, and fastened his safety belt.

"Stop complaining, Henry," Laura said. "You acted like the belle of the ball at the reception last night. I thought you were running for office."

She opened her new black-and-white handbag, took out a compact, and checked her makeup.

"I'm just a big ham. I'll be glad to get home," he said.

"I'll be glad to get home, too. I left the copy for next month's issue for the staff to put together. But all those bright college girls, so busy with their *terribly* important affairs—"

"You mean deciding which beds to hop in and out of."

"—that they won't get it finished till ol' momma bat comes home and starts bitching. That magazine means a lot to me. You have to admit *The Outrageous Decorator* is a fantastic success."

"Baby, anything you do is a knockout. Whatever you touch is a hit. I just wish you'd touch the pills you're supposed to take."

"Henry, everything on this trip has been great so far. Don't

253

spoil it with 'take the pills, check your sugar, knock off the salt.' Don't bug me, I'm managing just fine."

"Just one thing, Laura, and I'll lay off. You haven't taken your Orinase since we left New York, and the bottle of blood pressure pills in the medicine cabinet was empty when we left."

"I'll take care of it in the morning. Promise."

Smooth landing. Everyone a little impatient to get off the plane. People standing in the aisle putting on their coats while the stewardess announces how nice it was of them to fly whatcha-ma-call-it airline and asks them to remain seated until the plane stops. The passengers shuffle into the terminal in a crowd and then hurry away from one another like raindrops spinning off a twirling umbrella.

"Wait a minute, Laura, I'll get a porter," Henry said. "Laura, what's the matter—what the hell's the *matter?*"

She was standing. It was only a second before she fell, but in that second he knew it all. Her attractive, intelligent face twisted in silent protest. A slight shudder shook her frame before she fell, the brain's objection to having its blood supply cut off. She lay motionless on the floor. One hand was over her head, the other still grasped the black-and-white handbag. Her right leg had given way first, so she lay with her right leg under her left thigh. Maybe three seconds had passed. He bent over her to confirm what he already knew. Cardiac arrest in a hypertensive diabetic with coronary artery disease. The crowd hurried by, unstopped by the fallen figure.

Immediately, urgently, with panic gripping him like a vise, he flung off his coat and jacket to respond, shouting for help as he crouched over her.

Mouth-to-mouth breathing, then jumping to her side, external cardiac massage, straight arm pressure with the heels of the hands compressing the chest, over her heart. No response. He again shouted for help, and a guard came running.

"Call an ambulance! I'm a doctor. My wife just had a heart attack."

254

"I'll get the airport emergency team," the guard replied.

For ten, fifteen, twenty minutes, Henry continued the mouth-to-mouth respiration, then back kneeling at her side to pressure and plead with the heart to beat again. A group of guards surrounded him. Three members of the emergency team had arrived, lugging heavy first-aid kits.

"The ambulance is on the way," one of the men announced.

Henry turned his head. "Do you have a scalpel in there?"

"Yeah."

"Let me have it."

He cut away Laura's dress, slip and bra, and put his ear directly on her chest. No heart sounds.

Then, with no more than a second's hesitation, he made an incision between her ribs and pulled them apart. He plunged his bare hands into her chest and compressed the unbeating heart. With each compression less and less blood flowed into the heart to refill it. Further massage was useless.

He stood, not thinking what a sight he presented. His knees were shaking, his eyes were red and wild. He stared into space with his mouth hanging slightly open. Laura had become the latest in a long line of battles he had lost, battles that had left him physically intact but emotionally wounded. And it was then, at her side, that her torn body and his gashed soul bled into one another, and so infusing, made him for an instant mad.

A hand on his shoulder. Firm. It was one of the guards who had gathered around. They covered Laura with a blanket and carried her off. With guards supporting him, Henry followed, choking and sobbing as quietly as he could. For a moment, until the next rush of passengers, the center of the terminal was empty.

HENRY STOPPED ROLLING back and forth in Tara's chair. In the split second before he had made up his mind to cut into Laura's lifeless chest, an order had come out of a murky corner of his mind: Act or die. Now he heard the command again. His reason did not have the strength to rebut the command to act. What he

255

did in Laura's case was futile—as this would be.

It had taken him almost an hour to make the decision in Marlene's case that he had made in a second with Laura. Henry rose, closed the door to the office, and went to the elevator, knowing finally what he had to do.

# CHAPTER
# *THIRTY-NINE*

THE OUTPATIENT building was deserted at midnight. He walked quickly through the lobby. The cancer research building was also deserted except for a few maintenance people whom he had known for many years. He entered an elevator and got off at the fifth floor. The sharp concentration of animal smells mixed with disinfectants assured him he was in the right place. The concrete floor was still slightly moist from a recent washdown. In the large kennel room, he flipped on the lights. Yelping and barking greeted him. Henry walked to a work area and opened a refrigerator. He stopped for a moment as he calculated Marlene's weight and the concentration of repairin in the rubber-capped bottles. He filled a large syringe, covered the needle with a plastic sheath, and slipped it into his pocket. He retraced his steps through the main lobby and entered the hospital. He got off the elevator at Marlene's floor. He asked the nurse how she was, looked at her chart, and saw that the level of coma had deepened and that she was not producing any urine. Her parents were in the room. He asked them to leave for a moment while he did his examination. The contents of a bottle of intravenous fluid were dripping slowly into Marlene's veins. He injected the repairin solution into the tubing and threw the syringe into a plastic-lined trash can. He stood and watched her for a minute or so and then left her room. He had not noticed the nurse who stopped in the doorway of the room as he was slowly injecting the repairin. He told the distraught parents that they should go home and get some sleep. They would be called if there was any change. He made no note of the injection in the chart, but he gave the nurse some orders and told her to call him if anything happened. She understood what he meant. He went back and sat with Marlene for a while, and at 4:30 left for home. He did not undress but fell asleep on the couch. At 6:20 the nurse in charge called him to say that Marlene Lowell had died. Should she call the intern to pronounce her dead? Did he want to talk to her parents about an autopsy?

Yes, he would take care of that. And have the intern wait for him. Henry went back to the hospital. He looked at her chart. About an hour after he injected the repairin, the temperature and blood pressure had gone up slightly. Her pulse had quickened. The effects lasted two hours. She then became progressively hypotensive, and the nurse indicated that she had stopped breathing at 6:15 in the morning.

Her parents had been called. The intern was waiting. Henry and the intern walked into Marlene's room. The examination ritual was not necessary. Instead, he turned and walked slowly from the room, thinking he had about as much power over this disease as he had over the tides.

MISS FLANNERY HAD been in a lobby office when she saw Henry leave the outpatient building and walk toward the research building. The sight of him triggered a vagrant unkind thought. Then she dismissed him from her mind. However, when, twenty minutes later, she saw him again—this time with a large syringe protruding from his coat pocket—headed for the hospital elevators, her antennae started searching for suspicious signals. What was he doing here after midnight anyway? If there had been any hospital emergencies in the last few hours, she as nursing supervisor would have heard about them. No one in his right mind made rounds this time of night, not even that one with his bleeding heart worrying about his suffering patients. As if his patients were different from anyone else's or he could do something the other doctors couldn't. Nyren's patients died like anyone else's. And him thinking he could play God, deciding who's to live and who isn't. And why did he go to the research building before going to the hospital? After Henry entered the elevator, she left the small office and waited until she saw it stop on the eighth floor.

She arrived on the floor two minutes later and asked at the nurses' station where Dr. Nyren was. Standing outside Marlene's room, she could see Henry slowly injecting the contents of the large syringe into the tubing of the intravenous infusion, and she watched him as he threw the empty syringe into a trash basket. She kept out of sight. When Henry emerged from the room to go to the nurses' station down the hall to give some instructions, she quickly entered, retrieved the syringe, placed it in her pocket, and left the floor before Henry returned.

Back in the lobby office she called the eighth floor nurses' station and asked about Marlene Lowell. The floor nurse responded, "She's terminal, Miss Flannery. She doesn't respond, and her blood pressure is falling."

"That's too bad. And such a young girl. I see she's on the critical list. That's why I called. She hasn't been in any agony, has she?"

"No, she just became progressively comatose. There hasn't been pain."

"Is anyone with her?"

"Yes, Doctor Nyren is with her."

"Oh, good," replied the White Whale. "Did he order any medication for her?"

"No, nothing. She just has an IV running now."

"Do you know if he gave her any injections?"

"Not to my knowledge."

"Be a dear and take a look at the chart."

Flannery tapped her finger on the desk while the nurse went to

259

check the chart. In a moment she returned and said, "No. No new medications given."

"That's good. Be sure to call me if he orders any narcotics or a medication of any sort."

"He only asked that the temperature and blood pressure be taken every hour, and he ordered some blood chemistries. He said he'd be back."

"Fine, thanks. Be sure to call me if there are any problems. I'll see you in a while on rounds."

When Miss Flannery made rounds at 4 A.M., the charge nurse said that all was well, but that they expected the Lowell girl to expire any minute. Miss Flannery walked by the room and saw Henry sitting there. She thought to herself, Mister, I've got you by the balls!

Veronica Flannery did one more thing after she left the hospital floor. Following her instincts, she went back to the lobby and proceeded to the outpatient building. She took the elevator to the fourteenth floor, and with her passkey let herself into Henry's dark office. Using the flashlight she carried as night supervisor, she found her way to Henry's desk and the letter tray. One by one she scanned the contents. There were laboratory reports dealing with patients, letters from patients or referring doctors, and memos regarding hospital meetings. There was a carbon copy of a memo she was about to pass by because it wasn't addressed to Henry. But the location of the memo writer was just enough of a burr to catch the fabric of her suspicious mind.

> From: Avery Stemple, Animal Care Department, Cancer Research Institute

> To: Duncan Comfort, Chemotherapy Division, Department of Medicine

Near the end of the memo she read: "I know you want to try this in patients, but it's not ready yet." She carefully printed out the name of the substance on a pad she carried in her pocket.

260

# CHAPTER
## *FORTY*

THE NEXT morning Paul Rosen found Miss Flannery waiting outside his office, holding a large syringe as if it were a weapon.

"Good morning, Veronica. What brings you to my door this early?"

It was about an hour before the secretaries and research staff came in. Paul took off his coat. Little glistening drops of melted snowflakes stood in crowds on its shoulders. He shook the coat and hung it up, wiped his damp face and ears with a handkerchief, and slipped on a lab coat. With a friendly wave, he motioned the nurse in and asked her to sit down.

Holding the syringe at her side like a spear, Miss Flannery sat on the edge of the couch half-filled with small piles of magazines and manuscripts.

"I had the supervisor's duty last night, and there was a most serious breach of hospital regulations. An unauthorized medication was given to a patient. The patient died a few hours later."

"Veronica, you make it sound very ominous, almost as if someone was murdered up there last night. Exactly what happened?"

"Well, Dr. Rosen, I think I have all the facts but one. I have not added them up yet, but I know wrongdoing when I see it. Last night at two twenty-five A.M., Doctor Nyren injected the contents of this syringe,"—she held up the empty 50cc syringe for Paul to see—"into a patient on the eighth floor, Miss Marlene Lowell. He didn't obtain the medication from the nurse in charge, and he made no note in the chart of what he gave her. Only minutes before, while I was sitting in my office, I saw Doctor Nyren come from the research building with this syringe—filled it was, then—and proceed to the eighth floor. There he injected the contents into the patient intravenously. Then he had the nurse check her blood pressure every hour and take blood for research."

Rosen tried to reassure her. "Now, now, Veronica. I don't see anything so unusual in that. Doctor Nyren is in charge of new drug trials. If they run out of a drug on eight, he'd go over to pharmacy and get it. It was sloppy of him not to record what he did, but it's hardly sinister."

She started to get upset. "Please don't 'now, now, Veronica' me! I may not have such a fancy education as you doctors, but I know my business. Doctor Nyren did not go to the pharmacy. He went to the fifth floor of the research building, the veterinary department. The clean-up man told me so. I've put two and two together and I believe he gave the patient something called repairin, which is kept on that floor. There are still a few drops of the stuff left in the syringe."

There were a few beads of liquid left on the water-repellent inside surface of the syringe.

"If he had wanted to give her some new form of chemotherapy he wouldn't have to do it himself. All he would have to do is write an order. He's got interns, residents, and fellows to run around giving drugs," she continued.

"I don't know," Paul said. "Doctor Nyren has given patients chemotherapy himself."

"When's the last time you ran over to special pharmacy to fetch a medicine personally for a patient, in the daytime or at night? If he didn't send a fellow, he'd send the nursing supervisor, and that would be me. Besides, if it was a new drug, something the patient never had before, he'd have to get the consent of the family before giving it—the poor girl was in coma. Also, if you take a drug from special pharmacy, you have to sign for it."

"How can you be sure he didn't? Or maybe he just left a note," Paul said.

"You can check for yourself. But the fact is he didn't go to the pharmacy. As I said, I believe he went to the veterinary floor and took this repairin, whatever it is, and injected it without letting anyone know. His own personal, private experiment. You can analyze this liquid if you want to find out, but why don't you just ask him? Oh, he'll tell you, all right. The self-righteous kind don't bother to lie. They rationalize."

The freshness of the morning was gone for Paul Rosen as he reached for the telephone and dialed.

"This is Doctor Rosen, is Doctor Nyren there? Well, will you please ask him to excuse himself from rounds for a moment and come to the phone?"

Neither the nurse nor the Chief of Chemotherapy said a word while they waited.

"Hello, Henry. Paul. I have an important question, and I need a yes or no answer right away—I'll fill you in later. Did you or did you not give Marlene Lowell an injection of repairin last night?"

"I did, Paul."

"Okay. Please come by and see me as soon as you can."

He turned to the vindictive nurse, hoping she hadn't heard the response, but she had.

"Veronica, just let me handle this!" he said.

Miss Flannery's face did not show any of the satisfaction that was growing inside her. "I'd like to know what you're going to do about it."

"I'm going to look into it. I'm sure there is a straightforward explanation for all this."

"I'm not sure at all."

She got up. "Well, he is on your service, and what you do is your own business. But now that I have the information I came here to get, I shall write a complaint to the Ethics Committee, and I'll see to it they don't do a whitewash like they did the last time."

PAUL DID NOT wait for Henry to come to his office. As soon as Miss Flannery left, he went to the hospital where Henry was making rounds with the chemotherapy team. Henry excused himself, and the two went to Henry's office. Henry told Tara they didn't want to be disturbed and closed the door, and Paul related the details of Miss Flannery's visit.

"Henry, will you please tell me why you gave repairin to that patient? Is there some new development that I haven't heard about that would make you think it would be useful in malignant melanoma?" Henry was looking out the window at the bridge. "Are you feeling all right?" Paul asked.

"Fine," Henry said.

"There must be some reason you decided at one A.M. to use repairin for the first time in a human being and to choose as a subject a patient whose death was imminent?"

It was less than twelve hours since he had last stood here, Henry thought, looking out from his dark office at the bridge. Since that time someone had died, he had acted with poor judgment on several scores, and he hadn't had any sleep. He wasn't feeling fine. To tell Paul of Eve's hysterical rage, and to use the effect it had had upon him as an excuse, would have been to put his behavior on the same immature and irrational level as Eve's.

It had been just that.

"I knew Marlene was dying," he said. "She hadn't responded to any form of therapy we tried. I stood here last night and thought what more could I do for her, what last measure could I take? We had some brief tumor regressions with repairin, and the stuff is not toxic, so I used it. I just had to do something for that girl. I guess I tried too hard." He sighed. "You knew she and Eve were friends."

"Okay, I can see this as an instance of judgment clouded by overzealousness on the patient's behalf. But that isn't the way

264

Flannery is going to present it. She is going to paint you as some madman conducting unauthorized research on dying patients without getting the family's consent, without the consent of the hospital research committees, and then covering it all up by not making any record of what you did. Why the hell didn't you at least make a note in the chart? Maybe we'd have a leg to stand on."

"I don't know why. No reason. Bad judgment."

"What happened? Ordering the nurse to take the blood pressure and temperature and blood specimens every hour, that makes what you did look even more like an unauthorized experiment. I just can't see why you bothered. One shot of any medication into a patient about to die—that's no experiment."

"I *know* that."

"And you knew it last night?"

Henry looked at Paul a moment. Then he picked up the paperweight holding down the contents of his "In" box, and shuffled through some papers.

"Henry?"

Henry shrugged. "At the time it seemed like the thing to do," he said in a low voice.

"You weren't yourself," Paul said.

"I don't know how to answer that."

"You know what I mean!"

"The trouble is, you want to know why. All that's clear is that I wasn't thinking clearly." The emotional turmoil had passed through him, like some devastating storm, and its wreckage looked as grotesque to him as anyone else. "I can't defend what I did," he said.

"How do you want to handle this?" Paul asked softly.

Henry let the papers in his hand drift onto the desk and lifted his hands helplessly. "I can't tell you that, either."

"Henry, this is going to get to Len Boyer quickly, and God knows what else Flannery has in mind. But I want our version of this episode to be in his hands first. Please write up everything that happened, including your opinion about it being an indefensible action taken at a time when you were not thinking clearly. I'll add a postscript with my opinion that this was an act of therapeutic desperation, done on the patient's behalf, and that it was not carried out as a research activity. By the way, did you get permission for a postmortem?"

Henry nodded.

"Good. How did you manage it with that hysterical mother?"

Fatigue was beginning to show on Henry. His jaws were slackening slightly, and he had to fight to keep his eyes open. "I don't know how I got her parents to agree," he said. "We spent an hour together in the consolation room. I argued. I pleaded. Finally, I got permission for a limited post, everything but the head."

WHEN MISS FLANNERY had written her first memo of complaint regarding Henry Nyren, the issue, euthanasia, was a clear case of wrongdoing in her mind. But she understood that the incident involved a patient in extreme terminal agony, so the sympathy of those reviewing the complaint would not be with her. She had had a feeling of apprehension that time. Now she was exultant. With scrupulous attention to detail, she recounted the events preceding the death of Marlene Lowell and what she had uncovered. Then she let the Ethics Committee know she'd done her homework.

"There is more than one breach of conduct in these events. There is also a violation of federal law here," she wrote. "Almost all of the money to support the research at Curie comes from the National Cancer Institute, and they have strict rules for research on human beings: So does the Food and Drug Administration. I wonder what the people in Washington would say about all this?"

She chewed the end of her pen thoughtfully for a moment, then smiled as she closed in for the kill:

> My purpose in writing this is to see that Dr. Nyren is removed from the staff of this hospital. I address this letter to you because

266

you have the authority to remove him. But there are other authorities, such as the state's Division of Professional Licensing, as well as legal authorities that can take action that will lead to the same thing. This is not a veiled threat. I am perfectly prepared to take my complaint elsewhere, should you attempt another whitewash.

One final word. There may be those among you who feel I have a hidden motive in all of this. I want to advise you that Dr. Nyren and I are not socially acquainted, our paths have never crossed outside this great institution, nor have our families or personal interests any areas of contact of which I am aware. My first and last thoughts are of the patients who entrust themselves to our care.

Submitted with respect,

Veronica Flannery

Satisfied with what she had written, Veronica placed her pen in the drawer of the small, white desk in her bedroom. She felt completely at ease.

# CHAPTER
# *FORTY-ONE*

D
R. LEN Boyer took a seat at the head of the table. He put onto the table a folder containing Miss Flannery's letter, a signed statement by Henry with an addendum from Paul Rosen in the form of a memo, the autopsy report, a committee report, and the patient's chart.

"Gentlemen," he said, "what we have here today may be properly classified as a hot potato." He tried to force a small smile. Gregor Veit-Volpin took his usual place at the other end of the table and, pushing his chair back, sent forth staccato bursts of pipe smoke—his way of signaling distaste and his desire to remove himself as far as possible from the proceedings.

Peter Roland, the professional proponent of medical ethics, who considered himself to be the *de facto* head of the committee, sat as always at the middle of the table to the right of Dr. Boyer and facing the window. Also present were Paul Rosen, Ralph Hardy, and the attorney Gilbert Costaine. Others attending were the pathologist, Arthur Bancroft, a new member, and Jarrett Weil, representing the Curie Research Institute.

"I am going to distribute an account of the events involved in this grievance and attested to as substantially correct by the interested parties," Boyer announced. "However, Miss Flannery has requested that I read aloud to you her letter of elaboration, and I shall do that. But I reserve the right to determine if that letter shall be part of the permanent record of this meeting."

There was a knock on the door, and the secretary rose to answer it. She took a message to Dr. Boyer. He excused himself for a moment and then returned.

"Doctor Kolonymus is outside and asked if he may sit in on this meeting *ex officio.* Does anyone object?"

Dr. Boyer looked around the room. No hands went up.

"Good, I'll invite him in. Also, Henry Nyren is here."

There were brief greetings, and the meeting continued. Dr. Boyer read Miss Flannery's letter. There were head-shaking, jaw-rubbing, comments of disapproval, and some smiles. A few notes were jotted down.

"Well, that's it," he concluded. "It wasn't pleasant to read aloud, and I'm not sure it's all relevant, but I gave Miss Flannery my word."

"Better here than reading it in the newspapers," Dr. Bancroft remarked.

"I'm still not sure we won't!" Veit-Volpin was knocking the ashes out of his pipe and looking with surprise at a hole in the sleeve of his jacket.

Dr. Boyer turned to Henry and asked, "Do you have any comment at this point?"

"I do. What I did was stupid and irresponsible." His cheeks were sagging like the jowls of an older man. His black straight hair had fallen over the side of his face, but he ignored it. "I broke hospital rules as if they didn't exist, and please understand, I don't think of myself as a privileged character. I know my position on the staff imposes greater responsibility on me, not less. I had been up for twenty-four hours straight, and I believe I would have made a report of what I did after I had gotten some sleep, but in all honesty I can't be certain. I am certain that I did not plan that injection as an experiment."

Peter Roland looked severely at Henry. "Doctor Nyren, in all candor, did you have any emotional involvement with this patient?"

"No, none at all. I was never in her company alone outside the hospital."

"But you did know her socially?"

"She was a friend of my daughter's, and I had seen her for a few minutes in my daughter's company, never more than casually."

Veit-Volpin looked up. "Henry, why did you do this thing? Don't we have enough problems with cancer? Cancer is a crazy disease. Now we have crazy nurses and crazy doctors, too!"

"Gregor, I really don't know why," Henry answered.

"Any other comments or questions?" Boyer asked. He looked around the room. "Then we'll excuse Henry and continue our deliberations."

As soon as Henry left, Paul Rosen, who had been studying his hands, looked around at his colleagues. "I think Henry acted with misplaced zeal on the patient's behalf. It was not a clandestine experiment. However, I do recognize that important hospital regulations were broken."

Ralph Hardy half-rose from his seat, moved his chair closer to the table, and spoke up loudly.

"Look, doesn't every doctor, sooner or later, come up against a situation where someone is going to die and there is a gut reaction to try something different, something never tried before, to save that patient?"

"Miracles, he believes in," mumbled Veit-Volpin in the background.

"Ralph, don't roll out that old 'what-is-there-to-lose?' argument," Paul said.

"No, I think most of us have at some time acted with what could be called 'an excess of zeal.' Maybe this whole hospital is an excess of zeal, and Henry just gathered all the static into one spark." Ralph Hardy looked to his colleagues for assent.

Veit-Volpin said, "This reminds me of an old Russian proverb

—'Every doctor has his own private graveyard.'"

Dr. Boyer got them back on track. "I think we have to stick to the circumstances of the case and not try to establish conditional excuses. We're going to have to make a recommendation to the Medical Board. Mr. Costaine, could this episode be construed as malpractice?"

"I don't think so. One would have to show damage to the patient as a result of the act, and I gather this is not the case."

Dr. Bancroft, like most pathologists, had a juridical bent. "That's true. At autopsy she had enough tumor to kill her many times over. There was no evidence of organ damage that could be attributed to any cause other than the malignant melanoma."

"Isn't the damage induced by anticancer drugs always evident?" Boyer asked.

"We can usually tell," the pathologist replied.

"I feel we're getting off the point again," Roland announced. "Whether the drug killed her—even if the drug had cured her—is irrelevant to what was done. Hospital rules, medical society regulations, ethical codes, and international rules of medical conduct were broken just as surely as if one took a hammer and smashed a statue. There are always explanations, but they're not excuses and are never accepted as such unless we condone what was done. If you start to accept excuses, then there are no rules."

"From the point of view of the hospital, and especially the Board of Trustees, I hope we can keep it quiet," Gilbert Costaine said. He appeared a little nervous. "If it gets outside, it would be bad public relations and bad for fund raising."

Jarrett Weil was thinking of the effect of this episode on the Curie Research Institute. "Something like this gives research a bad name. It will make it harder for us to get grants because foundations may be reluctant to be associated with us. Also, there are always plenty of kooks around waiting to throw eggs at scientists or make them out to be ogres, and this will be grist for their mill. I must say as a scientist and as a member of the

271

Clinical Investigation Committee, I feel pretty foolish seeing how easily, almost casually, all the elaborate safeguards against this sort of thing were disregarded."

"There may have been an element of entrapment here on the part of Miss Flannery," Paul Rosen said. "If she was suspicious enough to follow Henry up to the patient's room, and if she stood outside and watched without questioning and interfering, I'm sure she was hoping to catch him in some act of wrongdoing. I'm also sure she was not interested in preventing it. In that sense she might even be considered some sort of accomplice, but in any event I believe we should also consider a reprimand for Miss Flannery in this matter."

Dr. Boyer took control again. "Gentlemen, we are at the point where we should prepare a resolution and vote on it."

Suddenly, Veit-Volpin pulled his chair to the table. "Wait, wait, wait! Listen, I too can stand only so much of this, and want a resolution, but before we get into that, I must get something off my chest. While you were all talking about your precious rules— my God, I'm sitting here thinking, where's the place for the hero in our society of committees? What would Jenner have done with the smallpox vaccine, or Ehrlich with salvarsan, or Pasteur with his rabies vaccine, if they had had to fight with clinical investigation committees demanding randomized clinical trials and informed consents? The world would be filled with rabid syphilitics with smallpox! I'm not voting for or against anything!"

Dr. Bancroft spoke up very quietly. "Unfortunately, there are no heroes in this play and no great discoveries. Nothing was achieved by breaking the rules. As an experiment it was trivial, as an act of desperation foolish, and as an act of therapeutic zeal it was misdirected."

A hand was raised from a chair set apart from the table. It was Kalman Kolonymus. "I am here unofficially, but I was Marlene Lowell's physician and referred her to Doctor Nyren. I felt compelled to come here this afternoon. Still, I did not intend to say anything. Correct me if I'm wrong, but I believe I am next to the oldest physician here and the one longest at this institution. In fact I have been here since I came to this country in 1939. I'll be emeritus in a few months, and I shall retire. I am not quite as old as Doctor Veit-Volpin. He will tell you he was a student of the great Semelweiss, which is nonsense. I will make no such extravagant claims."

"I don't make claims, only Hungarians make claims."

"But I do have a perspective that I wish to express," Kolonymus continued. "Many people have been criticized for their behavior in this case. The dermatologist who first saw Marlene Lowell has been criticized for not making a sufficiently large incision around the original melanoma. I have been criticized both for taking her leg off and for not taking it off sooner. The patient's mother is going mad with guilt because she made her daughter go to the doctor in the first place, and then again maybe she should have made her go sooner. The poor woman came in to see me after her daughter died, and I don't know how many times she has called. She says to me, 'Why didn't I leave well enough alone? Would Marlene have lived longer if you had not amputated? If Marlene had seen you first instead of Doctor Green, could you have saved her?' So it goes and it will never stop. Now Henry Nyren is under severe criticism for his unorthodox behavior during this woman's terminal illness. And I have just heard the suggestion that the nurse should be reprimanded too. I ask myself two questions. One, who is the villain here? Two, what kind of institution is this?

"The answer to the first question is—cancer. It was the malignant melanoma that destroyed this gifted young life, not the dermatologist, not the mother, not me, and not Henry. There is nothing any of us could have done, so malignant was this tumor. I see some hands raised. Please hear me out. My conclusion may not be what you think. It is clear in my mind, and I wish to express it in one piece.

"As to my second question—what kind of institution is this?—it is a hospital that looks like any other hospital. It has an admitting office, beds, nurses, doctors, operating rooms, and laboratories. By New York City standards, it is not large. It has only a quarter the number of beds of the University Hospital across the street. But we do five times as much surgery as they do, give ten times as many transfusions, do twenty times as many laboratory tests, and we have an astronomical death rate by comparison. Yet the seriousness of the cases is not the essential dimension of the difference. That lies in our special purpose and the nature of the disease we are treating. Now I will tell you something every one of us must have thought of at one time or another. We are a hospital devoted to a struggle with an evil force, and such a struggle requires a special effort, especially an emotional effort. We all carry a tremendous emotional burden but we never speak of it. It would require an inhuman heart not to be touched by the tragedies our patients endure.

"As a young man in Europe, I learned to drive a horse and wagon. The first thing my father taught me was to be very careful when going downhill, otherwise there could be a serious accident. On a steep hill, you must hold the reins tightly and push on the brakes to stay in control. The struggle we are engaged in against this evil force, this carcinoma, requires a great deal of emotional energy to hold the reins, to keep in control.

"One more digression. There is a story from the Middle Ages that tells of a mysterious garden that contained the secret of life. It was forbidden for man to peer into it. Three sages walked up to the garden and looked in. One went mad, the second went blind, and the third, the greatest sage of all, remained intact and sane, but he never told what he saw. Control. Without it, we and our patients are lost.

"I think what Henry did was very bad. The hill is steep here, the temptation to do desperate things is greater than in some other places. And so, much greater must be our effort to stay in control. We cannot help our patients with magic or special potions. Hospital rules of conduct are important legally, but they

274

are also important in helping us to keep our sanity. We must not break them. I am very sympathetic to Henry. But if you practice around here you've got to keep a tight rein on your emotions, and you've got to keep your foot on the brakes so you don't crash into situations where you are practicing desperate medicine."

There was complete quiet for a moment, and then Boyer spoke.

"Gentlemen, there are three issues here. One, the unauthorized use of an experimental drug. Two, the administration of an experimental drug without the patient's consent or that of the family. Three, failure to record and report the use of such a medication, in accordance with hospital regulations. The fact that there was no evidence that the medication injured the patient is irrelevant. Does anyone want to make a resolution?"

A resolution was made and seconded to the effect that Dr. Henry Nyren should be censured for breaking hospital rules and that the Board of Trustees and Chief Medical Officer would decide on the nature of the censure.

"All in favor, please raise your hands," Boyer said. An uncomfortable silence hung in the air.

"Come, gentlemen, we need a decision," he insisted. Finally, Paul Rosen raised his hand. Slowly the rest followed.

With the exception of Veit-Volpin. "I'm not voting for anything this afternoon, and as for you, Kolonymus, it's *you* that drive people crazy, not cancer."

"Unanimous with one abstention. Please record Doctor Veit-Volpin's abstention without his comments," Boyer said.

WHEN THE MEETING adjourned, Paul walked with Len Boyer to the Medical Department office. "I have a feeling we did not hear the whole story today," he said. I don't think Henry was being completely frank with us, and neither was Veronica Flannery. I feel they both had other motives."

Gilbert Costaine walked out with Peter Roland.

"There are implications in this case that are disturbing to me as an attorney," Costaine said. "It's not only the bad publicity that

275

could ensue from it, but in the Darlington versus Charleston Hospital decision, the hospital administration was held responsible for incompetent actions of members of its staff."

When Henry read the transcript of the meeting, he read it objectively except for the remarks of Kalman Kolonymus. These disturbed him deeply. He said to himself, He thinks I am Dr. Faustus and that I would sell my soul to find the cure for cancer. Goddammit, I would. And then a smaller voice within added: Maybe I already have.

# CHAPTER
# FORTY-TWO

THE FOLLOWING week the hospital's Medical Board suspended Henry from the staff for one year. Since he had no other hospital affiliation and no office outside the hospital, the action had the effect of forcing him out of the practice of medicine. This was underscored shortly afterward when the state revoked his license for a year.

"If you can use this year as a kind of sabbatical, devote it to research, go abroad and study, or just take a year off to relax and travel, you might turn it into something positive," Paul Rosen suggested. They were sitting in Henry's office where Paul had brought him the Board's decision.

"I've been trying to sort things out, trying to explain to myself why I acted against everything I advocate and believe. A bunch of thoughts crowd each other. First, there is Laura. I blame myself for Laura's death. She'd been having chest pains for a week. If we had stayed home I would have done something about it. But I was selfish. I wanted to go, and I didn't want to go by myself. I let her postpone her cardiac workup. I rationalize and tell myself that her life span would have been shortened anyway by the diabetes and heart disease, but somewhere inside me I believe she would be alive today if she hadn't gone on that trip.

"And then there's Eve. As a father I was lousy. All I did was

277

mess up her life. Finally, she finds some happiness with Marlene, who is dying of cancer. And I turn out to be Marlene's doctor. She goes berserk and blames me for worshiping cancer and killing the only person she ever loved. That night, sitting in my office with the lights out, I tried to think clearly. I just felt crushed—so many heartaches. I felt maybe if I made a gesture to show Eve that I did care and wanted to help, even at the expense of my own principles, she would understand. And that's when I did what I did. It's not an excuse but it's as close to an explanation as I can get." Henry, his eyes shut, ran both hands slowly through his hair, as if painfully squeezing out the thoughts.

Each of us accumulates his own set of guilts and regrets, Paul thought. Looking back was self-defeating. "I'm not much older than you, Henry," he said finally. "We've had similar educations, similar professional experiences, and on the personal level, well, everyone gets his share of knocks. But in your situation, I'd put things together differently. I would try to use the year constructively, spend as little time as possible roaming around in a hair shirt."

Henry paced behind his desk, shooting glances out the window. "This is what I'm going to do, Paul. I've giving up my practice, not just for a year, but permanently. I'm going into research, and I'm going to stick with it full time. Among the side effects of my stupidity was the bad light it threw on repairin. There is something in repairin, and I'm going to try to find out what it is."

AT FIRST, WHEN Marlene died, Eve would not speak to Henry. It was three months after her hasty departure from New York and return to Los Angeles before he was able to establish contact with her at all. Those were important months for Henry, three months away from patients and more than three months away from Donna. However, he was talking to Eve again. Whether their fractured relationship was healing or not was another matter.

"Are you feeling better?" Henry asked.

"Yes," Eve replied calmly. "I'm okay. It's just that I can't get that night out of my head. I keep thinking about it. Putting my hysterics aside, you'll never convince me that what I said wasn't right."

"You can't really think I love cancer!"

"The heart of the matter is that you, Rosen, Kolonymus, all of you, with your experience, your tests, and your statistics, you can tell when patients are going to die. Then why don't you leave them alone? You know damn well when your so-called experiments aren't going to work."

"It's not a simple black-and-white matter," Henry answered soberly. He remembered Ann Bauer and the time he did stop.

"You complicate it. Why couldn't you just have left Marlene alone?"

How much less complicated my life would have been if I had left her alone, Henry thought. "Eve, she wanted us to help her."

"That girl was strong. She could have faced the end at home with the people who loved her. What happened at that hospital— the amputation, the chemotherapy—was horrible, and you have the nerve to call it science? It was evil, it was cruel."

"Problems of good and evil are never simple," Henry said, trying to keep his annoyance under control.

"It seems cut and dried to me, or maybe cut and died," Eve replied sarcastically.

"There are no evil men in that hospital. Do you think Kolonymus enjoys amputating a leg, or that I'm pleased at making someone deathly ill? It's like the dilemma of pilots bombing cities to end a war. There are casualties we have caused, and I grieve for them, but it's my battle, Eve, and my burden."

"I don't see grieving doctors, only grieving families."

"Eve, I don't want to argue with you."

"My whole life has been an argument with you."

"I don't think at the end of a phone here, three thousand miles away, I can justify my existence for you."

"Why should you?" Eve replied. "It's none of my business."

"I just want to have a normal father—"

279

"—Daughter relationship. Please stop beating me over the head with your fatherhood again. It doesn't become you."

Henry sighed. "I can't seem to get through to you no matter what I say. Or do."

"I think it's time to hang up." And she did.

THE AIR WAS gray with anticipation of snow as Henry stood at the airport and awaited the arrival of Donna's flight. The memory of Laura's dying at the airport never left him, but it seemed further away than it used to. It was the anticipation of Donna's arrival that overwhelmed his consciousness.

Donna had told Rand she was spending a weekend in New York with her mother, and he raised no objections.

Mountains of dirty snow were piled against the airport buildings and between the cleared runways. The impending storm would give everything a clean, white look again, but that would be fouled in a few hours. The bad weather delayed Donna's arrival. When her plane finally landed, they rushed to an adjacent terminal and were barely in time to catch the flight to Saranac Lake.

Breathless, they strapped themselves into the small, high-winged Fokker commuter plane that would take them on the short flight upstate.

"I'm so glad you're here," Henry said. They were each sitting on the aisle, across from one another, and they reached out to clasp hands momentarily.

"Is it far from the airport?"

"No, just a few miles. The airport's at Saranac Lake. The hotel's actually closer to Lake Placid."

At the end of their journey they were ushered into an ample room with floral wallpaper, a four-poster bed, and a large bay window overlooking white hills garlanded with spruces. The solitude was perfect. Few people were in the hotel. They looked at and saw none of the other guests. For the moment, they were the only two people in the world.

280

They allowed themselves no interruption of their onrushing passions.

"Tell me—" she started.

"Later."

"But how about—?"

"It can wait!"

THEY SLEPT THROUGH the dinner hour and into a bright morning.

"Donna, I haven't felt this happy—this young—since I saw you last," Henry said.

"I have a fuzzy feeling in my head. Either I'm on cloud nine or else—I'm weak with hunger." She laughed.

In a short while they were sitting in the dining room of the hotel. Their table was next to a double window, the inside panel clear, the outer showing a halo of frost. Past the windows, a party of small evergreens dressed in sun-sparkling white nodded at them in the breeze.

Henry was sipping orange juice. Donna, looking tan and fit, was wearing a bulky blue-and-white Norwegian sweater. She was buttering an English muffin as she listened to Henry.

"I know it isn't going well for you in Phoenix, that's plain enough. But how do you size things up now?"

"Well, it was very clear from the beginning that the whole thing was orchestrated for my benefit. The move was meant to get me away from you, and from my mother, and to give our marriage another chance. Of course, it's no better out there than it was in Riverdale. What he doesn't understand is just how bad our marriage is. It's not my mother's fault and certainly not yours. What a lot of trouble he's gone to. That's his way. He thinks he can fix earthquakes with Band-Aids."

"You knew that from the start," Henry said.

"But *he* didn't. I went along for Randy's sake, and thank God, that's working out. That's one good thing. Randy really is fine. His hair has come in beautifully, and he has wonderful color.

He's growing. I really don't think the chemotherapy hurt him at all. He's doing great in school and has loads of friends. He's never home. I think he's forgotten he was ever sick. That would never have happened in New York."

"Unless you moved out of Riverdale," Henry interposed.

"You're right. Moving to any other community would have given Randy a new start. This was doing it the hard way. One thing you can't beat, though, is the weather. I don't have to worry about winter or sore throats or bronchitis."

The dining room was half-empty, and they ate slowly. Henry thought, this is how I need to start every day. "And what about Rand," he asked. "Have things worked out well for him professionally at least?"

Donna looked up at the ceiling. "It's been a disaster. He lasted only six weeks in architecture school. All that time he kept saying he was too old for classrooms and homework, but the truth is, he's a businessman, pure and simple. He might just as well have decided to be a space scientist, he'd have the same chance of success. So he's back in the real estate office, and he hates that, too. It has no class, he says. Doesn't compare to the real estate business in Riverdale and Westchester. No executives, just gray-haired couples looking to retire."

"Do you think there's a chance he'll decide to—"

"He'll never come back, he's too stubborn. And I can't leave. For the same reason I went. Randy." She sighed. "Oh, Henry, I don't want to talk. Let's enjoy ourselves. Take me for a walk. Better yet, take me cross-country skiing."

"Okay. First a walk around the town. It's a beauty. A little gem left over from the Winter Olympics. And then we'll ski, get soaking, sweating wet and tired. We'll take along a bottle of wine and some cheese and fruit in a knapsack and we'll picnic in the snow. When we come back this afternoon we'll be exhausted and high, and we'll love each other right through dinner, like last night, and won't get up till tomorrow morning!"

"It's already been more than I ever thought a weekend could be."

282

"Listen, I've been invited to give a talk in L.A. in April. That's just six weeks away. I'll stop over in Phoenix—if you think we could be together again."

"What I think is, I couldn't stand it if we weren't."

THE USUAL JOKING and bantering before a research meeting began was absent this morning. Avery Stemple was grim, and he wanted to be sure everyone knew Henry was the reason.

"The Scientific Advisory Board met last night to discuss Henry's wild caper. But do you know what they did? They voted to censure me because I didn't have the experimental drugs in the refrigerator locked up and because I didn't report any repairin missing."

Under discussion were Paul's not very promising results of treating animal cancers at Curie. The research group was gathered in the small conference room next to the Department of Animal Care.

Jarrett Weil directed the discussion.

"I hope you agree with us now, Paul. It's time to drop repairin, it just isn't getting anywhere. Henry, you said you had a different angle on repairin. If you still think it's worthwhile presenting, go ahead."

Henry was now a full-time member of the repairin research team. It took some accommodating for him since the research he had done before was always at the bedside and never at the laboratory bench. Working with Dr. Gomez in the dog lab was as far from the clinic as his research had ever carried him. Now it was tissue culture, radioimmune assays, and molecular biology. He was unsure of himself in dealing with seasoned laboratory researchers, so he was uncharacteristically reticent as he presented his hypothesis.

"I want to make a suggestion that could change the direction of our research. First I want to draw an analogy between reproduction and cancer. The ovum doesn't start to divide until it is penetrated by a sperm cell and DNA is inserted into the nucleus. The fertilized egg then undergoes a burst of new

283

growth. It starts to secure its own blood supply from the maternal host. When this mass of cells, now an embryo, reaches a critical stage in its development, labor commences and a child is born. There is another way to say this. The male deposits nucleic acids into the body of the female. One of these nucleic acids penetrates a special cell. The presence of the nucleic acid is a stimulus for the growth of this previously resting cell. A mass of dividing cells that is not subject to outside regulation grows into a tumor of considerable size and derives its blood supply from the body in which it is growing. After this tumor reaches a critical mass it is ejected from the site in which it developed." Henry looked around for a moment to see if he had everyone's attention. He had.

"Cancer starts with one cell also—one cell that has been penetrated by nucleic acids. This growth is also unregulated by the body in which it is developing, and it takes the nutrients it needs from the body. The tumor then continues to grow until it reaches a critical mass, when it too leaves the site of its conception. It will either burst through the surface of the body seeking to deliver itself, or it will be delivered inward—metastasize. To stop pregnancy we must use the same methods we resort to in the treatment of cancer—surgery, that is abortion. We cannot reverse it or hold it in suspended animation. We either have to kill it or let it follow its natural course."

Weil, annoyed by Henry's presentation, said, "Cancer is not a simple one-step transformation. Henry, all you did was show how much you don't know about how cancer develops. Besides, reasoning by analogy is something that the ancients used to do. It was quite suitable for the agora of Athens, but it's not part of the scientific method. Descartes, Claude Bernard, and Whitehead would turn over in their graves if they heard you."

"Jarrett, if you'll hold the attacks for a minute—there is a testable hypothesis that I'm trying to get to," Henry said. "You can't stop a pregnancy once it starts, except by destroying the tissue. The same holds true for cancer. But you can prevent

284

pregnancy with contraceptives, and what I'm suggesting is that repairin could be for cancer what 'the pill' is for pregnancy. We know that repairin is nontoxic, it is not species-specific, and it offers protection against all the cancer viruses we have tested it with. It also stays in the body at a measurable level for two to three months. Boost the dose and you'd have an effective level for from six months to a year."

"But it's not 'the pill' because it can't be taken by mouth," Frannie said. "You must give it by injection. Also, we don't know if it works for all known cancer viruses, we've only tried a few. We've been thinking only about treating cancer, not interfering with its development."

Frannie, or Fran Li Park, a young Ph.D. from Korea, was Jarrett Weil's assistant. She and Weil were inseparable, providing an agreeable amount of salacious gossip, something no decent institution could do without. When he heard this talk, Henry was reminded that once he and Janine were the targets. But that was ancient history, and new gossip was best.

Avery Stemple had been making notes. "I like the comparison with contraception," he said now. "The prevention angle is not often discussed around here. All we seem to do is try one drug after another, and we cure damn few animals, to say nothing of people. Speaking personally, I would prefer to prevent cancer in myself than have a chunk of me cut out trying to cure it. And that's not saying anything about radiation therapy or chemotherapy. The only handle we've got on infectious viruses is with vaccines and prevention. If smallpox ever came back, we couldn't treat it any better today than the Romans could. Yes, I like the idea of working on the cancer contraception angle. Did you know that it was a veterinarian who first noticed that ovarian cysts that produce estrogen kept cows from getting pregnant? That's what led to the development of 'the pill.'"

Weil now added indignation to his annoyance at Henry's presentation. He shook his bald head as he spoke. "My God, what do you propose, Henry, to give the whole world repairin? Or maybe just half will get repairin, and we will save the other half for controls? The implications are mind boggling."

"Jarrett," Henry replied, "you have one of the finest minds of the eighteenth century. I can hear a contemporary speaking to Doctor Jenner: 'My God, Jenner, what do you propose, to inject every child in the world with that smallpox vaccine of yours? The implications are mind boggling.' I'm not jumping to any conclusions at all. I'll be satisfied with planning just the next step, and that's what we're here today to do."

It was decided to inject susceptible mice with leukemia virus, plus varying doses of repairin. The protocols for these experiments had to be drawn up in detail. A supply of fresh repairin had to be assured, and laboratory technicians had to be instructed in the conduct of the new experiments.

Henry was pleased with the progress of the work. He had a small office now in the Curie Research Institute. Tara had decided to go with him. She had a cubicle with a desk and a chair, separated from Henry by a metal and glass partition. She had cheerfully accepted the change in both their positions. Her loyalty was a comfort to him.

This new work would take time, it would be at least two to three months before they could begin to see if repairin prevented the development of leukemia in mice. Waiting made the time move slowly, and it was a sluggardly six weeks from Lake Placid until the trip to Los Angeles. Donna was on his mind constantly— accepting the invitation to talk was mainly an excuse to see her—still he had to get his lecture ready. It could not be a routine presentation; Paul had been out there before him and would have set a benchmark of excellence for Henry.

Henry was putting together material for his lecture, using 35-millimeter slides illustrating the results of research projects he had been involved in. He examined the slides through an illuminated viewer, making his choices. One slide was from a patient whose first name was Donna, and that was enough to divert his thoughts. He glanced at his watch. It was 4:30, an ideal time to call.

"Hello! I'm back again."

"Darling, two calls in one day? I love it!"

"Something made me think of you. Anything and everything makes me think of you."

"And I was thinking about Eve. I'm glad you're trying to get together. I'm sure she doesn't hold what happened to Marlene against you."

"I don't know what she thinks. She doesn't know that what I did for Marlene was because of her. How the whole stupid thing backfired! What a price I paid! I'm tempted to tell her the whole story. That I did it to prove I loved her."

"I think the worst thing you can do is to tell children that you did something for them, when in fact they didn't ask for it to be done. And it's worse when the outcome is something they despise. You would just be lighting a short fuse. The whole thing would blow up in your face. Please don't do it." Donna pleaded.

"What do you think I should do? That child has me at my wit's end."

"First, she's not a child, stop thinking of her as one. Second, when you see her, don't rake over the past. She's trying to build a new life out there. Respond to her achievements. Be upbeat."

There was silence for a moment. Then Henry said, "Maybe I'll try your prescription. Mine have never worked."

# CHAPTER
# *FORTY-THREE*

A FTER HIS talk, Henry spent the day at the Los Angeles Cancer Center. As he looked around and spoke with colleagues, he thought of his first trip to Phoenix. He was still toying with the idea of leaving Curie and starting anew somewhere else.

The few hours with Eve were surprisingly cordial.

"Well, that's it," she said as she drove him to the airport for the flight to Phoenix. "You've seen where I work and where I live, and met my roommate. All's quiet on the western front."

"Do you like your work?" Henry asked.

"It's not bad. I was lucky to get the job. There aren't too many magazines published out here. Without the New York experience I never would have landed it."

"I'm proud of you," Henry said.

"It's nice to hear you say that. I can't recall your ever saying that to me before," Eve said.

As they walked from the parking lot to the terminal, Henry took her arm in his. On the uneven pavement, the late afternoon sun cast long undulating shadows that followed them like black sharks snapping at the heels of past regrets.

"We always got along better from a distance, didn't we?" she said as Henry prepared to depart.

288

He took his daughter's hand. As he did so, she drew back a little.

"I just want to see you doing well," he said, "and know that we can talk."

DONNA WAS WAITING for him at the airport in Phoenix. High color coming through her tan, her hair capturing the sun, her smile as warm as ever—he wanted to whisk her off to the hotel.

"It's early, Henry. Let's go to Incanto Park. I want to talk."

They leaned against the car and embraced again.

"I'm sorry about those phone calls before you left New York," she continued. "It's almost as if Rand knew when you would call. It's lucky I caught those two 'wrong numbers.'"

They drove to the park where there was privacy along the tree-shaded walks. Occasionally a toddler would pass them, chasing a ball, or some old-timers, who would smile and greet them as if they were recognized as a couple in love.

"I'm glad you gave me Doctor Kedar's name. He's been wonderful," she said.

They were strolling hand in hand.

"I think he's the first pediatric oncologist they've had in Phoenix—lucky he's a good man. He keeps in touch with me, so I know Randy is fine. Now, I want to talk about us," Henry said.

"There is something to talk about," Donna said, not looking at him. "But first I have to know about you. Our weekend—all we talked about was my situation. It's important for me to know—have there been any changes in your life? Especially," she took a heavy breath, "is there anyone else?"

"Of course there's no one else." He put his arm around her shoulders and pulled her to him. They walked in silence for a while. What else should he tell her? The details of his suspension? His theories about repairin, or that Mrs. West was still alive and living nearby in Denver? But that was just it. If he was going to change, if he meant what he had told her about sharing his life, he should tell her these things.

289

"You know," he began, "I never did tell you all the things that happened after I gave Eve's friend that new medication. The last time we were together I just glossed over it."

"I know you got a lot of the blame."

"Yes, but there's a lot you don't know—that you should."

Why did I start in this direction? He thought. This isn't the time or the place. What an idiot I am. She was holding his hand in a tense grip.

"Henry, you don't have to tell me everything. You told me what I needed to know. But there is something I have to tell you."

"What is it?" he asked warily.

"I'm pregnant." That was the high color in her cheeks. She stopped and looked at him.

Henry, caught off guard, looked as confused as he felt. Tentatively, then, he touched her cheek—as if she'd become suddenly breakable. "It seems so dumb to say I'm surprised. Is it good or bad? How do *you* feel about it? How does Rand feel about it?" Another defeat, he thought despondently. He felt her slipping away from him.

"Henry, Rand doesn't know. The baby's not *his*."

"Mine? Are you sure?"

For the first time, she smiled. "That weekend at Lake Placid. The baby's ours," she said.

"That's the greatest—I never thought—Donna, this is the best news ever!"

"I'm glad, too," Donna whispered. "But I don't know how to handle the situation."

"I want you with me, Donna," Henry murmured, reaching for her.

"I want to be," she said. "I also want Randy with me, and I want Randy with his little brother or sister, but how can I take him away from his father? What would Rand do? He'd do *something* crazy. I keep thinking and thinking, and it's driving me out of my mind."

"Donna," he began slowly, "did you mean to—I mean—did you mean to get pregnant?"

290

"Not consciously," she replied. "There was just once I didn't use my diaphragm. Maybe I was tempting fate."

"Well, we did tempt fate. And it's going to work out."

She was too distraught for easy optimism. "I'm the one who's making it complicated," she continued. "I didn't have to tell you it's yours. If I had just told Rand I was pregnant, and didn't say anything else, he'd be the one celebrating."

"And the pregnancy would have been a wall between us," Henry said.

"Instead, it's going to be a wedge between Rand and me. I don't care about that. The more wedges the better. I keep thinking of Randy. I *can't* hurt him."

They walked and sat and walked again, and every bit of conversation heightened their dilemma.

"I'll tell Rand this week," Donna said finally. "And you're right. I will see an attorney first. Someone who specializes in matrimonial and custody cases. Maybe with a professional ally, I won't feel so alone out here."

"Why don't you let me be with you when you tell him?" Henry said. "I'm the one who's your natural ally. I don't want you to have to face him alone."

"Please, Henry, let me do it my way. I think I can make it easier for Rand. He knows this marriage isn't working. If you're there, it would be like waving a red flag in his face."

"Where does he think you are tonight?"

"I told him I've got an 'Evening for Art' in Scottsdale. I don't think he believed me. But I don't care."

Henry kept at her. "Promise me that you'll be ready to leave when you tell him. I'll come right out and get you. I don't want you to be alone."

They drove back to the hotel. Silently, almost ritualistically, they prepared for bed. He approached her with a tender kiss, just touching her lips. Because of her condition he expected a tentative response. But as he brushed his tongue across her mouth he felt droplets of perspiration circling her lips. Her skin was covered with a film of moisture, and as her arms encircled him she commenced a gyration as old as the primal scream. She bit his neck and dug her fingers into his back. "Fiercely, darling! Do it fiercely!"

He rose to meet her passion. He entered and felt himself tumbling, falling, falling into the center of the earth.

SPENT, DONNA WAS asleep in his arms. Henry, for his part, was wide awake. This was a situation he was responsible for. It affected the lives of three other people plus an unborn child, and yet in the morning he would fly away, leaving Donna to bear the brunt of what must be the most unpleasant encounter of her life. She was going to do battle for them both.

# CHAPTER
# *FORTY-FOUR*

EVERY PHONE ringing in the laboratory interrupted Henry's concentration. Was it for him? It could be Donna. Finally, the call he was waiting for came. It was mid-morning—8:30 A.M. in Phoenix.

"I told him, Henry. Just before he went to work."

"What happened? Are you okay?"

"He didn't say much. Said he wasn't surprised. He told me he did know about us in New York. I was right about that. The whole move to Arizona was part of a plan to have us try again—a new start. And he said I pulled the rug out from under him."

"Just because you weren't seeing me didn't make things any better between you" Henry said.

"That's what I *told* him. He acted like everything was fine before this."

"Did he make any threats? What did he say about Randy?"

"He never makes scenes, I told you that. It's just nastiness and sarcasm and more sarcasm. He said he wasn't going to give Randy up. I asked him to meet my lawyer. He was pretty upset. We both were. I swear we were both so white, if you cut us we wouldn't have bled. He just walked out and slammed the door."

"What did your attorney tell you?"

"She said I should file for divorce and ask for custody. First I told her I was going back to New York, but she vetoed that. I've got to see it through out here."

"Do you have to live with him while all this is going on?" Henry was pacing back and forth as he spoke to her, pushing at his hair.

"Well, Phyllis Cowles—that's the lawyer—and I are meeting tomorrow to make some plans. I never knew how complicated this could be. I've got to watch every step I take."

"When do you think you'll have some more information?"

"Tomorrow night."

"I'll come out and and be with you."

"No. Please. I'll call you as soon as I know anything more. I love you."

She hung up.

FIVE HOURS LATER. "Rand took Randy! They've disappeared. He took him out of school, left me a note saying terrible things—I'll never see either of them again."

"Try to calm down. Don't jump to conclusions. And so much for not making scenes!"

"He drew a skull and crossbones on the note. Please come! I can't stand it. Maybe he's going to kill himself and Randy, too!"

"My guess is he just wants to frighten you into having a miscarriage. But of course I'll come. I'll get the first plane out. I'll be there tonight."

THERE WAS A seven o'clock flight to Phoenix. It was completely booked. He went to the airport as a standby and didn't make it.

"Where are you?" Donna asked anxiously when he called.

"Still in New York, damnit. I couldn't get a seat. I'm taking a nine o'clock flight to Chicago. I've got a better choice of connections there."

"I won't sleep any more than you will, so call me."

He did, from O'Hare. "The best I can do is stay overnight here, get a six thirty-five flight to Dallas, and make a connection that arrives in Phoenix at ten fifteen A.M."

294

"I'll be there. Try to get some rest. We'll go straight to the lawyer's office."

HENRY AND DONNA were two glum figures as they walked into the concrete and glass high-rise building where Phyllis Cowles had her office.

"She said she had a lot more information for me, but that the situation is touch and go."

"What does that mean?" Henry asked.

"We're here to find out."

The attorney's secretary took them into her sparsely furnished office with windows overlooking the city. Phyllis Cowles couldn't have been in practice long. Large, dark-framed glasses and a severely tailored suit did not succeed in making her look older. She sat behind a brown Plexiglas desk, clean except for a thin vase of flowers, a red phone, and a pad, and a large folder with STOCKMAN in block letters. She pointed them to some suede and chrome chairs facing the desk.

Donna brought the attorney up to date on what had happened and voiced her greatest fear. "He could hurt Randy for spite. I don't know what he would do if he was upset enough!"

"I think he's bluffing," Henry said.

"Maybe. But I can't stand it."

"I know you're anxious about your child. That would have upset me, too," the attorney said. "But I agree with Doctor Nyren, it's just a ploy. From what you've told me about Mr. Stockman, although he's vindictive, he doesn't act violently, and he doesn't have a psychiatric history. He's just trying to intimidate you."

"He's done that all right," Donna said, grasping the metal sides of the chair and taking a deep breath in which Henry could hear the wheeze. Henry leaned toward her. There was no way he could help her now, except to be there. Henry was used to being the central attraction. Now it was his turn to play a supporting role.

"Is there any way to contact him?" the young attorney continued. "Does he have an attorney?" Phyllis Cowles spoke softly to

295

reassure Donna. "When he contacts an attorney—any one—he'll find out he's made a big mistake. He's undercut his own position. If he had just taken the child from one residence to another, there would have been no question about the legality of his action. He could have claimed he had established another residence after separation. But to disappear and send such a communication makes it abduction. He's in a tight spot."

"There's not much comfort in that," Donna said. "It might just force him to do something desperate. If I had Randy, I wouldn't give a damn what he did."

"First of all," the attorney continued, "you mustn't leave Phoenix—I'm sure you wouldn't without the child anyway. Look, I've been through this situation before. Your husband has figured out by now that the next step is up to him. Go on home. Don't leave the phone unattended, but I don't want *you* to answer it. I'll have a suggestion about that. I don't want you to negotiate directly either with him or whoever calls on his behalf. Just refer them to me."

"Shall we go now?" Henry asked, rising from his chair.

"Don't be impatient, Doctor Nyren. We're not through yet."

Phyllis Cowles was making notes in the Stockman folder. Then: "Doctor Nyren, I don't want you to go home with Mrs. Stockman."

"You mean, leave her alone?"

For a moment, Donna looked desperate.

"No, but you shouldn't be with her at home. Mr. Stockman may have hired a private detective. I don't want any photos used as banners of righteousness, so he can claim he was provoked, had to protect his child from the iniquity of adultery, and all that. And I certainly don't want any confrontation, in case he comes barging in. I'm thinking of the child, too—and of the future. If Mr. Stockman has half a brain, he'll know this is a situation that can be worked out. It's not a novel event in the history of mankind. Now, as for being alone . . ."

She picked up the phone.

296

"Stella? This is Phyllis Cowles. Remember the Osborne case a few months ago? Well, we've got another one. Yeah. Call in sick. No, its not far. Right in town. I can't tell how long. The people are nice, but the husband's not—no, he's not violent. I know that doesn't bother you, but he's not. Besides, he's not home."

"Who was that?" Donna asked. Her breathing was noisy and sweat was trickling down her back, so that, despite the air conditioning in the office, her white silk blouse stuck to her skin. In addition, she had a sudden urge to go to the bathroom. Until then, she had altogether forgotten she was pregnant.

"Stella Razis is a retired weight lifter. She works as a security guard in this building. You'll be safe with her. She's a smart and resourceful woman with lots of friends on the police force. You'll have nothing to worry about, Doctor Nyren."

Henry used Donna's absence to press the lawyer on a touchy question. "If what you say is correct and what Rand Stockman did was illegal, couldn't he be arrested?"

"Yes, and I'll ask the court to issue a warrant for his arrest. Sending that note destroys his position totally."

"What happens next? Donna wants a divorce. I want to marry her. But the child is her first concern."

"I know. We have to move cautiously. Let's see how the first step works out. If he gets an attorney, it'll mean he's still got some smarts left."

DONNA AND HENRY picked up Stella and proceeded to Donna's house, a trim white ranch with blue shutters on a flat lot—attractive, but much more casual than the one in Riverdale. It was a clear day and slightly cool. Although it wasn't raining or threatening rain, Stella was wearing a tan Burberry raincoat and a rain hat, with her hair tucked under it. She looked like an obese private detective in a Grade B movie.

"I don't like them to know if it's a man or a woman going into the house," she said.

There was an occupied car parked down the block, whether by

chance or arranged by Rand they had no way of knowing. The two women walked into the house. Henry waited until they were safely inside and then drove Donna's car to the Hilton where she had booked a room for him.

The phone in his room was ringing. He ran to it, still holding the room key.

"He called. Stella took it. She was wonderful. A lot of nasty remarks. But Randy is fine, and he does have a lawyer. I called Phyllis. She just called back. We're going to meet in a judge's chambers at ten in the morning."

AT TEN O'CLOCK, Donna, Henry, and the attorney sat in one office knowing that Rand and his attorney were next door.

"Your husband's hired Martin Fleischer," Phyllis Cowles said. "He's a mean old bastard, but that's good. He'll be as mean to your husband as to us. He doesn't handle cases like this very often, and he doesn't know the family court judges like I do. Also, because this is not a big case for him, he'll want to get it over with. Still, he's a disagreeable man."

Judge Fogarty's secretary ushered Donna and her attorney into his oak-paneled chambers lined with law volumes. Henry was asked to remain outside. He protested to no avail.

The two women sat in cracked leather chairs on one side of the judge's large desk. Rand, glowering at them through his round, silver-rimmed glasses, sat on the other side next to his attorney.

"Where's the child?" Judge Fogarty asked. He had just come in from court and was still wearing his robes. He had lost an arm in World War II and wore a gray glove on the artificial hand that protruded from the robe. The half-clenched gray fist resting on his glass-topped desk became a scepter of authority.

"He's in good custody, Judge," Fleischer replied. He had bushy eyebrows, a gold tooth at the side of his mouth that showed when he spoke, and small, calculating eyes that matched his reputation.

"The Court will be the judge of that. Unless that child is back

298

home today—and I mean before dark—your client is in violation of the law and subject to arrest. Do you understand?"

"The father removed the child to protect him from the immoral conditions brought about by Mrs. Stockman's adulterous conduct and illegitimate pregnancy—"

"That doesn't excuse criminal behavior or threatening notes," Judge Fogarty replied sharply.

"My client was under extreme psychological duress as a result of his wife's disclosures of her depraved behavior. We can show there was no intent to harm."

"Now, Fleischer, we're here to cut through all that sanctimonious crap. You know as well as I that the child must be returned to his home. Do you want to make this worse than it is?" Judge Fogarty said, tapping his gloved fist on the desk top.

Fleischer got up, leaned over, and growled something in his client's ear. Then he turned to the judge.

"My client will return to his abode with the boy today. He, as well as the child, will stay in the home."

Donna put her hands over her mouth.

Mrs. Cowles spoke up. "Your Honor, my client is filing for a divorce and will ask for custody of the child."

Rand jumped up. "Over my dead—"

Fleischer snapped, "Shut up!" Rand sat down.

Judge Fogarty rose. "That's a separate issue. Counselor, you advised your client properly. He is avoiding a great deal of difficulty for himself although he has already compromised his position. However, I'm sure the court will take his psychological distress into account when the divorce proceedings are heard."

"I DON'T LIKE the way it ended," Donna said when they left the judge's chambers. "The judge softened up toward Rand. I can be made to look pretty rotten."

"Don't worry," Phyllis Cowles replied. "A different judge will hear the divorce case. Of course, Fleischer will try to make you look like the most wanton woman, the most unfit mother on earth, but the facts are otherwise. This isn't 1922 and it's not Saudi Arabia. You have rights. There's a proper legal format for handling a divorce. The pregnancy is only one part of it. His abduction of the child, and threats, are much more serious."

Henry joined them. "Fill me in—what happened?"

Before they had walked very far, Rand caught up with them, stepped in front of Henry, looked him in the eye, and spat on the floor. Then he turned and slowly walked away.

As a gesture of contempt, it was not without its effect on Henry. All during the proceedings, and in the hours leading up to them, Henry had been thinking: I am the author of this tragedy. I'm the one who broke up this family. I took the initiative toward Donna. Lake Placid was my idea. He had to keep repeating to himself over and over again that Donna's had not been a good marriage, that one way or another there would have been a divorce and a custody battle.

Outside the courthouse, Donna's breathing got progressively worse. Henry suggested they sit down a moment on one of the stone benches and that she use her Medihaler. It didn't help much. As they approached the car, Henry noticed that her color was not good and her legs were wobbly.

Henry and Phyllis both helped her into the car. She was gasping for breath and holding her abdomen.

"Is she having a 'mis'?" Phyllis Cowles asked.

# CHAPTER
# FORTY-FIVE

ONNA WAS not having a miscarriage, but a serious asthma attack. St. Joseph's Hospital was only a few minutes away. Henry ran inside for a wheelchair while Phyllis helped Donna out of the car. In the emergency room they started oxygen immediately. Then Henry told the physician on duty what the situation was.

"Well, first we'll get a chest X-ray, and then we should be able to break the bronchial spasms with some hydrocortisone," the young doctor said.

"No! I just told you she was pregnant. We don't want any X-rays. And no cortisone either. It could be dangerous for the fetus."

"Well, what do you want?" The busy young doctor, his white jacket and trousers soiled with the splatterings of eight hours in the ER, was obviously annoyed.

"Could you please just give her some intravenous aminophylline," Henry said, tempering his tone. "And then let's see what happens, okay?"

By this time the nurse had put in an intravenous line.

"Suit yourself," the physician responded, losing interest fast. He gave the order to the nurse and walked away.

In a few minutes, Donna was breathing easily. They got a

301

supply of Theo-Dur tablets from the hospital pharmacy, which would keep her aminophylline level up, and they were able to leave the hospital and go home.

Stella was in the house waiting for them. Rand and Randy had not yet arrived. Arrangements were made for Stella and one of her friends, another weight lifter, to remain in the house, so that there would be a 24-hour referee and bodyguard present.

Despite the lawyer's advice to stay away, Henry walked into the living room and sat down. He was in an armchair by the window overlooking the street and the path to the house. Stella was checking out the refrigerator.

"I'm going to stay where I am until that guy brings Randy back and I know things are quiet here."

"If there's one thing that will guarantee no peace and quiet, it's you being here when Rand arrives. Henry, I'll do anything to avoid a scene. It's no good for Randy or for me, either. Please go back to the hotel."

"I may as well go back to New York."

"Don't get angry. I've got to follow my instincts."

"We're trying to start a new family. We should start sticking together now. I've got feelings about this, too."

He was on his feet pacing back and forth.

She replied, "I know that, but you can't run everything, and you don't know everything! In fact, you're starting to sound like him. I feel like scooping Randy up and running away from all of you!"

"That type of talk doesn't hold too much promise for our future."

Afraid to carry the conversation further, their glances locked through a film of moisture.

"I'm sorry. I just wish I could whisk you out of all this, be alone with you," Henry said softly.

"And I've got such a longing to be held. But we can't, darling. If you love me, let's go along with what the lawyer said."

302

He kissed her lightly on the tip of her nose, held her to him for a long moment, and left without speaking again.

ABOUT TWENTY MINUTES later Donna's doorbell rang. She ran to open the door.

"Mommy!" Randy jumped into her arms.

"Are you okay?" she asked.

"Sure I am. Only I missed you."

"Where have you been?"

"A swell place with a swimming pool and a lot of people," Randy answered.

Stella had heard the doorbell and came out of the kitchen. Rand stood stiffly in the foyer, looking around.

"Well, *my* son is back in *my* house. It *is* my house. It's not joint ownership, you know that, don't you?!"

"My attorney told me not to talk to you when she isn't present," Donna told him.

"And is this bimbo your attorney?" Rand turned and stared at Stella.

"I'm her friend, *skata* face!" Stella walked up close to Rand, arms akimbo. She looked like a sumo wrestler dressed in a polyester pantsuit.

Rand walked through each room in the ranch house.

"I've worked for everything in here!"

Donna regretted the pain he must be feeling, but she knew that if she weakened, showed any softness now, it would make the inevitable much harder. She remained silent.

Randy skipped off to his room. Donna sat and waited. Rand had to do something. As he left, he stopped in the foyer. There were two small tables, one on which the mail was placed, and one facing it. On the second one was a large vase made into a lamp. He started to glance at the mail, then with a sweep of his hand, scattered it over the floor. As he opened the door to leave, he gave a backward thrust with his leg into the other small table, knocking over the lamp. With remarkable agility for one so large, Stella bounded over and caught it.

THE NEXT MONTH was a flurry of desperate phone calls and trips back and forth for Henry. There was a separation. Donna filed for divorce. There were many hearings. Fleischer was mean and did what he could to destroy Donna. She stood fast. The attorney could produce no witnesses with evidence that she was an unfit mother. Phyllis Cowles produced a great many witnesses who attested to Donna being a caring mother; but they could not impugn Rand's actions toward the child, except for the abduction episode, which Fleischer claimed was the result of his client's distress.

Henry did not escape Fleischer's scornful deprecations, and these had repercussions beyond the court. First, the attorney looked for malpractice suits that had been filed against Henry. Such an action might produce an antagonistic witness. But there were no such suits. However, the investigator that Fleischer hired did come up with something. He reported that Henry had a mistress in New York, one Janine Williams.

"Your honor, so far we have focused on Mrs. Stockman's fitness to continue custody. We hold that her illegitimate pregnancy is *prima facie* evidence that she is not a fit mother. I would now like to turn my attention to the man who impregnated her in an adulterous act, Doctor Henry Nyren. Doctor Nyren has a mistress in New York, a Mrs. Janine Williams. The evidence I will submit shows that this doctor's relationship with Mrs. Williams is of long duration and can reasonably be assumed to have existed prior to his wife's demise. Therefore this relationship, too, involved adultery. I cannot see how this Court can allow custody of a child to two individuals who are up to their navels in adultery."

That evening was rough for Donna and Henry. Added to the tension of awaiting the court's decision was Donna's distress at finding out—particularly the way she found out—about Janine.

304

"Why didn't you tell me about this Williams woman? What am I getting myself and Randy into? I asked you before if there was someone else in your life." Donna passed a handkerchief back and forth from one hand to another.

Henry wanted to go to her, but forced himself to remain seated. "It wasn't important, Donna. And it still isn't. Fleischer made a big ugly mountain out of a molehill."

"She is your mistress, isn't she—?"

"That's the way one of his investigators reported it."

"Well, is she, or isn't she?"

"She's an old friend, a fine woman. We have had sex, but I swear to you, not since you and I started going together."

"You still didn't answer my question."

Henry got up and walked over to a bookcase. "Is there a dictionary here?"

"This isn't English class."

"Look here. 'Mistress: a woman who has a continual sexual relationship with a man to whom she is not married, especially one who receives financial support from the man.' Our sexual relationship has never been more than occasional, and as for support," he had to laugh, "Janine wouldn't consider such an arrangement with anyone. Donna, she's a good person and a good friend."

Donna sat down. "I'm confused, Henry. I'm unsure of myself, unsure of you, unsure of Randy's future. Then something like this hits me out of the blue. It doesn't help."

Henry went to the kitchen and brought back some wine. They sat, and Henry told her how he had met Janine, the time he had helped her, and how Janine had helped with Eve when Laura died. So many mutual acts of friendship over the years. In the light of his candor the apprehensiveness melted.

WHEN THE DECISION was made, Judge Fogarty, who had taken an instant dislike to Rand, awarded Donna custody of Randy, with liberal visitation rights for the father.

This did not solve Donna's dilemma. She wanted to be in New York with Henry but moving would cancel Rand's visitation rights. Phyllis Cowles appealed for permission to move out of state, citing her client's pregnancy and forthcoming marriage. When the Court consented, Donna nearly fainted with joy. She could have her baby in New York.

Henry returned to New York immediately after the judge's decision. Donna and the child were to remain temporarily in Phoenix. There were details regarding the divorce that had to be settled. For Henry, there was an additional concern. He had to face the role of being a father, not to one child but two. He resolved to do better this time. He had to. He couldn't let Donna down. And he had learned something from experience—experience for which Eve had paid the price.

THE FIRST PERSON Henry had dinner with in New York was Janine.

"Well, how did it go?"

"Better than I expected."

"Is it okay if I cheer and cry at the same time?"

"I want you and Donna to get to know one another."

"I'm not a *ménage à trois* type, Henry," Janine said, quietly plucking artichoke leaves from her appetizer.

"I've got only a limited number of close friends, and I can't afford to lose any of them. Stick with me, be a pal."

"You know I will. We like each other too much to be anything less."

When they parted, four hands grasped each other tightly just long enough for a full measure of confidence to flow from one to the other.

GETTING BACK TO research was tough, but that also was a commitment to be kept. Repairin was on a fast-moving tide and it pulled Henry along with it.

The research with leukemia-susceptible mice was well under-

306

way. However, there was a cloud hanging over the repairin research as a result of Henry's suspension and the revocation of his license. Any research he was involved in might be suspect. Therefore, Jarrett Weil took extra precautions to see that no one knew which mice received repairin and which were injected with a placebo.

Mice started dying of leukemia a month after the experiment started. By the second month, large numbers had died. On May 31, at the end of the third month after starting the mouse experiments, Paul, Henry, Avery Stemple, Duncan Comfort, and two technicians waited in anticipation. They were seated outside of Jarrett Weil's office while he broke the code that indicated how the mice had been treated.

"Doctor Weil will be out in a few minutes. He's almost finished. May I bring you some coffee?" his secretary asked.

"We'll bring it." Rose Sylvester and LeToya Smith, two bright and energetic lab technicians, jumped to their feet.

"Hold it!" Henry said. "You two have done all the work on this research. If it's a success, we'll owe you an enormous debt of gratitude, and if it's negative, we'll still be indebted to you. The least I can do is get the coffee for you today."

The young women sat down, smiling. Appreciation was something they seldom received.

Henry had started to rise when Weil, with his usual serious demeanor and stiff motions, walked into the room. There were no preliminary comments.

"Under the conditions of this experiment, repairin prevented the development of virus-induced leukemia. The results suggest that repairin has some effect."

"That last remark sounds like an understatement to me," Henry said.

Paul heard the results impassively, then said, "Well, er, of course, the work has to be repeated, and extended, corroborated in another laboratory. We've also got to determine precisely how this substance works."

"Any other comments?" Weil asked.

Duncan was scribbling on a pad. He looked up. "You know, Henry and I have discussed what we'd do if the experiments came out this way. We are both clinicians, and we'd like to try repairin in humans. We have some thoughts about this, and very soon we'd like to present our plans for clinical trials."

"Henry, any other remarks?"

Henry was sitting back in his chair, looking up, almost daydreaming. He said, as if to himself, "I think this is as close to a star-burst as I'll ever get."

The others, puzzled, looked at him. Stemple had been sitting there awestruck by the possibility that his department could be in on something big.

"Avery, what do you have to say?"

"Hot shit!"

# CHAPTER
# *FORTY-SIX*

THERE WAS an additional finding in Henry's laboratory that Duncan Comfort was interested in. It appeared that in situations of stress and anxiety, repairin levels were severely reduced. Could psychological stress reduce repairin levels and thus have an adverse effect on resistance to disease, in particular, an adverse effect on resistance to cancer?

Duncan was in the hospital cafeteria trying to save a table for himself, Dr. Veit-Volpin, and a guest. He was standing and looking around so they would see him easily when they entered. The outspoken radiologist had invited Henry and Paul Rosen, but they had both declined, taking their usual working lunch in their offices.

Gregor Veit-Volpin and his guest, Dr. Maurice Gorski, arrived. Duncan apologized for not having a more private place for their discussion, and this struck a responsive cord in Veit-Volpin. He was one of the most vocal critics of the new order.

"Don't you know they hate doctors in this hospital? All our privileges they are taking away. It's those administrators. The hospital is their private *guberniya*. Little czars they are. They redecorate the whole place—starting with their own offices, of course. A dining room we used to have, now they make us eat with the peasants. And you know what? They don't clean up. No, not even paint. The doctor's locker room, the clock says ten o'clock. It hasn't changed for ten years."

Duncan smiled. "That's because you come into work at ten o'clock. There's nothing wrong with that clock."

"It's true, it's true. I like a leisurely breakfast. So, I'm ninety-nine percent right. No special parking privileges any more either. Some nerve. My wife parked my car only one little hour in front of Bloomingdale's, and a ticket she got from the Cossacks."

"Is that the administrator's fault also?"

"Of course. They are the czars. Didn't I just tell you that?

"Now, I want to finish the introductions. Gorski, my friend Doctor Duncan Comfort is a cancer chemotherapist and a recent addition to our staff. He works with Nyren and Rosen and that gang. Duncan, Gorski is Medical Director of the Matawan State Hospital, where he does psychiatric research. I want you to tell him about the Max Ledo case."

Gorski broke in. "Gregor, I am also a chemotherapist. I use drugs to treat diseases of the mind." Turning to Duncan, he added "Gregor told me about the autopsy findings, or lack of autopsy findings, in the Ledo case. He said that the case would relate to some of my own research. I gladly agreed to come for lunch, but I had another motive. I want to hear more about repairin."

"The Ledo case," Duncan said. "Well, Max Ledo was a patient with throat cancer who died unexpectedly a few weeks ago. Doctor Bancroft did the autopsy, and he could find no cause of death in the patient."

"Isn't extensive cancer alone sufficient cause of death?" asked Dr. Gorski, as he finished his soup and wiped his beard with his napkin.

"That's just it. Max did not have extensive cancer. This man was a sixty-six year old, small, tough mailman. He had had a left-sided neck dissection and removal of the larynx two years ago, and the tumor recurred. We treated him with radiation therapy and chemotherapy. He had a good response to bleomycin, the cancer regressed, and the neck looked very good. He was in good spirits too, looking forward to going home.

"Then one day his wife walks in and says 'Max. I ain't never gonna take you home. This is the last time I'm walking into this hellhole. You can drop dead for all I care.' She stands there and keeps cursing and cursing him.

"After that, Max stopped writing on his pad. He wouldn't look at anyone when they came up to his bed. He just lay there, morose and depressed. Four days later, he died."

"Abandonment, hopelessness, despair, and death," Dr. Gorski said, wiping his mouth again before dipping his spoon into some vanilla ice cream nestled in half a melon. "Gregor knows my research very well. I have been working with patients in nursing homes and mental institutions. It's the same sequence of events, only more acute in this case. His wife 'pointed the bone' at him. She cast the spell of hopelessness, and he died a voodoo death. The great physiologist Cannon described it in a nutshell. 'The victim pines away. Strength runs out of him like water, and in the course of a day or two, he succumbs.' And that's it. There is no adequate medical explanation. So, Gregor, if this is why you invited me for lunch here, it's a good reason, but that's all I can tell you."

Gregor Veit-Volpin had finished his lunch and was lighting up his pipe. "It's also cheaper to eat in the hospital dining room than to take you to one of those Second Avenue restaurants. What an appetite. That melon and ice cream would cost three dollars nowadays at any restaurant. But, the case. Oh, yes, the case. I knew you would be interested. This is not the only case where a cancer patient dies for no apparent reason." Turning to Duncan he said, "Maybe we could do some research along Gorski's line. What do you think?"

"I would like to work with Dr. Gorski. The psychological aspects of dealing with cancer are a particular interest of mine. But we don't get too many cases as blatant as the one I just described. Most patients here are encouraged by the fact that they are being actively treated, and we try to maintain this upbeat attitude. That's why this is such a great institution."

Veit-Volpin employed a range of about half an octave to reply, "Well, maybe not such a great institution. Sometimes a little too much smugness maybe. All kinds of czars we have here." He concluded his little aria with a puff of smoke.

Dr. Gorski turned to his host, saying, "Gregor, I enjoyed the lunch. And Doctor Comfort, it was a pleasure meeting you. Please call me if you think we can work out a joint research project. From what Gregor told me, repairin may be a link between cancer and mental diseases."

"That's a little premature. Doctor Veit-Volpin is a Renaissance man and he is fond of building global theories out of match sticks. But I will call you."

Veit-Volpin patted Duncan on the back. "Very good, very good. I couldn't have said it better myself. Young man, keep on being obnoxious, and some day you'll turn out like me!"

# CHAPTER
# FORTY-SEVEN

PHYLLIS COWLES'S work was not done yet. There were black scenes before it was decided exactly how Randy's time would be divided. In addition, both attorneys prevailed on Donna and Rand to speak to an experienced child psychologist. Donna worried that Rand would poison Randy's mind against her. Rand was upset that his role as father would be diminished. For the child's sake, they agreed to see the same psychologist, but not together.

Donna was packing to move back to New York, and Henry was in Phoenix for the weekend to help her. They sat in the living room amid packing boxes and piled-up luggage.

"You don't have to bother with the furniture, do you?"

"No, these are just personal things. Rand is going to live in the house for a while when we leave. But I didn't tell you the latest, did I? We haven't heard the last of him."

Donna looked exhausted. Chewed fingernails were a telltale sign of the pressures she had been under.

"What's he up to, now?"

"He's moving back to New York, also. What do you think of that? He got his old job back."

"I wasn't counting on that," Henry said.

"Well, the psychologist wasn't just working for us. Rand

313

insisted he wanted to keep up his visitation rights, and she agreed with him. I had a feeling he might move back to New York, anyway. The suggestion she made about moving into my mother's apartment when we get back will give Randy a chance to adjust to New York in familiar surroundings."

"Actually, if Rand could settle into a civilized pattern of behavior toward us and Randy, it's not a bad thing to have him in New York," Henry said. "I want to be Randy's friend, and I *will* be. But I'm under no illusion that I can replace his father. I have to admit to a certain amount of apprehension in that department. Parenting has never been my strong suit."

"Henry, as long as you do the best you can, and you don't ignore us, we love each other enough to make it work."

"Starting off at your mother's is okay. But as soon as we're married I want us to live together as a family. Randy has to learn to see me as a friend and not his doctor. He also has to see me as his mother's husband."

WHEN THE DIVORCE was final, Donna and Henry were married in Judge Lukan's chambers. Lukan was a former patient of Henry's, and although he hadn't performed a marriage since becoming a state Supreme Court Justice, this was an occasion he relished. He had an uncommonly large, window-lined corner office that was very suitable for this purpose. His law clerks and secretaries got into the mood of the occasion and were busy setting up a table in the corner of the office with champagne, crackers, cheese, and cookies. Donna had shopped for the prettiest maternity dress she could find, but her mother would have none of that, and made a high-waisted beige gown festooned with lace, which did not so much disguise her pregnancy as celebrate it. Randy was dressed up in a navy blue suit with short pants, high socks, and a red bow tie.

"What do I have to wear short pants for, it's not even hot outside!"

"That's how the suit came, Randy. The only long pants you have

314

are jeans. If you want to wear them instead, it's okay. I have a pair in the case outside. See which way you look nicer."

Donna won the day. In fact, she won all the way that day. She was radiant with the blush of pregnancy.

"I've never seen you look so beautiful," Henry beamed.

"Cut it out! All brides are beautiful, and most have butterflies in their tummies, but I've got more than that in mine."

He took her in his arms and waltzed her a few steps in an erratic circle. She broke away, laughing.

"The judge said it was okay to have some music in his chambers," Henry said, looking around for the musician.

"Don't worry, mother is reliable, and so is her neighbor. When she said she'd bring Sam Rizzo to play the violin, you can count on it. Stop acting the nervous bridegroom!"

"What'll he play, the 'Wedding March'?"

"How about 'I Don't Want Her, You Can Have Her, She's Too Fat For Me'?"

"For crying out loud, Donna, you've got to be a little serious!"

"Darling, this is so wonderful that if I get serious I'll never stop crying."

She rested her cheek on his shoulder for a moment. Henry, trying to be fastidious, brushed the face powder off his dark blue serge suit and straightened his tie. His thick, black hair was slicked in place. His apparent apprehension in this smiling group instantly gave him away as the groom. Judge Lukan's clerk made it official by coming over and pinning a small carnation on Henry's lapel.

"I feel bad that Eve didn't come. I wonder if she's angry," Henry said.

"If she were angry, she wouldn't have sent the flowers and the lovely note," Donna replied.

Paul and Joan Rosen arrived and, finally, Donna's mother, with Sam Rizzo and his violin. Rotund Judge Lukan determined that all was ready. He hitched his trousers up over his ample paunch. As soon as he put on his robes, he assumed a magisterial appearance, but when he stood in front of Donna, each in a ballooning gown, it looked like a vaudeville scene.

The judge winked at Donna, and she smiled back. Then he took a few steps backward and got into position. Sam made ready to play. Donna's mother touched a handkerchief to her eyes. Randy fidgeted with the ring.

Donna whispered to Henry, "We've made it, darling. I feel like we've finished an obstacle course."

"Specialty of the house," he whispered.

WILD ASIA AT the Bronx Zoo is a monorail that carries visitors through a forested area of the park where the animals roam free. For children, it is a ball. Henry just leaned back and let Randy enjoy it. Their first, few, short encounters without Donna had been tentative. Randy hadn't gotten used to Henry as other than a threatening figure in a white coat. This trip was a new experience for them both. Afterward, on the drive home, Randy sat in the front seat next to Henry, the seat belts wrapping him up like a package. For a while, he looked ahead silently, his eyes just at windshield level.

"You hurt me once," Randy said finally in a matter-of-fact tone.

"I remember."

"Will you hurt me again?"

"We're friends, and one friend doesn't hurt another."

"Are you my father's friend?"

"I don't know your father, Randy. I just met him two or three times for a few minutes."

"He says you hurt him, too. Did you do that test on my father?"

"No."

"Then how did you hurt him?"

"I guess he didn't want your mother to be friends with anyone else, and when she and I became friends he felt hurt."

"I got lots of friends."

"Sometimes when you have a special friend, you don't want to

316

share that special friend with anyone else. I'm friends with your mother because she wants me to be her friend. When your father can be friends with your mother and with me, then no one will be hurt."

Animation returned to Randy's face. "That's what I'd like. Then we could go places together, like the zoo."

THE PROTECTIVE EFFECT of repairin in mice was so impressive, the implications so far-reaching, it was inevitable that other laboratories would start similar experiments. The initial experiments were being confirmed at Curie and extended to other forms of cancer. Almost immediately reports began to appear of repairin's use in patients with far advanced cancer, but the results were not any better than they had been with Marlene. Still, the human studies had shown remarkably little in the way of toxicity. Henry was straining to find some practical application for his findings.

He was sitting one day in the office of Dr. Logan Conrad, the epidemiologist at the medical school. Dr. Conrad, a thin man with piercing eyes, had devoted his career to the study of cancer. Originally, epidemiologists were doctors who studied epidemics, the conditions under which they arose, how they spread, who was affected, and the toll they took. With the control of most infectious diseases achieved, epidemiologists were asking the same questions about cancer. Conrad leaned toward Henry and said, "And so you think this repairin might be useful to prevent cancer in man? You're setting a hard road for yourself. Even when we have something that's useful, like the Pap test, it's not easy to get everyone to use it."

Henry pushed back his thatch of hair and said, "I did some homework before I came here. You published statistics showing that about three adults per thousand will get cancer each year. That kind of startled me, because even if this material is good and could prevent the development of cancer in man the way it seems to do in mice, then I have to treat a thousand people to

317

prevent those three cases. And if it takes cancer many years to develop, then how many years do I have to wait, and how many thousands of people do I have to treat, to get results that anyone will believe?"

"That's what I meant when I said you've set yourself on a difficult road. You would have to have thousands of patients in your study and thousands in a control group, and you'd have to wait many years, perhaps the entire lifetime of individuals, to see if you've influenced the incidence of cancer."

Conrad leaned back in his old-fashioned, wooden, swivel chair. "I have another suggestion," he said. "There is a population that is ideally suited for your study. It has a very high incidence of cancer, and many of these individuals are already hospitalized and under continual medical supervision. I'm referring to institutionalized mentally deficient children, especially those with Down's syndrome. The incidence of leukemia in those children is forty to fifty times higher than in the general population. We think the leukemia comes up in them very quickly. You might be able to see some results in a year or two."

"With my sterling reputation, if I ever started an experiment with mentally retarded children, every editor, every clergyman, every prosecutor in the country would be after my hide. They would probably resurrect Torquemada for my benefit."

"I never said you wouldn't have problems, Doctor Nyren. You'll have one or another set of problems no matter which direction you go in. You could also look into clinics for workers exposed to cancer-causing substances in the course of their occupations, like asbestos or vinyl chloride. But if I were you, I'd try for the mentally retarded kids."

When Henry related this discussion to Rosen, Boyer, and Comfort, to his surprise they all favored the recommendation of the epidemiologist. The children were already under medical care and could easily be identified. It would not be difficult to get their parents to agree to an injection that could possibly help them and was without side effects. "If we can get the cooperation

318

of all the committees, we can be under way," Duncan said, raring to go.

The three others looked to Henry for a go-ahead. He studied some stains in the ceiling and slowly moved his fingertips across the top of his head, as if trying to push away insistent misgivings.

"It's up to you, Henry," Paul said.

# CHAPTER
# *FORTY-EIGHT*

D
RIVING INTO the grounds of the Matawan State Hospital, Henry had the feeling he was entering the campus of a large university rather than a hospital for the mentally ill. A series of large, red-brick buildings woven together by meandering stone paths and lush landscaping enhanced the impression of a campus. The driveway led to the administration building, which could have been on any college campus. Was that imposing building across the way the science hall? That lovely Georgian structure with the ivy-covered walls—perhaps the school of liberal arts? Ironic, thought Henry, that identical environments were used to house the two extremes of intelligence.

These feelings added to Henry's reluctance about the visit. On the trip up, Duncan had again stressed to Henry the advantages of using mentally retarded children. Dr. Gorski had arranged this meeting to discuss some of the problems they might encounter and how these could be handled. Henry was surprised to learn that the staff pediatrician Gorski had assigned to the project, if they did go ahead, was Roger Floyd. Memory lashed at him like rain against a windshield. Mrs. Kreutzer. Roger's refusal to administer an experimental drug, Roger's resignation and subsequent replacement by Duncan Comfort. He wondered if Roger

320

was still as opposed to experimentation as he had been. If he was, this trip would be a waste of everyone's time.

They parked in front of the administration building and spent a few minutes with Dr. Gorski in his office, then walked to the pediatrics building to meet Roger Floyd. Heavy wire screens on the windows, the guard at the door, and the urine and antiseptic smells in the halls dispelled the sense that they might be in a university. The sickness rate among these children, due to all diseases including cancer, was very high. Many of them had congenital defects besides those of the central nervous system. Cardiac, kidney, and skeletal abnormalities were widespread. Often these concurrent disorders reduced their life span to just a few years. It was apparent that Floyd was a busy pediatrician.

Floyd was waiting for them in his large, high-ceilinged office on the first floor of the sixty-year-old building. He got straight to the point.

"I know you have a problem in determining if repairin can prevent the development of cancer," Roger said. "I know also it's not like the Salk vaccine for polio, where you could tell after a single epidemic if it was going to work or not. Nevertheless, we have so many cases of leukemia here in our Down's syndrome patients, that it's the nearest thing you can get to an epidemic of cancer in human beings. I agree with Doctor Conrad's estimate that the incubation period of acute leukemia in these children is very short. You should be able to determine how effective your treatment is in a few years. Of course, there is the question of experimentation in children. But, if we plan carefully, I think we can overcome the problems."

On a coldly logical leve , Henry was pleased that the work would go forward. But, emotionally, he felt apprehensive about again being drawn into an area where science and ethics became a murky mixture.

"Roger," Henry said, "plainly your outlook on experimentation has changed since our last meeting. Well, so has mine. In fact there may be a complete reversal of roles."

321

Roger raised an eyebrow.

"When you were at Curie, you felt keenly enough about experimentation in patients to leave. It's clear that lots of things have changed since then. Doctor Gorski has said several complimentary things about how the quality of care for these children has improved since your arrival and about the research studies you've been doing here. He said you've helped put this institution on the map."

Henry's comments put Roger at ease.

"On the other hand," Henry continued, "I've been burned in the human experimentation area."

"I know how you must feel, Doctor Nyren," Roger said. "As far as conducting research with my children here, let me say that I agree completely that experimentation in retarded children that entails any degree of risk to their health is unethical. I also think it's wrong to involve these children in medical research just because they are mentally retarded or institutionalized. They're nature's victims. They shouldn't be ours, too. However, the repairin work has to be done here not because they are retarded, but because they have leukemia in great numbers. And the fact is, repairin seems harmless. Using it does not impose any risk."

Henry wasn't satisfied. "First, it hasn't been used in children. Second, if something goes wrong with the injection or the material gets contaminated, or if it is given improperly, or if anything remotely connected with the process goes wrong, then repairin will be blamed. Frankly, I don't see why you want to get involved with this."

"You *have* changed," Roger said.

Henry shrugged and smiled. "Not all that much," he said. "It seems the decision has been made, so let's get on with it!"

WHEN HE RETURNED to Curie, Tara called him in the laboratory and told him Jerry Connor, the hospital's public relations officer, was on the phone.

"I just got a call from a friend at the *Post*," he said. "She says

322

they got a tip from someone at Matawan that you are going to use repairin on mentally retarded children. It could be explosive if they want it to come out that way, or they could look like idiots if it's not true."

"In the first place," Henry said, "if by 'you' you are referring to me or anyone else involved in repairin research at Curie, then *we* are not going to do anything to mentally retarded children. We arc in thc proc3 of developing plans by which we would provide repairin to the pediatric staff of the hospital for clinical use."

He sounded so cool, he thought. But there it was. The trouble was starting already.

"Look, Doctor Nyren, those fine distinctions are going to be lost if the *Post* wants to play it for sensationalism. I think you should get together with the people at Matawan and come out with a joint press release—I mean now!"

Connor was right. Henry got right on it, and a joint press release from the Curie Cancer Research Institute and the Matawan State Hospital was sent out within hours. The copy was careful to state that the medical staff of the Matawan Hospital would be in complete charge. The evaluation would be done by the University Medical School Department of Epidemiology, and the Curie laboratories would provide research assistance. The release also made clear that nothing would proceed until an Investigational New Drug application had been approved by the Food and Drug Administration and the appropriate committees of the Matawan Hospital had reviewed the project. The safety of the material in adults was stressed, and the epidemic nature of leukemia in these special children was pointed out. Nowhere in the release was Henry's name mentioned. Dr. Floyd at Matawan and Dr. Rosen at the Curie Institute were named as the principal investigators.

The carefully worded, very accurate, and guarded release was picked up by the New York dailies and the wire services as well. Most papers printed the Associated Press material, which had the following add-on to the Curie-Matawan release: "The use of mentally retarded children in medical research has been severely criticized, particularly since the incident at the Shadybrook State Hospital where many children developed hepatitis as a result of a similarly well-intentioned medical research program. The difference in this project, according to medical sources, is that repairin has been used extensively in human beings in this country and in France, and while the promise of early claims has not been fulfilled, neither have there been any harmful effects to date. A Curie Institute physician, Dr. Henry Nyren, has been suspended from practice because of an unauthorized use of repairin in a terminal cancer patient. Although no longer practicing, Dr. Nyren is still associated with the repairin research program."

Fair enough. But the *New York Post* blared out the following version:

DISCREDITED CANCER DOCTOR
TO EXPERIMENT WITH
HELPLESS CHILDREN.

Dr. Henry Nyren, barred from the practice of medicine in New York for the unauthorized use of an experimental drug, is preparing to undertake a series of experiments with human beings, this time with hospitalized, helpless, mentally deficient children. In the episode that led to the suspension of his license by the New York State Department of Education, he used an experimental cancer drug, repairin, on an unconscious cancer victim who died almost immediately thereafter . . .

Although Henry and others on the repairin team had been on guard as to what the press might do with the story, they were nevertheless upset and angry when the hate letters started to come in.

Henry was bothered because, while point by point each criticism could be refuted, the grain of truth was there. He had

324

been discredited. This *was* an experiment; these children *were* helpless.

"Leaving the practice hasn't taken the pressure off, has it, Henry?" Donna asked one evening. They were having dinner at home. It was a late dinner, just as it had always been.

"Research is never helped when it's done in the glare of spotlights. We don't need newspapers or TV, they distort."

"I think you are more harried now than when I first met you," she said.

"There's something to be said for practice. You help someone. There's immediate satisfaction. Now I feel I'm battling the entire world."

# CHAPTER
# FORTY-NINE

THOUGH HENRY had been to Matawan several times for work sessions with Roger, he had not seen nor spoken with Irene. However, on this trip she called and invited Henry to visit. Henry and Roger were walking from the hospital building to the nineteenth-century frame house, one of several in a row, residences for the medical staff and their families.

"You seem happy here, Roger," Henry said. "I assume you have no regrets about having left Curie and changing the course of your career?"

"None whatsoever. I was not cut out to be an oncologist. It's hard on Irene, though. I mean staying home and keeping house. But she'll go back into practice when the baby is a little older."

"You know, when you left, I thought you would finish your residency in pediatrics and go into practice. From what Gorski tells me, this place is as much research-oriented as Curie. Do you find you are developing the same attitudes here that you did at Curie?"

Roger was amazed at what he considered Henry's obtuseness. "It isn't that I didn't like academic work or research—it's *cancer* I didn't like. I suppose for someone as dedicated as you, that's hard to accept. I'd come away in the evening jumpy and sullen. I was losing my capacity to laugh and joke, beauty and love and happiness stopped touching me. That goddamned disease was ruining my life."

Henry understood Roger's words, but not his attitude. "I think we got you at the wrong stage of your career. If you came back to Curie now you'd feel more at home. Research is the key that makes it possible to hang on. I'm sure if it weren't for the research you do, you wouldn't stay here, either. You'd say it was too damned depressing working with retarded kids."

"Sure," Roger said, "research offers hope for improving the lot of your patients. You feel it's worthwhile at Curie, Doctor Nyren, and I feel it's worthwhile here."

Irene, coming down the path to greet Henry, caught the last part of the conversation.

"Did you have the same feelings Roger did at Curie?" Henry asked her as they strolled to the porch.

"I still don't agree with Roger about chemotherapy," Irene said. "But, to be honest, it did get me down after a while. Still, I found Curie fascinating. I never worked anywhere else where science was right at the bedside, where everyone tried so hard. I really understood you, Henry. You didn't know that, did you? You were so busy fighting with one intern or another who hated oncology. You should have concentrated on those of us who were getting the message.

"By the way," she said, changing the subject, "I got a letter from Eve last week."

Henry leaned back in the tall wicker rocker. "Really! She doesn't write often. We phone once in a while."

"You know, Eve and I have kept in touch over the years," Irene said. "We've been friends since the days I helped her with her French lessons. Last June I gave her telephone number to Allen Bruce, one of our pediatric residents who was moving to Los Angeles. He finally called her, and they've had two dates, and she says he's a 'possibility.' A definite Category I, she said."

AS THE MONTHS of her pregnancy rolled by, Donna was busy

327

picking up the strings of her life in New York, making new connections for Randy and meeting Henry's friends. She also had a major task, finding a new apartment. They needed a third bedroom. Henry wanted to be closer to the hospital. Both felt they wanted a new start in a new home. During these months Henry spent most of his time shuttling back and forth between the Curie Research Institute and the Pediatrics Building at Matawan, monitoring the use of repairin and seeing that all the required data were properly collected and assembled. He threw himself into the work, like a predator rushing in for the kill. He couldn't imagine that he had ever been frustrated.

Henry had no clue as to how the results were turning out. Only Logan Conrad, who had the code, would know that. Conrad also had the data on the incidence of leukemia in the hospital for the last ten years and would use this as the basis for his predictive statistics. Henry wished only that he had more stamina. The schedule and pace he set for himself exceeded any effort he had made while he was in practice.

They found the apartment they had been looking for in a new high rise going up just a few blocks from Curie. Donna and Henry had just signed the contract and were having dinner in a Chinese restaurant.

"The lobby is magnificent, and the pool, what a bonus!" Henry said.

"It'll work just fine, even though the rooms are smaller, and the view isn't there."

"Think it'll be ready in time?" Henry asked.

"For me? In a month? Not likely."

After dinner they returned to the apartment on 81st Street.

"Donna, would you think me a boor if we went to bed early? I'm bushed." Henry was collapsed in his favorite armchair.

"Why, you dear old fool, I was hoping you'd say something like that. I'm feeling tired myself."

Hand in hand, like an old married couple, they went to bed.

328

NEXT THING HENRY knew, Donna was shaking his shoulder.

"Henry, wake up. Your pajamas are soaking wet, and you're making all kinds of sounds. Are you okay?"

"I'm fine. Sorry I disturbed you."

"At least get a fresh pair of pajamas, and I'll put some talc on you."

After that they went back to sleep.

But not for long.

First there was a twinge, then a cramp. Then Donna felt she had been kicked by a mule.

She shook Henry. "Darling, it's time."

"Are you sure?"

"I'm not a novice at this," she replied.

Donna was admitted to University Hospital that night and gave birth to a healthy, seven-pound baby girl. The next day, with Henry sitting at her bedside, Donna was beaming at the infant cuddled in her arms.

"Isn't she beautiful?"

"Lisa, say hello to your daddy," Donna said.

"She definitely looks like me. Hair over her forehead—big mouth."

"Did you tell Randy? How is he?"

"Excited to see his baby sister. Your mother's coming up in a few minutes. She's got everything figured out, how she can help. But I'm going to get a baby nurse, anyway."

"It seems like a miracle, doesn't it?" Donna asked.

"It is a miracle," Henry whispered.

FROM THE TIME his license was suspended until now, Henry had remained on the scene at the hospital, his visibility decreased very little. However, whenever he heard Tara say, in response to a patient's call, "Doctor Nyren is no longer in practice," he felt a twinge of shame, he felt diminished. His relations with his physician colleagues remained good, and they were generally sympathetic and could identify with his plight. The administrators of the hospital and institute, on the other hand, were distinctly cool toward him. Word had leaked once or twice that the Board of Trustees, while they would stand by him, would not be unhappy if he resigned and accepted an appointment at another institution.

Therefore, when Henry got a call that Dr. Morgan Evans wanted to see him right away in his office, he was somewhat apprehensive. It had been a long time since he had had a sit-down conversation with Dr. Evans.

Dr. Evans's spacious office, on the top floor of the research building, was filled with a heavy desk, a conference table, and comfortable chairs. The walls were bedecked with diplomas and awards. Henry thought this might be his last visit there. The Trustees and the Medical Board had not liked the idea of the Curie name being associated with research in mentally retarded children and disliked even more the fact that Henry was associated with the project. The fact that they could not do anything about it, since all the review committees had approved, only increased their frustration. Not only had public contributions fallen off sharply after the *Post* article, it seemed that a lot of the big corporate donors were staying away also. Henry had become the kiss of death as far as fund raising was concerned.

Dr. Evans's secretary showed Henry into the Director's office. As he came in, Paul Rosen and Dr. Evans stood.

"Henry, where the hell have you been? Logan Conrad said he had been calling you all day and couldn't get you."

Then Henry remembered Tara had given him a message that morning before he went to Matawan.

"I didn't know it was urgent, Paul."

Dr. Evans returned to his chair. "Henry, when Conrad couldn't get you, he called Paul and left the message with him. Repairin is okay. I mean, it works! It's going to prevent children from getting leukemia."

Henry just stood there for a moment. He couldn't understand

330

why he didn't share their elation. He wasn't sure how to handle successful research. He had had so little of it. His reply was almost distant.

"How can he tell so soon? It's just six months. Floyd and I had no clue anything was happening. There were so few cases."

"He could not speak with complete statistical confidence, of course," Paul said. "But for the same number of children of the same age and sex for the last ten years, there has not been a six-month period with no leukemia. Now, the number of cases in the untreated group is not large. He also threw out three cases that occurred in the first month in the repairin-treated group because he felt the leukemia had already started when they got the stuff. His exact words were that he was reasonably certain but that he did not have statistical confidence yet. He said he thought we should have the figures for that in three to four months. However there is very little question about it in his mind, and he thought we might want to know in order to do some planning ahead."

"Does anyone else know about this yet? Can they find out?" asked Dr. Evans.

"I don't think so," Henry said. "If anyone knew, it would be Roger or me, but even we don't know who is getting the drug and who is getting the placebo."

"That's good," said Dr. Evans, "because if word got out we would be deluged with frantic requests for supplies we don't have. Then we'd be criticized for not planning ahead. Also, I don't want us to be put on the spot and have to decide which research centers get it and which don't. That's a problem they'll have to face in Washington."

Paul Rosen had a different viewpoint. "I hope everyone sits tight for a while. It's going to take a long time to answer questions about the best way to use it. Also, we may find a way to give it by mouth. Tooling up to provide millions of injections each year could be done, but we don't want to fall into another swine flu trap."

331

Paul was a scribbler. Seated in a lounge chair, he held a pad on his crossed legs and was making notes in his microscopic handwriting. "We'll need two or three years to find out who really needs it, when, and how often. There also has to be strict control over production. I'm sure the pharmaceutical companies will be looking for ways to cash in on it."

Henry was methodically thumping his fists on the arm of his chair. Finally he stood up and started pacing back and forth. He was running his hand across his chin and mouth, as if trying to pull out a long thought in one piece.

"There is more. Preventing it isn't enough. We'll never get them all that way. There's got to be more. I can't forget the Kaprowski boy. There must be a way to get repairin in there after the cancer gets started. We're not close enough yet. I've got to get back to patients."

"Don't get hung up on the Kaprowski case," Paul said. "We still don't know what happened there."

Paul understood his friend's passion as well as anyone could. He looked at Morgan Evans, who was beginning to understand. Finally, Evans said, "You'd never satisfy Manolete by keeping the bull out of the ring, would you?"

332

# CHAPTER
## *FIFTY*

WHEN HIS punishment year was over, Henry kept on with the research and would see only patients involved in the repairin studies. He did, however, continue to see some old patients for follow-up. When he did, Tara would temporarily slip back into her old role, and he would borrow an unused office for the visit.

"Hello, this is Doctor Nyren's secretary," she greeted one such caller. "May I help you?"

"My name is Charlie Simpson. I'd like to make an appointment to see Doctor Nyren."

"Doctor Nyren cannot accept any new patients, he's devoting himself to research now."

"I think he'll see me—I'm one of his old patients. Tell him my name and that I've got a new problem."

"I don't recognize your name, Mr. Simpson."

"I haven't seen Doctor Nyren for several years."

"Oh. It must have been before my time. Excuse me, I'll get your chart." She managed to find it.

"Twelve years since your last visit, Mr. Simpson."

"I guess that's right. As long as I was okay, I was seeing my local doctor."

Tara made the appointment.

A few days later, a tall, well-groomed man with silver-rimmed glasses arrived and introduced himself to Tara. As she ushered him into Henry's office, she noticed he seemed agitated.

"Go right in, Mr. Simpson."

Henry was reviewing the chart of this patient whom he had not seen in many years. As he rose to greet Charlie Simpson, he stopped short, then stood stiffly behind his desk. "What are you doing here, Stockman?"

"I want to talk to you."

"Why didn't you arrange to meet me in an honest way?"

"Let's face it, you wouldn't have seen me alone."

Henry shrugged. Stockman was probably right.

Uninvited, Donna's former husband sat down across from Henry's desk.

"There are things that are bothering me, and they have to do with you. There's no use talking to the slut."

"*That's* the reason I won't talk to you." Still standing, Henry reached for the phone. "Security will have you out of here in two minutes."

"Don't! I'll just keep at it. I want to get this over with as much as you do." Rand was holding down the phone.

Henry let it go. "How do you know Charlie Simpson?" he said angrily.

"He works in my office. I knew you had been his doctor. When I called your office I took a chance that your secretary didn't go back that far and wouldn't know me."

"What is it that requires all these devious maneuvers?"

"Just one subject—Randy. You're a famous doctor, you've got a big name. You've started a new family. Where does that leave me? A sucker, a jerk, taken for a ride, my balls cut off by a surgeon, and my wife helps him."

"Cut out the dramatics," Henry said, sitting down on the edge of the desk as if he were in complete control of the situation.

"I was going to take an ad in the paper saying what I thought of you and her, but they wouldn't take it. I thought about walking in

334

front of the hospital wearing a sign saying what a wonderful man you are and what a sweetheart she is."

"Get to the point, Stockman!"

"I want my son, goddamit! He means nothing to you. The family you're setting up is going to rob me of him." The muscles in his face were so taut you could see their outline beneath the skin.

"You had months of counseling with experts about just that," Henry said. This was something he didn't need, didn't want, and hated to deal with.

"I don't want to take your place as a father. Randy knows who you are. You're the only one who can spoil that." Henry punctuated his words with a shake of the head that sent his straight black hair falling down almost to his eyebrows.

"You shouldn't have come here. You could have gotten the same results with a letter."

"You fool! Don't you understand that I'm ready to explode. Is a letter going to shout until you listen? Can a letter kill you? I'm warning you, Nyren, don't try to steal my son. You're not the only one with friends and connections. I can make it pretty miserable for you if you try to double-cross me."

Henry picked up the phone. "Tara, call Security and get this imposter out of here!"

"You're the imposter!" Rand flung the words at Henry as he slammed the door and left.

Stockman had done a good job of upsetting Henry. That passed, only to be replaced by anger at himself. Why didn't he manage to calm the man down? Why didn't he talk to him? He found that he was sympathizing with Stockman. Look at the desperate things he had done because of Eve and the efforts he had made to be on good terms with her. How could he not understand how another father felt? Why didn't he sit with him and tell him that he understood his pain? That he had been there. Why hadn't he shown him the simple compassion he showed any patient?

Everyone would have been better off if instead of reacting to anger with anger he had been understanding and sympathetic. Once again, Henry felt, he had been tested as a human being and found wanting.

WHILE DONNA WAS busy with the move to the new apartment, Henry was occupied all day and late into the night in his office, the laboratory, and the library. There was so much research for him to do, so many new approaches to cancer that repairin opened to him. Running at full throttle often found him returning home later than usual and physically exhausted but emotionally exhilarated. However, today's encounter with Rand assured that this evening he would return home just exhausted and annoyed.

When he told Donna what had happened she was furious.

"He's such a miserable bastard. What he did was pure harassment. Can't we get some protection against that sort of thing?"

"I don't want him bothering you," Henry said. "Somehow or other I don't think he will. He'd be afraid that if he got you upset, it would rub off on Randy. I think that's why he pounced on me. I tell you though, I want to put it aside. I've got a lot on my mind. The work with repairin is breaking wide open. I've got to keep on top of it. And right now I've got one hell of a headache."

"I'll get you some aspirin. How about going to bed early?"

"Let's make rounds first."

He took Donna by the hand, and they went to Randy's room. He was sleeping. Shoes and socks had been tossed by a chair. The room was perfectly quiet, suffused with the carefree sleep of youth. Protruding from the covers were the top of his head and an arm, healthy and paint-stained. Obviously he had missed his bath. They watched him for a moment, smiled, and walked to the next bedroom. The baby nurse was seated in a rocker giving Lisa a bottle. They squeezed each other's hands as they watched the little clenched fists and the eyes held tightly closed as the baby concentrated on the bottle. Then they nodded to the nurse and made a silent retreat to their own bedroom.

336

HENRY WOKE AROUND 3:30 A.M. in a drenching sweat. Aspirin always made him sweat, he thought. He got up, took a warm shower, dried himself off, dusted with talcum powder, put on fresh pajamas, and got back into bed quietly so as not to disturb Donna. He was wide awake—with what seemed like an intensified alertness. He perceived everything in the room with heightened feeling. The brass knobs on the bedroom furniture shone brightly. The white of the bedroom walls shimmered. The faint hum of the fluorescent light fixture in the bathroom was a penetrating electronic throb. He got up to turn it off. Sleep was out of the question.

"Henry, what's wrong?" Donna asked.

"Nothing—I can't get back to sleep."

"Is it Rand, did he upset you that much?"

"No, it's not that. I'm just restless. I've got to go out and get some air."

"I'll go with you."

"Not on your life. It's pointless. I'll be right back."

He dressed and made himself a cup of hot tea. He didn't know what to do at this hour. Then he put on his coat and left the apartment.

It was a clear fall night and he could use a walk. He lit a cigar, but he couldn't take the odor of the tobacco and put it out. He kept walking. He couldn't remember ever seeing the stars so clearly in a New York sky. This was what you saw from the top of a mountain.

Without thought, he had walked to the hospital. There was a guard at the front door who recognized Henry and let him in. He must have assumed Henry was making an emergency visit to a patient. In the lobby, to the left was the hall to the research building, to the right were the elevators to the outpatient building. Ahead was the bank of elevators to the hospital and the administrative offices for patient services and building management. There was a nursing supervisor in the office, a new person. Henry did not know her. Memories of the White Whale were fading. One year ago, as if her work here were done once she had damaged him, Miss Flannery had resigned. Someone said she had gone to England and was working in a hospital in Liverpool or Manchester.

He turned and entered the elevator of the outpatient building. The corridors were lit only by small lights over emergency exit signs. He took out his keys and went back into his old office. The outside office was empty of all furniture, in the process of being repainted. It had been left intact until he had announced that he had no intention of resuming practice. Then there had been a juggling of positions to get the office. Apparently they had assigned it, because his name was no longer on the door. Funny, he thought. That's how it had been over twenty years ago when he started at Curie. The building was new then, and when he had come up to this office it was empty and being painted.

He imagined Tara at the reception desk, then walked through the next door into what had for two decades been his office. He looked out the window at Long Island and the bridge connecting it with the city. How big the bridge seemed. The size of it was overwhelming, as if he were standing very close to it. In the river nearby, a large ship came into view. It appeared near enough to be silently sliding down an avenue. The appearance of a merchant ship so close to the streets of Manhattan was always somewhat startling, but now the ship seemed to jump at him. As the giant vessel continued its absolutely soundless slide beneath the massive arch of the bridge, he felt he could reach out and touch it. He held his breath as the ship disappeared down the river behind a curtain of darkness. His own desk was still there and the letter tray was on it, the same tray Miss Flannery had rummaged through when she found the memo on repairin. There was an old, metal wastepaper basket. The paint was burned off one entire side, the aftermath of a fire he had started while grinding out his cigar against the side of the basket. Tara had deliberately never replaced it. Incoming mail addressed to Duncan Comfort had already been placed on the desk. He could not concentrate, def-

338

initely did not want to think. If he let himself think, he would have to face a conclusion that he could not accept. He drew a deep breath. The stench of paint sent little spears of pain to his eyes. He fled from the office and down to the lobby. He continued walking, this time into the Curie Research building.

Henry had no special plan or destination in his wanderings. He entered the elevator, pressed a button, and, when the door opened, got off. The dog smells told him he was on the fifth floor. The lights were on. He walked toward the kennels; when he came to the door, the dogs started yelping. He walked in and noted that the refrigerator with medications and the cabinet above it were now locked. He left and went back to the elevator. He pressed a button and got off at another floor. All the lights were off except for one laboratory where the door was ajar. A beam of light could be seen within. Henry walked in the direction of the light.

It was a large laboratory with two waist-level tables cluttered with apparatus. The light was coming from another table; it was desk height, off by itself. On it was a large binocular research microscope with the illuminating lamp still on. Henry walked up to the microscope to turn off the light. First he looked around and called to see if anyone was there. Perhaps someone was working late at night—that would explain it. But no one was in the laboratory. As he put his hand on the light switch to turn it off, he peered into the oculars. There were images, moving objects. There was something on the microscope stage. He sat down on the laboratory stool in front of the microscope. His hand left the light switch and moved the focusing knob as he peered in. The images came into focus, but it was a phase contrast microscope, and he had to adjust the light diffraction rings under the microscope stage in order to see within the cells. When he did this, a sparkling array of jeweled forms appeared. The diffracted light revealed not only the outline of the cells but the nuclei and the chromatin material within. The protoplasm and mitochondria pulsated like the powerful engines of a majestic ocean liner.

Henry glanced at a notebook next to the microscope. These

were cancer cells from a woman who had died thirty years ago of carcinoma of the cervix. The book contained notations of hundreds of cancer cell lines kept alive in tissue cultures after the patients had died. They had achieved a grotesque immortality.

The living, naked enemy—its full shape and internal workings totally exposed before his eyes and his hands. How beautiful it was; each sparkling cell, in its amoeboid shape, a microcosm; each nucleus containing all the genetic material to reproduce an entire human being. How serene, tranquil, omnipotent. Henry stared with an intensity that approached ferocity as he grabbed the sides of the instrument. He lifted his head only once to wipe the beads of perspiration from his face and to shrug his moist shoulders. Then he projected himself again into the chamber, and the stars were still before him. Eternal life was not in heaven. These stars, these cancer cells, were divine. They had what no other living thing had, eternal life. How could you hate such power? Such perfection? It was a god you could see, believe in. What else was there? How do you venerate? By doing research. How do you pray? By reciting a litany of chemotherapy. How do you sacrifice? By surgery. Here was no stone idol, but neither was this god an abstraction. More numerous than the beings on earth, the great god cancer held sway over all of us and would never die. Sacrifices were taken randomly. Age or sex made no difference. There was no place on earth that offered shelter from its grasp, and no position or power provided protection. Mercy it had none, expiation could not temper this god's judgment. Certainly it was Moloch, the deity that required sacrifice.

Thus, through a long and tortuous route, Henry had come to the same conclusion that Mrs. Kreutzer's historian husband had reached in his moment of anguish. He stood up, stupefied, shook his head until his long black hair fell over his eyes and ears and he made an animal-like gutteral sound that originated as "No." He pulled the chambered slide from the microscope stage, let it fall to the floor, and crushed it underfoot. He had to think, and his thoughts were unbearable.

340

He turned to the microscope again. He had not turned the light off. There was nothing on the stage. One more look. He glanced through the oculars and saw perfect circles of white light, a gigantic blank screen. Then onto the screen came figures, people he knew: Ann Bauer, Sarah Kreutzer, Frank Walsh, and so many others. Holding onto a crutch but waving with her other hand was Marlene Lowell. There was Maria Fauci, at whose death he had wept such bitter tears. She was bright and cheerful, jumping up and down, so happy was she to see him. They were all part of his life, and they were waving to him, smiling at him. He turned off the light before they pulled him into their world. He put his elbows on the table, rested his head in his hands, and wiped his eyes.

For a moment all was quiet, so quiet that he thought he had lost his hearing, so dark that he thought he had lost his sight, so incredible that he thought he had lost his mind. He knew he could never tell anyone what had happened. Shaky on his feet, he reeled across the room and bent over one of the high tables to steady himself. Thoughts, sounds, images cascaded over him. Eve's voice screaming at him: "You love cancer. You love cancer." The newspaper headline: "Experiments with helpless children." Veronica Flannery: "Mightier than God, he decides who lives, who dies."

Henry walked to the hall, pushed the elevator button, stepped on, hesitated, got off, walked back to the laboratory and looked for the microscope. It was there. The light was off and there was nothing on the stage of the microscope. He could not be certain he had ever been in that room before. Slowly his fingers moved toward the microscope lamp and touched the housing; it was warm. He turned on the switch. A light of normal intensity beamed into the condenser. Henry looked and focused. Empty, bare, a clean circle of white light, not even a penumbra of distortion at the edge. This time he left the floor quickly and walked to the lobby. He passed the same guard, who thought Henry looked upset.

"Are you okay, Doctor Nyren?"

"Sure, I'm fine."

He went home, took some sleeping pills after all, and went to bed. He put his head on the pillow, then under the pillow. He curled up on his side in a fetal position. Perhaps he slept. It seemed like only a moment later he was awake. Henry sat up in bed once more, soaked with sweat. He wasn't concerned with what had happened. His grasp of reality had been challenged. And if he was firmly in control, then he had to face reality in all its aspects.

At last, morning light entered the room. He showered again, put on fresh underwear, and went back to bed in hopes of resting for a while. He folded his hands across his abdomen and took a deep breath. He sat up quickly, took off his undershirt, then lay back. He took his right hand, pressed his fingers into the abdominal wall just below the ribs on the right side and took a deep breath. He used to tell the medical students if they wanted to know what an enlarged liver felt like, to open their mouths, press the fingertips of one hand into the cheek, and slowly close the jaw. The fingers riding over the closing jaw would give the same sensation as an enlarged liver descending under the fingertips. And that's what he felt now. He had had night sweats for three months, and fatigue . . . it seemed forever. Now he faced up to what it meant. It was not that he had talked himself out of the significance of these symptoms, but simply that he had not admitted to himself that the symptoms had any significance whatsoever. He knew about denial of illness. Once, when he was an intern and working in a clinic, a young woman had slapped him in the face because he had examined her for stomach pains and told her that she was seven months pregnant. How could she be pregnant, she exclaimed indignantly, she wasn't even married! Denial was stronger than reality, he knew, and physicians were no more immune than anyone else. Now the unthinkable burst upon him in its totality.

# CHAPTER
## FIFTY-ONE

HENRY DRESSED quickly and went to the hematology laboratory at the hospital. He approached a technician he knew. "Felice, do me a favor," he said, "take some blood from me for a CBC, and do an SMA-twelve, too."

"Okay, Doctor Nyren, stick out your paw." He felt the sharp pain of the cold needle as it entered his skin and popped into the vein that had been distended by a tourniquet. How many times a day had he done this to people? It always surprised him how much it hurt and how little they complained.

"Have you seen our new blood sampler?", she asked. "One dilution and two steps with the same vial, and I have your hemoglobin and white cell count, too. Watch." A rush of dots flashed on a small cathode ray display tube, the digital counter raced along and stopped. The entire procedure took about a minute.

"Your hemoglobin is eight point six, and your WBC is fourteen thousand, four hundred and six. I guess you haven't been taking your Fem-iron, Doctor Nyren." She laughed. "I'll have the rest of the count and the results of the SMA-twelve this afternoon."

"Thanks, Felice." Henry went to his own laboratory, and to the list of things he had to do that day added: "Call Paul Rosen." He did not intend to discuss the matter with anyone else. Nothing looked or smelled unusual. Nothing was distorted or grotesque. Today's reality was enough to deal with.

HENRY WAITED FOR Paul Rosen to come to the phone. "Paul, can you meet me at Health Service? I'd like you to take a look at me."

"Anything special?"

"I think my Hodgkin's disease has returned."

"Don't jump to conclusions—let me examine you. Where are you now?"

"I'd rather wait till the place quiets down—how about Health Service at five?"

"Fine," Paul replied.

Paul was waiting for Henry in one of the Health Service examining rooms. Henry handed him the lab slips showing the presence of anemia and abnormal liver function tests.

"Any chance you were exposed to toxic substances in the lab?" Paul asked.

"I'd like to think that, but the time for evasion is over." Henry related the symptoms he had been having for the past several months and told Paul about the enlarged liver.

Paul examined him and found the spleen as well as the liver to be enlarged. There were also some large lymph nodes in the groin. The lymph nodes in the abdomen could be easily palpated. Paul didn't say anything, but he kept checking the same portion of the abdomen to be sure of his findings. Every second of no talking between the two made the situation more tense.

Besides, Henry knew. "Ouch, that hurts. I guess we don't have to bother with a lymphangiogram?" He was stretched out on the examining table in his socks and shorts.

"No, I'm afraid not. The lymph nodes are right here. I think you look a little jaundiced," Paul said. He stopped speaking a moment, then looked up at his friend.

"What would you do if it were someone else?"

Henry responded slowly. "I'd give them combination chemo-

344

therapy. Then, if there was any residual disease I'd clean it up with irradiation so that we'd have a complete remission."

Paul Rosen sat down at the small desk in the examining room and made some notes in Henry's chart.

"Well, that's exactly what we are going to do, and we're going to start right now with the chemotherapy. By the way, if this has been creeping up on you for months, why didn't you let me know about it?"

Henry shrugged his shoulders.

HE WENT HOME after the bone marrow biopsy and the chemotherapy injections. He knew it would be a few hours before the side effects of the medications started. His first impulse was to hide this from Donna, but it was not a boil that would be lanced and gone. He knew what he was in for. There was no way to protect her. He would have to tell her. He remembered Walsh's wife, Mary. He was not going to be a husband-patient who did not confide in his wife.

Donna greeted him cheerfully, sparkling with the hopefulness that came with the feeling that everything was going all right.

"Henry, you look kind of down. Anything wrong?"

She helped him off with his coat.

"We've got a new problem, darling."

"What's Rand been up to this time?"

"It's not Rand, it's me. Remember that Hodgkin's disease I told you about as ancient history? I'm afraid it's come back."

"Henry, is it serious? Have you seen Paul?"

He touched her face. "Don't frown so. You looked so happy when I came in. Yes, I did see Paul, and I've started chemotherapy. There's no reason to worry. I'll come around okay. This is just one more thing for us to go through together."

She appeared to weaken. He caught her and held her.

"Look, I've got a great model. Randy."

Donna sighed.

"He came through like a hero," Henry said. "And you know how competitive I am. I'm going to live up to the little guy's performance."

"I don't want you to be a hero about this, Henry. I just want you to be all right."

They stood next to one of the long windows, the warm sun streaking through. Her head was on his chest, her arms around his waist. Each had faraway thoughts. Donna's fears about Randy also having a relapse were stirred to life. If it could happen to Henry, she thought . . .

Henry's thoughts, as he stood holding Donna, were of another time and another situation, when he was not the patient. He was thinking about Frank Walsh. He felt a strong bond with that wise cop who had, through his wife's pregnancy, come to terms with his disease.

The nausea and fatigue came on after a while, and he threw up a few times. He knew the symptoms would last until the next day. He also knew he would be more tired then than he was now. His transition into a patient had been sudden and as upsetting as it would be to anyone else. But his knowledge and experience were resources. First, he was in familiar surroundings, he knew the people who were going to treat him, and there was comfort and affection to come home to. He knew the drugs, the side effects, how long they would last, and how severe they would be. He knew lots of little tricks he had learned from his patients, passed on to others, and now could use himself. For one of the medicines, procarbazine, he knew that breaking open the capsules and mixing the contents with applesauce, then eating a little of the applesauce all day long, would avoid procarbazine nausea. The nausea and vomiting he was having now were due to Cytoxan, and would pass in a day or so.

THERE WAS A letter from Eve on his desk. She apologized that she hadn't written before about her new friend, but now that it was serious she wanted him to know. The wonderful news was that

346

she was engaged. Wasn't it ironic that after all she had been through she was going to marry a doctor? "He is a pediatrician. He is going to do the same kind of work here that Roger Floyd does. All those mentally retarded children are so sad, but then I think, At least it's not cancer!"

Henry threw back his head and laughed. She's going to get more than she bargained for, he thought. Then he added half-aloud, "We get what we deserve." But he didn't believe that. He didn't deserve what was happening to him now and neither had any of his patients. The beautiful and the ugly, the saintly and the evil, the kind and the miserable—his entire career was a record of the unpredictable manner in which cancer selected its victims.

DURING THE NEXT weeks, Henry received injections and took oral medications continuously, but he did not go into remission. The anemia became a problem, and he required blood transfusions to keep his hemoglobin at an acceptable level. The bone marrow biopsy showed small clumps of abnormal cells; some were the characteristic Reed-Sternberg cells of Hodgkin's disease. The jaundice was getting worse. A car and driver now took him from home to the hospital each day: Paul Rosen insisted on examining him daily. They usually met between 6:30 and 7:30 A.M. before any of the employees appeared at Health Service, and they had the place to themselves. Their exchanges were controlled, limited to immediate objectives such as what medication to take today, or what to do tomorrow. Henry, like most patients with advanced cancer, started concentrating on the relief of his symptoms, preoccupied with whether today would be a good or a bad day.

Ralph Hardy was with Paul Rosen one morning when Henry came in. "I'm sorry you're not doing well, Henry. Mind if I check you over with Paul?"

The advanced stage of the disease was very evident, and there was nothing substantial that Ralph could offer; but the fact that he was there, that he was concerned, did mean something. So did

347

the daily morning visits with Paul Rosen. Paul insisted on these despite the fact that he had had a skiing accident in Colorado, was in continual neck pain, and had to wear an orthopedic collar. Although Henry had said it many times to others, and had long known it to be true, he now understood viscerally the need of the seriously ill cancer patient to maintain connections, to participate in the minutiae of everyday living, as if such contacts were assurance that he was still alive. He feared being cut off, abandoned, depersonalized. He did not fear anything else. Pain could be assuaged, bleeding stopped, tumors cut out, but for depersonalization there was no anodyne.

When he was finished with the examination, Ralph Hardy said, "Henry, you know my philosophy. There are only two kinds of patients, those who are doing well and those who are not. And if you are not doing well you need more attention. I think you should come into the hospital. Just for convenience, mind you. We'll fix you up with a suite on the tenth floor, move in your books and papers. You can go to any damned conference you like. We can even meet in your room. Then when you get better, or any time you want, you can leave."

"Thanks, Ralph. I think I'm about ready to take you up on that offer."

# CHAPTER
# FIFTY-TWO

I T WAS astonishing in how many ways Henry did not differ from other cancer patients. He allowed himself momentary flashes of hopefulness such as he had always engendered in his patients. Still, his experience and knowledge of the prognosis would not let him walk far away from the disease. All those months of denial—those were the months when the repairin work was culminating, when he had to supervise the work at Matawan and the research laboratories as well. Nothing could be allowed to interfere. Those were also the months when his relationship with Donna was culminating, when they married, and nothing could be allowed to interfere with that either.

And how about his cancer? How long had it been smoldering? Was it only a few months, or had it been much longer? Was it Laura's death that had slowly opened the cage and released the dormant malignancy? Was it his inappropriate behavior at the time of the Lowell girl's death, and the subsequent trauma of his suspension? Or was it the anxiety associated with Donna's divorce? Had it been any of these things that lashed the neoplasm within him into aggressive frenzy? What were his own repairin levels? Why hadn't he ever bothered to check them?

Paul Rosen used to examine him every six months, but he had missed the last examination. Henry let it slide, procrastinated.

Doctors are so good to one another, no bills, no sitting around in waiting rooms. Also, so casual—no definite appointments, no secretaries to see that schedules are kept or that records are made or that the right tests are done at the right time. The buddy system at its best and its worst.

Would repairin have helped him? If the disease had been lying dormant all these years and then reactivated, the repairin would not have helped. However, suppose Henry had been cured for these past twenty-five years, but remained susceptible and had contracted Hodgkin's disease again. Then it was conceivable that repairin could have prevented this from happening—one of the innumerable clinical situations for which repairin had not been evaluated and for which it might be useful.

Henry entertained these thoughts with neither regret nor remorse. As far as he was concerned, things had turned out satisfactorily. If his life was a sacrifice that this Moloch required, that was all right, too. He would not try to go back on his part of the bargain.

These thoughts were much more important to Henry than the occasional thought that treatment might yet save him, and soon he stopped thinking about treatment altogether. His present tranquility was a source of amazement to Henry. For the first time in his life he felt free of striving and anxiety. He felt sorry for Donna, but he felt no fear about what lay ahead for him. He gave it no thought. He was neither happy nor unhappy; he was serene. To those about him he seemed appreciative of every act of kindness or consideration. He was also uncharacteristically contained. He was glad that death had not wrenched him suddenly from life; that seemed to be what most people thought was the most desirable way to die, but not Henry. He had been fortunate in regard to many of life's great experiences—intellectual achievement, love, friendship. He had restored the dying to health and had given comfort to others. It was possible that he had assisted in an important achievement in the conquest of cancer.

There had been a price exacted for all these experiences. At present, he was also going through a remarkable experience, and the price did not seem too great. As he lay in the hospital bed, he was aware that his strength was rapidly ebbing, but he had no pain. In this, too, he was fortunate.

ONLY FOUR PEOPLE besides Logan Conrad had known the early statistical prediction of success of the repairin trial at Matawan: Henry, Paul, Morgan Evans, and Roger Floyd. When the second report came, the prediction was stronger. Roger told Irene but swore her to secrecy. However, he did think a small, quiet celebration, like going out to dinner, would not be out of place.

"The baby's sleeping. You call the nurses' residence for a sitter, and I'll get dressed." Irene was elated.

Roger was just hanging up the telephone when Irene came downstairs.

"Who did you get to sit?"

"Mrs. Stanley."

"Again?"

"Well, she came to the phone, and I couldn't very well say get someone else. Besides, the baby likes her."

"I know she's a fine nurse and a reliable baby-sitter, but she's a busybody. It seems almost every time we call we get her."

"She's okay."

A SHORT WHILE later Mrs. Stanley arrived. She stood at the door when Roger and Irene left. As they went down the steps, Irene took Roger's arm, "Whoever would have thought," she said, "that you and Henry Nyren would be involved in a breakthrough!"

A casual remark like that was exactly what Mrs. Stanley was waiting for. She was receiving fifty dollars a week from the *Post* to find out everything she could about repairin: the kids who were receiving it, what the parents thought, if anything bad happened, if anything good happened, any gossip, any rumors. She also kept an eye on the doctors. It took her less than five minutes to pass on to the *Post* what she just heard.

When the story was published the next morning, all hell broke

351

loose. Sound trucks with camera and crews converged on the Curie Institute like tanks at El Alamein. Logan Conrad was angry. His reputation—maybe his career—was at stake. There was a chance he was wrong. His friends at University Hospital had been right all along. "Don't get involved with the gang at Curie." "They're not gentlemen." "They're publicity seekers and unreliable as colleagues."

Irene and Roger had no idea they were the source of the leak. Nurse Edith Stanley continued baby-sitting for them. Both Henry and Paul Rosen were sorry the news was prematurely released, but both had more important problems.

Dr. Morgan Evans thought Henry was the source. "Can't say I blame the poor bastard. He wants a little glory before he dies. He always was erratic," he said to his wife. Dr. Evans had a lot to lose, and the odds of three chances out of four were not good enough for him to gamble. For a researcher to make a mistake is not unusual and not disastrous for his career. But for a director of a research institute to be labeled unreliable, there is not much left.

HENRY WAS SO ill now that he could not get out of bed. As Ralph Hardy had promised, they kept him as busy as possible. Donna stayed in the room much of the day, which was a comfort to him. Henry knew what his colleagues were doing and didn't object, but in his present state of detachment, it was all irrelevant. They had been trying to bring him in for a soft landing, and he had cooperated as much as he could.

After examining Henry one morning, Paul said, "Henry, something's come up, and I feel awful telling you about it at a time like this."

"You're not going to tell me you pulled a Henry Nyren and gave me the wrong medication?"

"I feel just as bad. I've got to go to California for a lecture series. I accepted the invitation a year ago. But to leave now—I feel I'm walking out on you."

"We've got a whole staff here," Henry said. "It wouldn't be right if you stayed."

"You're not just my patient."

"I know." They clasped each other's hands like brothers.

THE NEXT FEW days were not good ones for Henry. He slipped in and out of rational thought. People would appear inside his mind, and he would speak to them. One of these apparitions asked, "What are you?"

He replied, "I am a cancer chemotherapist."

"What do you do?"

"I treat people with cancer."

"Do you cure them?"

"Not always, but I give them hope to carry on."

"Is that all?"

"It's enough."

An hour later he was unconscious.

# CHAPTER
# FIFTY-THREE

**P**AUL ROSEN had been the missing ingredient during the critical days of Henry's illness. He had called regularly from California to get the news, none of it good. He hurried back as soon as he could. Now he was again participating directly in Henry's care.

"I just went over Henry's chart and examined him." Paul was speaking to Duncan Comfort outside Henry's room. "This may sound strange, but I can't reconcile the fact that all the involved lymph nodes are smaller, and yet his clinical condition is so poor."

"Poor is an understatement, Paul. I don't think he's going to last another week."

Paul, mumbling in his usual fashion, started flipping through the pages of Henry's chart. He kept repeating, "I'm missing something. I'm missing something."

He noted that Henry's temperature went down promptly after chemotherapy; all the lymph nodes decreased in size; the liver function improved dramatically—and then deteriorated again.

"Something's wrong. Everything seemed to improve, and then got worse," he said. He rattled off the peaks and valleys of the biochemical tests to demonstrate what he meant.

354

"It doesn't fit. Why did the liver take another nosedive? Did you do a liver biopsy?"

"With an elevated bilirubin and a prolonged prothrombin time? Nobody would risk it," Duncan answered somewhat defensively.

"I thought at first it could be hepatitis due to the transfusions, but I see the hepatitis profile was negative," Paul said. "The jaundice could still be something else besides Hodgkin's. You've had him on steroids, were you also giving him INH?"

"Of course," Duncan said. "He's still on it. In fact you told us to be sure he was getting it. You didn't want to take a chance with TB, you said."

"I know, but jaundice is one of the side effects of INH. Maybe he's as bad as he is because of isoniazid liver toxicity. I think he needs a liver biopsy."

Henry, in a comatose state, was taken into the operating room. A small incision was made in the right upper abdomen and a wedge of tissue removed from the enlarged liver. It was a simple procedure with no complications. Paul Rosen was right. The tissue showed plugged-up bile ducts due to an adverse drug reaction. There were also dead liver cells and scarring, signs that Hodgkin's disease had been there and left its mark. But Henry certainly didn't need the drug-induced insult to his liver.

The medication was stopped.

Over the next week Henry continued his slide in and out of coma, but he did not get worse, and the duration of the periods of consciousness increased. The liver function tests started to improve.


PAUL, DUNCAN, LEN Boyer, Veit-Volpin, and Hardy—the colleagues Henry worked with, fought with, and admired—in a sense, his family—gathered in Veit-Volpin's office.

Duncan spoke first. "If we give him maximum supportive therapy, he might just come out of it. But what for? The Hodgkin's disease is still in his bone marrow. The liver is so scarred it will never be normal. He'll never be able to go back to work. Do we fully appreciate what that would mean to him? That would be the real death sentence for Henry."

"We still can't be sure there is no residual Hodgkin's disease in the liver. I'm not sure we should stop the chemotherapy," Boyer said. He turned to Veit-Volpin.

"What do you think, Gregor? Would it hurt him to give some radiation therapy to the liver to make sure that we have all the Hodgkin's cleared up?"

"Ah ha! Here it comes again. Call in the Cossacks to finish him off! What are you trying to do, make me an honorary member of the KGB, I should give him the *coup de grace*? I remember how all of you acted with that crazy euthanasia business, and now Henry is on the receiving end. And still you can't leave him alone."

Hardy ignored this response, having already made a decision.

"Paul and I have discussed this at great length before we got together. There is no question what Henry would do—go full speed ahead. Paul, why don't you take it from here."

"Well, er, now speed is not the issue." As usual he spoke at a slow, uneven pace, as if inspecting each word before it passed through his lips. He put his large, beardless, Lincolnesque face into his hands and spoke through his fingers.

"Henry has had the proper treatment, and the response has been as good as we could have hoped at this stage of the disease. Even though the Hodgkin's disease is advanced and the chances of cure are not high, he could live and resume some level of activity as long as the remission lasts. How much activity depends on the degree of recovery of the liver."

Rosen stopped and took a deeper breath. "However, there's one point that hasn't been adequately stressed, and that is, he is not yet in remission. He's having bouts of fever again. The lymph nodes are not as large as they were, but they're not down to normal yet. He needs additional chemotherapy. I recommend that we treat him with a full course of streptokotocin."

Duncan had been standing in a corner of Veit-Volpin's office, holding Henry's hospital chart.

"Streptokotocin? Oh my God, I thought we were finished with that one. We did have some responses in lung cancer, but it's toxic as hell, and we haven't even tried to use it in Hodgkin's disease. We'd need approval from the Clinical Investigation Committee, FDA approval, the works."

Paul shifted in his chair. "It's effective in animals with lymphomas. We'll have no trouble getting the right committees to approve it," he said firmly. "Henry's blood counts are not bad—it's a calculated risk, but I think it's one that's worth taking. It's fitting Henry should be the first patient with Hodgkin's disease to receive that drug. I know he'd want it that way. I say we do it."

OVER THE NEXT three weeks Henry endured all the complications and side effects of streptokotocin. He also received the same care and support that he had administered to others. He suffered, he endured, and he improved. First his fever subsided, then the night sweats disappeared. More slowly, the still enlarged lymph nodes disappeared. Gradually his hemoglobin began to rise. Although Henry was far from well, the downward trend was halted, and he was slowly climbing back.

Paul walked into Henry's room one morning carrying his chart. "I thought you'd be encouraged if you saw the dramatic improvement in the lab tests."

Henry had been so thoroughly detached when he had been at the end of the line, he found recovery a difficult adjustment.

"You read them to me, Paul. I'm not up to looking at a chart."

"Well, the bottom line is you're going to shake hands with a remission."

"For how long?"

"That's not a question I've ever heard you ask. The last thing you need is a sermon from me, but think of all the people who asked you that question, and then recall how you answered them."

His improvement was remarkable—although everyone appreciated as much as Henry did that the remission was not going to be of indefinite duration. For the moment, though, it was enough that he had made the gains he had.

Duncan Comfort was walking down the hall with Paul.

"It's kind of awkward now. Do we continue to keep him in the hospital or send him back to his apartment?" Duncan asked.

Paul answered, "He's not ready to go home yet. Donna comes in to be with him every day. I keep her up to date on his condition. She wants him home, but he needs too much care now. Can you picture the situation with Donna, an infant, a second child, and a sick adult in the same apartment?"

Duncan couldn't disagree.

"Henry's comfortable here. Donna has breakfast in his room with him and sometimes Janine joins them. Those two have discovered one another, you know. If there's any problem, it's too many visitors. By the way, I was just in to see him with the metabolic team, and he was sleeping. They think he's sleeping too much. Part of it may be his liver, but he's still very withdrawn."

IT WAS 8 A.M. Donna walked in with fresh flowers and the *Times*. Henry was sitting up dabbling at his breakfast. There were two other trays waiting.

In a few minutes Janine joined them. She was an essential ingredient in their lives at this point. Henry's waking moments were concerned with Donna and the baby. He would be angry with himself, depressed that he had let her down. Donna, on the other hand, was continually preoccupied with Henry's condition and thought nothing of herself. Janine, more than anyone else, sensed that they were clinging to each other with desperation, knowing that one could do nothing for the other.

358

Donna sat on a low lounge chair and reached over to move the breakfast tray to her side. The tray slipped and crashed to the floor. Donna sat there feeling like a fool. Janine immediately jumped up, snatched a towel from the bathroom, and cleaned up, talking all the time.

"I must say, the best thing to come out of all this is that we have a private breakfast room," Janine said. "You know, Donna, my old buddy here and I would frequently meet for breakfast in the hospital. Well, the truth is, I detested eating in that miserable, smelly, noisy cafeteria all those years. Plus, I get perverse pleasure out of getting something for nothing from this hospital, even if it's only breakfast."

Donna managed to regain her composure, and Janine shared her breakfast tray with her.

Donna and Janine helped Henry into the vinyl-covered armchair next to his bed. He was wearing a maroon silk robe with blue stripes, which Eve had sent him. There were ankle socks over his still swollen feet, and his legs were raised on a hassock. He turned to the two women and said, "Do you know what's the worst thing about all this? It's being in limbo. When the Hodgkin's came back after all these years, I thought I was on my way out. Somehow I didn't mind. I felt I had done what I was supposed to do—someone who was religious might say, what I was put on earth to do. You know what I mean. I had no regrets. Now I've been given a reprieve, a limited reprieve. I'm out of the dog house, but on a short leash."

"Yes, that does stink," Janine said with typical candor. "Still, we like having you around on any terms. I know how frustrating not getting back to work must be for you."

Donna brushed crumbs off her skirt. Her emotions were fragile. When Henry spoke this way, it upset her.

"Henry, this doesn't sound like you. I want you to fight back," she said.

"I'm going to say something that may sound strange to both of you, even bizarre. I feel it's a privilege to be going through what so many of my patients endured all these years. I admired their dignity in suffering, and now I don't mind sharing their agony."

"I can't handle such conversations off a stage," Janine snapped at him. "Cover your feet!" she said, adjusting the blanket over his legs.

As the two women left the room, Janine turned to Donna. "I'm a strong right arm. Use me." She squeezed Donna's hand.

"Be sure to stick around," Donna smiled. "I need all the friends I can get."

"And another thing," Janine added. "Don't just sit there doing nothing. Dream up things to do, and don't feel sorry for him. He doesn't need it. Be tough with him—he can take it."

Henry remained in that withdrawn state characteristic of the terminally ill. He had reduced energy because of what he had been through, but he was not terminal. The only time he showed any life was when Donna came into the room. For her he tried his best to be cheerful.

He failed miserably.

# CHAPTER
## FIFTY-FOUR

O N A particularly grim day, with rain splattering wet pellets from a black sky against the windows of Henry's room, Father Noyes, full of ebullience, popped in.

"Oh, how I wanted to bring a bottle of Scotch along," he said.

"And how I wish I could handle it. What's new in the chaplain business?"

"Well, you're still around. Chalk one up for prayers being answered."

Father Noyes had come at a good time. Henry had been sleeping all afternoon and was in relatively good spirits. "Do you know why I have come back, Hector? To teach you the meaning of life."

"Does that mean you want to beat me at cards again?"

"Every time someone from the God Squad visits, he leaves me something to read. I found something I liked in one of those pamphlets. It said, 'God promises you three things—creation, revelation, and perfect peace.' That said it all to me. Life is a wonder of creation and revelation, and if at the end there is perfect peace, that's not a bad deal. What do you say, Hector?"

"Not a bad deal at all. But I say, let's play pinochle."

WHEN HE TRIED the routine out on Janine, he got an entirely different response.

361

"I can't stand it when you talk like that, Henry. When you sit there with that beatific smile on your silly face, wrapping yourself around with enlightenment like Siddhartha, I feel like bopping you on the head with a baguette. Now come on, you're not sick anymore. We're going to the theater tonight. Donna wants to, and Paul said it's okay to go out on a pass."

SLOWLY, HENRY WAS beginning to rejoin humanity. Paul Rosen would come in two or three times a day. They had agreed he would be able to leave the hospital any time now, and Henry was working himself up to that.

Paul was paying a late evening call. He thought a quiet evening visit would be the right time to tell Henry.

"Henry, I want you to be the first to know," Paul said. "I'm leaving Curie. When I was in California, I was asked to be Director of the new University of California Cancer Center. Run the whole program. Design it from scratch. Carry out cancer research the way it should be done—the Institute-Without-Walls approach—view the whole state as a cancer institute, link up researchers according to their interests, but don't move them from their home base. The Trustees bought it. I'm gonna do it, Henry."

Henry lay his head back on the pillow. Paul is doing what I couldn't, he thought, leaving, starting something new. An Institute-Without-Walls, what a grand vision. Collaborating, problem-oriented task forces tied together by instant communication, probably getting along better than if they were working in the same institution competing for power and position. Nature will reveal her secrets to you, Paul. How I wish I were going along.

Finally he said, "It's hard to believe you're going to leave Curie after all these years, but you're right, the idea of putting scientists in one building and saying, 'Produce!' is out of date. I just feel sorry to be losing a friend—and my physician."

"It won't be till the end of the year. Nothing is going to change

362

for now. Except for you. You can get up and around now. This Friday night Joan is making dinner for you and some of the old bunch. I want Donna to meet them. Everyone's agreed, we're going to get you out of this place!"

When Paul left, Henry felt what little strength he had accumulated had been drained from him. Paul was the only confidant who truly knew how the heady wine of research fired his spirit, how his restless soul could never accept defeat. Only Paul caught the Ahab glint when Henry was pushing too hard. So sensitive was Henry to the stabilizing effect of his friend, that a word, a nod, a gesture, was all it took to set him aright—at least most of the time. Now all that would be behind him.

HIS DISCHARGE FROM the hospital did nothing to improve Henry's frame of mind. Being home with nothing to do was not a happy condition for him. He had a few hours of energy each day but lacked the will to do anything with them.

One day Annie Janocek arrived with a cooking pot wrapped in a brown paper bag.

"Henry, you here? I've got your favorite dish."

"I'm here, Annie."

He came shuffling out of the bedroom in a robe and slippers. Only when Donna or his friends dragged him out of the house, would he dress.

"The cabbage is so strong you're gonna need a gas mask, but I'll betcha something. I'll bet you can't smell this for ten seconds without smiling."

And Henry did smile. All through dinner he was friendly and talkative. It just didn't last.

As they were going to bed that evening Donna said, "You've got another visitor tomorrow."

"Yes, I know. Mrs. West. I wonder why Tara gave her my number."

"You said it was okay, remember?"

"I guess I did. But she invited herself here."

363

The next day Julia West arrived, wearing a beige cloth coat trimmed with a massive white fur collar and carrying two gift-wrapped packages. Donna put the gifts down on the coffee table and went to get Henry.

"Your guest is here, darling. Oh, why don't you get dressed?"

"I'm just not up to it, and I'm not up to her either."

"Well, at least put on a turtleneck. You can't go out there in a bathrobe and undershirt."

Henry reached into a drawer, took the first turtleneck pullover he found, and put it on.

"HENRY NYREN, WHY didn't you tell me you were sick?" Mrs. West asked. "Not that I could have done anything. At any rate, doctors are not supposed to get sick. It shakes their patients' confidence, don't you know. Those packages—there they are —they're not for you. They're for Lisa. Can I take a peek at her?"

"Sure," Donna replied. "Come with me. She's sleeping."

"That's when they're at their best."

Henry waited in the living room while the two women went to look at the baby.

"I know everything that's happened," Mrs. West announced when she and Donna rejoined Henry. "Don't blame your secretary. She isn't a busybody, I am. I have this knack of getting information out of people."

"I must say, Julia, you are looking fine."

"I don't know what you told that cowboy doctor of mine to do, but it's working wonderfully well. In fact, I'm just passing through New York. I'm on my way to that sanitorium in Wengen again."

"Aren't there enough doctors for you between New York and Denver?"

"You, like most people, don't understand. Going there has nothing to do with medicine. It's all psychological. In fact, I admit, it's kind of neurotic. But I don't fight my neuroses, I live with them."

364

"Don't we all," Henry replied.

"I didn't come here just for a social visit, however. There is another purpose. You remember that cancer research foundation the Wests started? I asked you to be a scientific adviser? Well, the foundation voted $50,000 for your research, and I've come to deliver the check."

"I'm overwhelmed, Julia. That's a sizable sum. I don't know if I can accept it."

"What do you mean?"

"You're giving me that money with the assumption I'm going to be doing research again. And that's seriously in doubt."

"Look, I don't care if you just sit in an armchair and listen to Mozart all day."

Donna smiled, because that was exactly what Henry was doing.

"I'm sure that even if you're not up to doing the research yourself, you know what's going on. And I want you to use it at your discretion."

After Mrs. West left, Donna said, "Managing that money will give you something to do. It's a good motivation to get you involved again."

"It was a nice thing for her to do," Henry replied.

But, Donna could tell, the spirit still wasn't there.

THERE WAS ANOTHER visitor later that afternoon. Duncan Comfort.

Henry didn't feel the necessity for any formalities with his young friend, and the turtleneck went back into the drawer. Donna was busy with the baby, Randy had just come home from school, and the apartment was hectic and noisy.

"Duncan, let's go to the bedroom. There are some comfortable chairs there."

Duncan followed as Henry shuffled to a liquor cabinet and then to the bedroom.

"I'm up to having sherry again—not the hard stuff, and not these, unfortunately." Henry picked up a cigar from a box and sniffed it slowly. He then replaced it and took up the bottle of sherry instead. "Will you join me?"

"Sounds fine," Duncan answered.

"Now tell me, is this a social or a professional visit?"

"Social. Definitely social. Just came to say 'How are you?'"

"If one doctor visits another, and says 'How are you?' it's not a casual question. You're liable to get a full clinical report," Henry replied. "Come to think of it, with Paul leaving, I've got to have another physician. You're it."

"You're putting a lot of confidence in the youngest member of your staff." Duncan said. "Are you sure you want to do that?"

"There are two things I like about you. You're not afraid to let your patients know what you're thinking, and you pay attention to detail. Few of us have Paul Rosen's clinical intuition. That's a gift. And I don't think you've got the fire in the belly that I had at your age—you're cooler. Maybe that's better. At any rate, I think you're a fine oncologist."

"If I'm taking care of you, I'll have the advantage of my old teacher being at my side whenever I need any advice." Duncan set down the sherry glass and continued, "There's one thing, though. A lot of us are concerned about you being so depressed. No one seems to be able to reach you. Do you have enough confidence in me to open up a little and share some of your feelings with me?"

"Duncan, what can I tell you? I know I'm in some sort of remission, and should feel better, but I just can't find the starter to get the engines going again. You know what runs through my mind? Something another doctor who had cancer said." He leaned over and picked up a book from a bedside table. "'If it were a horse I was riding that went lame or broke its neck, or a ship on which I was travelling that sprang a leak, I could transfer to another one and leave the old vehicle behind. As it is ... all that I really am is inseparably tied up with the failing capacities of these outworn organs ... Poor viscera, I can hardly blame you ... only now it seems so silly that you must take me with you.'" He put

366

down the book. "I think right now I'm a better doctor than I've ever been. I know more than I've ever know. I can do more than I ever could, and yet I'm on a ship that's going down."

"You're not down yet, Henry. You've got a lot of life in you. Why not use it?"

"Duncan, right now I feel like I'm down in some sort of a valley and can't seem to climb out."

"Funny you should mention valleys. I think of life as a road between heights of hopefulness and valleys of despair. Every day I struggle for the heights. You know, *you* are one of those heights. I hope you won't let me down."

OVER THE WEEKS of his hospitalization, from stories told her by Paul, by Duncan, and by Henry's devoted historian Janine, Donna began to understand better what Henry's career had been like—his devotion to new treatments for cancer, sometimes using forms of chemotherapy that others wouldn't touch, what happened to Laura and to Eve's friend, but mostly how Henry and Paul had struggled to make medical oncology a recognized specialty. Knowing all that, and having herself been electrified by the sheer mass of the man's interests and initiative, and his emotional commitments, she couldn't understand his apparent mental deterioration. There was no explanation for his lack of motivation, his loss of interest in life; it was so unlike him, and no one could explain it.

ONE DAY, A few weeks after leaving the hospital, Henry was shuffling aimlessly around the cheerfully decorated apartment like a dry autumn leaf fallen into a spring garden. Even the baby would hold his interest for only a few moments. There was the rattling of a key in the door, and Donna came in from shopping.

"Henry, I've been thinking," she said, angrily thumping a bag of groceries on the kitchen table. "You know, everybody has said whatever could be said or done to put some life into you. The only people who are as out of it as you are, are drug addicts—I don't mean that the way it sounds. But damn it, Henry, you're the last person I would have expected to be like this."

"Don't lose patience with me, Donna," Henry said.

"I have lost patience with you," She replied. "You should be shouting from the rooftops, 'Hey, look, I'm proof that chemotherapy works!' You, Henry, are a vindication of your life's work!"

"I know I'm lucky," Henry said, watching Donna detachedly, listening primarily to please her.

"Lucky my foot! If this had happened to you ten years ago, even five years ago, would you have gotten out of the mess you were in?" Fear of losing Henry, and cues from Janine, had given Donna new aggressiveness.

"No, not likely."

"It was that stupid streptokotocin that finally put you into remission, wasn't it?"

"Yes, that, plus all the other chemotherapy," Henry acknowledged.

Donna sat down at the kitchen table across from him.

"That's point number one. I've heard you say it, and I've heard others say it about you—don't give up, never quit! You benefited from your own aggressive forms of treatment, and I know all the gaff you've taken over the years because of it.

"Point number two. Streptokotocin. Everybody hated that drug. You told me so yourself. Yet you stuck with it, you convinced Paul it was going to be accepted some day and that the bad side effects could somehow be handled. Paul thinks the world of you, but if you were wrong he wouldn't have gone along with you for a minute."

Henry was silent. Donna pushed on. "But you did convince him, and when your turn came, Paul did for you what you would have done for someone else, including sticking his neck out and getting approval for the use of a drug that had never before been tried in a patient with Hodgkin's disease. And it worked! Now don't you think you've got something to crow about?"

"You're right, I've got to write Paul a thank-you note," Henry said in a monotone.

"A thank-you note! Is that all you can think of? Henry Nyren, I could kill you!"

Henry shrugged. He got up and walked to the bedroom where he still spent a great deal of time just sitting.

The phone rang. Donna took the receiver from the white wall phone in the kitchen.

"It's for you."

"Take a message."

"It's Paul."

"Oh, okay."

He reached for the phone on the night table and sat on the edge of the bed.

"How are you?" Paul asked.

"Fine. Nice of you to call. We were just talking about you." No animation. No interest.

"Henry, are you up to talking about research?"

"I don't know, Paul. Its hard for me to concentrate."

"I think you'll concentrate on this one. If there was ever anything worth making an effort for, this is it, and its right up your alley."

"What is it?"

"Henry, I'm sure you didn't see the latest issue of *Science*. There's an article—they've isolated the cancer gene."

Henry sat up very straight. "Are you sure?"

"Yes. There's a second paper confirming it, published back to back."

Henry stood and began pacing back and forth restlessly. "That's fantastic! It's a whole new ball game!"

"There's more, Henry. It fits in with repairin, and it fits in with your fertilization theory, too. That's not all, there's going to be new chemotherapy that's specific, no more side effects."

"It's all coming together, Paul. For the first time in my life, it's all coming together!" Coming from down deep, where metabolism throbbed like the pulse of a great engine, his energy was flowing again.

"Incidentally," Paul said, "we're having a meeting this morning at ten-thirty. Too bad you won't be there."

"Ten-thirty! That's just twenty minutes from now."

"That's right."

"Hold them off. Do what you have to, but don't start without me."

He turned and shouted, "Donna! Help me get dressed! I've got to get out of here!"

While research is actively going on to develop new forms of chemotherapy and substances that enhance cell repair, the medications referred to as streptokotocin and repairin do not exist.